Tradewinds & Treachery

Tradewinds & Treachery

Drama and romance in old Fiji

Robert Campbell

Steele Roberts
Aotearoa New Zealand

National Library of New Zealand Cataloguing-in-Publication Data
Campbell, Robert (Robert Owen), 1934-1992
Tradewinds & treachery : drama and romance in old Fiji /
Robert Campbell.
ISBN 978-1-877448-17-1
1. Fiji—Fiction. I. Title.
NZ823.3—dc 22

Maps, drawings and cover artwork by Humph Holland.

STEELE ROBERTS PUBLISHERS
BOX 9321 WELLINGTON, AOTEAROA NEW ZEALAND
info@steeleroberts.co.nz • www.steeleroberts.co.nz

Editors' note

Although *Tradewinds & Treachery* is a historical romance and a work of fiction, its setting and historical context is authentic, and only the battle for Vatulevu is wholly fictional. Robert Campbell planned to create a fictitious family (the Cotterels) and weave its fortunes into the fabric of Fiji's history from before cession to Britain in 1874 to the present time. This book was written as the first instalment in a series.

The Denison and Cotterel families, Captain Bex and the Southern Cross Shipping Company, Elija Codrokadroka, Colonel Basil Gunning, MacDonald, Dr Matthews, and Horace Twyford are products of the author's imagination. The blackbirder Jack O'Hara and his vessel the *Philomena* are also fictitious but not unlike the real-life Bully Hayes and his *Leonora*. Most of the other key characters were real people listed below.

There is no Vatulevu — Robert Campbell's vision is represented in the map on page 83. The other places mentioned are factual (see map page 18). Levuka is now a sleepy tourist destination but in the mid to late nineteenth century it was truly a den of iniquity and intrigue.

Fiji-watchers will recognise many of the tensions alluded to as having influenced political events through the past 140 years, not excluding recent coups. The attitudes ascribed to European settlers were commonplace in the 1860s and '70s. When blackbirding was stopped they pressed for alternative sources of labour. The Colonial government's solution was to import indentured labourers from India, from 1879 on. Today, all citizens of Fijians alike are living with the consequences.

The following figured in Fiji's history in the roles ascribed to them in the book: Commander Boutwell USN, Ratu Seru Cakobau, King George of Tonga, Prince Ma'afu'otu'i'toga (Ma'afu), Rev Thomas Baker, Lord Belmore, W H O'H Brewer, William Burnes, SC Burt, JS Butters, Captain Chapman RN, Dr G Clarkson, Captain Douglas RN, WH Drew, IL Evans, Major Fitzgerald, Commodore JG Goodenough RN, Captain Harding RN, the Hennings brothers, R de Courcy Ireland, RW Keane (alias Smith), St John Keyse, EL Layard, Daniel O'Neil, Sir Hercules Robinson, JT Sagar, SA St John, JC Smith, RS Swanston, John Thurston, GA Woods.

Similarly, HMS *Cossack,* HMS *Dido,* HMS *Pearl,* HMS *Rosario,* the Fiji vessels *Vivid,* and *Volunteer,* and the USS *John Adams* and USS *Tuscaroa* featured in actual events, as did the Polynesian Company, and Godeffroy & Sons. A group of Europeans formed the 'British Subjects Protection Society' (dubbed the 'Ku Klux Klan') and met in Keyse's Hotel as described.

About the book

The editors, Peter Thompson and Derek Robinson, worked for the Fiji Department of Agriculture in the 1960s and 1970s. The heavily annotated manuscript of this novel was found after Robert's death and was later given to Peter. He had it typed up while working in Bangladesh in 1999 and showed it to a number of other ex-Fiji folk who agreed it should be published and helped with editing.

The editors are grateful to Robert's widow, Eileen Mather, for permission to publish the book in memory of him; and to a number of present and former Fiji residents who contributed greatly to the editorial process, including Charles Eaton, Rosemary Robinson, Bob and Jennifer Strick, Ian Thomson, Valerie Thompson, and Dick Watling. Thanks are also due to Naseem Uddin Pradhan and Reza Karim Md. Khasru of Dhaka, Bangladesh, who typed the original manuscript. Thanks also to Humph Holland for the maps, drawings and cover artwork.

A note follows on the pronunciation of Fijian and a glossary of Fijian and some English words used. Deryck Scarr's biography of Sir John Bates Thurston, *I, the very bayonet* (ANU Press, Canberra, 1973) has been used to verify historical facts.

Peter Thompson & Derek Robinson
Wellington, NZ
September 2007

Notes: Fijian pronunciation

Standard Fijian is phonetic, with the exception of the following letters:

b	is pronounced	*mb*	e.g. Ba becomes *Mba*
c	" "	*th*	e.g. Cakobau becomes *Thakombau* (hard *th* as in leather)
d	" "	*nd*	e.g. Nadi becomes *Nandi*
g	" "	*ng*	e.g. Turaga becomes *Turanga*
q	" "	*ngg*	e.g. yaqona becomes *yang-gona*

Vowels are pronounced:

a as in father
e " " let
i " " sing
o " " got
u " " flute.

Glossary

In this glossary Fijian words are in italics and translated in the context in which they are used in this book. Other words are in plain text.

Adi	honorific title given to a female of chiefly rank
bulamakau	cattle (lit. bull-cow)
bure	traditional Fijian house
Cakaudrove	major tribal district in southern Vanua Levu
carronade	short, smoothbore, cast iron cannon
copra	dried coconut kernel
dakua	hardwood, member of kauri family, *Agathis vitiensis*
dalo	taro — root of *Colocasia esculenta*
Degei	major Fijian deity
dina	right, true, correct
drua	twin-hulled war canoe
duck trousers	sailors' clothing made from strong cotton fabric
io	yes
i'saka	sir
Jisu Karisito	Jesus Christ
Kaba	Politically important village in Tailevu
kai	people
kai-colo	person from interior of Viti Levu
kai-Jiu	Jew
kai-loma	people of mixed European and Fijian descent
kai-si	slave, the lowest of the low
kai-valagi	Usually European, but can apply to other non-Fijians also *kai-vavalagi*
kai-Vatulevu	native of Vatulevu
kai-Viti	native of Fiji, a Fijian
kana	food, meal
kanaka	used to denote person of Melanesian origin

kawai	sweet root vegetable of yam family
kei	and
kemuni	polite form of 'you'
ki	to
Kubuna	Fijian confederacy headed by Bau
kuita	*w*hip made from knotted vines (lit. octopus)
lailai	little, small
lali	drum made from hollowed-out tree trunk
lesu tale	return again
levu	big
lialia	mad, stupid
liku	brief skirt usually of leaves or grass
lotu	religion, church
Lotu na Karisito	the Christian religion
Lovoni	valley in the interior of Ovalau
maca	empty
Macuata	major tribal district in northern Vanua Levu
magimagi	sennit — plaited coconut husk fibre cord
Marama	madam, lady
Maria Theresa dollar	a silver bullion coin used in world trade since 1780
masi	cloth made from the bark of the paper mulberry, *Broussonetia papyrifera* (tapa elsewhere in Polynesia)
mataka	tomorrow
matanivanua	herald or official spokesperson
Misiveka	Fijian version of Mr Baker (refers to Rev Thomas Baker)
na	definite article e.g. the, a
Nadroga	major tribal district in west Viti Levu
ni	formal prefix
nomu	your
Peritania	Britain
pineapple club	Fijian war-club with its striking surface covered in sharp projections
puggaree	muslin scarf worn around a sun helmet to protect the wearer's neck
Qaraniqio	place-name meaning 'Hole where a shark lurks'
raica	to look, see
Ratu	honorific title given to a male of chiefly rank

sa	verbal particle
sa bula	how do you do
sa moce	goodbye
sega	no
Siga Tabu	Sunday
sulu	wrap-around kilt
tabu	forbidden or sacred
tabua	whale's tooth presented in all important ceremonials
tagimaucia	rare flower from Taveuni, *Medinella waterhousei*
takia	outrigger sailing canoe
tanoa	large four-legged wooden basin carved from a single piece of wood — used for *yaqona*
tevoro	devil, evil spirit
Tovata	*(Tovata na Tokolau kei Viti)* Eastern Confederacy of Fiji
Tui	monarch or paramount chief e.g. *Tui Kaba*
Turaga	honorific form of address meaning sir, lord
Turaga na Kalou	God
Turaga na Talatala	Reverend, preacher
vaka-valagi	European-style
vale ni lotu	house of worship, church
vatu	a rock or stone
vinaka	good, thank you
vinaka vakalevu	thank you very much
Viti	indigenous name for Fiji
Vunivalu	'the root or source of war' the title given to the *Tui Kaba,* paramount chief of *Kubuna*
walai	vine, *Mimosa scandens*
walu	Spanish mackerel, *Scomberomorus commerson*
yaqona	ceremonial drink made from the root or stem of the pepper plant, *Piper methysticum* (kava elsewhere in Polynesia)
yavu	the raised foundation of a house
yavusa	clan

Prologue

THE AUDIENCE HOUSE MEASURED ten fathoms long by six wide and towered to a ridge pole thirty feet above the people sitting cross-legged on the mat-covered floor. At both ends of the undivided room fires burned in open hearths, acrid smoke drifting upwards to blacken the exposed beams and seep through the thatched roof. Firelight reflected from walls panelled with polished reeds bound by elaborate patterns of coconut fibre, and made death masks of the faces.

Ratu Seru Epinesa Cakobau, paramount chief of Fiji, a tall heavily muscled man, lounged on a pile of soft mats near the fire furthest from the single entrance. A grey beard could not hide the determination of his features nor mask the penetrating quality of the hard dark eyes. For the moment his mood was affable, but from time to time he swept the room with a searching glance which rendered even strong men cold and apprehensive.

It was said he was six years of age when he clubbed his first victim to death and joined in the cannibal feasting which followed. From then until his conversion to Christianity, more than 1000 human bodies had found their way to the steaming earth ovens of the island of Bau as food for his chiefly table. His name alone was sufficient to cramp the bowels of his enemies with fear and his people knew that instant obedience to his every command was expected on pain of death.

His Bauan people called him Vunivalu, the Warlord. Many, including some white settlers, were now calling him King of Fiji. Cakobau himself had yet to publicly accept or deny the title.

He wore a mix of Fijian and European clothing: a silk collarless shirt hung loose outside the bulky sulu of masi, cloth made from bark of the paper mulberry tree, which swathed his waist. He kept a British naval officer's full-dress uniform in a chest for ceremonial occasions. White men placed great importance on such things as clothes and when it suited Cakobau's purpose he was prepared to give lip service to their ideas; but to his mind clothes could not hide men's motives and nothing else was worth concealing. Even clad in a loin cloth and a slick of coconut oil he had natural dignity and majesty.

He had no love for the white men flooding into the islands. He knew they ridiculed him behind his back — not that they dared be anything but obsequious to his face. Ten short years before he would have had a white man clubbed to death with no greater thought than he would have given to the meanest slave. But times had changed; the execution of a white now brought a swarm of gunboats buzzing about his ears — though they would do well to remember that an accident at sea or deep in the jungle was easily arranged, and just as effective.

Whites had their uses. He owed his ascendancy over the other chiefs to the fact that a European had taught his Bauan people the advantages of the musket before the rest of Fiji. That particular pioneer had ended in the oven and his shin bones were made into needles and fish hooks. But by the time he came to the end of his usefulness there were others to take his place, to be used or discarded at Cakobau's whim.

Then there were the missionaries; it always paid to keep on good terms with them. Some were good, some bad, but all were gullible especially those of recent years. There were also a handful of white men whose advice was sensible and selfless and whom he knew he could trust. It was ironic that these men, on whom he would have heaped rewards, were those who refused all he offered while their insatiable fellows scrabbled about his feet for favours.

The British Consul and the chief missionary with their white houses on the Levuka hills, and the beachcombers wallowing in their filthy hovels on the flats, were all one in his estimation. They considered themselves creatures apart and vastly superior to the Fijian. That anyone in his domain could even think that was anathema to him — had it not been for his fear of the gunboats Cakobau would have wiped the settlement of Levuka from the face of the land.

Thinking of the white men caused his contentment to evaporate and his face set in a severe scowl. The room became silent; each man terrified that he might be the cause of his master's wrath. Only the matanivanua dared break in on the chief's meditation. As herald and chief officer of Cakobau's court, he had to take that risk. He crawled forwards on hands and knees in accordance with the custom which decreed that no man's head might be higher than that of the chief. Then he waited patiently until he was able to catch Cakobau's eye and whisper that a delegation from King George of Tonga waited outside desiring an audience.

The news did nothing to improve Cakobau's temper — if anything, he loathed Tongans even more than white men. They came from an island group 250 miles to the south-east of Fiji and were as much foreigners, kai-valagi the Fijians called them, as the whites and just as cunning and avaricious. Before allowing their admission he checked quickly to see whether sufficient of his warriors were present to impress the ambassadors with the size of his court. It was a source of gnawing irritation to Cakobau that the Tongan paramount chief had been recognised by the foreign powers and was now styled King George, whereas they still regarded him as a mere chief.

The Tongan party crawled into the chief's presence but once seated in their allotted places their leader, a minor Tongan noble, looked about him with an air of arrogance and ill-concealed contempt. They were fairer skinned people with much straighter hair than the crinkly black mops that Fijians combed to stand out from their heads in a huge halo. Their supercilious attitude made Cakobau's blood boil.

Tabua and other gifts from King George were ceremonially presented. Tabua, the teeth of the sperm whale, had more value in Fijian eyes than any amount of the white man's money. Customary speeches followed. The Tongan noble used all the correct honorific phrases, yet his attitude and tone of voice made it clear he thought King George was wasting his substance on these petty Fijians. In this he was relying on the hallowed tradition that the person of an ambassador was sacred — he might have been more careful had he been able to read Cakobau's thoughts.

The Fijian side made the usual reciprocal presentations and responses. As was expected, the matanivanua speaking on behalf of Cakobau, praised the courage, the nobility, power, wisdom and great generosity of the King of Tonga.

At his signal the tanoa, a huge bowl with four legs carved from a single piece of wood, was carried in and set in the middle of the room. A long cord of plaited coconut fibre decorated with white cowry shells was uncoiled and extended in a line from the bowl across the mats toward the chief. A great wad of yaqona, the root of the pepper plant, which had previously been chewed soft by Bauan maidens, was placed in the tanoa and, to the accompaniment of chanting and rhythmic hand clapping, water was added and an infusion prepared. Yaqona was an integral part of all Fijian ceremonies; it was non-alcoholic but slightly narcotic, deadening the limbs while leaving the mind clear and fresh.

The matanivanua closely supervised each stage of the operation and it was he who finally decided that the correct consistency had been achieved. The chanting and clapping rose to a crescendo, stopped abruptly, and the cup bearer sprang forward with the chief's bowl, a coconut shell scraped so thin and so highly polished it was like the most fragile Chinese porcelain. The bowl was filled until it spilled over.

The chanting began again and the cup bearer rose to his full height, the brimming bowl extended at arm's length. For what seemed like five minutes he advanced inch by inch towards Cakobau in a stiff-legged dance, the room reverberating to the deep booming of the ritual chant. Another crescendo and stop; and the cup bearer dropped to his knees and proffered the bowl, his arm muscles trembling with tension.

As Cakobau drank, a sharp staccato drumming began. He finished and with a great flourish sent the empty bowl spinning through the air to be caught deftly by the cup bearer.

"Sa maca!" shouted the assembly, acknowledging the cup was empty.

In customary style the next person served was the matanivanua, and only after he had drunk were the Tongans given bowls. Only the highest ranking on either side were served.

The formalities completed, the time had come for business and the Tongan ambassador began. He spoke fluent Fijian but, by giving exaggerated emphasis to certain sounds, made it obvious that he thought it a barbaric language.

He said he had been sent to complain of incidents in which Tongans had been killed or badly wounded by Cakobau's men and he insisted on punishment of the culprits and compensation for the families of those killed.

He went on to demand Bauan recognition of Tongan sovereignty over several islands seized by Tongan war parties. None of the islands in question were within Cakobau's immediate domains but, knowing his claim to the title of King, the Tongans wanted acknowledgement of their ownership so that they could hold what they had captured should a monarchy be established and recognised.

As demand was heaped on demand there was shuffling and indignant whispering among the Bauan warriors. But Cakobau allowed the ambassador to drone insolently on while watching him through half-closed eyes. He looked bored and half asleep; but he was seething inwardly.

Tongans had been coming to Fiji for centuries. To lead a raiding party into Fiji waters was part of every young Tongan noble's education and normally the first blood his club tasted was that of a Fijian. Some had stayed on and were spearheading the campaigns of Cakobau's enemies against him.

Most dangerous of all was the Tongan prince, Ma'afu, exiled as a pretender to the Tongan throne and now hoping to carve out a new kingdom for himself in Fiji. He had gathered about him a loose confederation of Cakobau's enemies dedicated to the destruction of Bau. It was obvious to the whole assembly that the ambassador was as much the representative of Ma'afu as of King George.

They must be very sure of themselves, thought Cakobau, for their ambassador to be so openly insulting. It could mean Ma'afu had settled his differences with his cousin King George and succeeded in welding his Tovata Confederacy into an effective fighting force. Unless he himself stood firm, Fiji would soon be little more than a subject province of Tonga. If they were preparing to strike, it was no time to show fear. And who better to carry a message of defiance than this wretched delegation.

"Hold your tongue!" he roared, slapping the mat beside him with his huge hand. "How long do you expect me, the Vunivalu, to listen to this groaning and whining, these insolent lies and threats?"

There was a hiss of appreciative excitement from the Fijians. They had been waiting for something like this, amazed by their chief's forbearance thus far. At a word from him they would pound the Tongans to a bloody pulp.

The Tongan leader, chopped off in mid-sentence, sat with his mouth open; his men looked anxiously around them at the hostile Bauan warriors. Everyone in

Tonga believed Cakobau lived in such mortal fear of King George that he would submit to anything. The merciless fury which now disfigured the Vunivalu's face was terrible proof that rumour had lied.

"You say you come from King George, but you are a liar," shouted Cakobau, his spittle hitting the mat near the Tongan leader. "I have met your King and he does things in true kingly fashion. He did not tell you to be insolent to me, Cakobau, Vunivalu of Fiji, his equal."

This was closer to the truth than Cakobau knew, for the ambassador had been told by King George to deliver a mild protest. It was Ma'afu, on whom the delegation had called at Lakeba, who had persuaded them to alter the tone of the message.

"Because you are the King's messenger you imagine you may insult your betters and hide behind your office. By your words you have shown yourself to be unfit for the duties you were appointed to perform."

"But … but my Lord," stammered the Tongan.

"Now it is 'my Lord', is it? You show honour at too late an hour, Tongan!" Cakobau bellowed, eyes blazing. "You and your demands! Everyone in this room, including you, knows that those dead Tongans got no more than they deserved; they were a raiding party which attacked the wrong village. Tell King George and that upstart dog Ma'afu that it is I, Cakobau, who should be complaining. But it is not my way to squeal like a stuck pig just because a few drops of blood have been spilt. Tell them that the next Tongans who invade my territory may expect the same treatment."

"Nor do I recognise Tongan sovereignty over one handful of Fijian soil. These islands belong to Fijians and no matter what has been conquered, nor how many puppet Tongan chiefs you may have installed, they remain Fijian."

"You imagine that I am blind to what happens in my own lands? Ma'afu boasts that he will rule Bau and that I, Cakobau, will cook for him — tell him from me that I am quite prepared to be the cook if Ma'afu is to be the food in the oven." Cakobau hoped that this last statement would not be reported to the missionaries or they would make his life miserable for days.

"Ma'afu is making trouble between me and the white men. He told the representative of the English Queen that only he can make the Fijians work on the white men's plantations. He wants them to make him King over Fiji. If that day comes we shall all be the slaves of Tonga and the whites. Tell Ma'afu that I, Cakobau, and my people stand in his path and while one of us lives no Tongan shall ever rule our land."

"You have brought your messages and now you may deliver mine!" Cakobau jabbed a finger at the Tongans and his warriors sprang forward to surround them with a hedge of spears and clubs.

The Tongans leaped to their feet but there was no avenue of escape. No move was made to touch them but all knew that Cakobau had only to say the word to set the clubs swinging and the spears stabbing. The Tongan leader, normally no coward, felt his courage ebbing before the malevolence in the chief's eyes.

"You cannot touch us," he yelled defiantly. "We are properly appointed representatives of King George. You would not dare harm us."

"So, I would not dare?" answered Cakobau softly. "You think that I, Cakobau, am so scared of a Tongan that I would not dare?" He knew it would do his reputation no good to kill the dog; but his Tongan masters must be made to understand that Bau had reached the end of its patience.

"Poasa!" he called. A warrior scarred from a hundred battles stepped out of the crowd and fell on his knees before his chief.

"Turaga na Vunivalu?"

"I want you to leave my mark on this Tongan pig. Should he live to be a hundred I want him never to forget the insults he once offered Cakobau."

"Turaga!" the Tongan pleaded. "I was only obeying the Prince's orders."

"So you finally understand that I mean what I say," said Cakobau with a sigh of deep satisfaction. "I am afraid you carried out your Prince's orders only too well.

"Beat him with the kuita. And when you have done that, remove his manhood so that he may never again father a Tongan brat or pleasure his Tongan wife!"

A roar of satisfaction came from the Fijians and a wild scream of terror from the Tongan. He flung himself towards the door but he had not moved a yard before he was felled.

"And the others, Turaga?"

"They go free," said Cakobau magnanimously, "but the Tongan chief must live, remember that. I want him to dream about me in the years to come."

Cakobau smiled contentedly. He had already decided to send a party of his own to Tonga to lay before the King evidence that Ma'afu was working against the King's best interests. It was highly improbable that King George would openly support his cousin, and if the Bauan delegation did its work properly it could drive a wedge between the two which would cut Ma'afu's strength by more than half.

The Tongans were dragged away yelling and screaming. For all the notice Cakobau took, the incident might never have happened. As he drank a brimming bowl of yaqona, the matanivanua was sent scurrying off to order the chief's sloop be made ready. The Fijian delegation would leave for Nuku'alofa that very night.

But it might be some while before the Tongans were able to follow, and by the time they reached home, his emissaries would have discredited them.

Part I

A new God

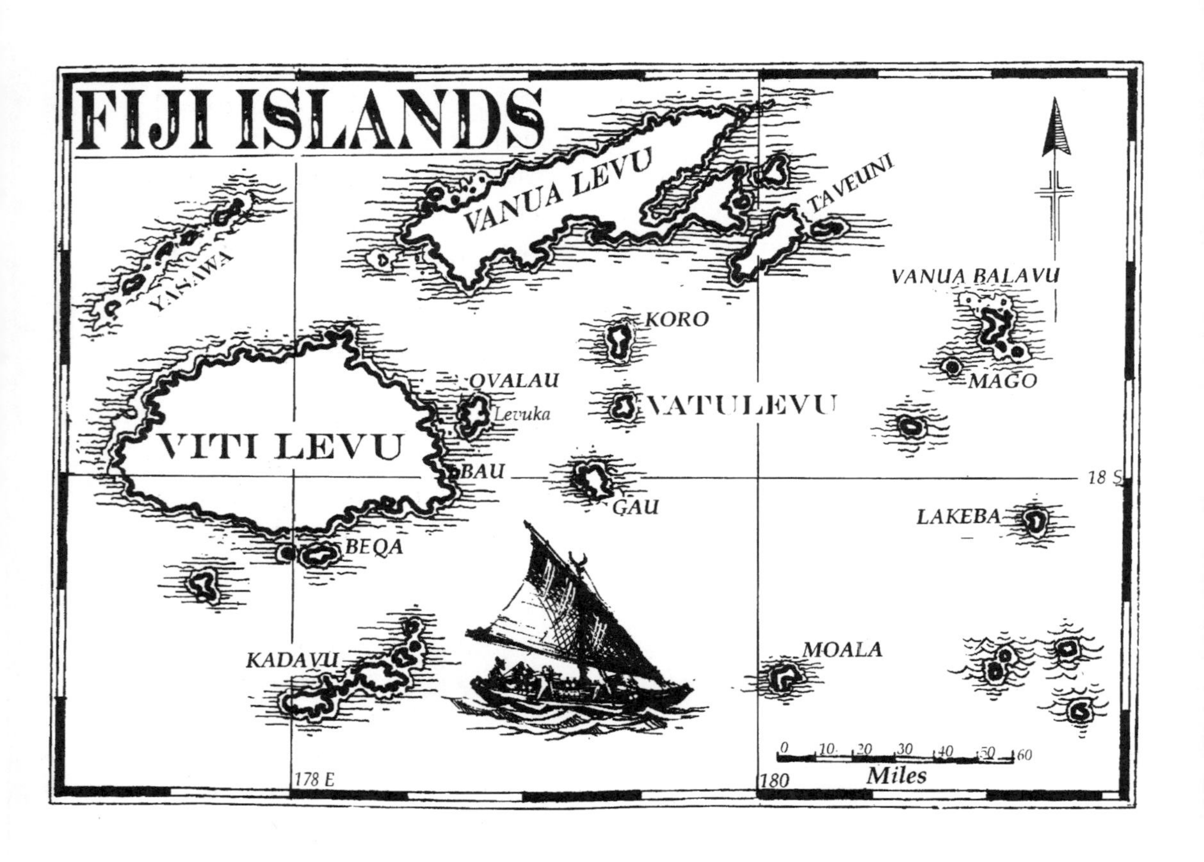
FIJI ISLANDS
VANUA LEVU
TAVEUNI
VANUA BALAVU
KORO
OVALAU
Levuka
VATULEVU
VITI LEVU
MAGO
BAU
18 S
GAU
LAKEBA
BEQA
KADAVU
MOALA
0 10 20 30 40 50 60
Miles
178 E
180

I

Fiji landfall

In years to come Katherine Denison would sail down this coastline many times, but it never again held the freshness of that first brilliant morning early in 1866. The long deep blue swells sweeping in from the ocean; the rolling, tumbling, dazzling, white foam on the offshore reefs; the still green waters of the lagoons; the golden sands and the graceful coconut palms fringing the land were a joy to behold. There seemed hardly any flat land, just soaring mountains and jagged purple peaks, forbidding yet exciting.

With her brother Tobias, Kate was accompanying their father, Rev John Cecil Denison of the Wesleyan Methodist church, who was destined to become a missionary in the far-off islands of Fiji.

From England, around the Cape of Good Hope, the Denisons had endured five months of gruelling weather, seasickness and cramped cabins to reach Sydney. There, after a short rest ashore, they transferred to the topsail schooner *Elizabeth* for the final leg of their journey from one side of the world to the other.

*****

Kate was escorting her father on their ritual morning walk around the deck. Normally Toby was with them, but there had been no sign of him at breakfast. Kate did not need to be told why — only an hour before dawn she had heard him stumbling and fumbling his way into the cabin next to her own which he shared with his father. That a clergyman's son but 19 years old should spend half the night carousing with the crew was a sad reflection upon her father's discipline.

But on such a beautiful morning, especially her first in Fiji, Kate had no intention of falling into a fit of the dismals on her scapegrace brother's account.

The deck was alive with colour, movement and noise — the snorting from the crated animals, shouting children playing tag around the masts, the crew working the ship, and the passengers excited by the prospect of landfall. Through her father's telescope Kate could make out clusters of grass houses dotted along the coast; and what had seemed to be black rocks in the lagoon turned out to be people fishing.

The scene might not have appealed to most young ladies reared in Queen

Victoria's England, but it struck a receptive chord in Kate's heart. She had never been truly comfortable among the teacups, sandwiches and polite conversation of London middle-class society; at times she had felt an almost uncontrollable urge to break out and do something utterly mad. In England, a parson's daughter necessarily kept her feelings well under control, but now these distant islands called to a kindred spirit within her which need no longer be suppressed.

As they circled the deck John Denison was accorded deferential greetings from his fellow passengers. These he returned politely but to his daughter's annoyance, he could never avoid a touch of pomposity. A tall distinguished man, his well-tailored clothes bespoke more money than was normal for a missionary. His attitude proclaimed that he, John Denison, was God's personal representative on earth and provided the common herd kept their place he would deign to intercede for them with his senior partner. Kate thought it highly unlikely her father would make a success of mission work, but well brought up young ladies did not presume to tell their fathers what they should or should not do.

Captain Peter Bex greeted them. Kate had been told by the mate, Mr Crosby, that there was not another man in the Pacific who knew the islands like Bex — hurricanes, reefs, cannibals the lot. It was said that he always had one eye cocked at the sky, the other towards the sea, and a nose which could smell trouble at 20 miles.

"Morning, Reverend. Morning, Miss Denison. Having a look at your new home?" he asked pleasantly.

Denison acknowledged the captain with a condescending nod whereas his daughter welcomed him with a warm smile. Despite the 30 years separating her and the captain Kate often felt they had more in common than she had with either her father or her brother.

"That's Viti Levu, the biggest island in the group and about the same size as Jamaica."

"Surely not, Captain?" Denison snorted. "These islands are not to be compared with those of the Caribbean." He had once read a book about Trinidad and, as usual, assumed that made him an authority on the subject.

"Well I don't know about that, Reverend, there's more than 300 islands in the Fiji group and three or four of them are pretty big. A few years back we had a Royal Navy survey ship out in these parts and it was her captain as told me." Bex did not like missionaries at the best of times, argumentative ones even less, but Denison was a cabin-class passenger and the Southern Cross Shipping Company expected its captains to be polite. "Still you could be right, never having sailed those parts myself I wouldn't know for sure."

Kate, thoroughly ashamed of her father, tried to change the subject. "Your ship is fairly flying along, Captain," she said smiling. "When do you think we shall arrive in Levuka?"

Bex glanced at the sails. "If we keep this wind, Miss, the *Elizabeth* will have you safe and sound in Levuka late this afternoon."

John Denison, however, refused to lose his place at the centre of the conversation. He had a deep fruity voice of which he was very proud and, though only his daughter and the captain were listening, he might well have been addressing a large congregation. He waved a hand vaguely in the direction of the land.

"Not the Caribbean, Captain, we are agreed, but very charming and picturesque I'm sure, a veritable paradise on earth. To a Christian nothing more clearly proclaims the wonder of the Almighty's creation."

Bex considered himself as good a Christian as most but the nonsensical platitudes mouthed by missionaries often made him feel ill. He could barely keep a note of contempt from his voice. "You're the expert on the Lord and His ways, Reverend Denison, but if you mean to last long in Fiji you would be advised to remember that beauty is often only skin-deep. A more murderous race of savages than the Fijians I've yet to meet. You and the other gentlemen may be able to teach them something about the Lord's mercy but somehow I doubt it."

Bex once owned a trading schooner that had been driven onto a reef in a storm. He and his crew survived the wreck only to fall into the hands of cannibals. With three others he managed to escape but 10 of his men had become the main course at a Fijian banquet.

John Denison, who was more used to giving advice than receiving it, ignored his daughter who was tugging on his sleeve in an effort to distract him.

"You have too little faith, Captain," he said coldly. "Some of what you say may be true, this is a savage land inhabited by an equally savage people, but you will not deny that the church has made great strides with the civilisation of the Fijians. The number of converts shows a considerable yearly increase and even such great chiefs as Cakobau are now Christian. Surely where he leads, others will follow."

"I wouldn't be denying anything, Mr Denison, nor is it part of my job as captain of this ship to lecture passengers on Fiji. All I know is that there are islands in this group where I wouldn't drop anchor at night if I were paid £10,000."

He continued, "I go by what I have seen myself and what I have been told by people whose honesty I vouch for. On my last voyage from Levuka to New Zealand I saw the burnt-out hull of a cutter on the coast of Kadavu. It was new since my previous trip, yet nothing was said in Levuka about any shipwreck, nor has anyone since heard of survivors. What happened to those poor devils I shudder to think."

"Just four months ago, three English families who settled near Viti Levu Bay were burnt out, clubbed to death, and eaten. Begging Miss Denison's pardon for raising such a gruesome subject but it's the truth, so help me God."

Denison blanched. Mission headquarters in England had assured him that murder and cannibalism were now virtually unknown and his work would be merely adding polish to what was already accomplished.

"Surely these reports are exaggerated, Captain. You don't know for certain that the crew of that cutter were murdered," he blustered nervously. As his self esteem reasserted itself he became more indignant. "You have just made this up; you are trying to frighten my daughter and myself with your fly-by-night stories."

"Father, please!" Kate protested.

Bex, temper and tongue out of control, exploded, "I'll have you know that Peter Bex does not tell fly-by-night stories. If you don't believe me then more fool you. Let me tell you something else, if it wasn't for British gunboats your church would have had damn few converts. For all I know Cakobau may be a genuine convert, but this isn't England. You'll find his writ carries no further than the circle swept by his club."

"In those peaceful looking mountains are people who have never seen a white man, never heard of the church, nor do they care tuppence for Cakobau. I'm just an ignorant sailor of course," he said with a sarcastic smile, "it's not for the likes of me to know church policy, but perhaps that's where they're going to send you, Mr Denison. After all that's what you came out here for isn't it? I wish you the best of British luck, because sure as hell is hot, you'll be needing it."

Denison, who had never entertained such an idea, was appalled. His fingers went up to his clerical collar, suddenly too tight, almost as if one of the captain's savages was already trying to strangle him. Even Kate was a little pale.

*****

The captain, in dire need of a stiff drink, abruptly excused himself pleading the press of work at the end of a voyage. He could not however resist a final thrust at this pompous parson.

"There's a small matter in which you could help me, Reverend."

"What's that, Captain Bex?"

"It's your son. It's coming to the end of the voyage and he'll be going ashore this afternoon. The mate tells me he has been gambling heavily and owes the men a packet of money. You might tell him that unless he pays up my crew could turn ugly. Deplorable I know, but I'm sure you understand how it is."

As Bex stalked off, he carried with him a picture of Denison's purple, outraged face which would be enough to raise a chuckle for many a day to come and in Levuka would make grand telling over a bottle of square gin in MacDonald's bar.

Nor was John Denison as lily-white as he made out; Bex had never seen him drinking but by evening a faint but unmistakable aroma of expensive brandy went with him wherever he went.

Denison stood spluttering on deck where the captain left him. "I'll report that man to his superiors for impertinence. How dare he speak to me like that!"

"Well, father, you virtually called him a liar and for all you know Toby may be in trouble with the crew. The captain was trying to warn you so as to avoid unpleasantness in public."

"Where is your brother?" snapped her parent. Having been humiliated by Bex he could vent his spleen on his son if no one else. "I'll give him gambling debts. As if his disgraceful behaviour in London was not enough, he has to continue here with a pack of low sailors. I tell you Katherine I've had all I can stand, I shall pay no more of his debts. If he lands himself in trouble he must get himself out, for I won't help him."

"I haven't seen him at all this morning." It was Kate's guess that her brother was still sleeping off his debauch of the previous night but she was not going to tell her father that. She could only hope that his luck had turned, otherwise the crew would not be the only ones he had to face. She had rarely seen her father so enraged.

"I shall find him," said Denison angrily, "and when I do, Master Toby is going to receive a real piece of my mind."

He disappeared below deck and Kate could only be thankful that for the first time she could enjoy the scenery without the intrusion of family problems. Twenty minutes later however she was joined at the ship's rail by her black-sheep brother.

Toby Denison was a slim young man with long pomaded blonde hair and handsome features, slightly marred by a weakish chin and a petulant mouth. Though so far from the nearest place with pretensions to civilisation, he still gave foppish attention to every detail of his dress. His beautifully cut coat and air of exquisite boredom would have been more appropriate to a St James's club than a schooner in mid-Pacific.

This particular morning the effect was rather spoilt by his bloodshot eyes, which nervously watched the movements of any sailors in his vicinity. Nor could he quite achieve the correct languid drawl, his was more the voice of a very worried young man.

"I say Kate, I'm in the very devil of a fix."

His sister made no attempt to hide her exasperation. She loved her brother, in fact since their mother left home she had virtually brought him up, but that did not mean she had any illusions about him. There were times when she would have liked to shake some sense into him.

"Oh Toby, does it have to be now? This is our first morning in Fiji and you want to ruin it for me. Why don't you see father?"

"See father? I've just come from him. Do you know he's flatly refused to give me an advance on my allowance."

"Which month's allowance would that be? I seem to remember other advances, you must already be six months ahead of yourself. Do you blame him?"

"Don't try to be funny, I must have that money. If I don't there's a couple of sailors aboard this ship who'll skin me alive."

"You should have thought of that before you started gambling. If I give you money father will be furious. You'll have to tell them that they'll get their money when you get your next allowance. Forget it for a while and look at this absolutely marvellous scenery."

"Your idea of what is marvellous and mine hardly coincide. I can conceive nothing pleasing about a parcel of scruffy islands and dirty savages. If it wasn't for father we wouldn't be marooned 1,000 miles from anywhere. Now he refuses to meet a trifling debt and gives me the most tremendous ear-bashing into the bargain. Do you wonder I can't concentrate on the scenery?"

"That's not fair and you know it," said Kate angrily. "If anyone is to blame for us leaving England it is you. Your scandalous behaviour had reached a stage where father could not have continued in the church much longer."

"I'm always the one at fault in our family. Did it never occur to you that our esteemed parent was looking for a place where he could quietly drink himself to death well hidden from the people who knew that his wife had run off with another man?"

It was the truth as they both knew but had always refused to admit, even to themselves. Toby at least had the honesty to look a little shamefaced. "Well you can hardly say father is imbued with missionary zeal."

At that moment he saw the boatswain bearing down on them, a hard and determined glint in his eye. Without a word of farewell to his sister he vanished at top speed.

*****

The *Elizabeth* sailed on down the mountainous coastline. Sails taut, her bowsprit split the sea at the bottom of each swell, her masts swung in majestic even arcs and a long white wake bubbled sweetly behind. The sun rose to its zenith and began to drop away again into the west.

At mid-afternoon the island of Ovalau emerged above the horizon. This was their destination and the 36 passengers stood in the bows watching it draw ever closer. They included eleven children and seven women, all married with the exception of Katherine Denison.

Captain Bex, watching from his station near the wheel, thought he had rarely seen such a motley, misbegotten lot. There were two other clerics apart from Denison: Partridge, a self righteous prig who with his massive wife accounted for most of the children, and young Burkit who had not opened his mouth throughout the voyage.

Of the other 14 men, two were farmers fed up with New South Wales and looking for better land in the islands. Then there was Colonel Gunning and his manservant, supposedly professional globe-trotters. Bex was prepared to take their word for it, but an inner voice told him that the Colonel was more than an ordinary tourist.

Each of the others looked as if he was on the run from something and in Bex's experience that usually meant one of three things, a bailiff, a judge or a razor-tongued wife.

Collins said he was a lawyer, and even boasted about the practice he was leaving behind. But from the way his wife jumped at every shadow it did not take great powers of deduction to guess that the man was some sort of embezzler.

Another, called Smith, an alias to be sure, had sufficient rum and square gin down in the hold to keep Levuka drunk for months. There were already 50 or more rum shops in Levuka and another would hardly make a difference and in any event, from the way Smith was sampling his stock, there might not be any left for customers.

Williams and his wife Polly were on the run from the New South Wales law; Crosby, who reckoned to know everything and everyone, had recognised them as keepers of a bawdy house near the Sydney docks. Bex had vague recollections of trying the place himself only to be put off by the filth and stench.

Polly had been plying her trade among the crew throughout the voyage and Williams was quite open about his intention of following his old profession of pimp in Levuka. It was none of Peter Bex's concern, he was running a trader not one of Her Majesty's gunboats. Not that he thought the Williams had a future in Fiji, after all who wanted to pay for sex when so many young Fijian women were eager to give it away free?

The rest were either army deserters or confidence tricksters who had outworn their welcome in Sydney. Apart from the two farmers, none of them would contribute anything to the islands. To them Fiji was just an escape hole and a land full of gullible savages begging to be fleeced.

Bex could see young Denison arguing with a crew member — that young fellow-me-lad had better watch his step; the crew were not noted for their lady-like manners.

*****

Colonel Gunning approached uninvited. Not that Bex minded — he was the least noisome of the passengers. Even out of uniform the cut of his clothes and his ramrod carriage portrayed an unmistakably military figure. He was very smooth-spoken and nothing seemed to shift the enigmatic smile from his face.

"If that's Ovalau, Bex, it's much smaller than I expected. After hearing about the island and Levuka for so long, I expected something larger. That other island, Viti Levu, seems quite continental in comparison."

"It's certainly not very big, Colonel," Bex agreed, "but it's in a good central position for trade. Levuka is the only real European settlement in the whole group."

"Why not pick one of the larger islands?"

"The settlements on the other islands are scattered plantations and open to attack at any moment. Not that Levuka's all that safe, they have had trouble from the Lovoni people but, generally speaking, being on a small separate island has kept the whites outside the mainstream of tribal warfare."

"What chance do you think Fiji has of becoming a stable country?" Gunning asked blandly. "This is my first visit, though of course I have heard a lot about the country's reputation. I'd be interested to hear what you, a man of experience in this part of the world, think."

Bex hesitated, Gunning was a very different kettle of fish from Denison but he had got into one argument already that day and didn't relish another. "Ah, it'd take too long in the telling, Colonel, and anyway it would only be my opinion."

"Come now, you are too modest," said the Colonel at his most charming. "I have a great respect for your opinion no matter what the subject."

"Alright then," said Bex, flattered into submission. "In my opinion Cakobau and his allies could stabilise the country provided he had solid financial backing and sound European advisors. His problem is that America is pushing him to pay debts at a time when he needs every penny to establish some sort of administration. On top of that he needs an army to bring the rebel elements into line and believe me there are plenty of them, both black and white."

"Rebellious Europeans! Surely it is in the interests of every white settler to help promote law and order?"

"Don't you believe it, Colonel. Most of the whites fear law and order far more than they do a cannibal's club. They're scared they'll be brought to book themselves. The first thing a sound administration would do is legislate for the repatriation of fugitives and Fiji's full of them!"

"I must say I have on occasion wondered about some of my fellow passengers. Your company is not particularly selective as to its clients."

"The Southern Cross Shipping Company is in this to make money and if I were you I'd be very careful to keep such thoughts to myself, at least until that law and order we were mentioning is a reality. The one thing you never do around here is enquire into a man's movements, his motives or his antecedents."

"I shall take your lesson very much to heart," laughed Gunning. "But please tell me more about these American debts."

"Well, there you have a right scandal, Colonel, and I'm sorry to say it reflects nothing but discredit on a great country. We had an American here called Williams, who set himself up as the US commercial agent. Believe me he was up to every trick in the book. One Independence Day he turned on a rocket display which got so far out of hand that his own house and stores were burnt to the ground. In the general confusion, a crowd of visiting Fijians made off with some of his stuff under the pretext of trying to save it from the fire."

"Those people had nothing to do with Ratu Cakobau, but Williams told the next American man-of-war that came along, the USS *John Adams* it was, that the chief's men had stolen $5,000-worth of goods. Commander Boutwell hauls Cakobau aboard; wouldn't even allow a couple of the missionaries who wanted to act as counsel to go with him. With the damages they added to Williams' figure, they finally told Cakobau he owed the American Government a total of $45,000. He of course denied any responsibility, but Boutwell ruled that because of his claims to be King of Fiji, he was responsible and threatened to deport him to the States unless he signed a paper acknowledging the debt and promising to pay within two years."

"But how fantastic! Did he sign?"

"He signed alright. There is nothing a Fijian fears more than being taken away as a hostage."

"Has he tried any other ways of raising the money?" Gunning seemed genuinely interested, yet Bex couldn't help feeling he knew the answers already.

"Cakobau has tried everything. A few years ago he wanted Britain to take over the debt and offered the islands as a colonial territory so that the pressure would be taken off him. They turned him down flat."

"It's all this damned liberal and humanitarian nonsense they talk at home these days. It's that man Gladstone who's responsible," snorted Gunning disgustedly. "If Britain doesn't take Fiji, Cakobau will be offering the islands to one of the other powers and you can wager France and Germany will not be bothered by a pack of middle-class scruples. With more settlement, investment, and a couple of battalions of regular infantry to keep the natives in their proper place, these islands could become a gold mine."

For the next five minutes they digressed on British politics and colonial policy, subjects on which they were in full agreement.

*****

Their discussion was interrupted by a cry from the lookout placed at the masthead by Bex to spot coral patches.

"Ketch closing fast from the port side, Captain."

Bex trained his glass on a the newcomer. Her trimness and the way she handled showed she was under the control of a damned good sailor. Soon she was close enough for him to make out a European at the helm with a crew of at least four Fijians.

"It's Jason Cotterel and the *Albatross,*" he announced to Gunning.

"Jason Cotterel?"

"He's got a plantation on an island called Vatulevu, about 40 miles east of here. He'll be on his way to Levuka same as us. He goes in regularly for stores and to sell cotton and coconut oil."

"Another of those fugitives you mentioned earlier, Captain?"

"Jason a fugitive?" mused Bex, "No, I don't think so. I don't know a lot about him of course; as I told you we don't pry into a man's background here but I would have thought that you could call Jason Cotterel the exception which proves the rule. A colourful character, most likely a little odd by your way of thinking, but according to my lights he's good man. I know that if I was ever in any trouble he's the feller I'd like to have standing behind me."

"He would be a supporter of our scheme for law and order I take it."

"Not if it meant becoming a British colony he wouldn't, Jason is a Yankee. Not that he wants to see Fiji under the Americans either, he wants to see an independent Fijian state with a Fijian government and an administration run by the Fijians. You might call it his hobby-horse; once you get him started he'll talk all night."

"If you're really interested in Fiji, Colonel, he's your man. A lot of the old timers reckon they know the lot, but for my money Jason knows more about the islands than that drunken bunch put together. And he's one of the few who aren't blinded by their own personal interest. So far as he's concerned, the Fijians and their interests come first."

"He must be quite a paragon, this Jason Cotterel. You are eloquent in his defence, Captain. He should congratulate himself on his choice of friends. So much so that I should like to meet Mr Cotterel when we get to Levuka, if that could be arranged."

The ketch was closer now and the man at the helm could be distinguished more clearly. Apart from a beard trimmed to a point, little could be seen of the face hidden in the shadow of a broad brimmed 'Tokelau' hat made from plaited coconut fronds. His only other garment was a pair of loose duck trousers, which terminated at mid-calf.

He was a man of tremendous physique, over six feet in height with a breadth of shoulder and muscles which would have done credit to a prize fighter. He stood on the port gunwale of his boat, one hand to a sheet while he casually controlled the tiller with a bare foot. He was so tanned that if Gunning had not already been told otherwise, he might easily have mistaken him for a lighter-skinned Fijian.

"That's some man," said Gunning, observing him through the captain's glass.

"Not someone to cross," laughed Bex. "I never heard tell of anyone who tangled with Jason and didn't come off the worse for it, nor for that matter one who didn't deserve all he got. He's not a man to go looking for a fight, but he's not one to step aside if a fight is offered."

Gunning lowered the glass and looked puzzled.

"I know it's against your principles to pry, Captain. You've already told me that several times this afternoon, but are you sure you don't know anything about this man's background. I'm sure I've heard the name Cotterel before."

"All I know is that he came here as a hand on a Nantucket whaler about 12 years ago. Why he dropped off in Fiji I don't know, nor have I asked. He can't have been much more than 20 at the time but already well able to look after himself. I'd say he came from a good home though, for he's well-educated — I've a parcel of books aboard for him now. I bring some every trip."

"But why should a man of education and ability bury himself in a place like this?"

"You're an educated man, Colonel, and it seems to me from what you've told me of your travels, you're not that partial to civilisation yourself. Maybe I'm fooling myself but I reckon I can always pick a fugitive; Jason Cotterel just doesn't have that apprehensive look about him."

Bex could have told Gunning a lot more about his friend but he hated people who gabbed about others. There would be plenty ashore ready to tell the colonel all he wanted to know, for Jason had plenty of enemies. As a trusted confidant of Ratu Cakobau the old-timers hated him for wanting to ruin their pitch through government interference.

The missionaries disliked him for his open criticism of their efforts to establish a theocracy. He hadn't stopped Cakobau becoming a Christian, but he had used every ounce of influence to keep the clergy out of the secular affairs of the islands. They in turn denounced him as a renegade and anti-Christ. This was partly true, for Jason had two mixed-race children and, because of him, Tui Navatulevu, the chief of the island where he had his plantation, had refused to admit missionaries or become a convert himself.

Bex could not go along with all of Cotterel's hopes and theories but he was still able to recognise and appreciate the honesty of the man. He also owed him a few favours, not the least of which involved an occasion when his life was forfeit to a gang of drunken sailors bent on knifing him. It was only Jason's dirk and his huge fists that had got Bex off with a whole skin.

*****

As the ketch came alongside, Cotterel's Fijian crew, all big men like himself, were laughing and yelling to the passengers and crew of the schooner. Bex stepped to the rail.

"Hello there, Jason," he shouted through his capped hands.

"Ni sa bula, Turaga," Cotterel shouted back the traditional Fijian greeting. "Good trip?"

"Not bad, how go things with you?"

"Same as ever," came the answer. Cotterel pushed back his hat and critically surveyed the line of passengers peering down at him. His deep laugh rolled across the sea, "I see you've got your usual cargo of jail-bait and bible-bangers, Peter."

There was an indignant stir from among the passengers and several heads ducked out of sight.

"Belay that sort of talk if you please. Remember there's ladies present or have you forgotten what ladies are?" yelled Bex gruffly. As much as he might agree with Jason's assessment, to say so would mean an avalanche of complaints to his directors.

But if Kate Denison was representative of the ladies they were not as annoyed as their menfolk. The giant's laughter was infectious and the discomfiture of her fellow passengers so ridiculous that she could not help laughing herself.

Shining blonde hair blowing about a face alive with enjoyment, she stood out like a golden dove amid a flock of crows. She was demurely dressed but the wind moulded the cloth so closely to her body a dead man could have pictured the perfection of the figure which lay beneath.

"Some very beautiful ladies too, Peter," shouted Jason appreciatively. He bowed with lithe grace for such a big man and kissed his hand in Kate's direction.

Enjoying every moment of the encounter, Kate blew a kiss back and waved. She had never seen such a man before; even at that distance she could feel his tremendous vitality.

"Katherine! How dare you!" She was unceremoniously hauled from the ship's side by her father who was livid with anger. "What on earth do you think you are doing?"

Kate came back to earth with a jolt and blushed furiously. Other passengers were looking at her as if she was some sort of traitor. For a moment she had been part of the freedom of the islands only to be snatched back a second later by the puritanism of the Methodist church and Victorian England.

"Go to your cabin this instant, girl," snapped her father. "Both you and your brother seem determined to disgrace me."

Kate fled, but even as she stumbled down the companionway she could hear the stranger's laughter hanging on the afternoon air.

The *Albatross* sheered away and Cotterel's stentorian voice drifted back across the waves. "See you in MacDonald's, Peter, try to bring the young filly with you if you can."

*****

To Gunning's amusement, Captain Bex spent the next quarter of an hour trying to placate his indignant passengers. Collins was the most vociferous, demanding that 'the Captain's hoodlum friend' be brought to task on their arrival in Levuka. Finally Bex had had enough and as they were about to round the point of land which would bring them in sight of their destination he brought the wrangling to an end.

"Please, gentlemen, you must allow me to attend to my duties or this ship will finish up on a reef."

"It is not good enough, I shall report ..." Collins began.

"Mr Collins," interrupted Bex, his voice heavy with sarcasm, "I can only repeat that there is nothing I can do and you may report to anyone you damned-well please. If you feel your personal honour has been injured why not take the matter up with Jason Cotterel himself, I'm sure he would only be too happy to give you satisfaction."

The thought of a duel with the young giant was more than enough to dampen the lawyer's ardour. He went off muttering about, 'due legal process for such rascals'.

Bex winked at Gunning who was no longer even attempting to keep a straight face, and couldn't resist a parting shot at Collins back. "As to legal process, Mr Collins, you'll find in the islands you have only as much process as your own two fists can enforce. I wouldn't try appealing to the native authorities either, Jason Cotterel happens to be a close personal friend of the paramount chief."

Then, seeing Crosby's face he switched his attack. "Will you kindly stop grinning like an idiot, Crosby, and attend to this ship. Prepare to enter harbour. Move lively, man!"

The air was thick with hurled commands and running sailors took over the decks. Most of the passengers scampered out of their way and, remembering last minute things to be done, hurried below. Gunning stayed near the captain as the *Elizabeth* rounded the point and swept down towards the harbour entrance.

Bex didn't bother with a pilot; as he explained to Gunning, the Levuka pilots were drunks scraped up off the beach to give the place a semblance of a proper port and likely to do more harm than good.

Gunning, his eye glued to the end of the telescope, surveyed Levuka the town which would be his headquarters for the next few months, "I've seen some godforsaken, nondescript dumps in my time, Bex, but this beats them all," he said in an awed tone.

Bex laughed. "It ain't the best, Colonel, and we're not close enough to get the smell yet. But outside of New South Wales or New Zealand, Levuka's the nearest thing to civilisation you'll find in the South Pacific"

"Then God help all civilised men," was the solemn reply.

2

The arrival

PART GRASS HOUSES, WITH SMOKE SEEPING through the thatched roofs from fires cooking the evening meal; part shanties of rusted corrugated iron; and part tent town, Levuka looked as if it might disappear in the next hurricane. The flat land was barely adequate for a single line of buildings to be squeezed between sea and mountains, the remainder were scattered over the lower slopes as if sprayed from a blunderbuss.

A few more substantial buildings were in the course of erection but were still of the wooden frame and iron roof variety. A single two-storied building sported an upstairs verandah of sorts and, right across its iron roof, a painted sign 'MacDonald's Hotel' could be clearly read from well out to sea. If, as Bex had said, every second building was a rum shop, Levuka must have the thirstiest population in the South Pacific, thought Gunning.

Yet the town also had the same air of bustle and movement Gunning had seen in the boom towns of the Californian goldfields. As they closed the shore he could see people on the move everywhere. The majority were Fijians with huge heads of hair, dark skins and in varying stages of nudity; but there were other dark-skinned people whom Captain Bex said were Tongans or islanders from elsewhere in the Pacific, and Gunning even thought he spotted a couple of Chinese, pigtails and all.

The clothing ranged from loin cloths, to various bits and pieces of European dress. He was especially delighted by the sight of a Fijian resplendent in morning coat and silk hat — needless to say he did not own a shirt though his shanks were decently covered by half a blanket.

The shipping added to the colour and general atmosphere of energy. Including the canoes pulled up on the beach, more than 70 vessels were in harbour. Fijians waded back and forth from the ships loading and unloading. It must have been slippery underfoot for Gunning saw one man go right under, bundle and all, and gales of unsympathetic laughter from his companions carried across the water to the *Elizabeth* as she turned into the wind and her anchor bit the mud.

"The canoes are from local villages," said Bex. "They're fairly primitive but quite adequate for fishing or short journeys along the coast and up rivers. On the other hand, those over there with outriggers, takia the Fijians call them, could be from as far away as Viti Levu or the other major island, Vanua Levu. They may not look much but their matting sails can really make them move in a good wind, I've seen them doing 15 knots, maybe more."

"Some of the bigger stuff is carrying cargo and passengers like us. That barque over there is the *William Jones* out of San Francisco and alongside her are two Nantucket whalers; they'll be after sperm whale or just laying up here for a rest before heading south towards the pack ice. I haven't seen that big white schooner that's flying the German flag before but it's even money she belongs to Godeffroy & Sons. They're from Hamburg and operate mainly out of Samoa and the islands to the north of Fiji, but you see the odd one or two down here looking for business."

Gunning pointed to a large double-hulled vessel. She was obviously of local construction but much larger than he would have thought primitive craftsmen capable of building. Her hulls, standing high out of the water, were at least 90 feet in length and she had a tremendous beam on the platform joining the two together. There was a mast and a deckhouse — it looked to be rough-hewn but for all that was solid and seaworthy.

"I'm amazed that savages are able to build such things," he said.

"They're quite something aren't they? Fijians are noted shipbuilders. Some say Tongans are the more intelligent, but they have to come cap-in-hand to the Fijians if they want a ship of that size. They tell stories about the old days when their ancestors used to travel the length and breadth of the Pacific. But you don't see as many as when I made my first trip to the islands a matter of twenty years ago. The chiefs all want cutters of European design now."

"Who does she belong to?"

"I'm not sure," said Bex, "She looks like one Fijians call *Senibiau*, Flower of the Waves. If so, she's Ratu Cakobau's, which means that either he or one of his lieutenants is in town."

"Which in turn means?" probed Gunning.

Bex shrugged his shoulders. "I don't know, something could be afoot. He doesn't come here just to do his shopping or pass the time of day with the missionaries."

The tops had come off the hatches and the passengers' heavy luggage was being swayed up out of the holds. The deck was littered with parcels, trunks and carpetbags. Those about to go ashore were dressed in their best; they might have been about to attend a garden fête rather than step ashore in the dirtiest, smelliest ramshackle hole in the Pacific. They scrabbled about among their bits and pieces, complaining bitterly of lost or damaged items as if they were as precious as the crown jewels. The sailors, anxious to get ashore to the women and rum shops, cursed them as they got underfoot.

*****

The Denisons sat on their boxes awaiting their turn to be rowed ashore in one of the ship's boats. Toby was in an absolute sweat; the cold sweat of fear. He rubbed his hands nervously against his knees and his eyes flickered from side to side alert for the approach of any member of the crew. They had been following him around all day and only the assurance that his father would come good had kept them off his neck this long.

John Denison stared at the shanty town which was to become the centre of his world. He refused to even look at his son; he had made up his mind and was determined not to give in. This did not stop Toby trying.

"Please, father, please. You don't know them like I do. I promise I'll never gamble in my life again if you'll only help me this last time."

Denison had reached the end of his patience and he turned on his son, his voice so loud that many passengers looked around to find out what was happening. "Your promises! Do you think I don't know how worthless your promises are?"

"Please, father, lower your voice," urged Kate, flushed with embarrassment. "You are attracting attention to us."

But this only made Denison more furious. "You keep out of this, girl. Your own behaviour has shown that you are as devoid of principles as your shameless brother. You are both determined to disgrace me and I am past the stage of caring who knows."

He shook his fist under his son's nose, "You, sir, are a consummate rogue. I refuse to accept any responsibility for your depravity and I shall not pay one penny of your gaming debts."

The other passengers enjoyed this immensely. Unluckily for Toby the crew were also listening. A seaman with a face like a battered copper kettle dropped down from the rigging and snatched a marlinspike from a rack at the foot of the mainmast. He advanced on the Denisons with obvious intentions and several women began to scream. One of the farmers' wives dragged Kate aside.

"So ye're not willin' to pay what your bloody whelp owes us?" snarled the sailor. "We have ways of dealing with welshers like him."

"How dare you!" roared Denison with a show of bravado. "If you do not get away from here immediately I shall report you to your captain."

"I'll get away from your Holiness when me and me mates gets our money."

"Father, please give him the money." Toby begged desperately.

"I'll do nothing of the sort, I do not deal with scum nor will I have any truck with gambling debts."

"In that case ye won't mind us havin' your brat's guts."

The seaman lunged forward and struck a wild blow in Toby's direction but the boy, with speed generated by fear, ducked and the heavy marlinspike missed his face by a matter of inches. As he dived away through the stacks of luggage his assailant was grabbed by a couple of well-meaning passengers, but other members of the crew took up the chase. Toby ran as he had never run before, the sailors after him like staghounds with the scent of blood in their nostrils.

"Stop those men, Crosby," roared Bex. Though sympathetic towards his crew he wanted no blood spilt on his decks. He plunged down on to the main deck, his bellow cutting through the hue and cry. "Any of you touch that boy and you're in irons."

The crew had cornered Toby Denison in the bows of the ship. He was terrified; there were at least eight of them, all armed with knives or marlinspikes. The captain's roar had stopped them momentarily but now they began to inch forward again.

"D...d...don't, come near me," Toby stammered hoarsely. "You heard your captain, you must leave me alone. I'll pay you, I'll pay you as soon as we get on shore, I promise."

"You snivelling, welshing little bastard," spat one crew member viciously. "You owe us a hundred golden men and we get them now or else." Even discounting the money they were enjoying seeing this London pansy squirm.

"Harrison, Davies, Johnson," yelled Bex as he barged his way through the passengers. "Belay that or you'll have me to reckon with."

Most of the sailors fell back rather than face the captain's fists. One, slower than the rest, Bex pole-axed with a hammer-like blow to the back of the neck. But he was not fast enough to stop Johnson raising a marlinspike ready to heave it at the cowering boy. With nowhere left to run, Toby yelled out and vaulting over the side of the schooner plunged into the refuse-littered waters of the harbour.

He surfaced, spluttering and choking from the water he had swallowed. The ship's rail high above him was lined with the jeering faces of crew and passengers. Despite the efforts of their officers to restrain them, the sailors threw anything that came to hand at Toby. Luckily he could swim well enough to save himself from drowning. He made for one of the ship's boats lying astern of the schooner but the rowers flailed at him with their oars.

Kate and her father stood white-faced at the rail, John Denison maintaining a deathly silence as if he was prepared to see his son sink beneath the surface of the dirty water without raising a finger to help him. Not so Kate. "Swim to the shore, Toby," she called anxiously. "We'll meet you ashore."

But instead of heading directly for the beach he swam with painful slowness towards the nearest ship, Jason Cotterel's *Albatross*. Cotterel and his crew, alerted by the uproar aboard the schooner, had seen the boy jump overboard and watched as he slowly approached.

Any help they might have offered was forestalled by a yell from the *Elizabeth*.

"Don't let him aboard, Mister Cotterel. "He's a bloody welsher, he owes us £100 and won't pay up."

Jason would not have seen the lad drown but there was a code governing gambling and he had as little love for a welsher as anyone else. He leaned over the side as Toby drew near.

"I'm sorry, son, but you heard what the man said."

"But I'll drown," Toby cried, thrashing feebly about in the water. "For God's sake let me come on board."

Jason felt pity for the frightened boy but he hardened his heart. If he had been gambling when he didn't have the money to lose he deserved to be taught a lesson. "You won't drown, you've swum this far and you'll make it alright. It's low tide, all you've got to do is head toward the beach and you'll be able to stand and walk before you've gone 50 yards."

"You Goddamned swine," Toby was weeping with mingled rage and fear as he struggled to tread water. "You are barbarian monsters, the lot of you." He turned from the ketch towards land, which still seemed miles away.

It was a wet and bedraggled young man, his beautiful clothes irreparably stained by the filthy water, who staggered up the beach. Regardless of the broken bottles, bones and all manner of human waste littering the sand he slumped down exhausted and putting his head in his hands cried like a baby, the first Denison to set foot on Fiji soil.

3

Levuka

Kate Denison lay on her bed in MacDonald's Hotel trying to close her mind against the damp heat. After the ship, where she had only to go on deck to find a cool breeze, Levuka was close and uncomfortable. The hills behind the town blocked the movement of air. Everything was slightly damp to the touch and the least physical effort caused her clothes to cling clammily to her body.

Wherever she went she wore dark clothes which would have made her feel hot on a normal summer's day in England. She had light, wispy muslins with her, but her father considered them too frivolous for a missionary's daughter. Kate envied the Fijian children gambolling naked in the sea.

Her only consolation was it was February and, according to the publican's wife, the wet season would soon be over and they would be into winter, a season of hot dry days and cold nights. Mrs MacDonald, a fat motherly woman, clucked and fussed about her the whole time. Salves for mosquito bites, sulphur to drive away the moths, lemon juice to remove mildew stains from clothing; Kitty MacDonald even seemed to imagine Kate needed protection against the wrath of her father.

Kate was no fool, she knew that those shrewd eyes had quickly calculated the depth of her father's pockets. Had Kate the normal threadbare look of missionary families her treatment might have been very different.

She needed no protection but in this heat it was easier to let the woman fuss. Though her father had the stubbornness of a weak man Kate knew she was more than a match for him when necessary. She had long since recognised that her menfolk were spineless. She was the strong one who bolstered their egos by giving them the impression that she was completely dependent upon them.

How her father would fare as a missionary did not bear thinking about for he was not in the least practical, indeed there were times she was convinced he had been born lacking basic common sense. The missionary position in Fiji had been the first opportunity to present itself at a time when he was desperate to leave London; there were a thousand more suitable places he might have fled to — he had signed the agreement before she knew a thing about it, otherwise for her father's sake she would have squashed the whole scheme.

Now that the full ramifications of life in Fiji were beginning to sink home, Kate could sense his growing fear and trepidation. He had already been told that, instead of the expected placement at mission headquarters, they were to go to a small island which had never seen a missionary before. The pagans of Vatulevu were to be brought into the Christian fold by John Cecil Denison.

It was not that Kate was worried for herself, far from it. The excitement conjured up by the very idea of the South Seas had overcome any qualms. At 22, bursting with health and an overwhelming desire to break free from stodgy London life, the prospect had been irresistible.

Neither was Kate frightened by decisions. In that respect she took after her mother who had run away with the man she loved in the teeth of public disapproval. Until Kate was ten she had supposed her mother to be dead, which was what her father had told her, but the truth leaked out from the servants. Toby also knew, but they both maintained the fiction of her demise whenever their father was present. It was just as well that her parents had been divorced by a private Act of Parliament for Kate could hardly imagine the beautiful Lady Sealwood settling in the Fiji Islands.

They had been in Levuka a week now. Kate's father spent the greater part of each day at mission headquarters only to lock himself away in his room as soon as he returned to the hotel. Toby was just as much a recluse. He was terrified that he would meet a member of the *Elizabeth*'s crew and be made to answer for his debts. Had he known it, he might have walked the length of the town without the slightest fear of assault for his sister had settled his account in full before leaving the ship. But, with bars and loose women abounding, Kate deemed it wisest not to tell him of his reprieve. Not even her father knew.

Kate hoped Toby would settle down once they were on Vatulevu. The family plan to buy land and set him up as a planter would, with any luck, keep him too busy to think about the fleshpots. In the meantime it was her self-appointed task to settle his shattered nerves and reconcile him to his life as a farmer. She had just come from one such session with him and felt emotionally exhausted by the effort.

"Goddammit Kate, what do I know about farming? Why do I have to be shut away on a blasted plantation for the rest of my life, I might just as well be in prison or dead."

"Don't talk like that, Toby. You haven't seen the place or even tried it yet. There'll be fishing, and father will buy a boat so you can go sailing, it won't be all work."

"Not half," he sneered. "I won't be forgiven my sins till the day I die, father will see to that. He wants to transform me into a country bumpkin."

Finally, Kate lost patience. It made her furious to see him slumped there in his chair. If she had been a man she would have known what to do with her life. "Well if you don't like it, why don't you do something about it? Tell father you have had enough; tell him you will not go with us to Vatulevu and that you are going to strike out on your own. Go to New Zealand or even back to England if you want to. Your trouble is you are too cowardly to do a thing for yourself."

"What am I supposed to use for money? Ask father I suppose. I know what sort of reception I would get."

"It would never occur to you that you might take employment here in Levuka and earn some money," she had snapped.

"Oh, don't you get at me too, Kate," tears of self-pity filled his eyes. "I know I'm no good, I'm a disgrace to the whole family. If only father had made me a soldier or a lawyer I'd have a profession to fall back on. I don't know how to work at anything. Oh God, what am I to do?"

Immediately Kate was all contrition and sank beside his chair an arm about his shoulders. "Don't worry so much Toby. You'll see, everything will turn out well and father will soon forget that business on the ship. If he doesn't I shall speak to him myself before we leave for the island. If you will only give planting a try I think you'll find it may solve all your problems."

"I'll help all I can and you can get advice from other planters. Why, some people have made fortunes from plantations," she said. Not that she had confidence that any project associated with her father and brother would do the same. "In a few years you may have made enough to retire to England and by then everyone will have forgotten what happened and you'll be able to leave a manager here and live in London like a nabob."

It was all highly improbable but it was sufficient to cheer him up slightly and enable Kate to escape to her own room where she bolted the door against intrusions. Her heavy clothes were wet with perspiration and she was physically and mentally exhausted. The dress collapsed in a heap on the floor and her shifts, corset and pantaloons followed. The water in the large ewer standing in one corner of the room was tepid, but a call for cold water would have meant at least half an hour of Mrs MacDonald's incessant small talk. She sponged herself all over and, feeling cleaner if not much cooler, stretched out on the bed.

Low rumbles of thunder along the hills, the rising humidity, and the sudden darkening of her room told her that the afternoon rain was approaching. Every day from three until four, as regular as clockwork, the heavens opened. Slowly it started, hard heavy drops, then the rain crashed down on the corrugated iron roof of the hotel.

Kate welcomed the drop in temperature. The water battering through her open bedroom window soaked the net curtains and the mat on the floor. She knew she should close the window but the noise of the rain on the roof had a hypnotic effect: she was powerless to move and her eyelids were too heavy to control any longer. Raindrops were blowing in on her but not even they could hold back sleep.

She dreamt that she lay on the deck of a ship which was carrying her away from all her family problems. Spray showered over the bows on to her naked body. It was exhilarating and she could not stop herself laughing deliriously, so great was the feeling of relief and freedom.

At the helm swayed a tall, bearded man, his massive shoulders shining golden in the sunlight. He laughed and blew kisses which fell all about her. He was everything the men of her own family were not and he was whisking her away to an island where she would never again have to worry about her father's drinking or her brother's gambling.

4

Conversations

While the rain poured and his daughter slept, John Denison was cooped up in the office of Dr Matthews, the superintendent of the Methodist Mission. The heat made his skin prickle uncomfortably and rivulets of perspiration coursed down his back, yet his tongue and throat were parched.

The lecture on the Fijian language and how to run a mission had been in progress for hours. Partridge and Burkit listened as if every word was a pearl of wisdom, whereas Denison had only managed to stay awake by concentrating on his personal predicament. If the harangue went on much longer he meant to excuse himself and seek privacy where he could sup from the flask which nestled in the inside pocket of his coat, so near yet so far away.

Fijian! What a barbaric language! Never would he be able to master it for conversation, much less use it for preaching sermons. Denison was proud of his command of Latin and Greek but this primitive gabble followed none of the rules which governed a civilised tongue. He could not pronounce, let alone understand it.

Dr Matthews explained that 'Na Turaga na Kalou' meant the Lord God Almighty. Denison could not reconcile himself to the concept of the Lord's name in a foreign language. The church taught that God was universal but he always thought of Him as an Englishman, a Victorian gentleman, the symbol of fair play, charity for the working classes, and the prop of Queen and Empire. There was something degrading about having to share his God with a pack of heathen cannibals.

Now the superintendent was expounding on the theme of rendering unto Caesar that which was Caesar's. They were to treat the chiefs with due deference and always accord them their proper titles. This, thought Denison, would present no problems for the others since both came from that stratum of society which was expected to tug its forelock to those in authority. But that he, a Denison, should be subservient to a black was an unbearable thought. He was quick to reconcile himself to it however when Matthews told them that the chiefs were extremely sensitive to anything which touched their honour — men had been clubbed to death for failing to observe proper courtesy.

"Vale means a house, and vale ni lotu means a church," Matthews was saying, "and your first tasks will be to construct a house in which to live and then a church in which your congregation may worship. I take it that you are conversant with such buildings and their construction, Denison."

John Denison sat up with a guilty start. It was as bad as being back at public school. Matthews was all too close an approximation of his old headmaster,

"Well, I have of course always been interested in church architecture, Doctor Matthews," he said with a show of confidence.

"I do not mean an academic study of the perpendicular, Denison, but your ability as a carpenter," snapped Matthews. He had been in a bad mood ever since this batch of missionaries had arrived. He didn't know what London was thinking of, sending men like these. If he had not been desperately understaffed he would have packed all three straight back to whence they came.

Denison's face registered bafflement, and to his profound annoyance Partridge sniggered. "As a carpenter, Doctor Matthews? I'm afraid I don't understand."

"You will have to build your own home and church using your own knowledge and mainly your own labour. Surely you realise that?" said Matthews trying to be as patient as possible.

"But I've never built anything in my life," Denison exclaimed. He was shattered by the idea. As a final degradation they meant to turn him into some form of manual labourer. "I don't know the first thing about carpentry."

"You surely didn't imagine there would be a ready-built house and church waiting for you on an island where we have never previously had a mission?" Matthews did not attempt to hide his exasperation.

Partridge's smirks and the vacant look on Burkit's face were just as infuriating. "What of you two? I suppose neither of you has ever handled a hammer?"

Both professed a keen interest but, as the superintendent suspected, neither had ever built anything, though Burkit said he had a book on the subject which he offered to lend to Denison.

Dr Matthews fell silent and studied the papers on his desk while the three novice missionaries fidgeted nervously. He was between the devil and the deep blue sea. The mission was at a stage where much basic work had been done but if they were to take advantage of the untiring, self-destroying efforts of the pioneers, he needed men to fill gaps in his ranks. What he would have liked were the sons of farmers, capable of standing on their own two feet; men who could show the people how to build better houses or how to improve their crops — the ability to read Hebrew or preach the Gospel was only part of the battle. These newcomers were babes in the wood and just as useless.

He had already decided that Burkit would go to Viwa, a small island just off the mainland of Viti Levu, to assist the incumbent John Hill, a man of almost saintly dedication who had wrecked his health in the fight against paganism.

Partridge, whose demonstrative piety failed to impress Matthews in the slightest, would stay in Levuka until work among the Fijians and European derelicts had toughened him sufficiently to face the work of the true missionary.

Denison was the real worry. He was very well recommended in England and even better connected. He came from the same public school and moneyed background as Matthews himself who had anticipated an equal reliability and efficiency.

He had been impressed with the girl's vivacity, friendliness and high spirits. The boy was sulky as a result of his present disgrace but if he came out of it, he could be of inestimable value to his father. Denison could not speak one word of Fijian, nor did he appear to grasp the problems which would confront him in the field. Yet Matthews had been angling for years to place someone on Vatulevu and now that the opportunity presented itself he could not afford to turn it down despite his lack of trained staff.

Others who might conceivably be transferred to Vatulevu were already fully involved in their present work, and the success or failure of a mission was so terribly dependent on the personal relationship between pastor and flock that to chop and change people around at this crucial stage might jeopardise much of what had been achieved.

"H'm," he mused while the others shuffled. "Well, Denison, whether you can handle a hammer or not I have no one else to send to Vatulevu; it will have to be you. I have an assistant I can give you who can teach you the language and basic carpentry."

"Thank you very much, Doctor," said John Denison, relieved. With another European experienced in manual skills he would be able to concentrate on those things which came within the proper sphere of a gentleman.

But the superintendent's next statement brought him sharply back to earth: "You can have my chief lay preacher, Elija Codrokadroka. But I must impress on you Denison, he goes with you as a teacher and not as a native labourer. Nor can I spare him for more than six months as he is due to go to England to complete his studies before being ordained as a minister himself."

While Matthews passed on to discuss particular problems with the others, Denison, sunk in the mire of his depression, let the conversation drift over his head. A Fijian! — when he had hoped for another European who might have provided some sort of companionship. A teacher-pupil relationship at that, and with him on the receiving end!

In England, 13,000 miles away, mission work in the South Seas had sounded romantic and uplifting; almost an atonement for his sins. But he could no longer delude himself, he was unfit to face what lay ahead. The honest thing would be to tell Matthews he had made a ghastly mistake. Yet he lacked the nerve to face the momentary but immediate humiliation.

But as much as he lacked those qualities needed for mission work, he also lacked the necessary moral courage to extricate himself. Denison could foresee himself being a complete and utter failure, shipped back to England in disgrace.

*****

John Denison was so wrapped in his own misery that he had failed to notice the departure of the others. He looked up to find that he was alone with the superintendent.

"Is something worrying you?" There was a solicitous note in Matthews voice.

"Er-not really, Doctor, thank you."

"You are not worrying about Vatulevu?"

Denison wondered whether he should let it all come pouring out and depend on the man's compassion.

"Well, no," he began hesitantly, "It's just that I begin to doubt my ability to come up to your exacting standards, I don't want to let you down."

Matthews smiled. He preferred to see his new people cautious rather than cocksure with confidence. He came around his desk to lay a hand reassuringly on Denison's shoulder.

"I'm sure you'll be alright, old man; would I send you to Vatulevu if I didn't think so? Come now, you must not worry, we all have much to learn when we first come here — it takes time. This Fijian I am sending with you is a very fine chap and I have absolute confidence in both him and you. What you don't know, he will teach you in no time."

Matthews could sense the man's desire to cry off but he could not afford to lose him. No matter how poorly shaped he might be, he needed every tool he could get. Taking the most cynical attitude, if he could get Denison to fill the gap long enough they would have a foothold on the island and once there no one would dislodge them.

"You realise, old boy, that it would be completely impossible to send fellows like Partridge or Burkit there," he said, laying on the 'old school' approach. "They're just not up to it like one of us."

Denison straightened slightly in his chair. The white man's burden, *noblesse oblige* and Dr Matthews acting as a father figure were more than he could resist.

Matthews followed up the advantage. "You are the obvious choice for a number of reasons, Denison. On Vatulevu, there's this American, Jason Cotterel."

"Jason Cotterel! He's the blackguard who insulted my daughter."

"Unfortunately Cotterel is a most important blackguard, and for years he has been a considerable thorn in the side of the church."

"And now in mine it seems," muttered Denison forlornly.

"He could well be," Matthews admitted. "It's because he has the ear of Tui

Navatulevu that we have been excluded for so long. But Ratu Cakobau is the Tui's overlord and at my insistence he has brought pressure to bear. Now Tui Navatulevu has agreed to accept and welcome the mission."

"With Cotterel working against me, I cannot see that I have much chance of success," Denison complained.

"You worry too much, my dear fellow, I hope I have fixed that for you as well." Matthews strode up and down the hot, stuffy office as he spoke. In his own way he was quite a general and so long as he could depend on the steadfastness of his troops there was little he planned which was not accomplished. "Cotterel is here on Ovalau at the moment and Ratu Cakobau will speak to him personally. The chief is certain that, even though he may not be able to win Cotterel's support, he can at least neutralise his opposition."

"You were telling me earlier that your son is interested in becoming a planter. If you want him to have proper training, you could not do better than apprentice him to Cotterel. He is one of the largest, if not the largest, of planters in the Group."

Denison's face was a picture of indignation. "You have formed a very poor opinion of me, Doctor Matthews, if you think I would allow any member of my family to associate with an anti-Christ such as this man appears to be."

"Don't take on so, Denison. I realise your natural repugnance, but for the sake of the church I ask you to think of the enormous benefits which could accrue if this man was won over. He has tremendous influence which would then be employed for us instead of against us. Your mission to evangelise the heathen will be only part of your duties; you must also bring Cotterel back to the church."

"Really, Doctor, I must protest! Expose my son and daughter to a low character like that?"

"Low character? You cannot have met the man, he is as well-educated as you or I. His habits and the company he keeps leave much to be desired but it would be a great mistake to place him in the same category as most of the white dregs who have washed up on these shores. Nor would he have anything in common with either Partridge or Burkit. But I am certain that a man of your scholarship and background could convert him where the others would fail miserably."

To Denison, the sound of Vatulevu and all it entailed became worse by the minute. His mouth was flannel-lined and the flask in his coat lay heavy against his ribs begging to be opened.

Matthews voice kept hammering away at him. "Just think, Denison, if you succeed you will have an educated and companionable neighbour on the island. By comparison to the rest of us I am told he lives in absolute luxury. He has a large home, an extensive library, and he sets a lavish table for those invited to dine."

By this stage Denison, desperate to escape, would have agreed to anything. He rose to face the superintendent.

"Doctor Matthews," he said, in his most pontifical manner, "I am not in the habit of associating with renegades and anti-Christs no matter how wealthy they may be nor how well they may have been educated. On the other hand, if you are sure our work in Fiji will benefit, I shall endeavour to befriend and reform this man."

"Bravo, Denison! I knew you would see where your duty lay."

Matthews was as anxious to be rid of Denison as the latter was to escape his superior. Dealing with the three new missionaries had made his head ache abominably. All he now wanted was to finish the interview and relax with the pot of tea he knew his wife must have ready. She would be surprised when he failed to take Denison with him, but he had had all he could stand of the man for one afternoon.

He led John Denison to the door, a hand on his shoulder, and said with a confidence he was far from feeling. "I'm sure everything will work out marvellously with you in charge and we can rely on Ratu Cakobau to see that Cotterel behaves. In fact I expect to see both you and your family travelling to Vatulevu on Cotterel's ketch; I understand he's leaving either tomorrow or the next day."

"So soon!" Denison was dismayed. He had expected to stay in the comparative comfort of MacDonald's Hotel for at least another month, when the mission's own cutter was due.

"If he agrees, we should be foolish to wait for the arrival of the cutter. Strike while the iron's hot, old boy! I'm sure you are eager to get started … first station and all that … always exciting …"

As Matthews was speaking he ushered Denison through the door shaking him heartily by the hand as if he was farewelling a trusted friend, while at heart cursing himself for his own hypocrisy. "Goodbye Denison, goodbye. My regards to your children."

Denison found himself outside the office facing a closed door. Within 24 hours he might be leaving this final bastion of civilisation and on his way to Vatulevu. He walked along the evil-smelling, refuse-strewn beach. On one side lapped the sea; goats and pigs scavenged around the buildings; and filthy natives and drunken whites were everywhere.

The town which he had once scorned as a flea-ridden slum, a stinking dunghill, and a haven for none but criminals and harlots, now seemed strangely appealing. The grass shacks and tin shanties were at least peopled by men who spoke the same language as himself. His stomach heaved nervously and, one hand holding the flask hard against his side he hurried, almost ran, to the hotel and the privacy of his bedroom and the oblivion that awaited him there.

*****

Meanwhile, elsewhere in Levuka, Colonel Basil Gunning was taking tea with Horace Twyford, Her Britannic Majesty's Consul in the Fiji Islands. Gunning never travelled without appropriate letters of introduction to ensure his comfort. Fijian porters had carried his baggage up the several hundred steps to the Consul's residence high on a hillside, overlooking and away from the smell and noise of the settlement. It was a small house built of the usual timber and corrugated iron — primitive by comparison to some of the residencies Gunning could remember — but it was luxurious compared with MacDonald's establishment.

They sat in comfortable cane chairs on a broad verandah commanding a magnificent view of the harbour. They could see, purple against the evening sky, other islands on the horizon. Even the town and huddled ships below them looked picturesque from a distance. In front of the house, the Consul's wife had used Fijian labour to slash a lawn of sorts out of a gentler slope and her gardens were a riot of colour. It was all very restful and arcadian.

Twyford, between sips of tea, was openly criticising his home government for refusing Ratu Cakobau's offer to cede Fiji to Britain and, far from being upset by such disloyalty, Gunning encouraged him. The Consul's attitude made his own task all the easier.

"I tell you, Gunning," Twyford was saying, "this place will never amount to a damned thing until we take over. The natives must be brought to heel and conditions established which will be attractive to investors and the big companies who know how to develop land and commerce. I've written dispatch after dispatch to London without the slightest result. In fact the mail bag on the *Elizabeth* had a memorandum for me from the Secretary of State which virtually told me to shut up."

"Quite apart from self-interest they should see it as their Christian duty to give the missionaries more backing and help in the conversion of the blacks."

"That would certainly help in the promotion of development and trade," said Gunning sardonically.

Twyford, a man of little imagination, missed the inflection and pressed on. "For all the good I do here, I might just as well retire. I have no proper authority even over British subjects. The one time I tried to crack down on lawlessness by setting up a Consular court I got a severe rap over the knuckles for my pains and an instruction to cease forthwith. There's no longer any point even trying."

"What about Cakobau, does he do anything?"

"Cakobau! Cakobau!" said the Consul scornfully, "everyone talks about Cakobau. I ask you, is it likely that a native can bring whites to heel when I myself have failed? He's calling himself Tui Viti these days, King of Fiji. He has neither the right to the title nor the power to back up his pretensions. If I have any say in the matter, the British government will never recognise him. What we need to knock Fiji into shape is not some petty black king but a regiment of British infantry and a couple of hanging judges, the same as they are using against the Maori in New Zealand. I tell you Gunning, force is all these blacks understand."

"Harsh measures," said Gunning smiling gently.

Horace Twyford started to protest, but his guest raised a hand to both reassure and silence him. "My dear Consul, I am all for any measure which will paint more of the world British red. You and I are in complete agreement and, if you will allow me, I may even be able to help you solve your local problem."

"Help me?"

"Yes, help you. I and the friends whom I represent should be able to give you just the aid you need." Gunning's smile never shifted despite his host's obvious scepticism.

"I'm afraid I don't understand, Colonel. I thought you travelled purely for your own amusement; who are these friends you represent?"

"I cannot reveal their names. You must take my word for it that they exist; that they are interested in these islands; and, like yourself, heartily disapprove of the government's refusal to accept the offer of cession."

Gunning was leaning forward over the tea cups, his languid manner had vanished and he spoke earnestly. "I could not say even this much to you were it not for the fact that your sympathies are well-known to us. You need not worry, I have not deceived you, I am what I purport to be; an eccentric who knocks about the world for pleasure. But I write long letters, call them reports if you will, to my friends back home and on occasion I execute commissions for them."

Twyford stood up and glared stonily down at his guest.

"Colonel Gunning," he said indignantly, "I think you have the wrong man. I am a civil servant and I hope an honest one. I have no desire to enter into business with secret cabals whose actions are meant to counter the policies of Her Majesty's government. I may personally disagree with those policies but, for all that I complain, I shall carry out my instructions to the best of my ability. You overstep your bounds as a guest and impose upon my hospitality by even suggesting that I should accept help from your friends."

The Consul's outburst did nothing to alter Gunning's smile, if anything it broadened. He waved his host back to his chair.

"Such heat Twyford, such heat!" he chuckled. "Don't be foolish. I'm every bit as loyal as you are and I have 20 years of army service behind me to prove it. If you must know, my friends are drawn from both the House of Commons and peers of the Realm, the only difference being that they represent Her Majesty's loyal opposition, not the government. All the main banking and business houses of the City have members in our ranks, but for the present we are unable to implement our ideas through normal parliamentary channels and are forced to bring pressure to bear in other ways. I need not tell you how strong such pressures can be, and the political pendulum is finally swinging our way. Mark my words, the next election will see us in office and whose instructions will you follow then?"

Twyford looked worried. It was clear that Gunning's friends were no hole-and-corner conspiracy, but a group of highly influential and respectable men. The elections were still some years away but governments could be brought down prematurely. His knees suddenly felt weak and he sat down again; it would not hurt to listen to what the colonel had to say and to antagonise him might well be disastrous.

"The present government have such limited imaginations, they are unable to see beyond their own noses," said Gunning. "They are little Englanders, whereas we believe that Britain must expand her possessions and trade to the most distant horizons if she is to maintain her position in the world. If there is unclaimed land lying about we intend to snap it up before anyone else has the opportunity."

"Who put Tahiti on the map? It was the British Navy in the shape of Cook the Navigator. But we sat back in 1845 and calmly let the French annex it. Well I can tell you here and now, Twyford, that my friends do not intend to see the same thing happen to Fiji."

Pausing to help himself to another cup of tea, Gunning continued. "We refuse to separate trade, commerce and religion, from politics and patriotism. If along the way we are forced to dispose of a thousand recalcitrant natives to guarantee our ownership and safeguard our markets, we can always salve our consciences by converting the remainder to Christianity."

Gunning's credo was cynical in the extreme, but the more Twyford listened the more he had to admit it matched his own views. Hadn't he himself spoken earlier about regiments of infantry and hanging judges? There was nothing he wanted so much as to see the islands under British government and he honestly believed it would be in the best interests of the natives as well as of his own countrymen. It was heady stuff and, for a believer in the divine mission of the British Empire, irresistible.

Had Twyford been able to see into the years ahead he would have ordered Gunning out of his house there and then; but he couldn't, and he didn't. Instead he swallowed the bait.

"Very well, Colonel, tell me more about this plan. I presume you have a programme of sorts. I shall help all I can, provided my name is kept out of it. You understand that I am a poor man, I have a wife and family to support, and I am wholly dependent on my career to do it."

"But of course, my dear fellow," answered Gunning with his cat's smile. "You have made a decision you will not regret. So long as this government is in power your name will never be mentioned but, depend on it, when my friends come to power the name of Twyford will be remembered and honoured. When that time comes you will find we are more than generous."

Poor Horace Twyford, his lack of means or family connections had doomed him to obscurity in the hidden corners of the world and now, out of the blue, Gunning was offering him access to unlimited patronage. He began to have visions of a brilliant consular, maybe even an ambassadorial, career. He had no idea what he would be asked to do, but so long as he could label his actions patriotic he was not likely to have scruples.

He listened intently as Gunning went on, "I plan to travel extensively throughout the islands, meeting and talking to as many people as possible; as a private person they will speak openly to me. We already know what we want, whereas the others don't. I shall soon discover who is for us and, if there is opposition, just how strong it is."

"I fear you will find more against us than for us," said Twyford.

"In that case we must discover their weaknesses. Show me their leaders and I shall deal with them. Some we can buy, others we can scare; with a little sound groundwork we can soon transform a majority against us into one in our favour. That is where you come in."

"But how?"

"You have been here for years and know everyone. Make me a dossier on everyone of importance, especially those who would oppose the annexation of Fiji by Britain. I understand that people in Fiji are very close about their pasts but I am certain there is plenty of rumour and speculation. If we can piece that information together it will be ready and waiting when we need to apply pressure."

To Twyford, the idea of treating human beings like pawns in a game of chess was repugnant, but he could see how effective it might be. "Yes, I could do that," he said uneasily. "It will take time of course."

"That is understood," said Gunning letting him off lightly. "There is another way in which you can help which is even more important. You have told me of your disgust at the drunkenness, the murders and the cannibalism committed every day in Fiji. We want to be kept fully informed of every incident which comes to your notice. The British government would like the public to forget that Fiji even exists, but the information you supply will keep the state of affairs here in the forefront of the British press. It will be a constant embarrassment to the government and we will ensure they carry the blame for it."

"Fiji has a far from salubrious name already." Twyford pointed out to his guest who was fast becoming master of his house. "The missionaries have been doing their best."

"No man preaching from a pulpit is as effective as one speaking from the floor of the House of Commons. We want to make the depravity of the islands a *cause célèbre* and to that end the occurrences you report will be raised as questions in the House. The government's majority is so slender that telling criticism from any source, coupled with a public outcry, might be enough either to make them change their minds on Fiji or, what would be even better, bring on an early election. Smaller things than this have brought down governments."

It all sounded innocuous and honourable. With relatively little effort on his part. Twyford had everything to gain and nothing to lose. What Gunning failed to say was that if incidents were too few and far between, he himself, with the assistance of his tame British Consul, intended to manufacture trouble that would fit the bill perfectly.

"I merely have to supply information on request to British Members of Parliament?" asked Twyford, justifying it to himself.

"My dear fellow," beamed Gunning. "That's it exactly, you will only be doing your duty as an officer and a gentleman."

Long after the colonel had gone inside to change for dinner Horace Twyford sat on alone with his thoughts. It all sounded easy, yet he knew instinctively it was going to be far from simple. But how could he have such forebodings when a fairy godfather had suddenly appeared with promises of a brilliant future.

He knew his wife would jump at anything which promised to further his career and consequently those of their children. It might be best to tell her nothing at this stage. Otherwise she would never let him rest.

5
Encounters

When Kate woke it was dark but she could hear servants banging pots and pans in the kitchen and Mrs MacDonald's voice as she bustled about organising dinner for the hotel guests. The afternoon rain had cooled the air considerably and Kate felt fresher for her sleep.

She washed and dressed by the light of an oil lamp. The evening breeze off the sea made the yellow flame flicker, and moths flew in through the open window attracted by the light. She could have shut the window against them but that would have turned the room into an airless oven.

Choosing a dress to wear, she considered the heavy, dark woollen favoured by her father but tossed it aside. He must understand that unless she wore sensible clothes she would soon be down with sickness and then where would he be? Instead she took up the muslin, the subject of earlier censure. Rather a lot of her shoulders and breasts would be on show, but it was beautifully light and she could carry a shawl to use if it became necessary.

As Kate brushed her hair before the speckled mirror she surveyed her reflection and tried to assess herself as objectively as possible. She was not unattractive — at least that man on the ketch had thought so. What a lot of fuss about nothing! No matter what Father might think, women liked to be admired; that was why they went to so much trouble with their dress and looks. Kate's hair was her best feature and it received much of her attention. She brushed it in flowing golden swirls over the smooth satin softness of her bare shoulders and instead of scraping it back into a demure bun decided to braid it into a single shining coil to lay along the side of her neck and breast.

Kate knew her father would have a fit when he saw her, but she was prepared to take that risk. Any day now they would be leaving Levuka and for all its drawbacks it was the last place with even a vestige of civilisation that she was likely to see for many a year. Kate wanted a last fling before they left and she might as well be hanged for a sheep as a lamb.

Her thoughts kept returning to the man on the ketch. She wondered if he would still like her at close quarters; her nose was a trifle too large and her eyes had none of the doe-like innocence men seemed to prefer. As Toby often told her, she looked 'too damned direct at people'. Evidently it made him and his friends uncomfortable.

She pulled a face and grinned, at least her smile wasn't too bad and her lips were full and soft. She had never been kissed by other than her father and brother but she had seen men looking at her as if they would very much like to try. To Kate's mortification, none ever had. Perhaps it was those eyes of hers; she must try fluttering them seductively. Perhaps in Fiji, where things were more primitive, even a parson's daughter would have a chance of romance instead of always being treated like a rare forbidden species.

Kate smoothed her dress over her hips, but then decided speculation should cease and that she should turn her thoughts to higher things. Victorian ladies were schooled to think it unseemly to let the mind dwell too long on matters of the flesh — not that Kate felt she had anything to worry about so far as her body was concerned. She was a healthy young woman whose constitution had so far met every demand put upon it without the slightest complaint.

Looking at herself again in the mirror she decided that discretion would be the better part of valour and draped a light silk shawl to mask the more daring part of her *décolletage*. She was now ready to face Levuka society.

*****

The upstairs verandah of MacDonald's Hotel was the drinking haunt for those Levukaites with any pretension to respectability. Not that it had any bearing on the meaning of the word 'respectable' as applied in London or Sydney, they were all renegades of some description and hardened alcoholics to boot. But the fact that they had money in their pockets and an almost clean, untorn shirt to their backs, set them apart from the scroungers and riff-raff of the rum shops along the beach. MacDonald, who sat at a table near to the door which led into the hotel from five o'clock every evening, saw to it that their alcoholic exuberance never reached the stage of murder, or damage to his property.

Kate walked calmly between tables full of men talking and busily emptying bottles as if she had never known any other type of society. Besides, there was no other place for her to go even had she wanted to. A beautiful girl, well-dressed and poised, was such a rarity that all conversation ceased as if sliced off by a guillotine. Behind her back one would-be cavalier got up to follow her but MacDonald was already halfway out of his seat and his low menacing rumble made the other sit down again. A whisper passed round that she was the daughter of a new missionary and therefore useless for their purposes. Apart from the odd whispered comment which brought forth a snort of appreciative laughter, she was allowed to pass unmolested and the men returned to the serious business of drinking.

Toby was sitting alone at a table with his back to the rest of the room, trying to be as inconspicuous as possible. Kate had no desire to hide herself away in a corner and instead she walked to the balustrade and looked out at the night sky.

It was a superb evening. The cool sea breeze blew away the street smells and the sky was a thick mat of stars, brighter and closer than she had ever seen them before. She could make out the Southern Cross, then Scorpio, linked together by the broad misty line of the Milky Way. Aboard ship she had tried to observe the stars using the mate's telescope but the ship's movement had made them swing wildly across the sky until she had felt quite dizzy. She promised herself that once they were properly established on Vatulevu, she would unearth the telescope from her father's boxes and amuse herself by identifying the different constellations.

Footsteps approached from behind her and, suddenly nervous that it might be one of the men from the tables, she turned abruptly. But instead of an amorous drunk it was Peter Bex and another man. The captain looked very distinguished dressed in a dark uniform coat and gold-braided cap.

"Good evening, Miss Denison," Bex smiled. "You shouldn't be out here alone. These ruffians haven't seen a good-looking woman for so long that given the slightest chance, they'd have you abducted and hidden in the hills before anyone could lift a finger to help."

"I'm sure they're not as bad as you say, Captain. I have been here for almost ten minutes and no one has attempted to molest me in any way. Even if they did, my brother Toby is sitting over there in that corner. So you see I'm not really alone!"

It was on the tip of the captain's tongue to tell her what he thought of her brother's protection, but he thought better of it. Bex felt at ease with Kate, whereas most European women made him feel like some monster just emerged from the sea. A nudge from his companion reminded him of his purpose in seeking Kate out.

"I'd like to present an old friend of mine," he said. "Miss Denison, Jason Cotterel. Jason is a planter on one of the islands."

"Your servant, Miss Denison," said the young man bowing formally.

Kate inclined her head graciously and smiled. She could not help thinking that this was exactly the sort of man she needed as a companion on her last night in civilisation. He had a strong and determined face with perhaps a suggestion of cruelty (or was it stubbornness?) about the mouth.

From the cut of his clothes he was well-to-do and something of a dandy, in fact not the sort of person she had thought to meet in Levuka where most people seemed content to wear any sort of old hand-me-downs. His shirt was obviously silk and he sported a large drooping bow tie. These were topped by a long white linen coat and narrow white trousers tucked into the tops of tall highly polished boots. In spite of his attention to the details of dress he gave an impression of strength and masculinity.

"I hope you don't mind us joining you like this, ma'am."

"Not at all, Mr Cotterel."

His voice was deep and powerful and he spoke with an unusual accent. Kate was sure she had heard that voice somewhere before. Good Heavens, she thought, surely this was … and hadn't Captain Bex called that other man Jason? But it couldn't be; that one was heavily bearded, a ruffian in torn canvas trousers, whereas the man before her looked and spoke as if he …

"But haven't we … ? Aren't you … ?" she began hesitantly.

Bex was laughing, "Jason asked me to introduce him to you, Miss Denison, so that he might apologise for his shameful behaviour the other day, and so he should, the rogue; 'twas disgraceful."

Kate felt herself blushing furiously and there was nothing she could do to stop herself. Jason Cotterel just stood there, looking down at her quizzically.

"But you had a beard!" she wailed.

Her face was a study of dismay and Bex and Cotterel burst out laughing. Kate, seeing the ridiculous side of their encounter, also began to laugh. People looked up to see what could cause such hilarity but not for long enough to make serious inroads on their drinking time.

"But didn't you have a beard?" Kate asked again when she recovered her composure. "Or did I imagine the whole thing?"

"Off it came, Miss Denison, when Bex demanded that I meet you personally and apologise." He had a reassuring smile and Kate decided that she liked tall men.

"There is no need to apologise I assure you. A great fuss was made about nothing. My father, as you must know, is a missionary and sometimes clergymen put improper constructions upon perfectly harmless incidents."

"There, Jason," said Peter Bex, "I told you Miss Denison would not be wanting an apology. You've renewed my faith in womenkind, ma'am; and to tell the truth it wasn't my idea to approach you, it was Jason's. I reckon all he was after was the introduction."

Kate's deep blue eyes gave her new acquaintance the same direct enquiring look that annoyed and disconcerted Toby and his smart London cronies, but it did not seem to worry Jason Cotterel in the slightest. He just gazed back with that rather droll, warming smile and lifted his hands in mock surrender.

"I choose my friends very badly, he's done for me again just when I was trying to prove that I can occasionally behave in a civilised fashion."

"You worry too much, sir," laughed Kate, "and if you do have faults they are to be found in the field of flattery not impertinence"

"Well, to prove that I am truly forgiven, Miss Denison," said Jason quickly following up the proffered advantage, "would you consent to sit a moment and join Bex and myself in some refreshment?" He saw Kate hesitate and look around at the crowded tables behind them.

"Believe it or not, Bex here is an excellent chaperone. He carries testimonials from leading mothers in Sydney and, even more unbelievably, Mrs MacDonald tells me she has made some lemonade especially in your honour."

Kate laughed at his concern. She was the sole woman in a public place dedicated to the demon drink. Her London friends would have been scandalised, but she knew that she was in no danger and for the first time in her life felt free. She could hardly have stayed cooped up in that hot-box of a bedroom that was the only alternative.

"It's just that I was wondering about my brother," she said. "He's at that table in the corner."

"If he's by himself then he needs company, why don't we join him?" From behind Kate's back, Peter Bex was pulling a sour face but Jason took no notice. He tucked Kate's arm firmly beneath his own and led her in Toby's direction.

*****

Kate knew that Toby was not going to thank her for breaching his anonymity, doubly so when one of her companions was the captain of the *Elizabeth*, but she refused to lose such personable company just because her brother wished to remain incognito.

"Toby, I have friends who wish to join us," she announced calmly. Looking up to see Bex above him, Toby sprang to his feet ashen-faced as if the axe of retribution was about to fall. But Bex was forcing a smile and Toby struggled to control the urge to flee.

"Good evening to you, Mr Denison," said Bex striving to make his normally gruff voice as pleasant as possible to ease the boy's obvious discomfort.

"Captain Bex … ah good evening, Captain … how are you, sir?" answered Toby in a voice hoarse with anxiety. "Won't you sit down? What can I get you to drink?" In his nervous state he hardly noticed his sister and her escort.

"For goodness sake, Toby, sit down yourself," said Kate embarrassed. "The way you're behaving, anyone would think Captain Bex was about to eat you."

"That's right lad, calm down. Your flutter aboard ship has nothing to do with me." If Kate had not sworn him to silence, Peter Bex could have put him at ease by telling him that the crew had been paid in full. Bex glanced at Kate as if to say, 'Well should I?' but she gave a quick negative shake of her head.

Jason Cotterel watched the interplay with close interest. Bex had filled him in on Kate Denison and her family — the parson who secretly hit the bottle and the good-for-nothing brother. It seemed a damned pity that such a beautiful creature should be saddled with such a family, but it did nothing to detract from Kate herself. The story of her paying the gambling debts had only raised her in his estimation.

Kate, remembering her duty brought him forward and introduced him.

"Toby, you haven't met Mr Cotterel yet. Mr Cotterel, may I introduce my brother Toby. Mr Cotterel is a planter. My brother also wishes to take up your profession as soon as we have settled down."

It was obvious to Jason that the boy, like his sister, failed to recognise him without the beard. It would have been better to leave it that way but a devil sitting on his shoulder forced him to remind Toby of their previous meeting.

"Your brother and I have met before, Miss Denison, but I admit it was not under very fortunate circumstances."

"Met before, sir? I think not," Toby answered coldly. Now that he knew he was safe from assault his normal insolence reasserted itself. He was furious with Kate for having given him such a shock and so far as he was concerned the sooner she and her friends took themselves off the better.

"But we have, you know," said Jason, refusing to rise to Toby's antagonism. "You swam up to my boat the other day and I directed you towards the shore."

In the last few moments Toby Denison's face had registered fear, relief, disdain, hauteur, and now, as he realised who his sister's companion was, it became suffused with anger.

"You are the barbarian who refused to help me when I was drowning!"

Jason, quite unconcerned, held Kate's chair for her to sit down. When he spoke his voice was the same calm drawl as before. His American intonation fascinated Kate.

"You weren't drowning, Mr Denison. If you were, we wouldn't be sitting down to join you now. Then again, even if you had been I don't know whether my conscience would have allowed me to interfere in a debt of honour."

"How dare you, Kate!" Toby's wrath exploded. He was now sure that his sister had brought these men to his table with the sole purpose of humiliating him. "I refuse to associate with your so-called friends!" he snarled, forgetting that a moment before he had been offering the captain both a place and a drink. "Father will be highly displeased if he finds you consorting with sailors and beachcombers! Isn't this the man who insulted you on the very same day he refused to help me?"

"Will you sit down and stop making such a spectacle of yourself" said Kate furiously. She turned to the others. "Gentlemen, if I had known my brother was going to behave in this disgraceful fashion I would not have inflicted him upon you. Please accept my apologies."

"How dare you apologise for me," Toby was nigh apoplectic.

Jason gazed at him as if he was something which had just crept out from beneath a stone.

"It is for me to apologise, Miss Denison. I seem to be the cause of your brother's outburst and to stop any further embarrassment I think it would be better if Bex and I took ourselves off."

"No, please, Mr Cotterel and you too, Captain Bex. If anyone should leave, it is my brother who has shown himself to be utterly devoid of manners." Kate glared at Toby and her expression gave fair warning of what he was in for when brother and sister were alone.

Toby threw caution to the winds. "No, please, Mr Cotterel," he mimicked savagely. "Don't move, Mr Cotterel. It's all my brother's fault. Anything which happens to the Denison family is his fault. It seems I must leave when I was sitting here minding my own business and you came barging in with this beachcomber. I'm at fault because, as your brother, I object to the company you keep."

Kate had her ears covered and her head down. Bex and Jason looked at each other grimly and the latter started towards the boy.

"That's alright. I'll go, I'll go," shrilled Toby moving quickly towards the door and out of range of the planter's doubled fists. "But don't think father isn't going to hear about this, sister dear. From now on, don't point a finger at me, you are nothing but a trollop yourself."

He escaped into the corridor just ahead of Jason and his feet could be heard running toward his room. The door slammed and the key turned in the lock a fraction of a second before his pursuer arrived. Jason was in a murderous temper though he knew that he was mainly responsible for the public scene. To smash in the door and give the boy a thrashing would only make matters worse for the girl.

*****

By the time he got back to the table the crowd, disappointed that there would be no fight to enliven the evening, had returned to their drinking; Kate was standing as she took her leave of Peter Bex. Jason took her firmly by the arm and sat her down again, her face white and strained. Despite her protests, Jason sent a waiter scurrying off for brandy for her and rum for himself and Bex.

Kate tried to apologise again but the men shushed her. That Toby should conduct himself thus in the presence of strangers and call her such names was unforgivable. It was her fault for not telling him that his debts had been paid and that he had nothing further to worry about — the strain of the last few days had been too much for him. He had been almost insane with anger.

Jason Cotterel laid a consoling hand on hers. In another country, an age away, it would have been an inexcusable liberty, but here it seemed only natural and very reassuring.

"I am truly sorry to have been the author of such a scene, Miss Denison. What I said provoked him. If I had known he held me in such aversion I would never have said what I did," he said gently. Kate gave him a tremulous smile.

"Just sit for a moment and have something to settle your nerves and you'll be right as a trivet in no time," Bex chimed in, genuinely worried by her paleness. "If you want my opinion, that young brother of yours is a villain to expose you to such a scene in public and I intend to tell your father as much when I next see him."

"Thank you, Captain, and you too, Mr Cotterel, but you must not say anything. That would only make my father furious at both Toby and myself, and I refuse to let you take the blame, Mr Cotterel, I was the one at fault."

"Your fault, ma'am? Indeed it was not," interjected Bex. "That young devil deserves a horse-whipping. Where would he be now if it wasn't for you paying those debts for him? If he thinks MacDonald over there would have been protection against my crew, he's much mistaken. Without you, the odds are he would be lying in an alley with his gizzard slit. I only kept it a secret because you were so insistent, but it's bound to come out — the crew know, and I admit to telling Jason here."

The look of admiration on Jason's face made her colour again and she mumbled that Bex should not have given away their secret.

"I cannot see that you have anything to blame yourself for," said Jason.

"But I have. Don't you see I should have told Toby he had nothing to worry about but I thought not doing so might keep him out of further trouble while we are in Levuka. Now, because of all the unnecessary worry and strain, he's made a fool of himself again and he'll never forgive me, especially if, as Captain Bex says, he discovers that I had already paid the debts."

"I reckon you pamper that lad too much, ma'am," said Bex. "If you'll excuse an old sailor shoving in his oar where I know it's probably not wanted, that's half his trouble. He's no longer a boy, he's a man; and he's got to be made to understand that he is responsible for the consequences of his actions. If he thinks he can come running and hide behind your skirts for the rest of his life he's in for a hell of a shock one of these days."

Kate was saved from having to answer by the arrival of the waiter with their drinks. She protested, but drank her brandy at the insistence of the others. Her father, who allowed her nothing apart from a little table wine, would have been horrified had he seen her on the verandah of this sleazy hotel drinking with strangers — though, had she but known it, he was even then drinking brandy in the solitary state of his bedchamber.

The raw brandy made her choke but sat warmly on her stomach and she felt much better for it. She looked across at Jason and for a moment their eyes locked as if each was seeing the other for the first time. Kate smiled her thanks.

"Oh! And I wanted him so much to meet you and like you, Mr Cotterel," she sighed. "As I told you before, father and I hope that Toby will settle down and become a planter. You could have given him so much advice."

"Before you push him into it, you'd best make sure it's what he wants," said Jason who considered Denison the least likely prospect for a planter he had ever met. He couldn't see Toby Denison stripped to the waist and hacking a plantation out of virgin jungle.

"You know, Fiji is not at all like the West Indies or the Southern States of my own country. Labourers are almost unobtainable and those you do get aren't at all keen on work. Neither you nor your family want to be under any false illusions about the life of a white planter in Fiji. For the most part it's exceedingly boring, back-breaking work."

"I never imagined it would be easy," answered Kate, "but Toby has no option. He never trained for a profession and I can see no other source of employment for him in Fiji. He must get used to the idea of hard work. After all, I don't suppose you would be doing it, Mr Cotterel, unless you liked the life and there was an adequate return for your labour."

Jason was not used to dealing with young women of her stamp and laughed at her business-like approach to the problem. "Yes, Miss Denison, the rewards are there but in Fiji there is also a very large element of risk and an equal amount of luck is required. But you must not get me on my hobbyhorse. As Bex here knows, once mounted I am liable to go on for hours."

"But I am most interested, Mr Cotterel," said Kate seriously. "Father intends to buy a plantation as close to the mission station as possible and I shall be as involved as my brother. What are the risks you mention? Tell me about the crops you grow and how many men do you employ?"

Turning to Peter Bex she smiled and said, "I'm sure the captain won't mind you explaining it all for … what is it? … a greenhorn?" Their laughter told her that she had the right word. "Yes that's it. I am a greenhorn now, Mr Cotterel, but I depend on people such as you to ensure that I do not remain one for longer than is absolutely necessary."

"Don't worry about me, ma'am," laughed Bex. "I think you are being very sensible and, if I may say so without Jason getting too swollen-headed, you couldn't ask a better man. Jason has forgotten more than most other Fiji planters will ever know."

"After that testimonial I can hardly refuse," said Jason, smiling at her. She seemed to have dropped the idea of retiring to her bedroom and for as long as she would sit opposite, him he was quite prepared to talk the night away. "There is so much to a plantation I hardly know where to begin."

Kate clapped her hands in delight and settled herself in the chair. "There, now I am comfortable. Mount this hobbyhorse of yours, sir, I want to know everything about plantation life."

*****

"First of all you must understand that what grows well on my plantation may not suit yours. Viti Levu and Vanua Levu have a distinct wet side and a distinct dry side and the side you are on determines the type of crops you grow. On the island where I have my own plantation we are unusual in that we have an intermediate sort of climate and are able to grow just about anything."

"We are going to a small island, Mr Cotterel," said Kate, "So, if we have some of your luck we should also be able to grow everything."

"The only mission stations on small islands are down in Lau," said Jason. "You'll find it quite a lot drier there than we do on Vatulevu."

He stopped, for Kate's face was a picture of delighted astonishment.

"Did you say Vatulevu?" asked Kate.

"Yes, Vatulevu, why?"

"But that is where father has been posted, we are going to Vatulevu. If you have your plantation there we shall be neighbours. Not only can you tell me about plantation life now but you will be able to give me a personally conducted tour of your own estate when we get there."

Jason was obviously taken aback: "You're going to Vatulevu? There must be a mistake or you've got the name mixed up. That's possible, you know, when you are not used to the sound of Fijian place-names."

"Jason's right, ma'am. I still get confused myself at times," Bex agreed. "Are you sure you don't mean Vanua Levu? The church has missions there."

"No, Vatulevu, I'm sure that was the name," Kate was emphatic, "and I know there is no mission station. Father is being sent to set up a new one. You must get to know one another, Mr Cotterel. I am sure he will be as delighted as I am to know we shall have you to advise and help us. We shall …"

Kate stopped as she saw Jason Cotterel's face, flushed with anger. He turned sharply to Bex, "Have you heard anything of this?"

"Now that you mention it I heard something yesterday of a new station. They did say where it was but I wasn't listening, it could have been Vatulevu. It's no use you flying off the handle, Jason, it has to happen sooner or later; you couldn't maintain your glorious isolation from the rest of the world forever."

Kate looked from one to the other, mystified. Something she had said had altered the atmosphere at their table. Whereas they had been happy and companionable, now the air was tense and hostile.

"I'm afraid I don't understand. Is something the matter?"

"Something is very much the matter, Miss Denison," Jason answered. He was still smiling but his eyes had gone hard and cold. "It has nothing whatever to do with you personally, but there are times when I would dearly love to get my hands on the people who run your church and wring the necks of each and every one of them."

"But why? All I can suppose from what you have just said is that you object to myself and my family." Kate had her own pride and while she had no illusions about the other members of the Denison family, she would not suffer them to be attacked without putting up a defence.

"Object to you? Of course I don't. I would object to any missionary pushing his way into Vatulevu no matter who it was. The people already have a religion of their own which serves them adequately. They want neither missionaries nor Christianity. I'm sure that Tui Navatulevu, the chief, has not agreed to the new mission station."

"Don't be so certain, Jason," warned Bex. "I'm sure the church wouldn't be setting up shop unless they had cleared it first."

Kate was on her feet now and highly indignant. "Do I understand you correctly, Mr Cotterel? Do you oppose missionaries because you are opposed to the conversion of the Fijian people to Christianity.?"

"I am opposed to the conversion of the people to a creed which does not fit their way of life. The Fijians have a perfectly sound economy and society which missionaries will do everything in their power to destroy." Jason was no longer excluding Kate from a share of the blame. "They are perfectly happy as they are. Why in heaven's name can't you leave them alone?"

"You, of course, consider cannibalism and the strangling of widows the marks of a perfectly respectable society."

"No I don't. There may have been a few widows strangled but there hasn't been an act of cannibalism on Vatulevu for years. And even if there was I don't see that any European has the right to barge in and tell them how they should live their lives."

Kate did not know whether to do battle on the spot, or flee from the verandah to her bedroom where she would be safe from heretical contamination. She was saved from a decision by the arrival of her father. He stood in the doorway for a moment chatting to MacDonald and then, after having their table pointed out, he made his way over.

The Reverend Denison was not intoxicated but if the flush on his checks and the slight in his walk were guides he had certainly been imbibing. He was in a good mood, had pushed his depression firmly aside, and for the moment was determined to look on the bright side of things.

"There you are, Kate," he said smiling pleasantly. "Have you eaten dinner yet? Toby tells me he's not hungry. Good evening, Captain Bex. How very nice to see you again. Won't you introduce me to your friend?"

No-one could have been more affable, but the faint slur to his speech and the heavy smell of brandy were confirmation of Kate's worst fears. She blushed for her family, one hysterical, the other a clergyman under the influence of alcohol. At least she could take comfort from the thought that her father always conducted himself in a gentlemanly manner. In fact he was more human when he had had something to drink than when cold sober.

"The Reverend Denison," said Bex apprehensively. "Reverend, may I introduce my friend Jason Cotterel."

Kate, the captain and Jason Cotterel waited for the explosion, but were disappointed.

"Cotterel, eh! You are from Vatulevu of course," he said, extending his hand for shaking, rather like the squire welcoming a new tenant to his rent roll. Jason, caught off guard, shook the proffered hand bemusedly. "We are well met, sir. I understand that you and I are soon to be neighbours. I look forward to seeing your island." Denison had learnt his lesson well and meant to follow Dr Matthews' advice literally.

Kate could not let this pass. "I must warn you, father," she said glaring at Jason, "Mr Cotterel does not like missionaries. He has just told me that in his opinion the Fijians should not be converted to Christianity."

"What I was endeavouring to make your daughter understand, sir," said Jason bowing politely in Kate's direction, "is that neither the people nor their chief need or want a mission station on Vatulevu. Without Tui Navatulevu's support your work is doomed to failure and you and your family will be in for a most unpleasant and uncomfortable time."

John Denison considered he was in a position of superiority from which he could proceed to put this young yokel in his place, and so when he spoke it was with all his old pomposity.

"That is where you are entirely wrong, Mr Cotterel."

"Wrong, sir?" Jason responded angrily. "I have lived and worked among those people for more than ten years. I think I can speak for them with more authority than you who have not been in the islands a week nor seen the island in question."

Denison refused to be ruffled. He knew what he was talking about and the brandy still glowed warmly inside him. Enjoying himself for the first time since he left England, he smiled benignly at his audience.

"But your information is sadly out of date; you have not been kept informed by your chief, Tui Navatulevu, that is his name isn't it? I'm never sure that I pronounce these Fijian names correctly."

"What about Tui Navatulevu?" Jason asked, suddenly wary.

"But I'm surprised you don't know, Mr Cotterel, if you have lived among these people for so long. The chief has not only agreed to the establishment of the mission but has also promised to give it his active support." Denison could not help a note of triumph creeping into his voice.

"I don't believe it," said Jason flatly.

"I am not in the habit of telling lies," said Denison calmly. "If you feel you cannot accept the word of a clergyman then I suggest you discuss the matter with Ratu Cakobau, with whom I am given to understand you are intimate. That you have not been told about the mission suggests to me you are not as close to these chiefs as my informants thought. Ratu Cakobau arranged everything for us as was of course his duty as a good Christian. He is in Levuka at the moment if you wish to take the matter up with him."

Jason was furious as he turned to Bex: "Now I understand — it was Cakobau who called me to Levuka. I can see that I am going to be given a heap of sweet talk and told to sit down and shut up. I've been trying to see him for the last five days but he's always been too ill for visitors. It's been a plan to get me away from Vatulevu so that they could put pressure on Tui Navatulevu without me getting in the way. Now that it is a *fait accompli* what I say doesn't matter a tuppenny damn!"

Facing Denison and his daughter, Jason gave a curt bow. "I must thank you both for your second-hand information but I would also warn you not to expect too much joy of your stay on Vatulevu."

Kate tucked her hand through her father's arm to emphasise her full support. She was frankly amazed that he had stood up to someone like Jason Cotterel, a much stronger character in every way, and she was pleased and proud that her father had been able to best him. On the other hand their argument had not lessened Jason Cotterel's attractiveness and she was secretly pleased they would be living on the same island.

"You may have your opinion, Mr Cotterel," Denison was saying, "but to be fair you should also allow us to maintain ours. My daughter and I must now go into dinner if you will excuse us. I look forward to the enjoyment of your company on Vatulevu. I am sure we shall all be the greatest of friends. Your servant, sir: Captain Bex, your servant."

He started to lead Kate away through the crowded tables whose occupants had been following the exchange with close interest, for there were many who were pleased to hear Cotterel receive a setback. Denison had only gone a few yards when he delivered a final thrust which he felt was certain to send his opponent to the floor.

"I completely forgot. We shall be seeing each other before we get to Vatulevu. I am given to understand by Doctor Matthews that we shall be all travelling together on your ship, the *Albatross* isn't it? I shall only wish you a very brief goodbye until then."

The mixture of outraged astonishment and fury on the planter's face was all he could have desired. "Come, my dear," he said happily. "Good evening to you, gentlemen."

6

Deeper currents

A relaxed Cakobau was drinking yaqona with a handful of his senior officers when a guard informed him that a kai-valagi wished to see him. "It is the man Jasoni from Vatulevu, Turaga," the guard explained. "He has been here every day for the past five days. He says that you sent for him. Shall I tell him that you are sick and unable to see him as we have before?"

Cakobau pulled thoughtfully on his beard. Cotterel must be truly angry by now. It had been necessary to keep him at arm's length so that he would not interfere in the Vatulevu negotiations. Nevertheless he liked Jasoni, as the kai-Vatulevu called him, and trusted him more than most white men. When Ma'afu's men had whispered treason in the ear of Tui Navatulevu it was Cotterel who had shown the old man where his true loyalties and advantages lay. Cakobau was grateful for such services and it would not pay to push Cotterel too far.

"He may come in, I shall see him."

The guard left and the others made signs of moving. Retaining only the matanivanua and the cup bearer Cakobau let them melt away. There were things he must discuss with Cotterel which would not bear repeating and he knew information was leaking to Ma'afu from a traitor among those closest to him.

Unlike most white men Cotterel had made a real effort to understand Fijians. He had prospered but so had the kai-Vatulevu, thought Cakobau. He could not bring to mind any other island where the people were similarly prosperous or industrious and it was undoubtedly due to Cotterel's advice and help. It showed what was possible if there were white advisors whose interests were not solely to exploit his people. Perhaps Cotterel's peculiar sympathy could be attributed to his Fijian wife, Tui Navatulevu's daughter. He remembered her as a great beauty and it was a great pity that she had died in childbirth.

But Cakobau could never understand why this man, who lived an exemplary life, should be so virulently opposed to the work of the missionaries, whereas even the lowest white drunk on the Levuka beach at least gave lip service to Christianity.

Most white men would have barged into Cakobau's presence without regard for Fijian protocol but Jason Cotterel, having first removed his boots outside, entered and sat cross-legged near the door awaiting the chief's summons. There was nothing servile about his manner; he observed custom but at the same time maintained his personal dignity. The other factor which predisposed Cakobau towards Cotterel was his fluent command of Fijian. The chief's English was very sketchy and he disliked having to conduct conversations through an interpreter.

"Jasoni," he said in a warm, welcoming tone, "it would please me if you would come nearer and have speech with me".

Jason crawled forward and took a place opposite the matanivanua. The cup bearer stirred the yaqona and brought forward brimming bowls, first to the Vunivalu, then the matanivanua, and then to the visitor. After drinking, Jason kept his head lightly bowed waiting for the chief to speak first. He was still smarting from his clash with the Denisons. He considered it an unwarranted slight that they should have known about the new mission while he himself had been deliberately kept in the dark.

"I regret that I have been unable to see you until now," said Cakobau, opening.

"For my part I was sorry to hear of your sudden illness. I hope you have fully recovered, Turaga." If this was the way Cakobau wanted to play it Jason would play along, but the slightly sceptical tone of his voice made it clear that he realised he had been fobbed off with phoney excuses.

"Quite well now, thank you," answered Cakobau graciously. "But I expect you have been able to keep yourself fully employed in the meantime. I know how you white men hate to waste a single moment of the day, unlike us."

"I had plantation affairs to attend to."

"And, of course, the attraction of the fair Miss Denison."

Jason looked up quickly to see the chief smiling at him. It was obvious that he already knew of their meeting at MacDonald's and that stupid business aboard the *Elizabeth*. This was not the first time Jason had been amazed by Cakobau's intelligence system.

"She could be a distraction I suppose but I doubt she would now welcome my company."

"Which means that you already know of my plans for Vatulevu and you are very annoyed and rather hurt that you were not first consulted," said Cakobau watching his guest closely.

This was what Jason had come for and whether or not his opinion was required Jason intended that it should be heard. "Turaga na Vunivalu," he said, giving Cakobau his formal title. "I do not presume to think you should not give orders with regard to Vatulevu without first consulting me, but on the particular subject of a new mission station I would be less than honest if I did not tell you that I think you will regret your decision. You know my opinion of missionaries and, having met the particular missionary appointed to the post, I see no reason to alter that opinion. He should never be allowed to set foot on the island."

"Why do you hate these men of God, Mr Cotterel? You are most unusual for a white man; your fellows enthusiastically support the conversion of my people to Christianity yet you actively oppose and hinder the missionaries."

"Perhaps I have seen more of them than most," said Jason without elaborating.

"Seen more of them?" Cakobau queried. "You amaze me. Hidden away on Vatulevu you see nothing of the good work they do and you avoid their company whenever you are in Levuka."

Jason hesitated. He had told no one in Fiji, not even Bex, that his knowledge of the church and its clergy was all too intimate and even after the passage of years his personal experiences were still painful. For the moment he confined himself to saying. "A great Frenchman once wrote, 'One day they will come, the crucifix in one hand and the dagger in the other, to cut your throats or to force you to accept their customs and opinions. Under their rule you will be almost as unhappy as they are themselves'."

"Jasoni, you may be correct, I cannot argue this subject on religious grounds. But you must realise that there are things at stake of even greater importance so far as the Fijians are concerned. On several other occasions you and I have talked far into the night about my plans for this country. Then, you agreed with me that we must have a sound government in these islands as soon as possible."

"I still maintain that is what we need," said Jason vehemently, "but it must be a government run by the people of Fiji, not a lot of pious missionaries and drunken foreigners. That was why I was opposed to your previous attempt to hand the country over to the British."

"I had no choice," said Cakobau irritably. "It is your own countrymen, the Americans, who cause trouble about the money I am supposed to owe them. My hand is still being forced. I am not prepared to name names, but there is a group of kai-valagi who might be prepared to pay off those debts in return for a land grant in the islands. If I can get that problem settled there is at least a chance we may set up a government which will encompass the whole of Fiji."

"As I see it, Turaga, if the present state of anarchy is not resolved quickly, one of the great powers is going to step in and snatch Fiji away from under your very nose. While there is no government, they can step into the vacuum. Our lack of a recognised government is an insult to their ideas of ownership and empire."

Jason had long since ceased to care what happened to the United States of America. The Civil War, only just concluded, had not touched him in the slightest and he considered himself to be a citizen of Fiji. It made him furious whenever he thought of the spurious American debt but at least it could be said in Washington's favour that they had no imperialistic designs on Fiji. Britain was not interested; she had her hands full in New Zealand and the various colonies in Australia. But the same could not be said for France and Germany, either of whom were liable to trump up an excuse for annexation.

"We both want the same thing; neither of us want to see Fiji made the plaything of the foreign powers. Yet you would play right into their hands," said Cakobau. "You are labouring under the illusion that Fiji and Vatulevu can isolate themselves from the outside world. You complain that the missionaries want to rule Fiji, but in the next breath you admit that there are others with the same ambition — France, Germany, Russia and your own United States of America. Sooner or later we shall fall prey to one of them if we try to hide in our shells like hermit crabs. "

"And there is an even greater and more immediate danger in the form of the Tongans. King George may publicly denounce Ma'afu but my informants say they are closer than twin brothers. A travelling entertainer once came to my island of Bau with little wooden people he called puppets. Ma'afu is like one of those puppets dancing on strings manipulated by his King in Tonga. If his puppet can destroy me, the Tongans will rule Fiji and I would rather the British than them."

"We on Vatulevu heard about the Tongan delegation and the answer you sent back," said Jason smiling. "If it is any joy to you, your Vatulevu subjects rejoiced that the Tongans can no longer insult Fijian chiefs and escape unpunished."

"It had to be done if we were to maintain our pride," said Cakobau pleased by the news of the favourable Vatulevu reaction. "But our missionary friends would not agree with you. Doctor Matthews came over to Bau from Levuka and for the rest of that week I had to endure lectures on the quality of mercy."

"No matter. I can endure their preaching — it is just words and has no effect on the day-to-day decisions I make. What I did may have been savage by Christian standards, but I would do it again if the need arose and that without the slightest qualm or fear of missionary displeasure."

Jason looked at the Vunivalu with increased respect. The man might be untutored, a reformed cannibal, but he had the makings of an astute politician. What he said about the Tongans was also true; Ma'afu and his Tovata Confederacy were slowly but surely nibbling away at Fiji's vitals. Every year another island or another yavusa came under their sway and their appetite seemed insatiable.

"These are weighty problems, Turaga. You will always be able to count Vatulevu warriors at your side if the need comes to repel the Tongans, but I still don't see how sending the Denisons to establish a mission station on Vatulevu will help. At a time when you may be desperate for fighting men they will all be in church learning to turn the other cheek. As of now, we could have men on their way to your assistance within hours of receiving your call for help. How many of your allies could say the same?"

"Your preparedness does Tui Navatulevu credit and I am sure you have had a hand in it yourself," answered the chief appreciatively. "Don't think I am unaware of your work on Vatulevu. The chief is an old man and could never have done it by himself nor could he have conceived plans like yours."

"Tui Navatulevu still has his wits about him, Turaga, but he is easily led," said Jason smiling. "Otherwise I'm sure you would never have been able to talk him into accepting this mission in the first place."

"Perhaps, perhaps," Cakobau was impatient with this continual harping back to the same complaint. "I must say that you disappoint me, Cotterel, you are blinded by your own prejudice. Can you not see our only hope of keeping Tonga and the other foreign powers at bay is by allying ourselves with the missionaries?"

"To prove that I am able to form a government acceptable by foreign standards I must show them I am capable of welding the islands and tribes into one nation. Even with the help of Vatulevu I shall never have sufficient warriors, muskets, or ships to do it by force. On the other hand the church and Christianity can give us that unity. By conversion to Christianity I was changed from the scourge of the church into its protector. No longer am I just the Vunivalu of Bau, I am now the Lord's anointed."

Cakobau continued "Wherever a mission station exists I have guaranteed its safety. The missionaries may preach against the evils of war but when it affects them personally it is a different matter. So long as war can carry the cloak of Jisu Karisito they lose their squeamishness. We can make war on anyone in God's name; every missionary is an outpost ready to report the movements of my enemies, and every enemy is a heretic and anti-Christ."

Shades of the Crusades and the wars of the Reformation, thought Jason. Those Europeans who said that Cakobau was nothing but a primitive savage incapable of ruling Fiji should have been listening. What he had just heard was amoral and Machiavellian but perhaps that was the mark of any effective head of state.

As Cakobau spoke he pounded the mat with his fist to emphasise points. Never had he appeared so impressive. "My country is divided against itself to such an extent that men travelling from one island to the next cannot understand the dialect spoken by their nearest neighbours. Not only does the lotu join men of all islands together under one faith, but the missionaries are translating the Bible into Bauan, the language of my own people. They preach in Bauan; and teach and speak to their converts in Bauan. Wherever the missionaries go they take a part of Bau with them. Soon all Fijians will have one language — my language."

Jason felt bound to check his enthusiasm with a word of warning. "Take care, Turaga, that they don't use you as you would use them. These people oppose the power of the chiefs. They want to rule and they, with more justification than you, can rule in the name of the church. Tahiti once had a monarchy but where are Queen Pomare and her sons now? They are dead and gone and those islands are ruled by the French and their church."

The cup bearer brought the conversation to a halt by ostentatiously stirring the yaqona, which he then served. So far as he and the matanivanua were concerned, most of what the Vunivalu had said was beyond their comprehension. They could see more sense in the white man's logic than their chief's subtle cunning.

Cakobau sat silent, pulling at his beard until the others had finished drinking. "Don't think that I do not see the dangers," he began again. "But the missionaries also taught me to read. I too can quote scripture to suit my purpose. Jisu Karisito told the kai-Jiu that what is due to a King must be given to the King and the Bible says that Kings are not to be disobeyed for they are ordained of God. I have spoken of these things at great length to Doctor Matthews and other missionaries. It is understood that we support each other; I protect the church and they recognise me as King."

Cakobau's methods were sometimes difficult to stomach but Jason could not help but admire his determination to weld the Fijians into a nation. Of one thing Jason was certain: Cakobau was the only chief with enough intelligence and strength of purpose to form a government. He would always have Jason's loyalty and support.

"Unless I deliberately antagonise the missionaries, they must support me and any government I form," said Cakobau, formulating ideas and clarifying his own mind as much as speaking to his guest. "I have them so deeply committed that they would now find it almost impossible to turn against me and still show just cause. But I watch and you may be sure I am careful, very careful."

Jason decided that it would be better to give in gracefully rather than wait until he was forced to the wall and made to surrender. "You play a dangerous game, Turaga, but it is not going to make it easier for you if I continue to put obstacles in your path."

Cakobau looked up quickly and his face lit up with a smile of success. "Ah! My friend, you agree to the missionaries going to Vatulevu, that is excellent."

"Did I ever have an option?" Jason laughed.

"Not really, but your assistance was essential. Your island is the key to the whole situation and your own role is vital."

"The key?"

"Vatulevu is my nearest island to Ma'afu at Lakeba. He has already failed to subvert the people and he will now try to achieve with force of arms what he could not do with words. At this very moment I have spies trying to find out when he intends to make his move. He will not wait for an excuse — as soon as his men and ships are ready he will strike like a ravenous shark."

Good God, thought Jason, this was another good reason why the Denisons should not be allowed near Vatulevu. It was intolerable to think of that girl thrown into the midst of a war; her father and that obnoxious brother of hers would be no protection.

"Turaga, if this is true, surely you cannot contemplate sending raw missionaries to Vatulevu at a time like this?" he protested.

"But this is why we must get the mission established," Cakobau explained patiently. There were times when he thought whites had as little understanding as newborn babes.

"As matters stand now, Ma'afu could use the fact that the kai-Vatulevu are heathen as a perfectly valid argument for his attack and there is little I could do to stop him. Once there is a mission on the island he will be attacking the church and Doctor Matthews will be screaming for the nearest gun boat to come to our aid. With any luck we might even talk the commander into shelling Lakeba for us." The Vunivalu's face displayed intense satisfaction at the thought of his enemies under attack from the guns of a man-of-war."

"But what of the missionaries?" asked Jason horrified. "They could all be killed. You can't send them to Vatulevu without making prior arrangements for their safety. You are using them like bait to catch fish."

Cakobau looked annoyed, the last thing he intended to worry about was the possibility that a few Europeans might be killed. It would be unfortunate, but dead they might be even more effective than when they were alive.

"Jason you are the most inconsistent man I have ever known. One moment you are castigating the missionaries and calling them all manner of names, the next you are worrying yourself sick lest a hair of their heads be harmed. If Ma'afu should do them any harm it could also result in his own execution. Anyway they will be in no danger," his tone brooked no opposition, "I hereby appoint you to watch over their safety on my behalf."

Jason gave up in disgust. He had been anti-missionary and anti-church for the whole of his adult life but now, not only had he agreed not to place obstacles in the way of the mission, but he was also to play wet-nurse to the missionaries themselves.

"I can take it then you will give these people your full support?"

This was going a little too far for Jason's liking. "My conscience forbids me to give them assistance, Turaga," he said, doggedly sticking to his principles, "but I will not actively work against them, and if it does come to a fight I'll see to it that they are nowhere near the firing line."

This was all Cakobau had hoped to achieve from the interview. "Excellent, excellent," he beamed at Jason, pleased with the success of his diplomacy.

"It is an honour as always to be of service to the noble Vunivalu," Jason said politely. "If you will excuse me I must return to my ship and prepare to leave as soon as possible. With this threat of war hanging over our heads the less time I waste in Levuka the better."

"So soon?" said the chief genuinely upset. "I had hoped we might share a bottle and discuss my plans further. You kai-valagi are always in such a tearing hurry anyone would think the sun could neither rise nor set unless you were present to assist it."

Jason was escaping when a further call from the chief halted him. "I was forgetting another favour I meant to ask of you."

Jason could guess what was coming but for the life of him he could see no way in which he could gracefully avoid it. "Of course, anything that is within my powers."

"The mission authorities wish the Denison family to go to Vatulevu as soon as possible. You would be helping me cement good relations with the church if you were to take them with you on the *Albatross*."

Jason bowed. "It shall be as the Vunivalu wishes," be said and added in an undertone to his own conscience, "and may they all be so sick they fall overboard and become shark-bait."

On a more serious note, he needed time to sort things out in his own mind. What were his relations with these people to be, especially the girl who kept intruding herself into his thoughts? What arrangements should be made with regard to the defence of the island? The main difficulty would be impressing the urgency of the danger on the chief and the people of Vatulevu.

7

Vatulevu bound

HEELED OVER, THE *Albatross* scudded along on a reach which would carry her to Vatulevu. Every seventh wave crashed over the bows and sprayed past the tightly sealed hatches and the cabin roof to drench Jason at the tiller. A fine layer of white salt encrusted his face and bare shoulders, his arm was cramped from a two hour spell, and he felt cold and chilled. But for all these discomforts he was contented and at peace with himself.

So far they had made a fast passage and his unwelcome passengers had not bothered him. He had not addressed more than five words to any of them since leaving Ovalau and had made it clear they were only aboard on sufferance.

He was glad to have the stench of Levuka out of his nostrils. The mud, the hovels, broken bottles and European derelicts hanging round the bars always depressed him; the animals rooting around under the buildings were cleaner than most of the humans. In all fairness he could not blame the vice and depravity of Levuka on the Methodist church, it was the European flotsam and jetsam who were responsible.

There had been a time when he too had wallowed in such a life, so he was in no position to criticise. He could thank his lucky stars he had found his salvation on Vatulevu. Although he still drank, the way they guzzled in Levuka sickened him. Here at sea he might be cold and wet but at least he felt clean.

Jason loved the sea. Not that he ever wanted to return to the searing cold and back-breaking work of a deckhand on a whaler, but he was never more in harmony with the world than at the helm of his ketch. Slicing through a white-capped sea, the *Albatross* was no racer, but he knew that she could carry him anywhere on the surface of the globe had he the urge.

More importantly, the *Albatross* was the product of his own sweat and the skill of his own hands. In those far-off days in New England, if any one had told him he had natural skill with wood and the temperament and patience of a boat builder he would not have believed them. Nonetheless, with the help of his Fijian friends on the island he had built the ketch from stem to stern.

They had even made her sister ship, the *Lovadua*, for Ratu Seru, Tui Navatulevu's younger brother and Jason's crony. Both ships had a barrel capacity of ten tons of coconut oil, but even with both on a constant shuttle run to Levuka they could scarcely cope. Now, production was increasing to a point where they would either have to build another, larger, ship or talk Peter Bex into picking up cargoes direct from Vatulevu.

From where he sat, Jason could look down the companionway into the cabin. He could just see John Denison's feet where he lay prostrate on the rudimentary bunk. To Jason's hard-hearted satisfaction, the missionary had been violently ill ever since leaving Levuka. Nor was it all seasickness — Denison had come aboard that morning looking haggard and smelling of stale brandy. Most missionaries would not touch alcohol, but it was evident from the ten cases MacDonald had delivered to the ketch that Denison was of a radically different persuasion.

The air down there would not be helping, thought Jason. Ships carrying coconut oil had its heavy smell soaked into their every timber; that, plus the odours of human sweat and cooking, must make the cabin particularly nauseating for someone with a queasy stomach. Denison was having a thorough initiation into island life. He would have to get used to it, his life was not going to be any bed of roses. Transport throughout the Group was only to be had on boats like the *Albatross* and the majority were infinitely worse.

Toby Denison was standing alone on the roof of the cabin, one hand holding on to the mainmast. At least he was a good sailor, swaying easily to the ketch's rolling and plunging. A few years before the mast was what that lad needed to straighten out his kinks. As Bex had said, the boy had never had to stand on his own feet. He lacked self-reliance and regarded the slightest setback as personal persecution.

But the fact that he kept strictly to himself meant he was still feeling sorry for himself. Unless he snapped out of it he would have a thin time once they reached Vatulevu. The kai-Vatulevu were a happy, friendly people, but if they once thought Denison looked down on them they would move heaven and earth to make his life uncomfortable.

Kate Denison staggered up the companionway from the evil-smelling cabin and heaved a bucket of slops over the side. The sleeves of her dress were pushed above her elbows and her hair was tied behind her head. For a moment she leaned pale and trembling against the cabin and her shoulders heaved convulsively as she fought to control her stomach. She had been tending her father ever since he started to vomit. Jason had expected her to collapse long before but somehow she had managed to continue.

Though he disliked the Denison clan generally, he could not help but admire her strength of character and he could even find it possible to feel sorry for her. For a woman used to having a flock of hovering servants, she was getting a rough introduction to Fiji.

"Miss Denison!" He shouted against the noise of the wind and the sea to attract her attention. She turned and gave him a rather wan smile — after the way he had deliberately snubbed her all day, it was more than he deserved. "Why not stay topside a while till you feel better? One of the crew can clean up down there."

She shook her head wearily but none the less emphatically.

"Well let me call your brother. He's up for'ard."

"Don't you dare," she even managed a weak laugh, "I'd have him on my hands too. One is quite enough, thank you. I'm alright, it's just that the smell down there is a trifle overpowering. I am about finished and father is asleep, thank the Lord." She smiled her appreciation of his concern and picked her way below to complete her noisome chores.

The only other member of the mission party aboard was the Fijian lay preacher, Elija Codrokadroka, and he was in his element. Regardless of the breaking seas soaking them, he and Jason's crew were comfortably settled forward of the cabin. Occasionally a burst of laughter drifted back to Jason at the tiller. There could be no doubt that the preacher was becoming a firm favourite with the men.

Elija was the first Fijian preacher Jason had met and, in spite of his own prejudices, he had to admit that the man was likeable. He had a happy, open face and a broad spontaneous grin which spread from ear to ear. It was perhaps his lack of pretension which was most impressive. He had associated himself with the crew from the moment he came aboard, ready to lend a hand with the sheets or swap a story with the best of them. He was quite different from other products of mission education Jason had met, most of whom set themselves up as superior beings.

Elija's popularity with the crew was partly based on his knowledge of fishing. As usual they set lines trolling behind the boat immediately they left Levuka, but with little success. Elija had asked politely if he could try his hand. Using the white, fleshy leaves of the viavia plant he had skilfully tied a lure, tossed it over the side, and within half an hour three torpedo-like walu, all 25 pounders, were hauled jumping and slapping into the cockpit.

Fijians were as curious as kittens about anything novel and Jason had no doubt that the preacher would have no trouble getting an audience once he started telling the thousands of tales which made up the Bible. He was honest enough to admit that with more preachers like Codrokadroka, conversion of the Fijians to Christianity might not be so bad.

*****

By the time Kate came on deck again it was late afternoon and the mountains of Viti Levu were a low grey cloud-covered line astern. Directly ahead a volcanic cone had come into sight. Its starkness leaping from the uninterrupted plane of the horizon was awe-inspiring, with golden slopes highlighted by the sun and slashed in places by black and purple gashes of shadow. Everyone aboard the ketch seemed hypnotised by the sight. The laughter and chatter of the crew stopped and all sat silently watching the mountain draw ever closer.

Jason tore his eyes from the scene to watch the girl as she stood not ten feet from him in the cockpit staring over the roof of the cabin. Now and then she was forced to duck her head to dodge the spray flying from the ship's plunging bows. To protect her hair and clothing she wore a full-length hooded cloak.

Seeing her wrapped up like that reminded Jason that he was cold and wet himself. He shouted against the wind for one of the crew to relieve him at the tiller and went below into the cabin. Taking good care not to wake John Denison he pulled on a dry woollen shirt; his canvas trousers were also wet through but there was no point soaking another pair when they waded ashore at the anchorage.

He returned and stood beside Kate. Then, in an effort to redeem his earlier rudeness, he said, "Quite something isn't it?"

She turned to him with eyes sparkling with excitement and a smile which had some of the attractive warmth he had noted at their first meeting. "I think it's absolutely marvellous," she said with genuine enthusiasm. "I have never seen anything so beautiful yet at the same time so terrifying. It makes shivers run up and down my spine."

"I know what you mean. I've seen the mountain from this angle a hundred times or more, but each time as we get nearer it shoots its head further out of the sea. Not that there's anything to worry about, Vatulevu hasn't erupted in the memory of man. It even has a small lake in the middle where you can swim. It's worth a climb up there one day if only to see the tagimaucia flowers."

Kate was entranced, "So that's Vatulevu."

"Vatu means a rock and levu is Fijian for big. So Vatulevu is the big rock or big mountain; Vatulevu, meet your new inhabitant, Miss Katherine Denison."

"Oh I want you to tell me all about it," said Kate, her excitement bubbling over. "I want to learn all about the people, I want to speak their language. You know everyone on the island, Mr Cotterel; do you think you could find someone who would be prepared to teach me?"

There were a dozen other things she wanted to say but she suddenly remembered their clash of the night before, "Ah, I forget. You do not associate with missionaries."

It was Jason's chance to be consistent with his principles but now he knew this girl's friendship was important to him — more important than any woman's since the death of his wife.

"I apologise for the way I spoke last night. My only excuse is that the whole thing was sprung on me suddenly and in my surprise and annoyance I forgot myself. Hidden away for so long on Vatulevu, I have forgotten how to deal with young ladies. I'm afraid you bore the brunt of it though it really wasn't you I was angry with at all, it was those fools of missionaries who run the church here."

No sooner had he said the last, than he could have cut his tongue off.

"Because I'm not a man, I cannot be a fully-fledged missionary," said Kate in a frosty voice which gave fair notice of battle, "but I have hopes that as soon as we have the mission operating, Father will allow me to start a school for the children."

"There is a difference between being a teacher and a missionary."

"It will be a mission school run on God-fearing lines and I shall be working for the mission," she said stubbornly.

The effect of her speech was rather spoilt when the ketch lurched in a heavy sea. If he hadn't grabbed her she would have finished up in the scuppers, as it was she finished her sentence in Jason's arms. It was difficult to argue with a man who had one strong arm about her waist and, to make matters worse, was laughing at her.

"There, Miss Denison, that just goes to show you shouldn't argue with the captain aboard his own ship. God may back the mission, but at sea Neptune looks after his own."

Jason set her back on her feet. His hair was wet and tousled and salt clung to his eyebrows; his clothes were a far cry from his sartorial elegance at the hotel; yet when he smiled her heart pounded, and she could not help but admire his rugged good looks and strength.

"If we are going to be neighbours we must be friends," said Jason. "I ask to be forgiven and, against all my principles and better judgement, here I am giving you and your family free passage on my own ship. You can hardly be less generous."

Kate never liked being at loggerheads with anyone and so she conceded. "Very well, Mr Cotterel, I hereby declare a truce but only on condition that religion and the mission are forbidden subjects of discussion between us. If we talk only of neutral subjects I am sure we shall deal very well together."

"You've no worry even there. I have promised the Vunivalu I will do nothing to obstruct the work of the mission. You can thank his persuasive tongue that you are all aboard now."

"I would certainly thank him if I only knew who and what a Vunivalu was," said Kate. "Whoever he is, he must be a great man if he can persuade Mr Cotterel of Vatulevu to change his mind," she said teasingly.

To explain the meaning of the title Jason was drawn into a description of the whole chiefly system. Kate's questions never let him rest and he found himself lecturing at some length on island conditions and the power struggle which might at any moment plunge them all into a bloody war. He took good care, however, not to mention Ma'afu's designs on Vatulevu itself. There would be time enough for that later, without terrifying her before she had even set foot on the island.

*****

An hour or so later, as they closed land, Jason reluctantly broke off their discussion to take the helm. The passage through the reef was narrow and dangerous and at this point he liked to pilot the ship himself. Discussing his ideas with an intelligent woman had been a new and stimulating experience. There were spheres where they would always disagree but they had established a relationship based on interest and mutual respect which might develop into a highly agreeable friendship.

For her part, Kate felt she had seen another side to his character. He might be a renegade and anti-Christian but that was not the whole man, he was more complex than that. He was sincerely interested in the welfare of the local people and any man whose hopes and ambitions were not centred purely on self could not be all bad.

She watched him standing at the tiller giving instructions to his crew. He seldom raised his voice yet there was no doubt that he would be obeyed. He was strong, capable and a natural leader of men; with him in command anyone would have felt safe. He was something new to her experience and although too disturbing for her emotional well-being, Kate knew she wanted to see more of him. Her father and brother would have been horrified if they could have read her thoughts but, except for his atheism, Jason Cotterel was her idea of what a man should be.

The reef opening, a small break only a few cables wide, lay between a small rocky island and the mainland. White tumbling water marked the line of the main reef stretching away into the distance. Elija came aft to pull in the fishing lines to prevent them snagging on coral patches in the shallower water.

"That's Vatulailai, the little rock," shouted Jason, pointing to the small island. "No one lives there — no water."

As they entered the lagoon the pitching and rolling ceased and the *Albatross* glided smoothly through the sheltered waters. Elija came and stood beside Kate.

"Did you enjoy the trip, Miss Denison?" he asked politely. The English he had learned in mission school on the island of Viwa was near perfect. According to her father he was one of Doctor Matthews' most promising *protéges*.

"I've enjoyed it immensely Elija, though I'm afraid father is still very ill." Much to his amusement she didn't make the mistake of calling him Mr Codrokadroka as she had when they first met.

Kate was worried about her father, more worried than she would admit even to Toby. Essentially a weak person, he had always taken pride in himself as an English gentleman. The fact that he had been slightly worse for drink the night before, and from his condition when they boarded the boat that morning had obviously been at a bottle again after he left her, was quite out of character.

She had known about his drinking but for someone outside his immediate family it would have been almost impossible to detect. Last night it must have been obvious to everyone, yet he had seemed past caring. If it got back to the mission authorities there was bound to be terrible trouble. Both he and Toby seemed to be disintegrating before her very eyes, as if Fiji was too much for them.

*****

Kate allowed the changing scenery to sweep her depression away. This was how she had dreamt a South Sea island should look. The mountain which had seemed yellow and bare from out at sea now proved to be covered with long waving reeds the colour of oatmeal; and strangely shaped boulders, some larger than a London mansion, were scattered over the slopes like a giant's playthings.

They passed a shallow bay. The sand on the beach was so white it looked freshly washed and bleached. She could make out green coconuts in clusters at the top of the palms. She had always thought coconut palms would be as tall and straight as guardsmen but these swayed and drooped in all directions like languid ballerinas.

"What do you think of it?" asked Elija.

"It's wonderful," she said, "especially after sordid Levuka. This is so clean it might have been created by the Lord just yesterday. I'm sure I shall be very happy here"

"There is certainly no comparison between Vatulevu and Levuka. That is an evil place, yet one of these days it may be different. When Ratu Cakobau is King and when the church of Christ has been accepted by all then Levuka will be as newborn as Vatulevu. It will be the capital of our country."

"Mr Cotterel has been telling me about Ratu Cakobau. He is the Vunivalu isn't he?" Elija nodded with pleasure at her interest. "It was clear to me he has great respect for your chief. What do you think?" she asked, trying to draw him out.

"Mr Cotterel and the Vunivalu are close friends and he will be able to tell you much that even I do not know. For me to pass an opinion is very difficult, even presumptuous. You see, I come from the island of Bau and Ratu Cakobau is my hereditary chief."

"As a Christian I know he is sometimes very harsh and cruel, and at one time he was a cannibal, as indeed was my own father. But those days are gone, Ratu Cakobau now rules in all things temporal. I am his loyal subject; whatsoever he commands I must do as he is the prince sent by God and I am sure that his orders, though somewhat difficult for Europeans to comprehend, are meant to further the best interest of our people."

"What about Mr Cotterel? What is he like? Is he respected by the Fijian people?" Kate was more interested in their captain than local politics.

"Well, as you know he does not love missionaries."

"I not only know," laughed Kate, "I have been on the receiving end of his views."

Elija glanced toward Jason as if making a final assessment. He was watching the shore, his profile to them; his face showed a determination which in opposition might be very dangerous.

"The people within the church do not like him," he said thoughtfully. "I think they are wrong. He has been in the islands a relatively short time, but he is already well-known and his opinions are much respected. Most Europeans treat us as if we are idiot children; they cheat and exploit us at every opportunity. Great masses of land are changing hands these days and often my people are only paid in trade blankets, rum and muskets. The majority of the planters treat labourers as little better than slaves and then wonder why people will not volunteer to work on their estates."

"Mr Cotterel is unique in that be does none of these things. If he was like the others the story would soon travel, we would know. Instead it is common knowledge that all Fijians get fair dealing and respect when they go to Qaraniqio."

"Qaraniqio?"

"That is what he calls his plantation. I have never seen it myself but the crew were telling me earlier that his home is always open and his hospitality is offered to any visitor, not just Europeans but Fijians as well. I have heard many stories of the ways in which he has helped the islanders."

"Vatulevu is one of the wealthiest islands in the group, thanks almost entirely to this white man. Not only has he developed his own estate but he has made sure that the people have advanced at the same pace. Is it any wonder he has much influence? When he speaks Fijians listen, not just out of politeness but because they know that his advice will be sound and in their own interests. Did you know that he was at one time married to a Fijian woman?"

"Married to a Fijian!" exclaimed Kate.

"That surprises you, Miss Denison?" Elija's voice was a little guarded.

"Er... Yes it does. I mean, no it doesn't," Kate was confused. "What I mean of course ... I knew many of the white men ..."

"Ah! That is where you are wrong. Jason Cotterel has nothing in common with those men of whom you have heard. They treat our women as if every Fijian woman was a harlot. Jason Cotterel was married to his wife not only according to Fijian custom but also by Doctor Matthews."

"A Christian marriage?" queried Kate. "But I thought he was anti-Christian."

"That is why I say many of our colleagues dismiss him too quickly. There is more to this man than can be seen at first glance. He is strongly anti-missionary but I do not think that we should necessarily assume that he is anti-Christian. He could well be, but if so then his church marriage was completely out of character. I think that if he was asked, Jason Cotterel would not be able to say whether he believed in God or not. His wife was never a Christian although she went through the church ceremony, but she was the most beautiful girl I ever saw."

"You keep saying 'was', did something happen to her?"

"She died giving birth to their second child."

Children! It was all too much for Kate to take in. This obviously well-educated American had not only taken a Fijian woman to wife, but had sired her children. In England she had been taught that it was a duty to take up the white man's burden but that implied a distinct and inescapable superiority of whites over blacks. She thought of herself as a liberal, even a radical thinker, but miscegenation was more than she could accept. Casual liaisons with Fijian women would have been more palatable than this perfectly respectable marriage.

"They had two children, a boy and a girl. The crew were telling me that the boy is now ten years old and the girl about seven. Evidently they are delightful children and Mr Cotterel takes great pride in them."

"There is another thing you should know," continued Elija. He knew that what he was saying came as a shock to the girl, but she had to learn sooner or later and better from him than from someone unsympathetic. "Mr Cotterel's late wife, Adi Ulamila, was Tui Navatulevu's only child. The Tui has many wives but only one child — perhaps a punishment from God for his heathen ways. There is a younger brother, Ratu Seru, who will be chief after the present Tui dies. But when Ratu Seru dies the succession will revert to Adi Ulamila's son and he will be installed as Tui Navatulevu."

"Surely he should be chief on the death of his grandfather," said Kate diverted by the strange system of succession.

"It is rather round about I agree," said Elija, "but it means that any sons who outlive elder brothers have a chance to rule and normally it avoids the succession to the title of a mere child. On the other hand the people can refuse to install a new chief. The chief needs a strong club arm and a loyal following if he wishes to stay in power. When a chief dies it is always a time of great turmoil, intrigue and uncertainty." Elija explained. "Often a contender will see to it that every other possible heir is put to death.

"Do you mean that when Tui Navatulevu dies Mr Cotterel's children may be in danger of being clubbed to death?" A moment before Kate had been horrified to know that the children even existed, now she was equally horrified that they might be in danger of assassination in a dynastic struggle.

"So long as the people keep to the old ways it is always a possibility, but in this particular case I think we can rely on Mr Cotterel to see that no harm comes to his own," smiled the Fijian.

*****

At that moment the ketch swept past a headland and into a large bay. "The Reverend Denison should be woken now," said Elija. "We shall soon be there and the people will have prepared ceremonies of welcome for him and the rest of us."

A welcome was the last thing Kate expected. She had thought the forcible introduction of a new faith was more likely to produce hostility than friendliness. "You mean they will greet us with open arms?" she asked incredulously.

"Did you think we should have to fight our way up the beach, Miss Denison? We are assured of a great welcome. We come accompanied by many fine omens. Not only are we travelling in Mr Cotterel's boat but we are under the protection of the Vunivalu; you could say we are his emissaries."

"A fast sailing canoe left Levuka before us and, if I know my people, the island will now be in a turmoil of preparation for our arrival. If we were enemies the clubs would be oiled and the axes sharpened. But they know us for friends and you are about to find out just what Fijian hospitality can mean — I think you will find it without rival; perhaps so excessive as to be embarrassing."

"My father will be relieved," said Kate happily, "I think he has been steeling himself for a cold reception."

"He need not worry. Some of the ceremonies he will find pagan and barbaric, even a little frightening, but so long as he remembers they are welcoming him with honour and if he follows my lead, everything will pass off well.

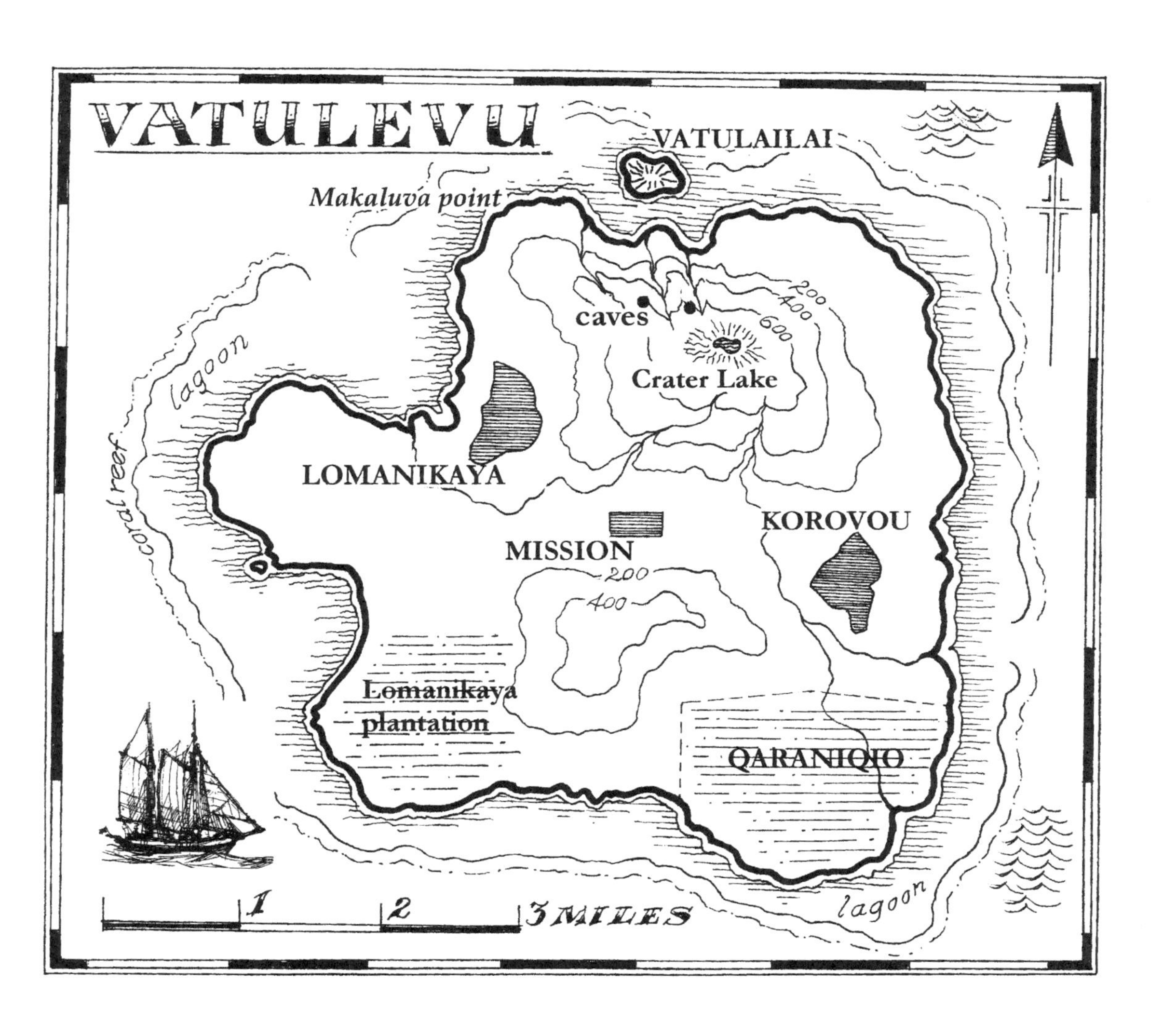
VATULEVU
VATULAILAI
Makaluva point
lagoon
coral reef
caves
200
400
600
Crater Lake
LOMANIKAYA
MISSION
KOROVOU
200
400
Lomanikaya
plantation
QARANIQIO
lagoon
1
2
3 MILES

8

A new home

FOR JOHN DENISON the whole day had been a never-ending nightmare. The act of stepping aboard that disgusting tub of a boat severed the umbilical cord connecting him to the rest of the world. The voyage and that revolting cabin would live in his mind as the epitome of misery and degradation. More than once he prayed the boat would sink and put an end to his humiliation and shame. After vomiting until his stomach felt torn asunder and his mouth was foul with bile, he was woken to find himself surrounded by black faces.

Fijians were clambering aboard even before the ketch reached the anchorage, making interminable and unintelligible speeches; and pushing whales teeth at him; which he had no idea what to do with. They were finally ceremoniously received by that Fijian preacher who, for a native, was much too forward. When Denison was told they expected a speech he had mumbled a few words. Then, without being asked, Codrokadroka had also spoken. Meanwhile, Cotterel watched with contempt on his face.

Ashore it seemed even worse. The Reverend Denison was carried to the beach on a platform by 50 shouting, screaming natives. More speeches followed, all of which were translated by the lay preacher. And for all their high-sounding phrases of welcome, Denison was sure he would be murdered in his sleep and eaten. Then he was made to drink loathsome stuff called yaqona which looked and tasted like filthy dishwater. Huge slabs of fish and half-cooked pork were pushed under his nose. After his seasickness it was a wonder that he did not vomit in front of the whole assembly.

The men were huge and ferocious and were either near-naked or festooned with coloured leaves and crudely patterned masi. The women seemed shameless in their nudity. They were totally bare but for a wisp of leaves about the waist. Breasts, breasts, breasts everywhere — long and wrinkled, fat and heavy, pert and provocative. It was sinful, a disgraceful flaunting of sex.

Then the thought came to him that his former wife would have been at home in an atmosphere like this. Whether fully-clothed in their drawing room or naked in her dressing room, she had exuded sex from every pore with an appetite he had never been able to satisfy.

To make matters worse the savages greased themselves all over with coconut oil which exuded the same smell which had so nauseated him aboard the ketch. As the night drew on and they sweated from the vigour of their pagan dances, the stench was such that he was sure he would faint.

*****

Toby Denison watched the young maidens dancing, his lips and throat dry, his loins aching. He was certain some were watching him with reciprocal thoughts. Their eyes and breasts were more provocative than an explicit invitation. He had heard stories about the women of the islands from the crew of the *Elizabeth* and he was not going to be inhibited by his clergyman father.

Nor did he intend to rot out his years on Vatulevu. He would learn to sail, then talk his father into buying a ketch like Cotterel's. Finally, he would get his hands on some of his father's money. Then, one morning they would wake to find no ketch and no Toby Denison.

He had to bide his time. Let them think he had turned over a new leaf and lull them all into a false sense of security. When his time came he would pay his father back for his humiliation. Cotterel was also on his list; that arrogant bastard had plenty coming to him. Kate had done nothing but make sheep's eyes at him all day — it would serve her right when Cotterel was shown for the ignorant Yankee pig he was.

Six months at the outside should be enough to bring his plans to fruition and in that time he might even manage to amuse himself. He thought of his father, John Cecil Denison, clergyman and English gentlemen; drunkard and hypocrite were nearer the truth. He knew about the brandy which had come with them to Vatulevu and he intended to have his own share of every case, whether his father liked it or not.

He needed an establishment of his own well away from prying eyes. Toby smiled to himself and licked his lips; the rhythmic thump of the drums made his pulse race and the hot feral smell of female bodies was full of promise.

*****

Near midnight Kate found herself alone, stretched out on soft cool mats beneath the protection of a mosquito curtain. The women had finally led her away from the main meeting house to a smaller thatched bure set aside for her.

She was surprised to find her personal luggage separated from the rest. A chair and a makeshift dressing table had been contrived from packing cases, a lamp was burning, and the house was inviting and friendly. As the entire missionary party had been present at the welcoming ceremonies it must have been Jason Cotterel, notable by his absence, who had organised this. Bone-weary, she blessed him for his thoughtfulness.

It had all been very strange and pagan but that did not really describe the welcome. This was a new world completely divorced from anything she had experienced previously — hundreds of huge muscular men and handsome strapping women. The Fijians she had seen in Levuka were drifters, cadging drinks from the bars or pimping for sailors, whereas the people of Vatulevu were proud and magnificent by comparison. Jason Cotterel was able to fit into such a picture without difficulty, but her own menfolk appeared puny and insignificant. Her father had been bemused the whole evening and Kate had felt shamed by the naked lust in her brother's eyes.

She was particularly interested in the old chief, Tui Navatulevu. He seemed to have shrunk with age and what must have once been firm muscles now hung in flabby wrinkled folds on his arms. But he had eyes like sparkling black beads which missed nothing. Kate could not understand a word he said but it was obvious that his people regarded him with great veneration and his slightest order was obeyed immediately. Most of the time he had spoken to Elija or through him to her father, but occasionally he had looked in her direction and smiled encouragingly.

The dances were quite hilarious. Some were performed by men and others by women, but each troupe included a clown who mimicked the other dancers to the huge delight of the crowd.

The young girls were beautiful and graceful, their hands and arms seeming to float as they danced. It made it all the more important that she should learn the language to understand what the songs were about. Their bare breasts and lissom bodies were so innocent and natural it was impossible to think of them in terms of sin. Kate herself had been so hot in the crowded meeting house that she had envied them their freedom from the heavy trappings of European dress. Sin could only be in the eyes of the beholder.

It would have been wonderful had Jason been there to explain everything. She had looked closely at the women trying to conjure up a picture of Adi Ulamila, the wife who had died bearing his child. The majority were rather Amazonian with blunt features but some were refined, proud and beautiful. It was not difficult to imagine a lonely white man falling in love.

Although Jason Cotterel had deliberately dissociated himself from the welcome, he had seen to her personal comfort which could mean that he was not entirely sorry to see her on his island. She drifted off to sleep thinking of their long, intimate conversation aboard the ketch and the way his strong arm had saved her from falling to the deck; she could still remember how safe and reassuring it felt.

9
Settling in

KATE HAD LONG BEEN responsible for the efficient ordering of her father's household, but now she had to supervise domestic arrangements for the entire mission compound. Nor was it catering solely for her own family and Elija. At every meal there were anything up to 50 extra Fijian mouths to feed. Bundles of dalo and yams, the staple root vegetables of the islands, plus fish and turtlemeat were constantly being presented as gifts to the mission.

Without them they would have been eaten out of house and home in no time. Visitors never arrived empty-handed but by the same token they expected the open house hospitality which was obligatory under the Fijian way of life. Kate was thankful she had included a large quantity of sugar in her stores for sweets, once tasted, were in constant demand from children and adults alike.

There was so much to be done and she was so weary every evening that time became blurred. One morning she stopped to calculate and was astonished to realise that ten weeks had flashed by since their arrival. One moment everything was strange and new and the next it seemed that she had never lived anywhere else. England was now a remote existence and somehow unreal.

Elija had engaged two young girls, Aloesi and Talei, to help her. At first they were not really much help, being unused to her ways. But at least they were able to relieve her of the drudgery of washing clothes and dishes. They giggled constantly and went off into fits of laughter at Kate's efforts to speak their language, but the compound was a happier place for their presence.

Because the girls were working at the mission, Elija insisted they be properly clothed. Much to the surprise of the menfolk, Kate objected. But when she saw the way Toby's eyes followed them around, she quickly changed her mind. The girls themselves did not care in the slightest, Kate's cast-offs gave them increased status in the eyes of their sisters. The fact that they wore nothing underneath and always forgot to attend to buttons and hooks meant little was left to the imagination. Had Kate but realised it, this modicum of veiling made them all the more desirable in her brother's eyes.

Toby was a changed person since they had been on Vatulevu. Not that he was any practical help to Kate, that was too much to expect. But at least he went out of his way to be pleasant and his sulkiness seemed a thing of the past. Apart from selecting the site for his own house — he had been most particular in choosing a spot isolated from the main body of buildings — he had shown no real interest in the mission. Every day he was out with the young men sailing or fishing. None of this was productive, but Kate at least had the satisfaction of knowing his time was taken up in healthy pursuits which had never been part of his previous life.

*****

Her father was the constant worry. The very first morning on Vatulevu — the morning following their never-to-be-forgotten welcome at what she now knew was Lomanikaya, the chief village of the island — he had woken ill and complained of severe pains in his back and legs. Thinking it was an aftermath of his seasickness Kate had been all solicitude and counselled him to stay in bed and recoup his strength.

But the next day he was still bedridden, and the next and the next and the next, leaving the whole burden of the work to Kate and Elija. Whatever his illness was it did not impair his appetite. He also managed to wash himself when Kate complained enough and, with the aid of a stick, hobbled backwards and forwards to a pit latrine which had been dug at the edge of the village for the convenience of the mission party.

He never ceased his querulous complaints and, in spite of all Kate did to ensure his comfort, was continually accusing her of disbelieving him when he said he was in a constant state of agony.

The last thing Kate wanted was to doubt her father. She could see no reason why he should want to feign sickness, especially after the warmth of their welcome. The island had been laid open to them and he had only to exert himself to control the whole of the moral and religious life of Vatulevu; what more could a missionary want?

When his illness entered the second week and neither she nor Elija could diagnose what was wrong, she could only accept his word that, imaginary or not, the pain completely incapacitated him. Whenever they managed to get him to his feet, he stumbled and hobbled about like a chronic invalid. Kate would have given anything for the services of a competent doctor, but the nearest was in Levuka. The medical books in their small library were no help.

Elija came up with the idea of massage, the Fijian panacea for almost any form of sickness. It took Kate three days to talk her father into trying it. He objected vehemently to being handled by a dirty Fijian, or being pummelled when he was ill. But eventually he agreed since it was either that or admit that he had no desire to recover.

Kate was not allowed to be present when Elija and an old man expert in the art of massage went to treat him but Toby gave her a graphic account of what happened. Evidently John Denison's screams almost brought the house down and, within two minutes of starting the treatment, the old man was scurrying backwards out of the door scourged by a fluent stream of non-clerical curses.

Kate would not have minded, but the extra work involved in nursing her father came at a time when she was terribly busy anyway. His drinking made it worse. When she took meals to him she could smell the brandy on his breath. At breakfast it was a sour sickening smell from the night before; by luncheon it was obvious he had been drinking again; and by evening when she carried in his dinner, his speech was slurred often to the point of incoherence. She could not fathom why he had turned to drink, nor for that matter did she know where he kept it, for she never saw a bottle.

Denison took no interest in the selection of the site for the mission nor in the construction of the buildings. The only work he could be said to have done took the form of perfunctory discussions on Christianity with Tui Navatulevu, using Elija as an interpreter. Even those were only performed under pressure from Kate and were of little positive value; Elija's personal interviews with the chief were much more effective.

She would have dearly loved to unburden herself to Jason Cotterel, but she had seen nothing of him since their arrival. It was as though he was deliberately avoiding her.

She even tried enlisting Toby's support but he was no help at all. "Me speak to him! My dear girl, you must be crazy, I'm the last person on earth he would listen to."

"If you could even get him to stop his drinking," Kate begged. "Find out where he keeps his supply and destroy it before it finally destroys him."

Toby knew exactly where his father stored his liquor, right down to the number of cases and bottles left. They were hidden beneath a stack of mats and luggage in the men's bure. Sometimes when his father was forced by nature to go outside he made a quick inventory.

He had no intention of interfering. Apart from the fact that he was systematically stealing bottles for his own use, Toby took a perverse delight in watching his self-righteous parent drinking himself to death. He would never forget the *Elizabeth* or Levuka, and once he developed a grudge against someone it was there forever.

He even tried to laugh the whole thing off. "You're making far too much of it," he said. "The old fellow's genuinely sick but he'll get over it. He is drinking too much, but if I was to try and tell him so he would crucify me."

Despairing of assistance from Toby, she tried Elija. To her surprise he also refused. "You must understand, Kate," — she had finally persuaded him to stop calling her Miss Denison — "your father is still in sole charge of the mission. I agree he is ill, perhaps not physically as he maintains, but certainly mentally."

"There is nothing I can do. I am living in the hope that once the mission buildings are finished and we can move your father out of Lomanikaya, his sense of duty will return and he will forget his troubles and continue the work ordained for him by the Almighty. I am his junior; it would be wrong if I, the pupil, began to read lessons to my master."

*****

So Kate took her courage in both hands and decided upon direct confrontation with her father. At first he bluntly denied drinking at all then, when it was obvious this would not serve, told her a long and garbled story about having visited a doctor in Sydney who had prescribed brandy for medicinal purposes.

"I have an extremely serious heart condition," he told his daughter, willing himself to believe his own lies. "I never told you, Katherine, I could see you had so much to do and I didn't want you worrying and fussing over your old father. Whenever I feel the palpitations coming on I follow the doctor's orders and drink a small brandy to settle my heart down again.

"I wasn't so bad, you know," his voice was near whining, "but your brother's dreadful behaviour on board the schooner, shaming me in the eyes of everyone, was the final straw. You'll never know how close you were to losing me in Levuka — I had an attack which all but carried me off. The heaving around in Cotterel's dirty little boat seems to have finally brought me to my knees."

Kate could only look and listen, flabbergasted. She instinctively knew he was lying. Even though he might have visited a doctor in Sydney without her knowledge, it was wholly out of character. Had anything been wrong with him he would have let the whole world know long before this.

She hardly recognised him as her own father. Her efforts made his drinking worse for, having created a good excuse, he no longer even bothered to keep it a secret; he was to be found at any time of the day or night with a bottle and a glass at his side. His heart became his hobby and he elaborated on the dangers of any exertion to the point where Kate began to doubt he would ever leave his bed again.

Kate had too much on her mind and too much work on her hands to brood. Half her day was spent chasing the two girls about trying to explain what she wanted done in her stilted but fast improving Fijian. She refused to be put off by people laughing at her mistakes. Her tongue became tangled in the jungle of grammar and pronunciation but she knew that if she once hesitated out of shyness, or fear of ridicule, she would never succeed.

Elija was a continual source of encouragement and, though he was worked off his feet, he made time every evening to give her another lesson. Kate at least had the satisfaction of knowing she was far more advanced than either Toby or her father, both of whom claimed to be scholars.

*****

The new mission station was the main interest in Kate's new life, perhaps as compensation for the lack of interest shown by her father and brother. Vatulevu had two principal villages, Lomanikaya and Korovou, situated on opposite sides of the island. Elija had selected a site near a river midway between the two so that the mission would serve both communities with equal facility.

He was careful to choose land away from that used by the villagers so that the mission, as it expanded, would have plenty of room for a school, dispensary and their own food gardens, without encroaching on those of the people. He explained to Kate that Fijians had a most uncertain temper on the question of land.

Every day Kate made the two mile trip to and from the mission to Lomanikaya. It was a long walk for a girl accustomed all her life to travelling in carriages but the going was easy and it was cool under the trees. Kate came to look forward to those few hours when she was spared her father's constant complaining.

She was impressed with the speed of the work. Hundreds of people seemed to be milling about aimlessly, shouting and laughing, but beneath it all there was an efficient organisation. Each person had his appointed task. While one group cleared away the jungle, others were levelling house sites, selecting and trimming posts, plaiting magimagi, the cord made from coconut fibre, or gathering reeds for the walls and thatch.

According to Elija they could have proceeded even faster if some of the labour force had not had to fish and tend food gardens. Another group of over 100 able-bodied men had been allocated to some project Jason Cotterel had in hand and spent all their time at his plantation, Qaraniqio. Kate could only surmise that either the work on the plantation was urgent or this was his way of deliberately retarding work on the mission buildings. Whichever it was she was sure it made no difference, for every day showed tremendous progress.

Kate was fascinated by all the activity. She could have stood for hours watching men chopping back the jungle, and teams dragging the heavy corner posts into position for another group to set them up in ready-dug holes. Elija was everywhere at once, instructing, supervising and where necessary labouring as hard as any of their helpers. She helped with the cooking and discussed with Elija the placing of each building.

Elija never stopped talking; every task seemed to have in it the makings of a religious story. When facing an elevated foundation for the church with river stones, he told them the parable of the house built on a rock foundation and of that set on sand. When they set the house posts, he showed them the folly of the old traditions which would have decreed the burying of men alive beneath each post. God's houses needed no other support than that of the Holy Spirit and His love of mankind.

He was tremendously popular and had only to join a group for a beam of pleasure to light every face and for the task to be completed in half the time it might otherwise have taken.

Kate discovered that the Fijians were master craftsmen who took great pride in their buildings. There were four sleeping houses, each four fathoms by three, one for each of them and another almost twice the size to serve as a dining-cum-sitting room. Two smaller ones were for use as a kitchen and office respectively. All of the buildings with the exception of Toby's were set along the edge of a large open area which stretched back from the river.

On slightly higher ground, at the end facing the mountain, the new church dominated the whole compound. This was Elija's pride and joy: not a post was set, nor a bundle of thatch tied without his personal supervision and assistance. Its large raised earth foundation, the yavu, was faced with specially selected stones and from this the walls and roof rose steep-gabled to ridge poles forty feet above the ground.

When the huge frame was in place Elija clambered to the highest point and there fixed a large white cross he had made and painted himself. Then, before the thatching commenced, he delivered the first full Christian sermon ever given on Vatulevu, explaining the significance of the symbol with which he had just crowned their labours.

The roof would have done credit to the thatchers Kate had watched while on holiday in Norfolk. Inside, stripped white reeds bound in intricate patterns by black and brown magimagi panelled the walls, and the exposed beams, bound with heavier material, were given an extra decorative touch by incorporating white cowry shells into the patterns.

The floor was of smooth white sand carried from the beaches two miles away in coconut-frond baskets on the backs of the women. Over this went a layer of plaited bamboo; and over that again covering after covering of freshly woven mats, a gift from the women of the island.

Elija vanished for a day and returned followed by a line of men carrying enough pit-sawn planks to make doors and shutters for every building, a distinctly European addition to the traditional Fijian bure. That he had been able to find such timber on a remote island was surprising enough, but Kate could hardly believe her ears when Elija told her it was a gift from Jason Cotterel.

The altar and pulpit were carved from local wood and stained with oil which left the natural grain but gave them a smooth, finished appearance. The building might have seemed rough-hewn and ugly to European eyes, but Kate felt it fitted into its surroundings whereas the finest English cathedral would have been out of place.

*****

When the time came to move into the new mission, the most difficult item to shift proved to be the mission's leader, John Denison, who protested for days beforehand that travelling was certain to kill him. Kate pointed out that unless he wished to remain alone in Lomanikaya, fending for himself, he would have to make up his mind whether the risk was worth taking or not.

"But you wouldn't leave me here by myself, Katherine? You wouldn't leave your sick father alone among these black heathens?" Denison exclaimed, sitting up in bed with more energy than he had shown for months.

Kate's sympathy was exhausted. This brandy-swilling old man dressed in a smelly, soiled nightgown bore little resemblance to the man she had known.

"The decision rests with you, not me." So saying she turned sharply on her heel and left to finish her own preparations for departure.

As expected, when the time came to leave there he was, acting out his part, staggering and leaning heavily on a stick and every few paces stopping to castigate his children for their lack of concern.

The Fijians were completely taken in. Anxious that their white Spirit Man should not die and bring down the wrath of his God upon them, they eased him gently over every slight unevenness in the path so that what was normally an easy hour's walk took them nearly half the day.

Even as egotistical a man as John Denison could not but be impressed by the new mission. The trim buildings and church with its tall white cross, looked clean, efficient and inviting.

Elija, dressed in his best sulu and shirt, was waiting to greet him. "Welcome, sir, to your mission. I am so happy to see you looking better."

"Who says I'm better?" Denison snapped. He had thought it better not to drink in front of the Fijians and had thus been without sustenance during the journey. "I am far from well and I'll thank you to remember it. That cursed goat track has done nothing to help me, I can tell you."

Elija looked questioningly at Kate who shrugged her shoulders in despair.

"Would you like to look around, sir?" Elija tried again. "Without your experience and advice to guide us we have been severely handicapped. However we have kept you always in mind and tried to plan what we thought you might have done had you been here to supervise the work yourself."

Denison looked around at the neat new buildings. Even a brick church in a

London slum would have been more to his liking, but at least this was better than the dirt and pandemonium of the pagan village he had just left.

"It will do, it will do," he said munificently. "There are changes I shall have to make of course but as a temporary measure it is quite satisfactory."

Kate's face was flushed with anger and Denison knew that unless he showed more enthusiasm she was liable to turn on him there and then. "You have done very well, my boy. I am very pleased, very pleased indeed," he said to Elija hastily. "I shall tell Doctor Matthews in my next report that you have been of great assistance to me."

"Now if you'll kindly show me to my house … I must rest … my heart you know." He hobbled off, leaning on Elija's arm for support.

How the Fijian could have so much patience with her drunken, hypocritical father was more than Kate could fathom. Perhaps, if she were a better Christian like Elija, she would be able to find compassion for his mental breakdown, if nothing else.

*****

That was a week ago and they had now been in the mission long enough for a routine to be established and for it to take on the atmosphere of a home. Being able to have her personal possessions about her for the first time since she had packed them in London made such a difference, probably more for her than for her father or brother.

Toby was never about when he was needed and her father pretended to be as decrepit as ever. He had managed only to change his position from lying to sitting and from where she stood near the kitchen she could see him on a bench Elija had built around the base of a large dakua tree. There he could look across the river to the jungle and the mountain.

Now, his excuse for not working was that he should perfect his command of the language, and so he sat all day in the shade with a book open on his lap. Kate had yet to see him make an attempt to read it; he either slept or, she suspected, closed his mind to his surroundings and imagined he was still in London.

Kate had given up trying to reason with him. She desperately needed advice but had no one to ask. The news Elija had given her about Jason's part-Fijian children had come as a shock, but the man had been properly married and the more she thought about them the more common sense overcame ingrained prudery. He was an amusing and interesting companion and potential adviser who, sadly, she appeared to have lost.

Not that Kate was unhappy; she loved Vatulevu which she was coming to understand increasingly as her grasp of the language improved. What was more important, she felt that the people liked her. She was working harder than she had ever done in her life and manual work at that, but it was very satisfying to have a sense of achievement in a worthwhile cause.

The work seemed to agree with her, for she had never been in such good health. Her cheeks were blooming, her figure had lost a few pounds of unnecessary weight, and apart from some hardening of her hands she had never felt so feminine or so alive. Though she would not admit it even to herself, she started the day by making sure she looked her best and there were frequent repair sessions. If asked, she might have said she was determined not to lower her personal standards; but in truth it was the off-chance that Jason Cotterel might come visiting and catch her looking like a work-worn shrew which frequently sent her back to the mirror.

On Sundays, Kate dug into her chests and brought out her finery. Bonnets and lace shawls might have seemed out of place on a lonely Pacific island but the Fijian ladies appreciated them and were soon trying to imitate them in masi. For church at least, they covered their breasts in imitation of Kate, long before Elija raised the subject as a moral issue.

As John Denison still hardly grasped even the basic elements of Fijian, sermons were given by Elija. People flocked in from both villages; even old Tui Navatulevu made the two mile pilgrimage. Three chairs were set at the front of the congregation for the Denisons; beside them on a mat sat the chief, his wives and his officers; and the rest of the church was filled to overflowing with the island's population.

Elija's deep booming voice dominated the room. He was a born orator carrying his audience along with him. When he told them of God's love, they smiled and bathed in the warmth of his message; and when he roared of hellfire and damnation they huddled closer together and looked apprehensively heavenwards.

Kate's Fijian was only sufficient to grasp the bare gist of what he said but his display of sincerity and fervour would have convinced an audience of deaf mutes.

*****

Tui Navatulevu and his people sat drinking in every word. It was only a matter of time before there was a wholesale conversion of the island to Christianity, but none would or could move before the chief himself gave the lead.

Kate thought of Elija's own words on the subject: "The chief is an old man, Kate; he was born, nurtured and has lived under the shadow of the old gods. He will make no change until he is absolutely convinced. If I know my own people, he has already made up his mind but is waiting for a sign from the new god which will tell him that he, Tui Vavatulevu, is acceptable as a member of the new faith."

"The others will follow like sheep, but we must go carefully. I fear your father does not understand this. He would baptise them into the church in one large group to get it over quickly. But we should only accept into the fold those who take conversion out of deep conviction. I am not trying to belittle the authority of the chief, but we must make it absolutely clear that acceptance of the Holy Spirit and admission to Christianity is a matter for individual faith and not mere obedience of orders."

How Kate's ideas had changed! In England she had thought of all Fijians as heathen cannibals, small, wizened, ugly men. Instead they had proved to be tall, handsome, magnificent specimens; men like Ratu Cakobau fighting to maintain his independence; Tui Navatulevu venerated by his people; and Elija who had a more profound knowledge of Christianity and a greater capacity to live according to Christian mores than she herself would ever have. It was all very humbling for a girl brought up to believe that God was an Englishman.

10

Toby's agenda

THE SHADOWS LENGTHENED as another day drew to a close. Kate could smell the heavy scent of frangipani and hear the cawing of parrots and the bubbling notes of the golden doves in the nearby jungle. It was so peaceful and benign she sometimes thought the tales of war and violence for which Fiji was famous were the fabrications of a Baron Munchausen, and the mission an intruder in the Garden of Eden.

She sat, tired but content, on a bench outside her sleeping-house soaking up the atmosphere of the evening. It was a magical part of the day. Unlike the long summer twilight of the Northern hemisphere it flashed by quickly, yet somehow its brevity made it all the more precious.

Toby wandered into the compound along the track from Korovou. He was a different person from the pale-faced dandy Kate had known in London. He walked with a spring in his step, his face was bronzed from constant exposure, and he looked brighter and healthier for the South Pacific air.

It was all the sailing — he seemed to have developed an absolute mania for boats. Anything to do with the sea and he would devote hours of painstaking effort but when it came to work about the mission it was a different story, and the proposed plantation was not even mentioned. So long as sailing was not another of his momentary crazes it might even be put to use. From what Kate had heard, the islands needed good coastal shipping services both for inward delivery of household goods and equipment and for the outward shipment of produce to Levuka. It might be wiser for her father to set Toby up in a shipping business than force him into farming.

She watched him slip into the kitchen where Aloesi and Talei, were preparing vegetables for the evening meal. Soon she could hear scuffling and giggling, then Talei shot through the doorway laughing and holding the front of her dress together with Toby running after her.

"Toby!" Kate was on her feet, her voice sharp with anger. "Stop that this instant!"

Both Toby and the girl halted in their tracks at the sound of her voice. It was obvious neither had thought Kate was anywhere in the vicinity.

"Talei! Lesu tale ki na nomu cakacaka!" said Kate, ordering the girl back into the kitchen. She obeyed, but from the way she flounced off with buttocks rolling provocatively, it was obvious that she enjoyed Toby's attentions and thought his sister a spoilsport. Once safe inside the kitchen the girls' laughter only served to infuriate Kate further, for she knew they were laughing at her.

"Do I need to remind you that this is a mission compound, not some low sailor's haunt?" she stormed at her brother. "Why am I continually having to talk to you about your behaviour? I sometimes think you do not have a single gentlemanly instinct."

"Come off it, old girl," laughed Toby, "I was just having a bit of fun with them, there was no harm done."

"You needn't try to pull the wool over my eyes. I know exactly what you were trying to do, and I tell you I will not have it! If you don't leave those girls alone I shall send both of them back to the village and they can stay there."

"You're imagining things Kate," Toby blustered. "I tell you I was only having a little fun. Are we not allowed to laugh any more? Has the church made that a sin as well?"

"That's not what I meant and well you know it," she answered furiously. "You seem to have no pride left at all, running around after a couple of native girls like a broken down beachcomber."

Toby had every intention of running after them and running them to ground at that, but like his father he had very healthy respect for his sister's temper and what she had just witnessed had her really roused.

"Running after black wenches? Good God, you must be mad to even to think such a thing. I was only having a joke with them and it was more their doing than mine; one of them grabbed my hat and I chased her."

In truth both girls had their backs to him when he entered the kitchen and creeping up on Talei he had deftly slipped a hand around her, through the front of her open dress, and on to a firm young breast. His hat had fallen off in the scuffle when he tried to kiss her.

Kate recalled seeing him wearing the hat when he entered the kitchen and he certainly did not have it now. "Alright then," she said accepting his story reluctantly, "but kindly remember I will not tolerate you interfering with my house servants."

"I won't go within a mile of them" he assured her.

He slipped an arm through Kate's and smiled down at her, exerting all of his considerable charm to put her back into a good humour. "Come on Kate, smile and be friends, there's been no harm done and if you are nice to me I have some fantastic news to tell you."

"News?"

"Not unless you say I am completely forgiven."

"Oh, you're forgiven you silly boy," laughed Kate, who could never be angry for long, even though her temper was usually fierce while it lasted. "So long as it doesn't happen again. Now tell me your news."

"It's just that I met your beau today," he said, leering at his sister as if they shared a secret.

"My beau?"

"Who else but His Grace, the Duke of Vatulevu, Jason Cotterel."

"Jason Cotterel is not my beau," Kate snapped indignantly snatching her arm from his grasp.

"Oh I'm so sorry," he said with mock humility, "but from the way you were chatting in Levuka and on the way over here, you must admit it was a natural mistake. I apologise and, of course, if you have no interest in him it follows you won't be interested in what he was doing."

Kate was deeply interested in anything Jason might have been doing but she was determined not to give Toby the satisfaction of admitting it.

"You can tell me or not, just as you wish. Jason Cotterel is not my beau, nor is anyone else for that matter, but as he is the only other European on Vatulevu of course I'm interested. Anyway, since when have you been able to keep anything to yourself? You are bursting to tell me — it's only a matter of time and I'm in no hurry."

Her unemotional air deflated Toby who was set on teasing her, especially after the roasting she had given him. "I think you like Cotterel more than you say. Anyhow I will tell you. You know I've been out fishing several times? Well last night father was in a more expansive mood than usual and I got him to agree that we should have a boat like the *Albatross* for our own use."

"He's going to buy a boat!" she said incredulously. "Why Toby that's marvellous, I knew you wanted one but I didn't know you'd actually asked him."

"See, I don't tell you everything," he laughed. He did not add that he had put it to his father when he was pie-eyed with brandy and the argument he used was the procuring of regular supplies once the present stocks were exhausted. "Both of you think I'm a useless fool but for the first time in his life father admitted that I had a good idea. I'm to be captain and it should make a tidy profit." A profit for him, for once he had a keel beneath him Vatulevu would never see Toby Denison again.

"But how does all this affect Jason Cotterel?" Kate asked.

"Don't you see? He built the *Albatross* and the *Lovadua*, so I went to see if he would build another for us."

"I can imagine the reception you got. If he thinks it's for the mission he'll never do it."

"That's just where you are wrong," said Toby triumphantly. "He agreed to build her so long as we are prepared to carry general island produce when the mission isn't using her. That was no problem. After all, I said, we wanted to make her a paying proposition and the more the boat is employed the better."

"But Toby, the mission won't be able to charge."

"Of course we shall charge for freight; and in any case the boat won't belong to the mission, it will belong to father and myself as a personal venture." He was so carried away with the idea of a shipping empire that for the moment he even forgot that the whole point of building the ketch was to escape from the island.

"I'm so pleased for you, Toby," said Kate, genuinely excited.

"Of course it won't happen overnight," he said a little mournfully, as if he had hoped to be commodore of his own fleet within the week. "It will be upwards of six months before he can deliver. Most of the timber has to be pit-sawn by hand and dried, though he has some drying now. He'll do alright out of it; he's not building her for nothing, you know. They get another freighter and on top of that he's charging us £150 paid in Maria Theresa dollars. You wouldn't call that cheap."

"Well I think you're lucky he's even agreed and as for getting father's consent, I just don't know how you did it. It's a miracle."

Toby decided that was a subject which would not bear enlargement so he changed the conversation. "And the new boat isn't all I have to tell you about. What do you think Cotterel was doing when I got there this morning."

"For goodness sake don't ask me," laughed Kate. "Weeding his plantation or building another boat I should think."

"Neither of those," he said excitedly. "You'll never believe this, nor could I at first. He had with him about 100 Fijians, all with muskets, and he had them formed up in ranks teaching them to fire in volleys. Cotterel is training a private army."

11

Danger looms

THE MESSENGER WHO preceded the *Albatross* to tell Tui Navatulevu of the missionaries' impending arrival had also delivered a warning from the Vunivalu of the danger of Tongan invasion. As he sat at the helm of his ship on the way to Vatulevu Jason thought of little else, except when the unsettling fact of Kate Denison's presence erased this and all other subjects from his mind.

Out of politeness, the news was not allowed to interfere with the arrangements for the mission's welcome but Jason had been closeted the whole of the next day with the chief and his officers explaining his plan for repulsing an attack.

He knew that Fijians would comprise the majority of the opposing force but the real cutting edge of Ma'afu's war axe would be provided by Tongans, most likely under the leadership of his bloodthirsty lieutenant Semisi Fifita. The Tongan warriors were renowned for the fanaticism and unbridled ferocity of their assaults and Jason dared not risk a head-on confrontation between Ma'afu's men and the local warriors. The islanders were not lacking in courage and the will to fight, but in hand-to-hand battle Ma'afu's more experienced shock troops must inevitably triumph.

It might be different at sea. It would take a sizeable fleet of even the best double canoes to transport an invasion force and any local army travelling by sea was bound to be disorganised and chaotic. If they could convert the confrontation into a naval battle, there was a fair chance of cutting the attacking force to pieces, thus blunting the edge of that war axe before it even reached land.

Explaining this to an assembly of senior kai-Vatulevu Jason stabbed his crude map with a forefinger to emphasise his points. "They can only come at us from two directions: the northern passage by Vatulailai or the main passage opposite Lomanikaya, with the off chance that they may split their forces and try both at once. We can forget the small channels on the other side of the island, I doubt if they know of them and even if they do they're far too small to be negotiated by a war canoe."

The Fijian elders nodded their heads. They had no illusions about their chances against the Tongans and if Jasoni had a plan they knew from past experience it would be worth listening to.

"We need cannon. The Vunivalu has some and I intend asking for them. We need gunpowder, shot and a hundred or more of the best muskets. These will all cost money," he told them bluntly. "I can pay for some, and if you, Turaga," he said addressing the chief directly, "agree to use the money you got as your share of the last two cargoes, we should just about manage."

That money had been intended for the construction of a larger ship and proper wharf facilities on the island, but the defence of their homes came first and other things must wait for peaceful times. Tui Navatulevu nodded his agreement but he was not prepared to say anything until he had heard the rest.

"That is agreed then," said Jason, relieved at the lack of opposition.

"It is all very well having cannon," said one old man from the floor," but how will they be used?"

"We shall set up two on Vatulailai and the other two on the mountainside opposite. Between them they can close the northern channel completely. The other two will go on the *Albatross* and the *Lovadua*. It will mean strengthening their foredecks but that is no difficult task. I also intend to raise a shield of hardwood around the decks of both ketches behind which we can put men with muskets. Our men will be well protected and if they fire together in volleys we should decimate the Tongans in their crammed canoes.

There was an excited buzz of appreciative interest from his listeners, only for them to fall respectfully silent as Tui Navatulevu intervened.

"Perhaps I am just an old man whose courage has drained away with his strength, Jasoni. But there are cracks in your plan which must be mended if it is to hold water. They will be attacking in great numbers and if they choose the main channel your two small ships may delay them, but I doubt that they will be enough to stop the advance. Another thing, our weapons are the club, the spear and the axe, not muskets and cannons. There are less than a score of men on Vatulevu who have ever fired a musket."

The room became a sea of mournful faces as this truth was acknowledged.

"We must train them," Jason had interjected firmly. "This is the time of year for hurricanes and it will be another two months before the season ends. With any luck they won't attack before then; we may even have a month or two more — you know yourselves how long it takes to get a Fijian army organised and ready to move."

"If I can have a 120 men, or as many as can be spared for that long, I will teach them. Both ketches should leave for Levuka immediately to start hauling in all the weapons we shall need. Give me the men and I'll start building the gun emplacements. Then, with the few muskets we've got I can begin teaching them the rudiments of war kai-valagi style."

"But two boats are still not enough to stop a whole Tongan fleet" the chief objected.

"With respect, Turaga," said Jason patiently, "you are presuming they will all strike at once through the main passage. Sailing from Lakeba, the first and nearest passage is the northern one which we can block no matter how many of them there are. Some of their fleet are bound to try that route and provided we achieve an element of surprise we should damage them considerably as they make the attempt."

"So far as the main passage is concerned, the Tongan ships coming through the passage one at a time will have to run a gauntlet of fire. If we have those cannons loaded with grapeshot we can damp their ardour to such an extent they will think twice about pressing home their attack."

"I have another idea: there are at least 50 outrigger canoes on Vatulevu and there are none more skilled in their use than the kai-Vatulevu. If we put a musketeer aboard each — two on the larger ones — they will be able to sail rings around the Tongan ships picking off the helmsmen and chiefs."

The older men had looked at each other askance for certain rules applied to island warfare one of which was that chiefs' persons were sacred. Yet here was Jasoni suggesting they be deliberately targeted.

"It is no use trying half measures if you want to beat Ma'afu," argued Jason vehemently. "He and Semisi Fifita are determined to take your island and if they do so your own chief, Tui Navatulevu, will be shown no mercy. We are defending our homes and, no matter what we have to do, the means we employ justify that end."

There came a murmur of agreement and Jason did not take this delicate point further.

"With luck the Tongans, who are bound to be the spearhead of any attack, will be decimated in the passages; and those who do make the beach will be so demoralised and disorganised our own men ashore should have no trouble stopping them. We can set traps on the beach and, provided we can get enough guns, we can let them have another volley as they step ashore."

What alternative to we have, Turaga?" Jason had asked the chief. "If we try to fight the Tongans using traditional Fijian methods of war we are bound to be defeated and Ma'afu's banners will fly over Lomanikaya. I agree there are many risks in what I propose, but there is also a chance we may beat them off. Unless someone has a better plan, and I am ready to listen to any plan at all, I advise you to do as I have said."

For a moment there was silence; then the whole room broke into groups all speaking at once arguing the pros and cons backwards and forwards. Jason had let the debate stream over his head unanswered. He knew that Tui Navatulevu was the one who would make the decision and he could only hope he had been convincing enough.

He was certain in his own mind that his plan was the one feasible way of meeting the attack. The ifs and buts lay in the control of the various parts of the defence force. Fijians were liable to do things on impulse. Unless they made a plan and kept to it, they would be beaten by their own lack of discipline long before the Tongans arrived.

Tui Navatulevu slapped the mat to attract the attention of the assembly and there was silence. "Have any of you a better plan?" he asked his elders.

Silence. Some looked meaningfully at others who had opposed Jasoni's plan but for all their objections they had nothing better to offer.

"Sa dina," said the chief, signifying that silence was what he had expected. "If that is so, we must follow Jasoni's advice. He is the only man among you who can think in terms of a whole battle and not just of each man's skill with club and spear. We will do as he says and the money will be used to buy guns."

"Vatulevu will fight the Tongans vaka-valagi and Jasoni will be your Vunivalu. I am too old to be your leader in this fight; but I order you all to remember that Jasoni was the husband of my only daughter and one day, when I and my brother are dead, his son will be your chief. You will obey him in all things as you would me. The man who disobeys his command will be a meal for the sharks before the same sun sets. Are my instructions understood?" he said coldly, daring anyone to object.

"Sa matata vinaka, i'saka," they said in unison, signifying that all was clear.

"What of the missionaries, Jasoni?" asked the chief. "The Vunivalu has ordered us to build their houses and a temple for their god."

Jason thought for a moment. The perfect opportunity was his for the taking, but he decided it was not worth it. Talking to people like Kate Denison and Elija Codrokadroka was even making him rethink some of his ideas about the church.

"There should still be more than enough people to build the mission, Turaga. Give me the men I want and the rest can attend to the other work. On the other hand missionaries are against all forms of war and if they know we are preparing to fight they may try to stop our preparations. I would like you to forbid all your men and women to mention our plans or even talk of a Tongan invasion."

"It is agreed," Tui Navatulevu had said solemnly. "It shall be as you say."

*****

So it was settled and since then both Cotterel ketches had been hard at work ferrying supplies from Levuka. Each trip they returned heavily laden with lethal cargo — muskets, gunpowder and ball, even a few rifles. The large order was no problem — Levuka merchants traded in little else but guns, rum and square gin.

The Vunivalu had even gifted six old cannon, once the pride of an East Indiaman which had come to grief on a Fiji reef 20 years before when the sandalwood trade was at its height. They were brought over in two separate shipments. When Jason saw them he feared they might burst in the faces of their crews, but the risk had to be taken.

The important thing was that the programme was under way and, having chosen the youngest, strongest and brightest of the warriors, training with the new weapons was made easier by their enthusiasm. Jason even consented to handing over the captaincy of his vessels, busy as he was training his 'private army', as Toby Denison put it.

At least Vatulevu's defence was forewarned and Jason was determined to maintain that advantage. Lookout posts were placed at the summit of the mountain in the north and on the hills to the south. He had to be satisfied with a system of smoke signals. He would have preferred some form of heliograph or semaphore but that was beyond the comprehension of the locals without spending scarce time training signallers.

Tui Navatulevu agreed that at the first sign of the Tongan fleet the women, children, and all those too old or infirm to fight would be evacuated to caves high on the western side of the mountain. The caves were large enough to hold the entire population. There was water aplenty and their food supply would be yams and kawai, which could be stored indefinitely, plus what the women could find in the jungle.

Then the warriors would be able to concentrate on the battle without fearing for the safety of their families. Even if the Vatulevu troops were defeated there was always the off chance that their loved ones might escape detection. He was uncertain how he would manage it, but Jason was determined that when the hour of danger came Kate Denison and her family would be up there too; there could be no turning the other cheek when the Tongan divisions struck.

Jason kept in touch with the progress of the work on the mission. He gave Elija the timber he needed. He knew of John Denison's simulated weak heart and felt sorry for Kate, but there was nothing he could do to help; he was so busy himself that a 24-hour day was all too short. But from the moment Toby walked in on an arms drill at Qaraniqio it was no longer possible to keep the missionaries in the dark; the most he could hope was that they would remain neutral and not interfere.

Even if they did, ten weeks had been enough to drum the elements of his plan into the heads of the Vatulevu defence force and he doubted the missionaries could undo his work at this late stage. What was needed was practise and more practise, not only to make his men ready but to keep them sharp and alert throughout the period of waiting. This might be easier to achieve if the veil of secrecy was lifted.

Also, Jason wanted to see Kate again and now that the basic work was done he needed to relax. If he explained the situation adequately he might even win the missionaries support, thus turning the fight into the 'Holy War' envisaged by the Vunivalu.

12

Interlude

JASON LAY IN A HAMMOCK on the verandah of his house. Set on a hilltop, it commanded a marvellous view over acres and acres of young coconut palms. For the past ten weeks the plantation had been neglected, the grass was high under the palms and uncollected nuts lay everywhere. But his own safety as well as that of every man, woman and child on the island was at stake. His property might have gone to the devil but behind the house, in hastily thrown up shelters, were 120 musketeers and riflemen, the like of which had not been seen in Fiji before.

For weeks he had lived, eaten, drunk and dreamt war. The sea was no longer a symbol of peace and freedom but the arena for the coming battle, reminding him of his fleet of takia and the dozen-and-one flaws evident on their last exercise. Using the *Albatross* as a mock Tongan war canoe he had manoeuvred the outrigger canoes in squadrons to the beat of a big lali. Two at a time they had swooped like striking barracuda, fired, and wheeled away to reload while another two took their place.

But in spite of the skill of their helmsmen, excitement and misunderstanding had resulted in four capsizes and two collisions. There was also a problem keeping powder dry on such flimsy craft. The marksmen had carried their powder in pigskin bags slung around their necks but it was an unsatisfactory arrangement and he would have to think of something better.

Only those who had proved their ability as marksmen were assigned to the canoes; even so there were 50 percent misfires and their reloading speed left much to be desired. If they kept their heads when the Tongan ships bore down on them, and concentrated solely on the chiefs and helmsmen, they might be effective.

He had experimented with the cannon settings until they could drop shot and grape just where the enemy must pass. For the most part they had practised their skills with dry runs to conserve shot and powder. And, despite his forebodings, none had exploded in their crews' faces when they were live-fired.

So long as the gunners held their fire till the enemy ships reached the agreed spots — Jason had done all he could to drum the landmarks into their heads —

any ship trying the northern channel would face annihilation. The batteries were invisible from the sea and with any luck the Tongans would make the attempt on the passage before they discovered what was coming to them.

Any number of things could ruin his plans. He would be trying to control the whole battle from the deck of the *Albatross* and if the men lost their heads and gave the game away it would be too late for him to remedy the situation. Not for the first time in the last few weeks, Jason found himself wishing he had not lost his belief in the power of prayer.

Beside him on a table was a bottle of rum, a jug of water and a partially emptied glass. Jason had not been a heavy drinker for years, but he enjoyed the relaxation of an evening drink after a hard day. Bathed and clad in a clean sulu, he could feel himself uncoiling as he sipped that first glass.

He would not have traded the half an hour before and after sunset when the whole island settled into a quiet peace, for fame, fortune and the finest mansion in the whole United States of America.

Once, when asked why he did not take more interest in the Civil War being fought in the States, he had answered. "They can fight all they damn well like for all I care; I've no wish to be mixed up in the argument and sure as anything if I start worrying about what is going on there I'll take sides myself and want to be in it. Here, I'm my own man minding my own business and I intend to let others mind theirs. The only war I'll fight is when someone tries to push me off my perch; let someone try and may their god help them!"

This was what the Tongans were aiming to do and he was determined they would be defeated and would never try the same thing again.

*****

His reverie was interrupted as an elderly Fijian woman came onto the verandah leading two children. They broke away from her and leapt into his hammock demanding that he play with them.

"Lala! Lala!" he laughingly admonished the nurse. "What have I done to deserve this lot? Get off you rascals you are tearing me to pieces." He grabbed each child in turn and, standing, tossed them in the air and caught them again to screams of delight.

"More, more, Father," they yelled.

They were handsome children and lighter-skinned than their Lomanikaya cousins. The girl, named Ulamila in memory of her dead mother, was plump, jolly and completely spoilt by every adult on the island. She had the look of her mother and already knew she could twist her father round her little finger.

Jason's son's full name was Aporosa Jason Cotterel. As Tui Navatulevu's eventual successor, he had been named Aporosa after his grandfather and the

Fijians addressed him as 'Ratu Aporosa'. He was a sturdy ten year old, normally rather solemn, as if the burden of his future duties had already descended on his young shoulders. But when he was with his father and sister he was just another young lad demanding affection and his share of any fun on offer.

"They wanted to say goodnight, Turaga. If I had known how busy you were I wouldn't have brought them," the old woman said with mock sarcasm. Lala had come with Adi Ulamila as her personal servant when she first married the white man and had remained after the death of her mistress to watch over her children. In Lala's eyes neither Jason nor his children could do any wrong, but that did not mean that men did not have to be put in their places occasionally.

Jason smiled. With two bundles of energy pulling at him he had time for no one and nothing else, even war, for they would never have tolerated it. For half an hour father and children romped together. Then, they were taken off to bed protesting at the top of their voices.

By now it was dark and a lamp burned on the table as Jason sat on with his drink thinking about the children whom he loved dearly but nevertheless were a constant worry. He always spoke to them in English but they were with Fijians all day and, even though they tried hard, when it came to explaining anything complicated they reverted to Fijian. He knew both needed more than his perfunctory efforts at education but he just didn't have the necessary time. If Kate Denison did open a school they would attend, no matter what his opinion of missionaries might be.

When Aporosa was a tiny baby, Jason and Ulamila had discussed their son's future by the hour. Fiji was changing so swiftly that if the future Tui was to give his people the leadership they needed, he must have education and training so that he understood the new way of life. It seemed heartless to toss a healthy young savage like Aporosa out into the world but Jason knew he must one day send him to school in New South Wales or New Zealand. If Kate Denison could teach him his three R's first, so much the better.

These days he hardly ever thought of Ulamila — how callous the human mind, anything painful was forced further and further into the background until all but forgotten. Yet just a few months before his grief had been insupportable and her face continually before him. He had walked the lonely moonlit sands and her spirit had joined him. On his solitary bed it was almost as if her long cool body still lay close to his.

Now she was becoming a vague dream, a life lived by another, younger, different Jason Cotterel. Any of the island girls would have come to his bed — Jason only had to show a preference and Tui Navatulevu would send her, willy-nilly — but the urge had never been there. Somehow it would have been sacrilegious to bring another woman into the house built for Ulamila even though she had not lived to occupy it herself.

Aside from Lala, Kate Denison was the first woman to whom he had spoken more than ten words since his wife's death. A greater contrast between Ulamila and this young English girl could hardly be imagined. Ulamila had been a wild pagan, passionately eager for love; the other was a Methodist missionary's daughter, a product of Queen Victoria's England. He could not imagine her racing along the beach in the moonlight as naked as the day she was born.

Or could he?

There was no denying the girl had hidden qualities. She had courage and was loyal to her own no matter what they did. It had been a pleasure to talk to someone intelligent — one thing Ulamila could never give him was intellectual companionship, but there had been no need for intellect in those days.

Yet Kate Denison had something of the pagan in her too, or at least a desire to throw over the traces imposed by her background. The day she had thrown a kiss to him from the ship and the way she had dressed her hair that night in Levuka were hardly appropriate for a staid daughter of the church.

He had only to visit the mission to see her again, but the very thought of what would be involved made him feel ill. Her father would be pompous or complaining, according to how much liquor he had beneath his belt. It was the church, as represented by John Denison and his breed, which Jason was recognising as his basic anathema, rather than Christianity. A couple of nights before he had even dug out a copy of the New Testament from among his books and begun to reread the story of Christ. It sat on a table beside his bed and every night he read a little more before sleep. He was able to look upon the Bible as an important philosophy even if he no longer accepted its divinity.

Two problems remained: He had to explain the Tongan danger to the missionaries and, perhaps even more important, he had to talk to Kate Denison again. If he didn't want to go to the mission the only alternative was to invite them all to Qaraniqio and hope that John Denison would be put off by the prospect of the three mile walk.

*****

Jason Cotterel's invitation came as a welcome break to the Denisons and Elija after the backbreaking work of getting the mission established. It also meant they would see more of the island.

In Toby's view, "Cotterel would never have invited us if I hadn't found out about his soldiers the other day, so you can all thank me." On the other hand Elija, who had also been to Qaraniqio and had seen neither hide nor hair of an army, said they should take the Christian view and assume that Cotterel wished to be friendly.

As Jason had hoped, John Denison declined on the grounds that his heart could never stand the exertion. He tried to talk the rest of them out of it and, when he saw that neither his children nor his assistant meant to miss the opportunity of sleeping a night in a civilised house, complained bitterly of their unthinking cruelty in leaving him to the none too tender mercies of Aloesi and Talei.

He was slightly mollified however by a letter from Cotterel which assumed that he must refuse but said the bearer of the invitation had a parcel which might compensate for the absence from home of the others. In it were preserved foods and a bottle of cognac the like of which Denison had not tasted since leaving Europe. It was so charmingly done that he could hardly object to Kate and Toby going without appearing less gracious than the man he considered a beachcombing American.

Kate was interested to see Jason Cotterel's plantation, which she remembered Captain Bex saying was the finest in Fiji, and how he lived. But the thought of meeting his part-Fijian children by his first wife scared her and she knew that in seeing Jason again there was a risk of emotional involvement, at least on her part. She had problems enough without that.

*****

Their journey was both an education and a delight. There was no rush and they took frequent rests. Kate made Elija tell her the Fijian names for every plant, bird and insect they saw, recording them in a notebook she carried for the purpose.

They went first across the island to Korovou. They passed 50 or more people on the way and Kate was amused how each asked where they were going, why, and how long they would be there; and then explained their own journey without waiting to find out whether or not the mission party might want to know. It wouldn't have occurred to them that anyone on Vatulevu might wish to be apart and private and Kate derived a warm feeling of belonging from their unconscious friendliness.

From Korovou they headed south towards Qaraniqio. The track was deserted and Kate was at the stage of imagining she was a female Crusoe and her party the first to set foot on a deserted island. But her illusion was rudely shattered when around a bend came a column of 20 men travelling at a steady trot. They carried muskets and powder bags slung across their shoulders and each had a short throwing club in his right hand. Their very un-Fijian uniformity, and air of discipline and purpose made them frightening.

There was insufficient room on the track for the two parties to pass and, after a startled look of recognition, the leader of the warriors signalled his men to halt and move into the jungle verge. Kate could no longer doubt Toby's report; these men were part of an army.

Elija greeted the leader, "Ni sa bula, kemuni. Where are you men off to in such a hurry, and why are you carrying those guns?"

Others along the way had been only too ready to volunteer such information, but not these. They looked at each other and back at the missionary as if in some awful quandary. The leader looked confused and worried then shrugged his shoulders fatalistically as if to convey that the worst things always happened to him.

"I'm sorry, Turaga, but we are not allowed to talk to you about these things." He smiled to show that their warlike trappings were not meant for use against the mission.

"Not allowed to talk to us?" Elija was both surprised and somewhat annoyed. As the only Fijian on the mission staff he prided himself that in a short time he had managed to get close to the people. Yet they had kept him completely in the dark on an important matter like this. He had even refused to believe the truth when Toby Denison had told him.

The spokesman for the warriors could see the annoyance on the preacher's face and mistook it for anger against himself. The last thing he wanted was to upset the emissary of the new god.

"We do nothing bad against your god, Turaga," he hastened to reassure Elija nervously, as if at any moment a bolt of lightning might strike him down. "We are just simple people. We obey the orders of our chief, Tui Navatulevu."

Kate understood only part of what was going on until Elija translated. "You were right, Mr Denison, and I am deeply ashamed that I did not know of this sooner. It seems that the Tui is in it as much as Jason Cotterel. Their orders are to keep this matter a secret from members of the mission."

"It would seem we are not to be trusted," said Toby dryly.

The leader of the troops could not understand English but he was able to pick out the word 'Jason'. "Jasoni is the man you should speak to, Turaga," he said, happily, "he will tell you all you want to know." Having managed to shift the responsibility, and rather than face more embarrassing questions, he signalled to his men and the troop made off down the track at double their original pace.

"Do you think Mr Cotterel will tell us, Elija?" Kate asked.

"I imagine that the main purpose of his invitation is to do just that," he answered. "His hand was forced when Mr Denison saw them."

Kate was disappointed — in her heart of hearts she thought he might have wanted to see her again as much as she wanted to see him.

They walked on down the path beaten smooth by generations of bare feet. Directly above their heads a sliver of pale blue sky was visible but on either side the trees formed a complete canopy. Parasitic plants with enormous green and yellow leaves crawled up the trunks whilst vines festooned the branches.

Elija slashed one large vine as thick as a man's arm into sections and water, clear and drinkable, poured out. He explained this was the walai and so long as they could find it they need never be thirsty in the jungle. Small brown and purple bush orchids were everywhere, and Kate renewed her barrage of questions.

She learnt the names of trees such as damanu, kauvula and enormous giants called dakua. Some were used for house-building, others for canoes, and a few were good for nothing at all. They came across a new tree and Elija took his clasp knife again, cut off a piece, and gave it to Kate to smell. Immediately her nostrils were filled with the most exotic perfume. "Sandalwood!" she cried, "I have a fan made of it."

"Correct. We call it yasi. It has brought more bloodshed to our islands than any other single thing. White men came from everywhere to buy it for shipment to China. They chopped down the yasi forests and even dug up the roots, until now only a few remain deep in the jungle."

"It must have been profitable while it lasted," said Toby.

"For the white men, yes," said Elija with a touch of bitterness. "They say the profits on a single voyage were as high as 800 percent. The Fijians were paid in rum or muskets; and in some cases ships' crews helped the chief in wars against his neighbours. If it hadn't been for that tree, Fiji might have continued for another hundred years without foreign powers bothering her."

Kate listened sympathetically. From his expression there could be no doubt that he regarded the advent of the European as a very mixed blessing.

Then his face lightened again and he smiled at Kate. "But I forget that if the Europeans had not come to Fiji my people would still be lost in the pagan darkness of the past. The white men not only brought guns, they have also brought us salvation, Jisu Karisito and his message of hope for all men."

*****

Further along the path the trees began to thin out. Soon they arrived at the edge of extensive groves of coconut palms all of a uniform size, and set in planned lines instead of haphazardly like those near the villages where the palms were of all shapes and sizes and planted by nature rather than by man.

Many were already carrying bunches of nuts near the crown which, from what Elija had told Kate of the life cycle of a coconut palm, meant they were at least eight years old. When they had planted coconuts at the new mission compound Kate had found this fact rather daunting for she had fondly imagined she would be eating her own fruit within twelve months.

Their guide was the Fijian who had delivered the invitation and Kate asked him in his own language whether the extensive groves belonged to Mr Cotterel but he looked questioningly to Elija for translation. "I can see more work is needed on your pronunciation," said Elija consolingly, "but having been here before, I can answer your question myself.

"When I first came I assumed that these groves were part of Qaraniqio but I was soon set right on that score. Mr Cotterel was the leader and instigator of the work but all of these palms belong to the kai-Vatulevu. For the next mile it is all like this. I have travelled widely among our islands and believe me there are no other Fijian plantations like this. Our guide says this is communal land belonging to the people of both Lomanikaya and Korovou and at this point the palm groves extend as far as you can see."

Through Elija, Kate asked the guide, "Who planted the nuts?"

"We all did," he answered proudly. "My brothers, our cousins and our friends. For months we worked to clear the jungle, prepare seedlings, and plant and care for them. It has taken a long time but now we come every day to gather the reward which our labour has provided."

"What of the white Turaga, Jasoni? Does he help you?"

"But of course," his tone suggested he found such a question ridiculous. "No man works harder than Jasoni; even on our land he works harder than three ordinary men."

"And do you help him on his land?"

"When he needs us we do. In return he gives a share of his crop to Tui Navatulevu who decides how our profits are to be used." Clearly, so long as the chief and Cotterel were in charge he had no doubts about the fairness of the deal.

Elija added, "Even before we came to Vatulevu I had heard of all this. Mr Cotterel is one of the few white men who deals honestly with my people. He helps them and they are therefore only too willing to help him in return."

"It looks more to me as if he and Tui Navatulevu are on to a good thing themselves," said Toby sarcastically. "They divide the proceeds and don't pay their labour a single penny of real money."

"I don't think it's as bad as you imagine, Mr Denison," said Elija. "It would be senseless to give the people dollars or pounds; where would they spend them? The only logical person to take the money is the chief and they trust him to spend their share on things which will benefit them all. Even if he should use some for rum or articles personal to himself, they would not begrudge him these things. They would accept it as due recompense for the responsibility he bears."

"Nor do I think much has been wasted. Every man on Vatulevu has his own steel axe and digging spade whereas the rest of Fiji is still using wooden digging sticks. You must also remember these groves have only just started to produce and they will keep producing for two or three generations. The spending of this money will be a heavy responsibility for whoever holds the chieftainship."

But Toby was determined to put the worst possible construction on anything associated with Jason Cotterel: "Spades and axes are only tools to make them work faster and more productively, I should think their sweat also paid for those muskets we saw. Tools to make them work harder, guns to make them fight. I still say Cotterel and the chief have a very lucrative set-up here."

Kate hoped that Elija's picture was the true one. At some time during their visit she would get Jason Cotterel's version; she had still not given up hope that one day Toby, and perhaps she herself, would have an estate and she wanted to know all the problems involved in the operation of a commercial plantation.

Whatever the motives, credit was due for the enormous amount of work which had been done and, as he led them through the groves, their Fijian guide certainly had no doubts.

Kate had a fair idea of the amount of manpower involved from her experience in establishing the few acres around the mission compound; these groves, stretching as far as the eye could see, must cover hundreds. Clearing the jungle, let alone the planting and maintenance involved, must have taken up the organised labour of every able-bodied man and woman on the island. Clearly Jason Cotterel or Tui Navatulevu, whoever was responsible, was an organiser of ability.

"This Jasoni, he is a good man?" asked Kate, trying her Fijian again. This time she spoke slowly and simply. The broad smile which split the guide's face showed that she had managed to get her message across.

"Jasoni is a great man, Marama. He has done much for Vatulevu, Jasoni is our very good friend."

"So much for your theories, Toby," she said, translating for her brother,

"Maybe so, but you wouldn't need to be overbright to pull the wool over the eyes of these yokels."

Kate ignored this; no profit was to be gained from argument with Toby. They came out onto a clearing, about 20 acres in extent, completely planted with low bushes.

"Cotton," Elija explained. "Since the war in America, cotton from Fiji has been in demand. I don't know much about it but I've been told Fiji 'Sea Island Cotton,' is of very high quality. Most of it goes to France."

Kate was amazed that they managed to cultivate such a large area with hand implements but then saw the answer for herself. Grazing beneath the trees at one side of the field were six monstrous working bullocks such as she had previously seen pulling wagons in New South Wales. The sight of those huge barrels of muscle standing docile in the shade made her feel she was at home.

It was marvellous to see animals again after so long — somehow they seemed even bigger and stranger for the fact that they were the last thing she had expected to find on a Pacific Island. If she ever had a plantation of her own she would stock it with every conceivable type of domestic animal; cows, horses, goats, turkeys and fowl. Though born and reared in a city she knew that this was how she wanted to spend the rest of her life.

She hardly knew Jason Cotterel but already she was asking herself how she would like to be the mistress of Qaraniqio. She had been told the name meant 'hole in which a shark lurks' and referred to a pool in the river which flowed through Jason Cotterel's plantation and near which he had built his homestead.

Before the mission party saw the house they knew they were close as they heard shouted commands and the crash of musketry. The first volley startled the party but their guide continued along the path towards the noise, quite unperturbed.

"Whatever this is all about it must be something very big," said Toby excitedly. "They are deadly serious."

Rivers on Vatulevu were waded if shallow enough or, if deeper, a large tree was felled so that its trunk spanned both banks. Across this the traveller was expected to do a high wire act. On Qaraniqio, by comparison, several trees had been felled and placed in parallel and the surface decked with rough-hewn timbers. It was the first structure Kate had seen in Fiji which could, with justification, be called a bridge.

On an open space directly beyond it a group of 50 Fijians were drilling with firearms under the direction of another Fijian. "That's Ratu Seru, the Tui's younger brother," said Elija.

When Kate had met Ratu Seru previously he had been trying to advise her on the mission vegetable garden. They became so tangled in her limited vocabulary that the lesson had ended in gales of laughter on both sides. He had been full of fun and so friendly it seemed hardly credible that this could be the same man.

Toby drew their attention to the *Albatross* and the *Lovadua* which were tied up alongside a small wooden jetty near the mouth of the river. Wicked looking cannon had been mounted just forward of the forehatch on both ketches, and men were practising gun firing and sponging-out drills.

"My God, who is it they are taking on?" cried Toby.

Elija frowned. Blasphemy was unforgivable from a clergyman's son and he worried for the thousandth time about the bad example set by the Denison men. The scene before him could hardly have been more damning but an understanding began to dawn. The kai-Vatulevu were not given to raiding other islands and if they did not intend to attack they were obviously expecting to be attacked themselves. As allies of Bau — and he was a Bauan himself — there could only be one enemy.

"I feel our questions will be answered in the Lord's own time," he told Toby.

Toby laughed sardonically. "If Jason Cotterel is the mouthpiece of the Lord, all I can say is He is a poorer judge of character than I have been given to believe."

"Oh shut up, Toby," snapped Kate. She could see that Elija, who usually enjoyed a joke, was shocked by her brother's sacrilegious language.

Ratu Seru saw them cross the bridge and dismissing his squad he walked over to meet them. "Ni sa bula, na Turaga kei na Marama," he greeted them smiling.

Around his waist was a broad leather belt from which hung a murderous, short-handled, broad-bladed axe and across his chest, bandoleer fashion, was another belt holding two pistols and satchels for powder and ball. His only other clothing comprised a scanty loin cloth and a chiefly necklace of boars' tusks. Ratu Seru could never have been described as an insignificant man but Kate could not but admire his magnificence when dressed for war.

The chief and Elija were conversing in Fijian and too quickly for Kate to glean anything but the odd word here and there. However it was obvious that they were near quarrelling. "He won't tell us anything either," Elija finally told them disgustedly. "Mr Cotterel is away but is expected to return soon. We are to go straight up to the house and he will join us there when he arrives."

13

Jason at home

Ratu Seru led them up a small hill following a path with borders of flowering hibiscus. Kate counted seven different varieties, big red double blooms, yellows, pinks and a beautiful white with a blue centre. She called over her shoulder to Elija that they must not leave on the morrow without cuttings to plant at the mission. They passed through a group of flamboyant and frangipani trees and onto the small headland where Cotterel had built his home.

Kate gave an involuntary gasp. "But how absolutely beautiful," she said.

The house was neither large nor pretentious but it was obvious that a lot of thought and love had gone into it. It seemed to combine the best of both worlds. The walls were of timber, pit-sawn and dried on the estate. Any imperfections were hidden beneath white paint and the flowering vines which had been trained to cover the areas between the windows.

The windows must have been brought in from Sydney or Auckland — most likely by Peter Bex, thought Kate; they were small-paned and the sills had been painted bright green giving the whole house a cottage-like appearance.

Its thatched roof distinguished it from Levuka's where even the better houses had hideous corrugated iron roofs. Somehow the thatch completed the picture for Kate. It might have been lifted out of the Cotswolds: there were window boxes, well-tended gardens, lawns and hibiscus trimmed into hedges. The only thing which would have been out of place in England was the deep verandah which ran the full length of the front of the house. Another open porch at the rear connected the main body of the house to a smaller building, probably the kitchen.

River stones had been used for the steps and the low wall around the verandah. The roof was supported by ten white pillars. From a distance it seemed they might have been hewn from marble but in fact they were matching tree trunks which had been smoothed and polished until they looked machine-lathed.

"My, my. Cotterel certainly does himself well," Toby whistled. His previous visits had been purely on business and Cotterel had not offered to take him to his home. He was very impressed; this was no beachcomber's hut, but a gentleman's island residence.

"And he built it himself" said Elija, who had been there for a meal on the day of his own visit. "His friends helped of course but the method of construction is so different from Fijian styles, he must have done most of it himself. He even made the furniture."

Toby sneered to himself: it was all very well to own a place like this but that the man could use his own hands to build it showed he must come of damned common stock.

Inside, everything was cool, spotlessly clean, and with the exception of a few books carelessly dropped on tables it seemed too tidy for a man living on his own. The furniture looked solid and comfortable: hammocks, long chairs with wooden frames and canvas seats, low tables to match, well-stocked bookcases and a huge desk covered with papers and ledgers.

The overall effect was one of industrious, yet homely and wholesome, good living. Kate knew before she arrived that anything Jason Cotterel did would be out of the ordinary but she had not expected anything like this.

An elderly Fijian woman came forward from the rear of the house, dropped to her knees and gave three slow claps, the Fijian cobo of respect. "Ni sa bula, Marama. On behalf of the Turaga I welcome you, the Turaga your brother, and Turaga na Talatala," acknowledging Elija's special status as a preacher.

The woman's speech was in slow distinct Fijian which Kate easily understood. It was unusual however in that it was addressed to her rather than to Toby. It was if she was the guest of honour whereas normal Fijian custom would have reversed the order of precedence. Kate could not help wondering whether this was the old woman's idea or Jason's, but whoever was responsible it made her feel genuinely welcome.

They made the correct responses and Kate thanked her in Fijian. Rooms led off the main sitting room: the men were shown into one set aside for their use, and Lala ushered Kate into her own room. It was as big as the bedroom she had in MacDonald's Hotel when she last slept within conventional walls. There were net curtains and the window was of glass, rather than covered by a wooden shutter.

On a table beside her bed was a large bowl of the hibiscus blossoms she had admired on the path up to the house. The bed was more of Jason Cotterel's own handiwork but instead of mats it had a soft mattress and crisp white sheets. It made her remember the way her things had been laid out on their first night on Vatulevu. Jason Cotterel was full of contradictions: renegade, anti-Christ, at that very moment training an army, yet he could still find time to think of the small touches which might make her, the only European woman within 40 miles, feel more comfortable.

The housekeeper was speaking again and Kate had to concentrate to understand her. "The men bathe and swim in the river," explained Lala, "but the Turaga has built a special place for you."

Kate had forgotten just how hot and dirty she was after their long walk. It made her thankful that their host had not been at home to see her arrive grubby and dishevelled. She now had a chance to clean up and appear before him as best she could under island conditions. That he had made special provision for her bathing showed greater consideration for her comfort than would her own father or brother.

Lala took her to the most extraordinary shower contraption Kate had ever seen. It had four tall wooden uprights with mats of freshly-plaited coconut leaves nailed between, making a screen stretching from mid-calf to neck. At the top of the stand was an iron drum which swivelled on an axle when a cord was pulled, cascading cold water all over her.

She revelled in the luxury which not only washed away the dust of the journey but seemed to revitalise her whole body. She decided that as soon as they returned to the mission she would have a replica built, even if she had to ask Jason Cotterel to make it.

An hour later, wearing the same muslin dress she had worn in Levuka but this time with her hair demurely tied in a neat coil behind her head, she emerged onto the verandah. The men were still absent but Lala was there with a tray of freshly-made tea and scones, the recipe for which could never have originated on a Pacific Island.

Sitting back in comfort sipping tea from fine china, Kate enjoyed a sense of peace and security. Her father had money enough for such refinements, but no matter how many years they might live on Vatulevu he would not have the initiative to achieve this standard of living.

The book on the table beside her was a well-thumbed copy of *Religio Medici* by Sir Thomas Browne with many notations in the margins. 'The Religion of a Doctor'? Strange reading for an agnostic! Then there was Jason's marriage, a Christian ceremony whereas a pagan Fijian girl would have been content to accept whatever local custom decreed. What lay at the bottom of this enigma called Jason Cotterel?

There was a scuffle near the steps leading to the verandah. Kate could see no one, yet she could hear urgent whispering behind the low stone wall. There was a burst of excited giggling, then mops of curly black hair and two pairs of bright eyes popped above the wall but, seeing Kate looking them straight in the eye, they disappeared just as suddenly. It was so comical Kate could not help laughing.

With her laughter as proof that the atmosphere was friendly the heads slowly reappeared. "Sa bula, children," said Kate smiling and held out her hand. "Won't you please come and see me?"

The heads disappeared again and from the buzzing conference behind the wall it was obvious that the children were arguing whether she was friend or foe. They were Jason Cotterel's children, of this there could be no doubt. Kate felt heart-easing relief; for all they had mixed Fijian and European blood her reaction was exactly the same as it might have been with any others. They were normal healthy children.

Most likely they had been told to keep away from the visitors but, like their counterparts anywhere in the world, had been unable to resist a small peep. Nor were they being annoying. Having seen them, Kate wanted to meet them, to get to know them, and if possible to win their confidence. She prided herself on being a firm favourite with children and it was this love that made her so keen on the idea of a mission school.

She waited, certain that curiosity would overcome their apparent shyness. Patience had its reward when the boy, leading his younger sister by the hand, marched up the steps. They wore only brief loin cloths and both were quite beautiful. Kate smiled at them encouragingly and beckoned them forward.

"Good evening, Miss Denison," they piped together in English. They had evidently been schooled beforehand though Kate guessed that their greeting had been meant for much later in the day, by which time they would have been specially scrubbed, polished and dressed for the occasion.

"Good evening, children," "Kate answered solemnly matching their formality. "How nice of you to come and see me."

"My name Ratu Aporosa," said the lad importantly. "My father, big Turaga. My…my…" his command of English failed him and he lapsed into Fijian. "My grandfather is a big chief, he is Tui Navatulevu. One day I shall be Tui Navatulevu."

Kate fought to control her amusement for she knew that she must not laugh. "But how nice for you," she smiled. "And shall I call you Ratu Aporosa or just Aporosa?"

"Oh, here in the house I am just Aporosa and father sometimes calls me Jason" he said, climbing down off his high horse now that his status was confirmed.

The girl pulled free from her brother's hand and running forward climbed on to Kate's lap. "Me, Ulamila," she said proudly.

Kate, absolutely delighted, gave her a great hug, "So you are Ulamila," she said using her best Fijian. "I have heard much about you and I am so happy to meet you." Aporosa, still rather conscious of his own dignity, hung back for a moment, but Kate patted the arm of her chair and the small boy triumphed over the heir apparent.

"Vinaka vaka levu, Marama," he said as he perched close enough for Kate to slip an arm about his waist while she held Ulamila on her knee with the other.

Ulamila passed a hand over Kate's smooth golden hair and touched her dress. "Very pretty," she sighed. Kate hugged the warm little body to her again and laughed, "I think that Ulamila and Aporosa are very pretty too."

She found it impossible to understand her own feeling of happiness. It was not that she had ever had anything against children of mixed blood, but she now realised that it was because these children were Jason Cotterel's by a former marriage and she had been terrified they might not like her. They were the final touch which made his wonderful house a home.

"Tell me all about your home and what you do each day" she asked them, "but you must speak very slowly, for I am a silly person who cannot understand if you speak too fast."

Neither required a further invitation. They began to chatter like monkeys in a mixture of Fijian and English. There were times when they all became hopelessly lost but rather than cause embarrassment it only generated gales of happy laughter. Lala, attracted by the noise, came out to scold but three concerted voices quickly consigned her back to the oblivion of the kitchen and for an hour they played and laughed together. Aporosa and Ulamila were less inhibited than English children and obviously thoroughly and understandably spoilt by every adult on the estate.

A deep voice, which sent a shiver down Kate's spine, broke the spell and sent the children flying from her lap. "I hope these brats of mine aren't annoying you, Miss Denison." Jason grabbed his son and daughter as they charged and swung them in turn high into the air. They babbled away nineteen to the dozen about their new friend.

Kate used the diversion to stand, smooth her dress, and pat her hair back into place after the rough treatment it had been receiving.

"My apologies for not being here to welcome you," said Jason with his well-remembered smile, "but it looks as if these rascals have done the Cotterel honours. Are you sure they haven't been too much of a nuisance?"

"Not at all, Mr Cotterel. We have been getting to know each other. You are a very lucky man to have such delightful children."

"Rather naughty children," he replied. "Lala is in the kitchen going mad, now off you go brats, your kana is ready." He aimed a playful slap at their bottoms to speed them on their way. "You can come and say goodnight to Miss Denison before you go to bed." This promise coupled with their hunger sent them flying off into the house, followed by Kate's and their father's laughter.

"The one time I have no disciplinary problems is when food is in the offing."

"They are really lovely children. They must be a great solace to you."

"Solace?" For the moment Jason did not catch Kate's meaning which made her blush and wish she had never mentioned the subject, no matter how obliquely.

"I mean the death — the passing — of your wife."

He smiled to relieve her embarrassment and confusion. "Ulamila died six years ago last April. The children have been a great comfort to me." Jason agreed. "My worry has been whether I have been able to adequately fill the dual role of mother and father. I don't want them to forget their mother but I try to avoid constant reminders which might darken their lives."

"You'll find they're unruly young devils. When are you going to start that school of yours? Mission or not," his smile took the edge off the qualification, "count my two as your first pupils. They can hardly string a sentence of English together and I doubt they can count beyond 20. Now they have met you I'm sure I won't have trouble with truancy; you have obviously made a great hit with them."

"I shall love to have them at the school," she said. "The delay has been the establishment of the mission and my own lack of Fijian. I can hardly hope to teach children when I cannot speak to them in their own language."

"That's not what I have heard," Jason retorted. "Lala tells me that the kai-valagi Marama speaks very good Fijian. By the way, you have made a conquest there and Lala is very hard to please. She says you have a great way with children, especially mine. We shall have to watch out or she will try her hand at matchmaking."

Kate blushed and turned away to hide the guilt so evident in her cheeks. To her relief Jason immediately changed the subject again.

"What think you of my view?" he asked. "I chose the site especially even though it can be inconvenient being away from the river. Every drop of water we use has to be carried up the hill. Of course I could have had a corrugated iron roof and use it as a catchment, but I dislike iron roofs even more than the inconvenience of carting water. You'll really see the view at its best about an hour from now when the sun is setting."

"Tell me what else have you seen? What do you think of my plantation. Rather unkempt at the moment I'm afraid, but it cannot be helped, I've had more pressing matters to attend to."

Kate, only too glad to avoid such subjects as matchmaking, his late wife, and the 'more pressing things', entered into a lively discussion on the problems facing a planter on a South Pacific island. Jason Cotterel should never be allowed alone with impressionable young women; he was too strong yet too gentle, too ruthless yet too considerate. A hero to the locals, a loving parent, but on top of all else still the epitome of everything she was supposed to abominate.

Jason found himself talking incessantly like an uncouth adolescent. It was as if he was unable to stop his tongue running away with itself, a defence mechanism to hide his own confusion. He cursed himself for a fool, talking about Lala matchmaking — he could well imagine what Kate's father would say to such a misalliance.

Seeing her there playing happily with the children had undone him; he had suddenly seen how much they needed a mother and, looking at the girl herself, how much he needed a woman — not any woman, but Kate Denison. She could put warmth and meaning back into his life, where at present there was just work, more work, and efficiency for the sake of efficiency.

What made it worse was the hopelessness of the whole thing. No prim and proper young miss from a mission compound would look twice at a beachcomber like him. For all their easy prattle about the plantation he was beginning to wish he had never invited them to Qaraniqio. Seeing her again made matters worse instead of better. The very nearness of Kate Denison was a temptation he doubted he had the strength to resist.

Their conversation was beginning to founder when they were saved by the arrival on the verandah of Elija and Toby Denison.

"Evening, Denison, you'll have a drink won't you," said Jason relieved that his duties as host led him away from Kate's dangerous presence. "What about you, Elija? I know you won't touch alcohol but there is a fruit drink made from our own oranges."

"Whisky and water would suit me," said Toby, happy that the occasion was not to be kept dry just because of his mission associations. "I must say you have a marvellous place here, Cotterel. I'd heard most of the Fiji planters were near bankrupt but you live like a veritable nabob."

14
Cards on the table

Dinner over, cigars had been lit, and Toby and Jason had brandies at their elbow. Toby had overindulged and Kate prayed he would not make a fool of himself as he had in Levuka.

Jason appeared to keep him company glass for glass but whereas Toby was bleary-eyed, their host seemed unaffected. He was dressed very much as when she had been introduced to him in Levuka. The candles highlighted the prominent bone structure of his face and etched deeper the lines about his mouth. He was a charming host and the meal had been excellent — better than anything Kate had thought possible under local conditions.

They were dying to get Jason to open up on the subject of the military preparations which were tying up half the island's labour force and Elija was no longer prepared to be put off with the inconsequential small talk Jason had employed to deflect questions. "Now, Mr Cotterel," he began.

"Come Elija, I thought we agreed that between us there should only be first names. Your 'Mr Cotterel' sounds too serious; in case you have forgotten, mine is Jason."

"Jason it shall be then," said the Fijian smiling at his host," but let us have no more rigmarole and fobbing off. Tell us what we want to know. Why has Vatulevu suddenly become an armed camp? Why do we meet armed men when we travel? Why is there a conspiracy to hide everything from the mission?"

Jason looked at his three guests. Even at this the eleventh hour he might have managed to fool the Denisons, but there could be no deceiving the Fijian. He put on as cool a front as possible.

"I would have thought the reason was obvious, Elija." He drew on his cigar and calmly exhaled a plume of blue smoke. "As a Bauan all you have to do is put two and two together. There can only be one answer surely."

"I admit to having my own thoughts on the matter but I would prefer to hear it directly from you."

Jason leaned forward. Although his tone of voice did not alter, Kate noticed that his eyes were now cold and rather forbidding. "As you will, then. To put it bluntly, the people living on Vatulevu, with the possible exception of yourselves, face annihilation. We are about to be attacked by an army of Ratu Cakobau's enemies led by the Tongan prince, Ma'afu."

"There has been no act of provocation on our part unless you count the fact that we remain loyal to the Vunivalu. Ma'afu intends to swallow us in the same way he has swallowed half the islands in Lau. He will kill the men who oppose him, carry off the women into captivity, replace the rightful chief with his own Tongan puppet, and divide the land among his followers."

Jason watched Kate's face go pale and drawn beneath the weight of his words but there was no way he could soften the message. "This time, however, when he bites we shall give him such a mouthful as will break every tooth in his head. That is why we are arming and preparing. Does that answer your question?"

Elija's face was a pattern of conflicting emotions, on the one hand inbred loyalty to his chief and hatred of the Tongans, and on the other his calling as the messenger sent among the heathen with God's word.

"Ma'afu! It had to be Ma'afu and the Tongans," he sighed. "You understand my position in this, Jason?"

"Oh! I understand," said Jason bitterly. "Shall I quote you Matthew Chapter 5, verse 43: 'Ye have heard that it hath been said, thou shalt love thy neighbour and hate thine enemy. But I say unto you, love your enemies, bless them that curse you, do good to them that hate you and pray for them which despitefully use you and persecute you.' Surely you, Elija, a Fijian, are not trying to tell me you think we should sit back and let the Tongans ride roughshod over us? Do you want to see the Fijians slaves to the Tongans and Fiji a province of Tonga?"

Jason continued "Anyone can quote the Bible for his own purpose. I give you Proverbs Chapter 6, verse 16. 'These six things doth the Lord hate; yea seven are an abomination unto him: A proud look, a lying tongue and hands that shed innocent blood, an heart that deviseth wicked imaginations, feet that be swift in running to mischief, a false witness that speaketh lies, and he that soweth discord among brethren.' If those words do not describe the Tongans and Ma'afu's intentions I would like to know what does. If that is not enough a final quotation from Genesis 9:6: 'Who so sheddeth man's blood, by man shall his blood be shed'. "

Kate, Elija and Toby Denison sat looking at their host as if they were unable to believe their ears. Cotterel was quoting the Bible with as much facility as a professional minister. Elija was too torn by his own internal conflict to answer immediately and it was left to Kate to restore normality to the tense situation.

"How long have you known of this threat, Mr Cotterel?" she asked in a quiet, dispassionate voice. "When do you expect the attack to come?"

Jason thanked her with a smile; he could not hope to convert her to his point of view but at least she now understood his position.

Before he could answer, Toby, his voice thickened with brandy, broke in: "But why keep the whole thing such a deadly secret, Cotterel? If there's a fight coming up I want a part in it."

"One question at a time please," said Jason with a wry laugh, trying hard to regain the amicable atmosphere which had prevailed throughout dinner.

"You first, Miss Denison. I have known about this danger since the night before we left Levuka when Ratu Cakobau told me what was in store for us. Ma'afu tried to subvert Tui Navatulevu to his own ranks about a year ago but the chief refused to listen to his emissaries. Since then I suppose an attack has been inevitable."

"Ma'afu controls the whole of Lau, Cakaudrove, Macuata and Bua. Vatulevu is just the next step in his march on Bau. When we refused to submit to Tongan rule it could not be hidden from others; within a month everyone in the Group knew of it. In exactly the same way, Ma'afu is unable to prepare a warfleet to avenge the insult without our knowing. Having failed with words he has no option but to use force."

Jason paused to sip his brandy then continued, "I hate to destroy your illusions, but one of the reasons the Vunivalu was anxious to have your mission on Vatulevu was to forestall Ma'afu. One of his favourite ploys is to attack an island on the pretext that it is heathen and that he is converting it to Christianity. Isn't that right, Elija?

"It was certainly his supposed reason when he conquered Matuku," said the Fijian sadly. "Dr Lyth, who was superintendent of the church then, expelled him from the society of the church for that very reason."

"But for all that Ma'afu is back in the church again and a Tongan puppet still rules Matuku," Jason pointed out. "I tried to explain some of this to you the day I brought you here on the *Albatross*," he said to Kate.

"As to the second part of your question, we would have been attacked before this if it hadn't been that a Fijian army is never on call when it is needed. Local armies are loose federations of petty chiefs and they take a lot of getting together. A large fleet is involved and they were not likely to risk the ships during the hurricane season. That season is now past and they could strike at any time.

"We have guards standing beside signal fires at both ends of the island to warn us of their coming so we are not likely to be surprised. With luck and sound preparation, the boot may well be on the other foot."

"I think you are right," said Elija. "If an attack is to come it will be within the month; this is the season for war."

"But what about me?" asked Toby excitedly. "I could help sail one of the ketches."

Jason felt sorry for the boy but he was too great a risk and it was too late to alter his plans to fit in an amateur. "I'm sorry, Toby, but that is completely out of the question. The Vunivalu has given me strict instructions that none of the missionaries are to be in any way endangered."

"But I'm not a blasted missionary," said Toby sitting forward in his chair, his face suffused with anger and disappointment. "You don't trust me, that's what it is, isn't it?"

"Toby!" said his sister sharply, "Don't be so stupid, and remember where you are; you know father would never consider it."

Jason made a mental note to thank her later. The trouble was the boy had struck a little too close to the truth. Thus far he had not seen Toby demonstrate either moral or physical courage, but he could hardly destroy the boy's ego by telling him so to his face.

"Don't be a fool, Toby, it's not that at all." He pushed the brandy towards him. "Have another drink and simmer down. Whether you like it or not, so far as people in the islands are concerned you are as much a part of the mission as your father or Elija. The fact that the mission is here and has been accepted by Tui Navatulevu is supposedly proof that the old pagan ways are at an end, so we can spike that particular gun. But apart from that the mission is not to be involved in any way."

"I've just quoted from the Bible; if you had known about all this previously, Elija might have been quoting it at me and the people. We couldn't afford that nor, now that the time of the attack is imminent, do we want church interference in any way. The mission must stay neutral."

"I find it very hard to stay neutral, Jason," said Elija. "I agree with all you have said about the Tongans. Although any war is wrong, I can hardly sit here and condemn you and the people for wanting to defend yourselves even though I am precluded from taking up arms and standing at your side as a soldier. If there is such a thing as a just war it can only be from the side of the defenders."

"Thank you," said Jason. "You know what a Fijian war can be like. Some drag on for years and are just petty skirmishes and a few treacherous murders. Sometimes a whole village is surprised and wiped out. But the majority are a great flourish of challenges; a couple of people are killed and, honour being satisfied, everyone goes home."

"That is not likely here," Elija replied. "The Tongans are determined to conquer Ratu Cakobau and if they once set sail against Vatulevu it would be a tremendous loss of mana for them to return home without a decisive victory to show for their pains."

"I concede that, but the majority of his force will be Fijian, not Tongan. If we can show them from the very beginning that we mean business and that the capture of the island is going to be bloody and all but impossible, Ma'afu's Fijian allies are going to think twice before they press home the attack, especially if we can show from the start that Tongans are as vulnerable as anyone else."

"Let's get one thing understood: this war is none of our choosing. If no attack comes no one will be happier than ourselves; we shall be the first to start beating those muskets into ploughshares as it were. On the other hand, if we are attacked Vatulevu will give the Tongans the biggest shock they have had since they first appeared in Fiji waters."

Elija looked at him approvingly, Kate admiringly, and Toby sat head down, sulking.

"What I find difficult to understand," said the Fijian finally, "is why you are taking such a great interest in something which is after all a Fijian affair. As a white man why are you interfering at all?"

"I am as involved as anyone else on this island, maybe more so. The chief and people of Vatulevu took me in and gave me a home when I was a footloose scavenger. They set me up, befriended me, and I have prospered here. I married a woman from this island and one day our son will be the chief. I have obligations to discharge and my son's patrimony to protect. What would you have me do, put my children on the ketch and run for Levuka at the first sign of the enemy?"

"There are many white men who would."

"Well you can take it from me, I'm not one of them. I don't hanker after being a hero, nor am I partial to the thought of Tongan spears flying in my direction. But if I were to desert my friends at this stage I would never be able to show my face here again, quite apart from the fact that I wouldn't be able to live with myself."

"What of the women and children?" Kate asked coolly, as if the arrangements for a Sunday School outing were being discussed. Her matter of fact tone again brought back sanity and a sense of proportion to the discussion.

What a wonderful woman, thought Jason. There was no hint of fear or panic; the concern she felt was not for herself but for the safety of others. In the setting of his home she shone like a luminous jewel; never had she seemed so beautiful or desirable as at that moment when they were in complete communion one with the other. For a second they might have been alone in another world. It was Kate who dropped her eyes and broke the spell. Released from the compelling magnetism of her eyes, Jason hurriedly composed his confused thoughts and concentrated on her question.

"The women and children have been provided for," he said. "At the first sign of the enemy they are to withdraw to caves high up on the mountainside, taking with them the old people. The caves have been stocked with food and they will be well away and quite safe there."

"Would it be of any help if I went with them?" Kate asked.

"It would indeed; some are bound to get panicky and most will be worrying about their menfolk. We need someone who can keep her head and generally organise the others. It will also be used as a hospital; any wounded on our side will be sent up to the caves out of the way. You could help with the nursing if you would."

"I suppose I go up there with the women and children too," said Toby bitterly. "You talk about not being able to live with yourself, Cotterel; what about me? I'll be the only able-bodied man on the island not engaged. I'm supposed to hold hands with a pack of frightened women and wipe babies' bottoms. The great Mr Cotterel can't run away but I've got to. Do you think you have a personal monopoly over courage?" His usual truculence was now aggravated by Jason's brandy.

Jason could see Kate was about to reprimand her brother but he got in first. "Alright, suppose I did say you could come with us, what could you do? Do you know how to use a rifle, or handle a cutlass; can you fire a cannon?"

"Well no, of course I can't," Toby had to admit, "but dammit all man, I could learn."

"The time is past for learning. You heard what Elija said, for all I know the Tovata fleet could be at sea while we sit here over our brandy."

Suddenly Jason thought of a way that Toby Denison might be of real value and at the same time assuage his wounded pride and yet be well out of harm's way. His change of mind must have shown even before he spoke.

"Jason, no, please," said Kate anxiously.

"There is something Toby could do if he had a mind to."

"You keep out of this, Kate," said her brother, brightening up.

"It's not fighting, Kate," said Jason reassuringly.

"Well if it's not, I'm not interested," said Toby disgustedly.

"Fighting isn't everything, you young fool," said Jason exasperated. "This is something that you and you alone could do, and it could mean the difference between success and failure. You would have to get your father's permission."

"What is it? If I'm going to do it, leave the permission part to me."

"Do you know what a heliograph is?" asked Jason.

"A system of mirrors used for signalling, isn't it?"

"Exactly, a system of signalling. The weakest link in our whole plan is the complete lack of any communications apart from rudimentary smoke-signalling. If we had a heliograph which could relay the minute by minute movements of the enemy, we would always be that much ahead and ready to meet them. Without such information our whole defence could come unstuck."

"If you could rig up a heliograph station on top of the mountain where the main lookout is situated and work out some sort of code, you could relay messages to me on the *Albatross*. There's no question of this being unimportant, Toby, if you can do it. Accurate information sent quickly could he the key to the whole battle."

"It's not fighting," said Toby stubbornly.

"Fighting is the least of my worries; in fact the one thing we shall try to avoid is hand-to-hand fighting. If it does come to that I can find 200 men more powerful than you and twice as skilful with arms, whereas it would take me months to find and train just one to operate a heliograph. Anyway, make up your mind," said Jason testily, "will you do it or won't you?"

"I'll do it," said Toby in a condescending tone of voice which made Jason long to slap some sense into him. Gradually, however, the heliograph idea took shape in Toby's own mind and he began to look happier now that he was not to be left with the women and children.

"Do you have a code?" he asked. "And we'll need two heliographs, you know — one on the ketch to acknowledge my signals and ask questions."

Kate and Jason both laughed; one moment her brother was depressed the next, enthusiastic.

"What do you think, Kate?" Jason asked. "Will your father object?"

Surprisingly it was Elija, not Kate, who answered his question. "You can take it there will be no objections from the mission, Jason." It was as if he had made the decision for them all, knowing this could not be left to John Denison.

"We are in much the same position as yourself. We came to preach the Gospel, to show the people a new and better way of life. Now, at the first sign of adversity, we can hardly desert them. Mr Denison senior and Kate will look after the women and children and any wounded there may be; Toby will be in charge of your signalling; and I shall be with the warriors."

"That's one thing I can't agree to," said Jason frowning.

The Fijian looked at his host coolly, "I don't particularly care whether you agree or not," he said.

"Oh don't you?" Jason was taken aback.

"Men will be going to meet their Maker that day and they will need a man of God to help them prepare for that moment of confrontation. If men must die, let it be with some hope of a life hereafter. Then there will be the wounded; I can also arrange for their transportation away from the battle-lines. I shall be there to serve the enemy in exactly the same way, not just the men of Vatulevu."

"When I was a boy I saw the war between Bau and Rewa. For two years the cannibal ovens were never cold. War was an excuse for every conceivable extravagance of cruelty and the people sank to the lowest depths of depravity. Not being the aggressor in this war you still have your honour intact. If the people of Vatulevu can start off their Christian lives by acting in a Christian manner towards their defeated enemy, it will count strongly in their favour on the Day of Judgement."

"I note you say 'defeated enemy', are you so sure we shall win?" asked Jason, amused.

"If you are so sure that you fight on the side of right you need have no fear of the outcome. God will be at your side to help defend the righteousness of your cause." Elija answered, convinced that what he said was the literal truth. He stood up to take his leave of the company. "Thank you for being so frank with us, Mr Cotterel."

"We may be on the same side now, Elija," laughed Jason, capitulating, "but we are hardly going to be friends if you will insist on calling me Mr Cotterel."

"Alright, Jason," the Fijian smiled. "Now if you will excuse me, I would like to spend the rest of the evening talking to Ratu Seru and his men. Don't worry, Jason," he said anticipating the frown, "I shall not teach them to turn the other cheek. If anything, I shall breathe the fire of the Lord into them."

15

A new understanding

THE DINNER PARTY BROKE UP, Elija going down to the lines, whilst Toby begged the use of Jason's desk and immediately had his head down determined to produce a functional plan for a signalling system even if he had to work until dawn to do it.

Jason and Kate wandered out on to the verandah. The evening breeze was blowing in off the sea and there was not a cloud in the night sky. The brilliance of the moon outshone all but the brightest stars and imparted a patina to the sea.

Jason placed a hand beneath Kate's elbow and led her down the steps and across the lawn to the edge of the bluff. There, they looked down on the deserted beach and the swirling wavelets where the river poured into the lagoon. Had the scene been painted on canvas it might have been thought a figment of the artist's imagination. For several moments they stood there in silence, lost in the beauty of the night.

Their stillness became more charged with emotion with every second which passed and Kate finally felt she had to break the silence. She gently disengaged his hand from her elbow and stepped a few paces apart so that she could be free of his physical presence and think clearly.

"Mr Cotterel ..."

"Jason," he smiled reprovingly.

"Jason," Kate began again, "I want to thank you for a marvellous evening and above all for being so understanding with Toby."

"You don't need to worry about him."

"But I do. No one knows better than I how difficult he can be and you have had to put up with so much from him on every occasion you have met that I sometimes wonder where you find such patience. You have given him something useful to do; I was so pleased. It would have been impossible for a young man to sit twiddling his thumbs with the women, knowing all the time that the rest of you were risking your very lives to keep the island safe."

"I must be absolutely honest," said Jason capturing one of her hands. "I gave him that task simply to stop another scene such as the one he turned on in Levuka and which caused you so much embarrassment. The more I think about it the more I realise just how crucially important he will be. But perhaps I've made a mistake; suppose he makes a mess of the signals? It could well be the end of us all."

"But you surely wouldn't change your mind now?" Kate was aghast that he might be having second thoughts. "Having given him this responsibility, you cannot turn around and take it away from him again."

"No, I won't do that," said Jason wryly. "But I don't mind you knowing that your brother is going to give me some sleepless nights. As it is, I lie awake wondering whether I have made the proper decisions or whether I am leading this whole island into disaster."

"I didn't want the responsibility, the Vunivalu and Tui Navatulevu just expected it of me. Left to themselves the people here are so disorganised it would have been a walkover for the Tongans. Done my way we have a chance, an outside chance, of winning, nonetheless it's going to be a bloody business. You heard what Elija had to say on that score. Maybe if I hadn't become involved it might have been an easy victory for the enemy; the people would have been subjected to Tongan rule but a lot more of them would be alive under the Tongans than will live to enjoy freedom under my plan."

Jason needed to explain. "All our preparations are made, the training's finished and it's too late to change even if I wanted to, but I still wonder if it is going to be a bloody fiasco. What do I really know about war? A few minor skirmishes and the odd barroom brawl and here I am setting myself up as a seasoned general. The people have done everything I've asked as if I was some damned oracle."

His uncertainty made him all the more human and understandable. Kate knew instinctively that he desperately needed her to bolster his confidence to face what lay ahead. She had thought it would be marvellous to have the security a man like Jason could offer, yet it seemed that he was more in need of her than she was of him. Back in England, if anyone had told her that she, a missionary's daughter, would be urging a man to war before the year was out, she would have thought them mad. Kate wondered how many women down the ages had been faced with the same problem on the eve of battle.

She placed her other hand on top of his, "You must not worry so much, Jason," she said with a show of conviction. "If you appear indecisive at this stage the morale of the whole island will crumble. The face you show will give them the spirit to win. Toby too; if he sees you have confidence in him he'll give you the results you want. However, if he thinks you distrust him, not only will it destroy him as a man but he will make a mess of everything."

She gazed up at him. With the moonlight reflecting in her hair she looked ethereal yet her spirit was like tempered steel. "You have thought of every eventuality and have prepared as best you can. It now remains for you to lead the people with that absolute faith in the righteousness of your cause which Elija spoke of. You will throw the enemy back — I am sure of that — no Tongan will ever rule Vatulevu. Even though I shall be with the women and children, I shall be praying for you and the others all of the time."

"Will you really pray for me, Kate?" Jason's fit of depression was already passing.

"You know I will," she said, squeezing his hand.

"You poor thing, being burdened with all my problems." His eyes burned down into hers; he had to physically restrain himself from folding this angelic creature in his arms. "I have been bottling these things up with no one to talk to — I haven't dared speak like this to any of the islanders."

"I'm pleased you feel you can talk to me, there is little else a woman can do at a time like this."

Jason laughed. "You will never know just how much a help you have been. I feel a new man; you have revitalised me. You can tell your father when you return to the mission that the great Jason Cotterel, Lord High General of the forces of Vatulevu, the scourge of the missionaries, now has to depend on the missionaries to provide him with moral backbone."

This was the wrong note. He felt Kate stiffen and start to pull away from him but he held her hands tightly in his own.

"Don't misunderstand me, Kate, I meant what I said sincerely. Listening so patiently and talking to me the way you have put new heart into me. Just look at the night," he pulled her around to look out to the sea. "Have you anything as beautiful as this in England? We cannot ruin a night like this with argument."

*****

"It's time I was going in. Toby will be wondering what has happened to me," said Kate uncertainly. Her thoughts and emotions were in a state of chaos; she needed time to sit quietly by herself and reassemble her thinking on more sober lines. It occurred to her that Toby was not the only member of the Denison family who might have drunk too deeply of the wine.

"Don't worry about Toby. You were the one who said that he now has a task to keep him occupied. The last thing he wants is interruption from us." Jason pointed down to the empty beach. "Have you ever walked on the sand in the moonlight? Come along now, we shall settle our dinner by walking to the point and back."

He could see she was tempted; the sand and the moonlight had hypnotic qualities which could not be denied.

"I shouldn't," said Kate weakly, allowing herself to be pulled in the direction of steps leading down to the beach. She searched her mind for an excuse but it refused to function. “I haven’t got a wrap with me and my shoes weren’t made for walking in the sand.”

“Why worry about shoes? Take them off and carry them. The sand is soft, we can paddle in the sea, and if you feel cold you can have my coat.” Her arm was tucked firmly under his and he led her off willy-nilly.

Kate knew that this was either moon madness or the effect of the wine, but for the life of her she could not stop herself.

Once on the beach Jason dropped his coat, took off his shoes and socks, and rolled up the bottoms of his trousers. Kate hesitantly took off her own shoes and passed them to him; she could feel the cool sand through her thin cotton stockings and that was enough to tempt her further. Turning her back on him she quickly hoisted her long skirts and rolled down her stockings, in a moment she too was standing barefooted on the sand.

Instead of being appalled by the enormity of her behaviour she was revelling in it. The feel of the sand between her toes was marvellous; it was like stepping into another world free of the taboos and shibboleths of workday existence. Jason stood watching her changes of expression as one new experience followed another and Kate could not stop herself smiling back at him.

“You see that coconut palm,” said Jason, pointing to one which curved out over the beach about 200 yards away. “Lets get some clean fresh air into our lungs, I’ll race you to it.”

“Race you to it?” Kate hadn’t run a race since she was a small girl at school and even there it had been thought unseemly for young ladies. “But I couldn’t possibly.”

Her words fell on space. He was already off, running down the beach, the sand spurting up behind his bare heels.

“Jason come back,” she called, suddenly feeling lonely and lost on the beach all by herself. He only waved an arm and his laughter drifted back to her. She started after him, slowly at first, but hitching up her skirts she began to move faster and faster until she was running as if Ma’afu and his whole Tongan army were after her.

Jason gave a whoop of excitement and it was so infectious Kate could hardly breathe for wanting to shout and laugh herself. Untrammelled by skirts, he was miles ahead and she put every ounce of effort into catching him up.

Splashing through the edges of the waves, shying like a nervous horse at a crab which scuttled across her path; floundering and all but falling in a patch of soft sand; Kate was too exhilarated and intoxicated by the moment to worry what her brother or her father might have said. Had they seen her they must have concluded that island life had addled her brain.

When she reached him Jason was leaning against the coconut palm roaring with laughter. At the very last moment she became entangled in her long dress and would have tumbled headfirst at his feet had he not reached out and caught her. Laughing and panting she was pulled towards him. Her prim, ladylike bun had come adrift during the race along the beach and her hair streamed loosely about her shoulders.

"I could kill you," she exclaimed, her eyes sparkling. Her breasts heaved against his chest as she fought to regain her breath. "I haven't run like that since I was a child; you were an absolute beast to run off and leave me there."

"From the way you were running, if I hadn't got that head start I reckon you might even have beaten me," he laughed. "You looked as though the devil was at your heels."

His arms held her tightly to him and as Kate looked up into his eyes she saw the laughter suddenly change to hunger and longing; his grip on her tightened; one hand dropped to her waist, the other came up to the back of her head.

"No, Jason, no!" she cried, suddenly frightened. The hand on her head held it firmly and his lips came down on hers. She struggled feebly, beating at him with her clenched fists but his moving lips seemed to burn the strength from her bones and she found it impossible to resist. All at once she was kissing him back with a passion as fierce as his own; her arms were no longer striking at him but were behind his neck straining him ever closer.

She was crushed against his hard maleness. Her head spun in a world of pure senses; she wanted to give and take and the whole world surged beneath her feet. When his lips started to part from hers it was as if her very soul left with them.

They were both momentarily exhausted by the unheralded explosion of feeling. Jason cradled her head against his shoulder whispering her name over and over again, his lips against her hair.

She might have broken away and run for the safety of the house and her brother but she was paralysed. Never had her name sounded so sweet. She clung to him engulfed by her need for his love, and she sobbed against his shirt, not from shame or fright but from reaction to the emotion which had overtaken and destroyed her when she had least expected it. The suddenness and the immensity of the moment was beyond comprehension.

Jason put a hand under her chin and forced her face up until he was looking deep into her eyes again. The hunger had gone and in its place was a warmth and love such as Kate had never before dreamt existed.

"Should I say I am sorry?" he asked gently.

Kate shook her head and her arms, belying her tear-stained cheeks, pulled his head down to hers. This time there was the same fierceness, but also a sweetness and love so intense it was exquisitely painful. She knew she loved Jason Cotterel as she had never loved anyone before in her life, nor would she ever love another like this — the wonder was that he loved her just as much. Neither had to put it into words; words were for a later place and time when they could both think coherently.

When Jason's hand slipped gently inside the low neckline of her dress and found her breast, far from rebuffing this further violation of her body, a tingling fire which burned from her nipples down to her loins, welcomed his caresses. His lips were on her throat and head thrown back and eyes tight closed in ecstasy Kate's hands clutched deep in his hair and held him against her. He eased her down to the sand and Kate knew that if he wanted to take her there and then she was powerless to resist. Indeed her own need, this bewildering new force, was every bit as strong as his; her senses, quite independent of her mind, were in compulsive control of her limbs.

It was Jason who broke away. Heaving himself to his feet he staggered several paces in the soft sand fighting for self-control. Kate lay sprawled where he had abandoned her. Slowly she sat up, her shoulders shaking as she gasped deep shuddering breaths and struggled to regain her composure. Still inviolate she felt, not relief, but a deep sense of loss.

*****

Minutes passed before either spoke and even then Jason's voice was hoarse. "As God is my judge, Kate, I had no intention that anything like this would happen when I suggested we come down here." For a kiss he had been unrepentant, but a moment later he had been about to seduce her as if she was no more than a dockside trollop. It was not a question of morals, it was unforgivable of him to have taken advantage of Kate's innocence. He was appalled by what he had done.

"You do believe that I didn't plan this, don't you Kate?" Jason pleaded.

"I believe you," answered Kate in a small voice. He knelt beside her on the sand.

"I just couldn't help myself," he tried to explain. "I knew what I was doing yet I couldn't stop myself. Kate, I want you to know that I love you with my whole heart and soul."

Slowly Kate raised her head and looked at his troubled face. This giant of a man was waiting for her reply, terrified that she might rebuff him. She smiled tremulously and reached out to touch his face.

"Don't you realise that I love you too, Jason," she said. "Whether you planned this or not, I must have wanted it to happen or I would have refused to come with you in the first place;" and then they were in each others arms again.

This time Jason, his body firmly under control, was not taking chances. He sat with his back against the round bole of the coconut palm, Kate lay against him and his hand was softly stroking her hair. She realised that in a roundabout way he was proposing to her. She had often wondered what it would be like when her future husband proposed, but she had never imagined it might be on a lonely moonlit beach and she wearing neither shoes nor stockings. The slightly ludicrous side to it made her smile contentedly as she lay there listening and lapped in love.

"You were made for the life here, Kate," Jason was saying earnestly. "Between us we will make Qaraniqio the finest plantation in the Pacific. The children already love you as much as I do and we will have another dozen of our own to keep them company."

"Oh will we?" Kate laughed up over her shoulder.

"But you want children of your own don't you?"

"We can hardly have children without having first been married, Jason, and you haven't even asked me to marry you yet." He began to protest. "I demand that you ask me properly."

"Miss Katherine Denison," he said with mock solemnity, "will you do your humble servant, Jason Cotterel, the honour of bestowing upon him your hand in marriage."

Now that he had formally proposed, Kate suddenly realised that there were serious problems to be resolved. She sat up. "Of course I will," and she leaned forward and kissed him on the cheek, quickly jerking back again before he could catch her. "But we must be serious. It's not as easy as you think and I can get nothing straight in my mind if you are kissing and touching me."

"Ordering me about already!"

"Well first there is the war. I don't think we should do anything until you have this Tongan business finalised."

"Agreed," said Jason firmly.

"The really difficult question, Jason, is our marriage itself;" her voice expressed worry and Jason knew that she was genuinely serious. "I could not be married in anything but the church and for all my father's failings, I would want him to marry us and give us his blessing."

"But I wouldn't object to being married in a church if that is what you want, Kate. After all my first marriage was consecrated in a church."

"Why did you insist on a church marriage?" This was a question which had always intrigued her. "It can't have been out of any desire for consecration before God; you have always been consistent in your denial of God."

"I don't think I do deny God," he objected. "I wanted the church ceremony not for my own sake but for Ulamila and any children we might have. Even then I was determined to build the finest plantation in the islands, but life in these waters is a precarious affair at the best of times: I could have been killed in a skirmish or drowned at sea on my next voyage. Fiji was filling up with Europeans and I didn't want some sly white man cheating her or the children out of their inheritance. With a properly performed church marriage, there would be no danger of that."

"But I couldn't go through a ceremony like that, Jason. To you it was just another legal process, to me the marriage ceremony is full of meaning."

"How much does Christianity and the church mean to you Kate?"

Kate had never attempted to appraise her faith before, it had been with her and a very real part of her life since she could first remember. The fact that her father was a broken reed did not alter her faith in the essential truth of the Christian doctrine. She had absolute faith in the risen Christ and at times when everything in her family seemed to go wrong, that faith was her one consolation in a sea of troubles. Her faith was something she could never renounce, not even for Jason.

"Christianity is something real and dear to me," she said with quiet sincerity. "The love I feel for you, Jason," she said, "is no less real because of my love of God. They are separate but at the same time complementary things. I want to consecrate our love in the sight of God and I will want our children to be baptised in the Christian faith and brought up to believe and love the Lord as I do myself."

Jason started to speak but she laid a soft hand over his mouth to silence him. "I could no more run away from the church, Jason, than you could run away from this war against the Tongans. Somehow the fact that father has failed makes it all the more important that I should stay on to help him regain his senses and make up for his desertion of his duties.

"I only wish I could find such simple faith," said Jason, his voice harsher, "I have tried; I have read; but I have also seen and suffered too much for it to come easily."

"As long as you are trying, that's the main thing." Kate was clutching at any straw which came to hand. "What about the life you lead? Look at the way you have helped the people here; there are many men walking about professing Christianity who haven't had a single Christian thought or impulse in their lives."

"Look at the books you read," she said, thinking of the well-thumbed volume back at the house, "I saw one today, *Religio Medici*. You are not as ungodly as you make out. For a man of intellect and sensibility it is harder than for people like me who have never been given cause to doubt."

Jason laughed, "So you saw old Thomas Browne eh? You know, he and I are similar characters in a way. He wrote that book with all the slaughter and hatred of your English Civil War swirling about him. He had trouble reconciling religion with his scientific beliefs. But he was luckier than I; when things got too rough he had the power of prayer to fall back on. He could always go down on his knees and refurbish his faith. That is the thing I have lost; I have too many doubts and I suppose I am too damned arrogant to go down on my knees any more."

Kate framed his face with her hands and kissed him softly. "But you aren't on your own any more, darling," she said, wanting desperately to bring ease to his tormented mind. "You have me to help you now. Surely our love is something we can thank God for with an easy act of faith."

"My Kate," he answered wistfully. "I wonder … Will you ever really be my Kate?"

"Oh Jason, I so want to be," she said fervently.

"But only if I can be a good Christian into the bargain," said Jason ruefully. Clouds were coming up to blanket the moon and it seemed as if her moment of exquisite happiness was also fading. He continued, "It's not so much Christianity, as the church, which sticks in my throat."

"But you say you love me and I know you respect Elija. My father is not the whole or even a large part of the church." Kate argued, an ache in her throat threatening to choke her and tears welling up in her eyes. "The church itself is secondary, it is purely a vehicle for my own faith. That is why my father's conduct does not make me too depressed. There are the others, like Elija, who more than make up for his shortcomings."

"The church and I have been enemies far too long for it to be something I can undo overnight." It seemed only a day or so before that he had been on the point of saying much the same thing to Ratu Cakobau; Kate had an even better right to know. "You see Kate you are not the only one who had a clergyman for a parent: so was my own father. I was supposed to become one myself." It was her turn to be silent so that he could tell his own story.

"I was raised in New England. If you don't know America and you don't know New England it is almost impossible to understand what that means so far as religion is concerned. It is a land of bigots and dark narrow minds, where the Bible is used to cloak sins against mankind. As a child I had the Bible and John Calvin's Institution thrashed into me with a leather belt. Play and freedom were synonymous with sin and my every waking moment was governed by the rules of the church."

Jason continued, "An hour in the morning and another hour at night kneeling on a cold stone floor listening to my father communing with his God. Midweek prayer meetings and four services every Sunday — my only prayer, as I remember, was that my sainted and self-righteous father would come to the end of his sermon. I knew the Bible from end to end; I don't doubt I could still compete with your father if it came to quoting scripture."

From the coldness of his voice and the grim expression of his face, it was evident that as he spoke he relived his bitter childhood. "My father's God is hard, unrelenting, cold, bigoted, narrow-minded and hateful. He seeks to destroy all that is good, all that is warm and enjoyable in life. The one thing he hates above all else is pleasure."

Kate was holding Jason's hand tightly as he continued, "As a child and even as a young man I was terrified of my father and his vindictive God; the two were bound so closely together that I had difficulty at times distinguishing which was God and which the man. I believed blindly, fearfully, in those preordained footsteps and parrot-fashion I echoed everything he said."

"I had no separate identity of my own. He sent me to a Theological College to be indoctrinated so that I could become a minister in his image. But it was there, away from my father, that I began to think for myself. I broke free and became my own man for the first time. I rejected his God, his ministry and his church. In payment for my desertion my father disowned me as his son. He threw me out of his house without a cent in my pocket and just the clothes I stood up in."

A cold shiver ran down Jason's spine as he thought back to that night and his father's terrible wrath. In the years which followed he had been in a dozen fights and tight corners which had needed all the strength and courage he could muster. But he knew that his greatest moment of personal courage was the night he told his stone-faced father that the God he worshipped was but a false, empty shell.

He told her the whole bitter, twisted tale including personal details he had never told anyone before. But he was asking this girl to marry him and the complete truth was the only possible course. His hatred for his father and church bigotry poured forth; the punishments heaped on a child by a father crazed with piety; the fact that he could hardly look at a church now without feeling physically ill; the abuses and stupidity he had seen during his travels.

Kate finally understood what made up her man and her tears flowed with compassion for the frightened little boy in far off America. Her own heart hardened at the thought of the father who had expelled his son from his home at a time when he should have found enough love and enough Christian understanding to help him. If anything, it made her own love all the greater.

*****

When Jason finished his account his face looked lean and drawn and his eyes were hard with the bitterness of his memories.

"My poor darling," she whispered.

"I can only say I'm sorry for what I did tonight, Kate. If it hadn't been for my unthinking stupidity we should not be faced with this."

"Now you are being even more stupid," Kate forced a laugh which ended in a sob. "If you had not kissed me tonight there would have been another night. I think I must have loved you since the first time I saw you. If you had not found the opportunity I should have made an occasion to force myself upon you. I love you so much I feel absolutely shameless about it."

"But it is hopeless."

"It isn't hopeless at all and don't you say so," said Kate fiercely. "We both need time to think. If you can't pray, I can pray for both of us."

Jason pulled her to him and they kissed with a passion and meaning deeper than before. Her courage was such that even he, the professional cynic, had to believe that her determination, if nothing else, might pull them through.

They stood up and arms about each others' waists slowly retraced their steps along the beach. The deep imprints from their race earlier in the evening were still there but they now seemed to belong to different people and a different age. They reached their shoes and climbed the bluff, every step heavy with reluctance. At the house they stood gazing into each others eyes for a long moment.

"Can I come and see you at the mission, Kate?" Jason asked humbly.

"Of course," she whispered. "And if you don't I shall have you dragged there. I shall always be waiting for you my darling."

"You know we may even manage that marriage one of these days," said Jason with more optimism than he really felt.

Jason was going off to fight a war; and now the stories Kate had heard of Tongan ferocity had a new and more dreadful meaning.

"Jason, when the Tongans come, you will be careful won't you?" she said anxiously. "You won't do anything reckless. If anything happened now I don't know what I would do."

Jason could only see the funny side of this and chuckled softly. "You are the girl who was whipping me on earlier this evening and now you want me to take care I keep a whole skin. Something must have happened in between." His teasing drew the answering smile which had been his main purpose. "Don't worry, Kate, I'm not likely to throw myself under the Tongan axes, especially now I have you to come back to."

Kate had another request: "Jason, may I take the children back with me? You will be busy and they will be safer at the mission. As soon as the Tongans come I can take them to the hills with the others. It will also give them a chance to know me properly. I'll look after them and love them as much as their own mother would have."

"Of course," he agreed, "they will be a bond between us and I shall always have a perfect excuse to come visiting."

"As soon as you can," she whispered, and turning away she fled up the steps and into the house, almost bumping into her brother Toby coming out.

"Kate! You've been out a long time. Where's Cotterel?"

"I'm here, Toby," said Jason quickly to divert attention from Kate who was near tears as she fled.

"Ah! Jason, it's about time too. Have a look at what I've done," he said excitedly. "So long as you can supply me with a couple of decent mirrors — we have two at the mission I can use — and then I'll give you the finest heliograph outside the British army."

*****

Safe from scrutiny in her bedroom Kate collapsed on the bed exhausted. She lay there listening to the rumble of the men's voices in the lounge. It seemed hardly credible that her life could have been so utterly transformed. From the moment Jason's lips had touched hers everything had turned topsy-turvy; her whole life had a new direction, purpose and responsibility. It might be an age before she and Jason were able to marry, but he was no less her responsibility now than if they had been wed 30 years. She even had a ready-made family: a sturdy little boy, so like his father, and the most beautiful daughter. She would make them love her as much as she loved them already.

She pulled herself up with an effort and washed her face with water from the ewer beside the bed, changed into her nightgown, then knelt to say her prayers. Poor Jason had lost the power to find relief in prayer, but the children need not be the same; her own mother had taught her and she would teach them. In the meantime she could pray for them all.

"Dear Lord," she whispered, "thank you for this marvellous love you have bestowed upon me — make me worthy of this great blessing. Protect Jason from all danger, Lord, and bring him back into your fold that he may once again live in peace with himself. He is a good man and he tries hard to live a good life, a life that would do honour to any Christian. Grant him the blessing of true faith. Protect the children, Lord. Make them love me as their mother and give me the patience and skill a mother needs."

"Lord have mercy upon my poor father and restore him to his normal health and sanity, that he may work to further the success of the mission. May my brother learn to love the life in these islands as I do and settle down to a useful and fruitful existence. These things I ask in the name of the Saviour, who taught us when we pray to say, 'Our Father which art in Heaven'..."

16

Battle-lines

In Levuka, the coming battle between Ma'afu and Vatulevu was the main topic of conversation and heavy odds were laid on Ma'afu to win. As soon as the opposing camps began to buy large stocks of arms and ammunition the merchants had known, and Ma'afu's men openly boasted that they would be bedding the Vatulevu girls before the dry season was over.

The Vunivalu spent hours closeted with the superintendent of the Methodist mission. Not only did he want the missionaries to avert the attack but he wanted the blame placed where it properly belonged.

Two Europeans who took an inordinate interest in the coming war were Horace Twyford, the British Consul, and his house guest, Colonel Basil Gunning. Gunning had spent the last few months travelling extensively throughout the islands making himself an expert on Fijian affairs. He had even visited Ma'afu's headquarters at Lakeba.

"Ma'afu's men will go through them like a sword through butter," said Twyford, "I cannot say I'll be sorry. Not only will it be a slap in the face for Cakobau but it will put paid to that arrogant Yankee, Cotterel."

"My dear chap, you really must try to think more subtly if you want a career as a diplomat," purred Gunning. "It will not suit our purpose if the Tongans are victorious. Ma'afu constitutes as great a threat to us as does Cakobau; maybe more if he manages to conquer Vatulevu."

"Well there's no doubt that he will, I can tell you that."

"I wonder."

"You wonder?" Twyford looked at his companion to see if he was ill or had drunk too much rum. He stood in considerable awe of Gunning's cunning and amoral ruthlessness and this was hardly in character. "Vatulevu won't even make an impression on Ma'afu, so don't look to see him weakened there."

Gunning rolled his glass in his hands, thinking. "I'm not so sure about that," he said slowly as if savouring a pleasant thought. "They know he is coming and reliable reports suggest they will defend the island. I think it all depends on Cotterel. I haven't met him but from what I hear he is no fool and a determined devil when he sets his mind on something. Even you have said the man's capable and behind the scenes I have given him some help."

"You helped him?". This was news to Twyford but it did not astonish him as much as it might have a few months previously. This was the sort of thing Gunning was always coming up with, such was the deviousness of his mind.

"Ma'afu would have attacked earlier if it hadn't been for me. He was waiting for a shipment of arms and I got Cotterel an extra month by the simple expedient of persuading Henderson, the trader in question, that it would be wiser to hold the shipment up. It was either that or our fat friend would have been on the next British man-of-war back to Sydney to face a charge of murder."

"Henderson a murderer?" Twyford had always thought of him as one of the few respectable traders.

"You gave me the clue yourself in the dossier you prepared. I had enquiries made in Sydney and it seems that Henderson's wife died in very interesting and bloody circumstances. He was very willing to do anything I wanted."

"Nevertheless, we should get the man shipped back," spluttered Twyford.

"My dear chap, play fair. Henderson has done all I asked and you never know, we may yet wish to use him again."

"I hope to God London never finds out I'm sheltering murderers and dabbling in local wars," said Twyford taking a quick, nervous gulp at his glass.

"You have nothing to fear. As soon as Henderson outlives his usefulness of course he will have to face the charge. When Sir Horace Twyford is Her Majesty's Governor of Fiji we shall not want murderers around the place."

Twyford shuddered but looked to see if Gunning was joking. "Me as Governor?"

"Why not?" smiled Gunning. He enjoyed manipulating the emotions of this little man, so gullible and innocent yet gifted with a rapacity which outweighed any principles he might have had. "Sir Horace Twyford KBE, Governor of Fiji, Commandant-in-Chief in the South Seas; I think it sounds rather well."

So did Twyford and his pleasure would have been small beside that of his lady wife had she heard it. Nor did he doubt Gunning's ability to get him the post; he seemed able to do anything. "You really mean it?"

"If you play your cards right old fellow, it won't stop there: Fiji will only be a stepping stone to greater things. You might even end up as Governor of one of the Indian presidencies. Gunning could read his host's mind and was happy to build fool's dreams for him if they served to dissolve his scruples; but in truth he really thought 'Sir Basil Gunning' had a more likely ring to it.

"But such spoils are for the victors," continued Colonel Gunning. "If you and I desire them we must first earn them. For a start, there's our little project with the hill tribes of Viti Levu."

"Ah! The hill tribes," said Twyford returning to earth. That was one project he had intended to back out of. The plan was to foment trouble among the fierce, cannibalistic tribes of inner Viti Levu. Cakobau would have to lead an expedition against them to prove he could keep the peace and at that stage he would be soundly repulsed by those same tribesmen who had been armed in the meantime by courtesy of Twyford and Gunning. The risk was that once those savages went on the warpath, not only would the peaceful tribes suffer but the lives of every planter and missionary on the main island would be jeopardised.

"What have you done so far?" asked Gunning sensing Twyford's fears. He was interested to see which would win, the safety of a few, or a knighthood.

"You don't understand, Gunning," said the Consul stalling for time, "it's too damned risky. Finding someone to act as our agent is impossible. They're still out and out cannibals up there. He's likely to finish up in the pot himself."

"There's only one thing I do not understand," Gunning's voice was suddenly harsh as if he was reprimanding a junior subaltern, "and that is, how much you want Fiji to be a British Colony and how much you want to be its first Governor?"

The Consul wiped beads of perspiration from his forehead with a large red handkerchief. "Don't worry! It can be done," he said, chasing hard after those dreams.

"It must be done. Cakobau will be defeated in the hills and Ma'afu will be defeated at Vatulevu. Once we prove that neither is capable of ruling these islands, then we step in."

"When Cakobau fails to control the hill tribes, the settlers and missionaries will create such a tremendous fuss it will be heard in Westminster. The other dispatches we wrote must be in London by now and I have placed copies in all the right quarters. The government will be under so much fire that this could be the last straw. Our friends on the beach don't yet know it, but when their crimes and depravity are splashed across the pages of *The Times*, every inhabitant of Levuka will bear the brand of social pariah which he will never lose this side of the grave."

"When Cakobau does move against the hill tribes ..." began Twyford.

"Unless we move ourselves, and quickly at that, Cakobau will never move," snapped Gunning. "For God's sake man, we don't want a European as our agent, we don't want to broadcast our part in this. Use a Fijian, a chief if possible. Someone who has a personal insult to avenge. Give him ample funds and whales teeth, fill him up with rum, and leave the rest to his own barbaric imagination."

"You would need hundreds of tabua to get the results you want," Twyford objected.

"What if we were to give him a tooth ten times bigger and finer than any other in the islands?" Gunning asked slyly.

"What do you mean?"

Gunning began to unwrap a long parcel which had been intriguing Twyford since Gunning's servant had first placed it on the table. He drew the paper aside to reveal a long teak box, "Come here, I have something to show you."

With a dramatic flourish he opened the lid. Nestling inside on a lining of black velvet were two elephant tusks. By African standards they might have been thought small but they were perfectly matched and had been polished till they glowed with an opalescent bloom.

Twyford whistled appreciatively. "But they're elephant tusks not whales teeth." He argued half-heartedly, already knowing what was in Gunning's mind.

"So what? Elephants, whales, the Fijians will never know the difference. They've never seen an elephant: they will think these came from the biggest whale that ever lived — show these to your chief and see his reaction. There's one for the man who does our work, and the other is for the tribe which starts the raids."

"It'll work, the idea's not even new. During the sandalwood days some of the skippers coming here used to chop tusks up into tabua and they were in huge demand, the Fijians fought to get them. One bright spark presented a whole tusk and entire villages changed hands. No one seems to know where that one got to, most likely some chief still brings it out now and again to gloat over; in all probability he is too scared to admit ownership in case his neighbours dispute his claims."

It was true, thought Twyford, Fijians placed tremendous value on these chunks of ivory. If these two were accepted as authentic, the ramifications were such that the mind boggled. "One of these could fire the hills of Viti Levu from end to end," he said fearfully, "hundreds of men will die."

"Come now, Twyford," laughed Gunning, slapping the Consul on the back, "you mustn't be morbid. Think of the cause; think of the glory for the Empire when you add Fiji to its list of jewels."

The soft glowing ivory tusks in their cocoon of black velvet looked infinitely evil. All the treachery and infamy of Africa and Asia lay there ready to poison the islands. Horace Twyford recognised what they could do, but he also knew he lacked the moral courage to stand up to Gunning and stop their use.

"Having provided the materials I leave it to you," said Gunning. "I shall be too busy myself. I think it is about time the Vatulevu Defence Force was reinforced by the addition of an experienced professional gunnery officer!"

*****

When Colonel Basil Gunning, late Royal Artillery, arrived unexpectedly at Vatulevu on the *Elizabeth*, he somewhat nonchalantly explained to Jason Cotterel, "I heard you were about to have something of a scrap, old boy. Having fought in every other damned place, I could hardly turn down a chance of keeping my eye in whilst in the Pacific."

That evening Jason and Peter Bex took Gunning up to the house and, as they sat over drinks on the verandah, tried to get to the bottom of the man. "If you wanted a fight why didn't you join forces with Ma'afu?" Jason asked. "From what I know of the scum in Levuka, I'll bet they told you his was the winning side."

"My dear Cotterel, you might sound a little more enthusiastic," Gunning said. "If you must know it was all a matter of shipping. Bex was sailing for Vatulevu and there was nothing available for Lakeba."

"You're a cool one anyhow," laughed Jason.

"Well, I've always had a sneaking respect for the underdog. The betting in the Levuka bars is 20 to 1 against you and it only seemed right to do what I could to redress the balance. I'm a fool when it comes to long odds and I put 100 guineas on you. So you might look on me as a gambler who has come to safeguard his bet."

Any further inquisition was against Jason's ideas of hospitality, so he let the matter rest. His private view was that Gunning was just too good to be true. But there was no doubt the man knew his business. When Jason showed him the gun emplacements and the drills he had taught the crews, Gunning stripped to the waist on the spot. Within a matter of hours and with some amendments to the drill, he had the gun crews operating with far greater efficiency than Jason had ever been able to achieve.

His methods were effective but expensive on powder and ball for he didn't believe in dry shooting. As he told Jason, there was no possible chance of a drawn-out gun battle: their whole defence was dependent upon surprise; they would have but one chance, and when it came whatever shots they got off had to be dead accurate.

Jason had established a routine of twice-weekly visits to see Kate and the children at the mission; though had it not been for pressure of work and a desire to keep their love personal to Kate and himself, he would have been there every day. Their discussions were always held in full view but usually down near the river bank, far enough away to forestall eavesdroppers. They were unable to touch each other, but were content to keep it that way for both knew that another passionate encounter like that on the beach at Qaraniqio could only lead to consequences which would make them feel even more frustrated and miserable.

On his next visit he shared his doubts with her. Kate had known Gunning on the voyage to Fiji, and since he had landed on Vatulevu he had been to pay his respects to her father. She tried to be objective in her judgement but she too felt that a second person lay behind the front the colonel presented to the world.

"I know what you mean but I think you are worrying unnecessarily, Jason. You can't afford to spurn his assistance and you can see no way in which he can damage your position. If I were you, I would let him know in an indirect sort of way that treachery on his part would mean his immediate death at the hand of his own gun crews. That way you can make use of his knowledge and experience without fearing that he is suddenly going to let you down."

Her ruthlessness no longer surprised Jason who now knew that when danger threatened she had as much if not more strength and purpose than he had himself.

"I would look on him as an unexpected blessing if I were you. You will just have to accept his story that he is an eccentric, foot-loose, rich man with too much time on his hands and not enough regard for the value of his own skin."

"I hope you're right."

"You can't afford to look a gift horse in the mouth, darling, and you have no evidence that he is in league with the Tongans." Despite the fact that her father might well be watching, Kate laid a consoling hand on his arm, "Don't worry, Jason, you've done everything one man can do. Use Colonel Gunning if he can help you and if he can't, ship him out with Peter Bex when he leaves."

"That's the trouble," Jason laughed ruefully, "I really cannot afford to turn his offer down. I don't know, may be it's just my ingrained distrust of the English."

"Just don't let your prejudices extend to Englishwomen," Kate countered.

Two days later, the *Elizabeth* had to up-anchor for her run to New Zealand. Bex had hung on for as long as he could hoping the Tongans would arrive while he was present so that he could play a part. But there were his owners to consider; they would be highly displeased if he delayed. Gunning was left behind, a rather unwelcome guest at Qaraniqio, but one its owner could ill afford to do without.

The island settled down to wait. With each dawn men wondered if they would live long enough to see the sun set; and at sunset they waited tensely for the dawn.

*****

As a house guest Basil Gunning was no problem, in fact with Lala absent with the children at the mission his manservant took over as cook/housekeeper and proved to be a chef of no mean ability. Gunning liked to talk before and over dinner, but once his cigar was ended he excused himself to write letters. As he followed the same routine night after night, Jason could only assume that he had a staggering list of correspondents. Jason could have found company in Ratu Seru's camp, but it suited his present mood to be left to his own devices.

Since tearing himself free from his father's domination, Jason had lived exclusively in a physical world and had not felt a need to justify his actions in philosophical terms, but meeting Kate had changed all of that. He had not been conscious of any vacuum in his life yet, on reflection, he realised that even before Kate's advent, perhaps since Ulamila's death, he had been reading more philosophy than other subjects. Now the importance which Kate placed upon religion made him review his whole attitude.

Jason's European contemporaries seemed either to have been believers since childhood, or to have experienced some form of religious revelation which made disbelief impossible, whereas he could only make a value judgement on the evidence available. There was much which led the mind towards belief in a God; the unity and perfection of the universe, the symmetry and order of existence, and the factors which set human beings apart and above all else in the world they inhabited.

If the Bible was accepted as an historical document, there could be little doubt that Jesus Christ had lived and had died upon a cross. But divine? The son of God? Had he really been resurrected to sit upon the right hand of His Father? The problem was the reader had first to accept the divinity of the Bible before it was possible to accept the proofs offered. There were many things that Jason knew he could never accept no matter how much he tried, though if a God did exist there was no such thing as the impossible.

But Jason felt certain on one point — there could be no divinity about the church. The church was a mean vessel shaped by inexpert human hands in which man had endeavoured to confine his religious ideas. This was very evident in a place like Fiji where rival churches scrabbled over the bodies of the poor Fijians with little regard for their souls. Each sect maintained that they alone held the key to salvation and confidently prophesied eternal damnation for their opposition's converts. If ever he did find it in himself to profess faith in a religion, Jason swore that he would never chain it down with church dogma.

Jason desperately wanted to believe. But he could not slough off years of doubting as a snake does an old and unwanted skin. If there was a God, at least Kate's prayers were already interceding for him. He could almost wish that the Tongans would hurry their coming and still his turbulent mind in the din and chaos of battle.

17

Action stations

IT WAS IRONIC THAT, when the call to arms came, Jason was the one person caught napping. Instead of being at his post at Qaraniqio or Lomanikaya he was at the mission, the place he was supposed to abhor. Though Jason imagined his love was a secret, in reality it was being openly discussed throughout Vatulevu. The only person still fooled was John Denison who thought Cotterel came to see him; he was even writing a report to Dr Matthews predicting the planter's early return to the fold.

Kate and Jason were at their favourite spot by the river, oblivious to anything or anyone other than themselves. If they had looked towards the mountain they would have seen the fires and the heliograph flashing madly in its search for the missing commander. It was the heavy beat of the lali and the long wailing note of the conch shells calling the warriors which finally penetrated their consciousness.

One moment, Jason could think of nothing but the girl looking into his eyes; the next; "My God, Kate, that's the Tongans!" He spun on his heels and the long spirals of smoke from the mountain top confirmed it. "I must go, God knows how long they have been waiting for me." He was off and sprinting towards the jungle edge.

"Jason, Jason!" called Kate hysterically running after him. He stopped and regardless of watchers she threw her arms about his neck and kissed him hungrily; they held each other as if it were their last moment. Then he put her firmly aside.

"Be careful, my darling," she implored.

"Don't worry, love," he smiled, "I've you to live for, they won't get me." He was away again and Kate watched until the first bend swallowed him from sight.

*****

It lacked two hours to noon, the sky was a washed out blue and a stiff wind was blowing. Up on the mountain Toby Denison was almost beside himself with excitement and impatience. It was just the sort of day Cotterel had said they would need, yet the only people the wind was helping at that moment were the enemy.

From his perch, Toby could hear the lali and the conch shells. He felt like a hovering eagle watching ants enact a play far below him. He could see for miles and, like a magician, by putting his eye to the telescope he could turn ants back into people — people scurrying about in the village, the women and children leaving for the jungle and the takia being launched.

Even if he could raise no one with the heliograph, at least they had seen the smoke from the fires. This time it was no false alarm, they had better move smartly.

Toby estimated the enemy were still 12 miles off; one of the Fijians said they would reach the reef by noon. He could see 10 vessels loaded to the gunwales with men and arms; he had expected more. According to Cotterel, Cakobau had over 100 when he attacked Verata twenty years earlier.

On the other hand the Tongan fleet included a large schooner, a sloop larger than either of the Vatulevu ketches, and eight massive drua, the double-hulled canoes. The closer they came the more detail he could make out. They were dressed overall with flags and long streamers of masi. It took Toby back to his schooldays and a book he had on the Crusaders and the Saracens. In it there had been a picture of ships bedecked with the banners of the knights which looked just like these.

According to his Fijians, eight drua could carry upwards of a 1000 men. When he thought of 1000 men determined to destroy Vatulevu, his stomach churned, for all that he was far from the frontlines. With a century of victories behind them, the Tongans would be convinced of their invincibility and when dashing full tilt into the assault confidence like that was worth an extra regiment.

"Dina, i'saka!" called one of his men pointing to the south where the *Albatross* was leaving the river mouth at Qaraniqio, the heliograph fixed to its deck flashing. Toby settled himself beside the telescope to take the message onto a pad. Whoever was on the other end was slow and stumbling and it took two repeats before the message was clear: "COTTEREL / ABSENT / SHIFTING / KETCH / LOMANIKAYA / THEN / MOVING / NORTH / BATTERY / GUNNING."

Toby flashed an acknowledgement. If Cotterel was not at the plantation there was only one other place he would be — poodlefaking at the mission. He trained his glass on the tiny scar in the jungle — there was no one in sight, the women, children and old folk must be making their way up the mountain by this time.

He could only pray that Cotterel had made for Lomanikaya knowing that Gunning would shift the *Albatross*. He wrote Gunning's message out on another piece of paper and giving it to one of the Fijians told him to run like hell back to the village, and give it to Jasoni. Off went the messenger, leaping and bounding from rock to rock regardless of risk as he flew down the slope.

The thought that the omniscient and all-powerful Jason Cotterel might for once prove fallible was no consolation. Too much depended on Cotterel's leadership and quick wits for that. If the island did fall, Kate and his father would be quite safe but Toby had compromised himself by joining forces with the defenders and he could expect no more quarter than the meanest warrior.

"Where are you, Cotterel, you blasted fool?" he said out loud. The Fijians looked at him questioningly though none could understand English.

At least the other defenders weren't sitting down until their commander arrived. The sailing canoes were manoeuvring into position; ten were already outside the main passage and the others were just passing out through the northern entrance near the guns. How useful they would be remained to be seen. With two men per canoe, the outer defences totalled 40 men — a mosquito bite — annoying but not lethal.

To the north of Makaluva, Toby saw Gunning transfer from the *Albatross* to a sailing canoe which took him winging across the lagoon to the battery on Vatulailai. The ketch turned back again for Lomanikaya where, God willing, Jason Cotterel would be ready to board.

Ratu Seru on the *Lovadua* had taken station with a contingent of 15 armed canoes halfway between Makaluva and Vatulailai. There they sat on the wind-ruffled water, sails down, awaiting the signal from Cotterel which would send them at top speed towards whichever passage was most heavily under attack. It was Toby's job to feed this information to Cotterel but he could hardly send messages to thin air.

Minute by minute the enemy fleet was closing. The sounds of the lali from Lomanikaya were now mingling in the wind with the drumming and chanting from the enemy ships, sounds which seemed to echo off both the sea and the mountainside, until Toby could have sworn it would take 50 ships to make noise carry such a distance. They had seen the signal fires and, either knowing Vatulevu was forewarned or perhaps scorning the need for surprise, they meant to take the island by storm!

He could see now that the decks of the Tongan vessels were jammed tight with warriors and there was virtually no freeboard on any of them. It would have taken more courage than Toby had to have gone to sea like that.

The sun, coming high into its noon position, reflected from polished musket barrels and axe blades. Boom-boom, boom-boom; the rhythmic beat of the Tongan drums sounded more like an army on the march than an armada. On the foredeck of the schooner there were at least three cannon and there could have been more.

Toby's only consolation was that they could not have artillerymen of Gunning's capability. Not that precision would be needed — if they ever came within Gunning's range those packed decks would be a perfect target.

Toby held his breath and waited — the enemy navigators were as familiar with local waters as the defenders. They were at the point where if they intended to attack through the Lomanikaya passage they would bear south — if they did, the defenders would have an extra half hour, but it would also mean an attack at their weakest point. The shorter distance was along the cliffs on the northern side and in through the Vatulailai passage where they would have to pass right under Gunning's batteries.

He watched for the slightest alteration of course, his fingers tightly crossed. The Fijians beside him were just as apprehensive; they had no need of telescopes and stood like statues, eyes fixed on the approaching ships.

"Turaga!" shouted one, spotting the move before Toby. The sloop and two of the double canoes were splitting off from the main force and heading south. It was to be a pincer attack.

Toby thanked God; there was the *Albatross* surrounded by a small cloud of gnat-like canoes, coming out from Lomanikaya towards the main passage. With the heliograph oriented on the cabin of the ketch, Toby sent off a steady stream of information. "SLOWER / REPEAT / SLOWER" came back Cotterel's acknowledgement.

Toby cursed Cotterel as he transmitted. If the man had only been where he was supposed to be at the proper time, there would be no need for all the hurry now. "ENEMY / SPLIT / TWO / FORCES / THREE / UNITS / ESTIMATE / THREE / HUNDRED / MEN / MOVING / SOUTH / STOP / SEVEN / UNITS/ ESTIMATE / EIGHT / HUNDRED / MEN / MOVING / VATULAILAI / INCLUDES / SHIP / WITH / CANNON"

This took all of 15 minutes to send and be fully understood. Then a signal came flashing crisply back from the *Albatross*: "QUERY / ARRIVAL / TIMES?"

Toby scanned the advancing prongs of the attack and had a hurried conference in broken Fijian with his fellow observers. Cotterel had written down key phrases and he had memorised them. The difficulty lay in Fijian vagueness when it came to time; he had to equate sun movements with the mathematical precision of his pocket watch.

The flashing began again on the *Albatross*, impatiently this time.

"Damn Cotterel," thought Toby trying to work the problem out as accurately as he could. He finally turned back to his home-made heliograph and sent: "VATULAILAI / FORTYFIVE / MINUTES / SOUTH / SEVENTYFIVE."

He repeated it twice. By the time he was sure they had received the message properly, a further 10 minutes had been lost and Toby could only hope Cotterel had enough sense to allow for this. He need not have worried, for a fast sailing canoe had shot away from the ketch in the direction of Vatulailai even before the second repeat was completed. A large red flag had also been hoisted to Cotterel's masthead; this was Ratu Seru's signal. There was a flurry of hoisting sails and they too moved north to reinforce Gunning.

Toby was now scared that Ma'afu might sail straight past Vatulailai. It that happened the *Lovadua* could be recalled, but their main guns would be rendered impotent. Then, those precious cannon might just as well be children's pop-guns for all the use they would be.

*****

Crouched beside those guns, Gunning was thinking much the same and, comparing his command with some of the magnificent ordnance he had commanded in the past. If only some of his toffee-nosed friends in their London clubs could have seen him now, stripped to the waist, hiding out with a parcel of cannibals waiting to spring an ambush. He laughed at the thought. The gun crews looked at him astounded; they had heard that the kai-valagi was a great warrior in his own country and now his contempt for the approaching enemy was proof of it.

What a battery! Two old trader's guns mounted on makeshift wooden carriages, set in an embrasure of volcanic rubble. Directly opposite on the mainland was a similar set controlled by a Fijian who, until a few weeks before, had never seen an artillery piece in his life. Gunning and his companions were in greater danger from their comrades than the enemy.

The whole set-up seemed more ludicrous than alarming. His men had plenty of enthusiasm but none of the speed and precision of trained artillerymen. It would be interesting to see how they reacted if the batteries came under fire — rock splinters could be very nasty.

The trap was baited. Ratu Seru with the ketch and its attendant guard of canoes waited just inside the reef. They looked so weak and pitiful that the enemy, it was hoped, would regard them as an incentive to attack rather than as a deterrent. When they did, if the old cannon did not split and explode in their faces; if their camouflage was enough to keep the guns concealed; and finally, if the gun crews kept their heads and did exactly as they had been instructed, then Ma'afu and his men were in for the greatest shock of their lives.

One of the men began gabbling excitedly and pointing north. Sure enough there they came, rounding the point — 'all the Saints and Gods be praised' they were setting a course straight for the channel: two big drua in the van, then a large schooner fairly bristling with men and guns, while in the rear were four more drua. The enemy were still more than half a mile away but their drumming and chanting made the air throb with menace.

It was no longer a laughing matter and Gunning, as always in those few endless moments before an engagement started, forced his tense muscles to relax. He had fought through the Crimea and on the burning plains of Bengal but he knew that he would never be in a stranger battle than the one about to be joined. If he lived to tell the tale, his friends would never believe him.

*****

"Raica na vei takia," yelled one of his men, pointing at the outriggers they had stationed outside the reef. All 10 were flying straight for the enemy fleet. Gunning waited for them to fire and swerve away to safety but they kept on, skimming straight for the leaders. The gun crews were leaping up and down screaming encouragement to their brothers already striking at the invaders.

"Cease that noise and get your bloody heads down," roared Gunning, recognising the danger of giving their position away. Not one of them knew a word of English but they had no trouble grasping his meaning from the flashing anger in his eyes. They dropped back, silent now, but their eyes remained glued to the gun ports and the tiny canoes.

A ragged fusillade of shots from the leading ships peppered the sea around the scouts. One veered suddenly to starboard and capsized, its helmsman dead and the rifleman struggling for his life in the water. The rest kept straight on undeterred. To Gunning it seemed a useless gesture but it was still the act of exceptionally brave men.

They were right under the bows of the big ships before their rifles barked and they swung away, their outriggers high out of the water on the turn. One miscalculated or perhaps a stray bullet had put paid to the helmsman, for it kept straight on and crashed into the side of one of the double canoes. Two others were crippled by the fusillade of musketry which followed their retreat. Only six of the ten survived that initial charge.

But the very audacity of the strike had its effect: Ma'afu's army were more accustomed to attacking than being attacked and a shout of rage went up from the whole fleet whilst every available gun, rifle and musket blasted away at the fleeing takia. Gunning smiled with grim satisfaction. It would take that undisciplined rabble an age to reload and when they entered the channel most would still have empty muskets.

The scouts had also scored a few hits. Several men on the leading vessels had fallen overboard — at that range and with such densely packed decks it would have been almost impossible not to hit someone; he could only hope they were men of importance.

The first Tongan drua had momentarily swung off course, spilling the wind from its great mat sail and losing headway in the process. It quickly righted itself but it seemed likely at least one helmsman had been hit. From what Cotterel had told him about Fijian warfare, the mental affect of the strike could be even more important than the number of casualties. The challenge had been flung straight back in the enemies' faces and first blood was to the defenders. If nothing else it might make Ma'afu's Fijian allies think twice about the invasion.

Reloading as they went, the Vatulevu takia were swinging in again towards the schooner and the rear drua. This time it must be suicidal!

But now, neither Gunning nor his men had time to watch; in line ahead the first drua were running into the channel — their own moment of truth was upon them. The enemy could see Ratu Seru and his men waiting for them and, as Cotterel had planned, the sight was like a red rag to a bull. Warriors were jumping up and down screaming curses and firing muskets though still well out of range. He could not understand the insults but they must have been effective for he had to speak sharply to quieten his stirring men. Gunning checked his watch for the fiftieth time and sighted again. It would be open sights at point-blank range. A prize idiot could be an effective bombardier, so long as he had patience enough to wait for the critical moment.

The first gun thundered, not Gunning's, but the cannon mounted on the deck of the *Lovadua.* It missed the first drua and splashed harmlessly into the sea on the landward side of the second. Unless Ratu Seru's men reloaded smartly or the batteries managed to halt the Tongans in their tracks, that cannon might never fire again.

The Tongans jeered and laughed at the miss; their vision confined to the defenders ahead, blind to the danger hidden on either side of the narrows. They disdained to check their forward speed though in tricky waters. A mass of streaming flags, beating drums and a hullabaloo of noise, the famous Tongan spearhead came under the guns.

A match was applied to the touch-hole, the cannon crashed backwards on its mounting, and the first shot smashed into the crowd of warriors just at the foot of the mast. Simultaneously the mainland guns spewed grape in a murderous swathe across the enemy decks. The mast and sail collapsed and the huge double-hulled drua slipped sideways out of control, blocking the passage.

Gunning leapt for the second gun which was trained on the other drua now driving in on an irretrievable collision course with its crippled leader. His shot crashed home on the crowded platform linking the hulls, spraying bodies in all directions. Then he was screaming for the gun crews to reload with grape before the enemy had a chance to drift beyond point-blank range.

The surprise could not have been more complete — the middle of the channel was confusion and bloody carnage. Dozens of Tongans were dead or dying and the chaos was compounded by the rending crash of the two drua colliding. The second rode up over the side of its helpless leader; the platform split right down the centre and the hulls turned turtle, throwing men into the sea. The Vatulevu takia moved closer, pouring ball into the shambles.

The five cannon, one on the ketch and four in the shore emplacements, roared again and the seemingly invincible attack became a frightful massacre. Gunning's men screamed with excitement and bloodlust; they reloaded and fired again and again. The sea reddened and was soon slashed by the dorsal fins of sharks and grey torpedo-like barracuda coming to finish what man had begun.

The gun pit was a dense fog of smoke and reeking gunpowder fumes. Basil Gunning leapt to the top of the front wall to get a clearer view of the overall picture. The first attack had been smashed and, without firing a shot, the schooner and the remaining drua were clawing away, desperately trying to avoid the reef and reach the safety of the open sea.

Ma'afu and his chiefs must have been stupefied by the sight of their vanguard disintegrating in a matter of seconds before a defence which should have crumbled at the first touch. In less time than it would have taken to read the death roll, they had lost over 200 of their finest warriors. Win or lose, this moment of carnage would be remembered forever in the history of Fijian warfare.

The Vatulevu outriggers picked their way among the survivors in the water, clubbing and shooting. A small group tried to make a stand on a coral outcrop, water up to their waists. No quarter was asked and none given; at Ratu Seru's order they were annihilated by a well-directed blast of grape.

How many casualties was the Tongan prince prepared to sustain, Gunning wondered? Now he must realise that he could only take the island at tremendous cost to his forces and his prestige, if he managed to take it at all. Would pride make him try again or would discretion be the better part of valour?

He remembered his own lecture to Horace Twyford — they wanted the Tongan weakened and humiliated but not destroyed. Standing on the top of the parapet, blackened by gunpowder, he looked down at the results of his own handiwork and could not help feeling he might have been a little too efficient.

On the mountain, Toby Denison and his men were yelling themselves hoarse with jubilation. They had watched it all from start to finish; no victory could have been more decisive. "TWO / UNITS / ENEMY / DESTROYED / OFF / VATULAILAI / PASSAGE," Toby flashed off to Cotterel.

"REPORT / MOVEMENTS / REMAINING / UNITS," came the answer, reminding the lookouts that the day was far from being ended or won.

The schooner and its four attendant drua were standing off to the north of Vatulailai not daring to run the gauntlet of the channel guns. The tiny takia which had struck the first blow for Vatulevu had disappeared without trace — 10 canoes and 20 men — the island had also suffered its losses.

*****

There was no telling what the enemy might do now. They could try to force the north passage by taking the batteries on Vatulailai from the seaward side; they could join forces with the sloop and the other canoes from the south and strike through the Lomanikaya passage; or, best of all, they might decide it was not worth the inevitable losses and sail for home.

Toby relayed the facts, leaving Cotterel to do the guessing, and returned to the watch ready to catch or anticipate significant moves.

`Ma'afu still had three quarters of his army intact and Jason had no doubts that a second attack would come, this time through the Lomanikaya Passage where it was liable to be a very different story. They might be able to inflict further severe losses, but so long as Ma'afu was determined, he knew they could not hold them off for long. If the sloop and schooner used their own cannon, the defenders would receive a taste of what they had served out.

A yellow flag at the masthead recalled Ratu Seru and his squadron. While he waited for them to join him, ideas rushed through Jason's head. His main objective was to keep casualties on his own side down to a minimum while ensuring the Tongan defeat. He had to remain where he was but someone with a cool head was needed ashore to take control if the enemy broke through the forward ranks of the defenders. Neither Elija nor the Tui could be relied upon for the plan he had in mind.

He scribbled a note and sent it by messenger to Gunning on Vatulailai. He had served his purpose there and now could be better employed at Lomanikaya. "ENEMY / MOVING / LOMANIKAYA / JOINING / SOUTH / FORCE."

Before the message had been completed Jason could see for himself the sails converging from north and south. With Ratu Seru he had a total of two armed ketches and 40 takia, 10 of which were outside the reef. Those in the lagoon he arranged in two lines to form a corridor of fire through which the incoming ships would have to pass if they wanted to reach the beach.

They were as ready as they would ever be. The enemy were not as cocksure as before and the Vatulevu men were determined to give a good account of themselves. The musketeers and riflemen knelt behind the barriers in the midday sun, their naked bodies gleaming with nervous perspiration. The waiting was telling and, from the way they constantly licked their lips, Jason knew they were as parched and hot as he was.

The cannon in the bows, an old brass six pounder and the pride of its handlers, was polished till it was hard to look at in the brilliance of the midday sun. It was loaded with grape and spare charges and canvas bags full of musket balls were stacked nearby. Jason had decided that there was no point in using ball — unlike Gunning he was no professional gunner. Grape gave him a greater margin of error and would do far more damage to the enemy troops even if their ships were left undamaged. He also wanted Ma'afu to have something left to sail away in when he finally decided he had had enough.

Jason had strapped about his waist two long-barrelled Colt revolvers that Bex had given him. He felt a regular desperado but their weight on his hips was very comforting and at hand-to-hand range they would be deadly. Once they were empty he would fall back on the heavy dirk which hung beside them.

*****

Ma'afu did not make the same mistake twice. This time he waited patiently for his other ships to join him and then slowly approached the reef opening, the schooner and sloop to the fore, the war canoes to the rear. There would be no more surprises.

Jason saw the puffs of smoke before he heard the flat banging of the guns. The shots fell harmlessly between the two lines of defending boats but the enemy's strategy was clear: they meant to stand off and pulverise the defence before risking the passage. There was no hope of answering such fire. Even if Jason decided to change from grape to ball, the Tongan vessels were well beyond range.

He yelled to the nearest canoe to pass a message down the line to disperse during the bombardment to reduce the chance of a hit then, at the first sign of an enemy advance, to resume their present station. But he was too late; skipping shot from the next salvo crashed into three canoes huddled together and smashed them to pieces. The others scattered like a shoal of terrified fish, leaving the *Lovadua* and the *Albatross* to face the enemy barrage alone. Jason knew they would return once the attack started, but he also knew that he would be unable to use them as a disciplined force.

The next salvo splashed into the lagoon well beyond them, clearly the previous shot had been a fluke. The sea was calm where the *Albatross* lay but Jason could see it was choppy outside the reef. If he himself needed a large margin of error firing from a smooth base, it would have taken an expert to be effective from the pitching deck of a schooner. Unless Ma'afu had pressed a naval deserter from Levuka as a gunner, the enemy had no one of Gunning's class, which was something to be thankful for.

Ratu Seru did not have his friend's patience. At hand-to-hand combat or stealthy ambush in the jungle the average Fijian was without peer, but he had never been trained to stand steady while the enemy poured shot down on his head. The cannon on the *Lovadua* barked, belching grapeshot into the sea, none coming within 300 yards of the sloop.

"Hold your fire, damn you!" yelled Jason through cupped hands. "Reload, and hold your fire till they come at us."

The takia, taking Ratu Seru's shot as a signal, skimmed off towards the schooner. It was Vatulailai all over again. Jason had meant to use their speed and manoeuvrability against the drua, firing from a safe distance, swinging off to load and then back in again. In the event the first strike halved their numbers, and on the second, the attack disintegrated into so many floating logs and dead bodies. They must have targeted the gun crews instead of the chiefs and helmsmen, for there was a lull in the cannonade but not for long, as others took the places of those killed or wounded.

At the sight, tears started to Jason's eyes and his heart ached knowing that he had ordered them to their death. The enemy were cheering and Jason's hands clenched in determination that every one of his dead friends would be well and truly avenged.

Ma'afu's men were as little able to bear the inaction as the defenders. With the destruction of the takia being taken as a favourable omen, the drua left the shelter of the larger ships and made for the channel, massed voices roaring out a war chant as they surged down on the two small ketches.

"Up sail," ordered Jason, deliberately keeping his voice as calm as possible. The mainsail creaked up the mast and, cautioning the helmsman to keep her head right up into the wind until he got the signal, Jason ran forward to the gun. "Quiet, friends, your chance is coming," he called to the men crouching along the decks. "Hold your fire until you could spit on them just as easily."

The mainsail rattled and slapped in the wind and the sun shone down brilliantly on the lagoon — a kaleidoscope of yellows, browns and greens — while overhead the sky was a clear blue. No day to die on, thought Jason, but if it was to be, he would take a full bag of Tongans with him.

*****

He felt a sudden terrible need for prayer. It was an involuntary, elemental thing and nothing to do with books, philosophers or organised religion. Nor did he want to pray for himself; having vilified God for most of his adult life he could hardly turn around now and beg for mercy. Jason deeply wanted to pray for the lives of the men he was leading into battle, for the women and children on the mountain, for his own children, for Kate, and he could even find room in his prayer for those of the enemy who would be dead before the day was over.

In the comfort and silence of his home the concept of God seemed hopelessly remote, yet in the very cannon's month God was self-evident and undeniable. War, far from disproving the creative genius of God, only seemed to illuminate his greatest gift to mankind — free will. God created men and gave them freedom. War was not God's creation, it was the product of man's abuse of His great gifts.

Jason's lips moved soundlessly, it was hardly credible that his road to this point could have been so hard and so long. The big drua were at that very moment entering the channel but they had shrunk in significance before his greater moment of truth. He smiled ruefully; was it fear of imminent death which had shocked the truth out of him?

Jason lifted his hand as a signal to the man at the tiller. The ketch swung, the sail bellied and they closed with the enemy.

A hail of bullets and arrows showered down on them, smacking into the ship's timbers and tearing at the sail. A man fell coughing and wailing at Jason's side, blood bubbling from a great hole in his chest; but he had to lie there alone, there was no one who could be spared to tend to him. Now the first drua was broadside on to them, a huge stage crammed with howling faces. The distance closed rapidly. Some of the riflemen opened fire, coolly seeking their targets as Jason had taught them. Jason held the cannon's fire knowing that a second shot was out of the question.

100 yards, 75 yards, 50, 40 … "Fire!" he yelled at the top of his voice. Cannon and muskets crashed in unison, blasting the enemy faces into a gory, screaming pulp.

As the gun fired the helmsman set the tiller hard over and just managed to miss the drua's twin bows without colliding. There was only 10 feet in it — an athlete could easily have jumped from one ship to the other. A few blood-crazy Tongans tried, only to be shot down by Jason's revolvers as their feet touched the *Albatross*'s deck.

As if to make amends for his earlier impatience, Ratu Seru's attack was just as coolly delivered. His cannon and musketeers cut bloody corridors through the virtually defenceless warriors packed together in the second drua. The discipline and training of the previous months made 50 men more effective than 500 untaught irregulars.

Just as Jason thought they had pulled if off, Ratu Seru was in serious trouble. He managed to clear the crippled war canoe but his helmsman, killed by an arrow, fell forward across the tiller and the ketch crashed out of control on a jagged outcrop of coral. Everyone jumped clear and swam for the takia.

The crippling of two of his drua might have caused Ma'afu to call off the attack had he not seen disaster overtake the *Lovadua*. Instead, in spite of the shambles in the passage, the flagship was advancing to pick up survivors and press home the attack.

Jason had no hope of stopping the Tongans reaching the beaches without the help of the *Lovadua*. The takia were no longer a disciplined body; they were buzzing about the wrecks firing at any target which presented itself, regardless of his instructions to keep to chiefs and they had no semblance of formation which might be organised for an attack.

Should he attack again on his own or join the forces ashore where the issue would finally be decided? With no time to waste he gave his orders: the *Albatross* heeled over and raced up the bay towards Lomanikaya. As they went he explained to his men what he wanted done in the simplest language possible so that there would be no mistakes. He and the riflemen would join Tui Navatulevu, while the *Albatross* and the gun crew made a wide sweep coming up behind the Tongans, collecting the takia as they went.

Then, making sure they kept out of trouble themselves — and Jason threatened to shoot any man who disobeyed this order — they were to harass the enemy from the rear. Ma'afu could hardly commit his whole force to the landing at the village while his ships, his only means of retreat to safety, were menaced. If possible, the *Albatross* was to pick up Ratu Seru who would then take command of the seaborne forces leaving Jason free to operate ashore.

*****

Jason considered his position anew. By now the Tongan prince must be breathing fire and brimstone. If he took the island he would wreak a terrible vengeance for the casualties and humiliations he had suffered — no man, woman, or child could expect quarter at his hands. He would want to get to close quarters and settle the issue by hand-to-hand fighting and this was exactly what Vatulevu could not afford. Already 50 or more had been killed and they could not afford to lose another man.

The rules Jason had laid down for the sea forces must apply even more strongly on land — hit and run, hit and run, making damned sure there was always a safe distance between themselves and retribution. Already the Tovata losses were ten times higher than was normal in a local tribal war and it would not take much more to make Ma'afu's Fijian allies turn tail and run.

It must be personal pride which drove Ma'afu on. One small mountainous island could hardly be worth the loss of so many of his best warriors. It might be wisest not to push the Tongan too hard, thought Jason; in fact it might even be best to give him some means of saving face rather than make him determined to destroy the kai-Vatulevu regardless of the cost in men and ships. Ma'afu's pockets ran a lot deeper than Jason's and Tui Navatulevu's.

A possible solution was a complete withdrawal from the villages, leaving them to be burnt by the invaders; that way Tovata honour would be satisfied and they could withdraw claiming a technical victory. It might also save hundreds of lives.

But after the initial victories at sea Tui Navatulevu would not take kindly to the burning of their homes. Nor were homes the only things involved. In the centre of each village, on ground sanctified by generation after generation of worshippers, were the ancient Fijian temples and holy places. A year ago it would have been unthinkable for them to be left undefended and open to the defiling touch of strangers; it now remained to be seen just how effective Elija Codrokadroka's preaching had been.

*****

Early in the battle Kate was with the women and children, settling them into the caves. The distant roar of guns filled their ears and it was all she could do to stop them racing back to the village. The women cried and keened for their men as if they were already cold and dead; and the children followed the examples of their mothers until she had more than 400 hysterical people on her hands.

Kate then had the bright idea that her father should hold a special service to pray for the safety of the menfolk. She explained it in broken Fijian, refusing to heed her parent's protests. At once they quietened down, not that they understood a word the Englishman was saying. Kate could not even be sure that they were all praying to the same God, but at least everyone was down on their knees.

It was Kate's own patience which then broke. Hemmed in by the jungle and packed into a dark cave with dozens of other women the rumbling gunfire and, even worse the silence which followed, was more than she could bear. She did not have to be on her knees to pray for the safety of Jason and the others, but she had to know what was happening. It would be some time before any wounded arrived and the women were calmer, so Kate slipped away taking a small boy with her to show her the path up the mountain.

"I thought it wouldn't be long before I saw you up here," Toby said, giving her a hand up to his perch. "Welcome to the royal enclosure. I feel like an umpire sitting here by myself."

"What has happened, Toby? We heard the guns but now there is nothing."

"There hasn't been any more. We won the first round hands down. You've got to give the laurels to that chap Gunning; he fairly blasted the daylights out of them."

Excitedly, Toby pointed out to his sister where the first engagement had been fought. It made it all the better to have an audience other than the Fijians, none of whom understood a word he said. Through the telescope he showed her the Tongans regrouping prior to their attempt on the Lomanikaya passage. She was just in time to see the schooner open fire on the tiny craft in the lagoon.

"Our people haven't a chance, Toby," she cried aghast. As if to confirm her assessment she saw the next shots scatter the takia destroying three and then, a few minutes later, the suicidal charge of the 10 scout canoes outside the reef. Her stomach cramped with a terrible fear.

"Where's Jason?" Kate asked, her voice trembling with anxiety.

"That's him on the *Albatross* just inside the reef to the north. They'll be coming down on top of him any moment now, I don't like to say it but I don't think he has a chance against odds like those."

"Please God, no!" Kate whispered. Her eyes misted over and she could no longer see through the glass. She felt physically ill from worry and knew then she should have stayed with the other women.

Toby looked at his sister, suddenly sympathetic; she was obviously going through hell. There were times when he could not stand the sight of her, nevertheless she was the only soul on earth who cared a tuppenny damn about him. If he had affection for anyone other than himself, it was her.

He put an arm protectively around her shoulders, "You like him, don't you Kate?"

"Like him? I love him," said Kate fervently, still mesmerised by the scene below them. "I'm going to marry Jason Cotterel." Even as she spoke she could see the Tongan war canoes moving into the passage and the *Albatross* swinging to meet their charge.

"Marry him?" said Toby incredulously. "You! Marry Jason Cotterel! You must be out of your mind. Father would never agree for a moment. You, marry a man who is against every principle you believe in?"

"I don't care what father thinks, or what you think for that matter," said Kate with cold determination. She had just made up her mind, or what she had just seen had made it up for her. "When this is over I am going to marry Jason. I don't care if he hates every church in Christendom. I shall still be a Christian, but he can be anything he pleases so long as I can be with him."

There was a flurry of explosions and the battle was blanketed from sight by dense smoke. Kate was unable to distinguish friend from foe. Her lips were moving in silent prayer and it seemed as if her heart had stopped beating. They saw Ratu Seru commence his run, then the wind blew the smoke away to show the *Albatross* crossing the bows of its opponent.

"My God, they'll hit," Toby yelled, only to be proved wrong the next second. Then a few moments later the *Lovadua* struck the reef like an unmanageable toy, spilling its crew into the sea.

Kate turned away, her stomach wrenching. Toby looked at her, startled, and it sank into even his insensitive mind that his sister should not be allowed to witness a holocaust such as this. "Kate, you can't stay here," he said emphatically; for once worried about someone other than himself. "This is no place for a woman."

Kate needed no second urging and she stumbled down the hill, her eyes blinded by tears, trying to block the roar of the guns from her ears and erase from her mind the memory of what she had seen. It seemed impossible that Jason could live through that inferno. She had told him everything would be alright, yet she had known nothing of war. What a fool she had been. She had fired him with confidence and told him where his duty lay and now he was most likely floating dead on the surface of the lagoon, along with a hundred others.

18

Unfinished business

UNSCRATCHED, JASON WAS STEPPING ashore at Lomanikaya to be embraced by Tui Navatulevu. "You have done well, my son; the Tongan pigs and their kai-si will never forget today."

"So far we have held our own," answered Jason, his face was blackened with gun-smoke and drawn from weariness and worry. He nodded to Gunning and Elija who were also on the beach to greet him. "But we have lost a lot of men and there is still much to be done if your people are to be saved from the invaders, Turaga."

"In fact we haven't done well enough. Gunning will tell you that I speak the truth. The English soldier killed many Tongans at Vatulailai and my men killed more, but it still was not enough; they are too many for us. If one of our men falls there is no one to replace him, but Ma'afu has three times our number who have not even tasted battle yet. Out there we slowed them down; they are no longer charging in and they are more cautious, but that does not mean they will not come. In just a few minutes from now they will be landing on this very beach."

Gunning nodded in agreement; he was waiting to hear what came next.

"But we shall cut them down on the beaches in the same way that you did at sea. Our forces will be victorious." The initial success had gone to old chief's head just as Jason had feared. "What you have begun, Jasoni, I and my men will finish."

"You are wrong, Turaga," said Jason emphatically. "Even if you did win, it could only be at the expense of three quarters of your best and strongest men. It would be a very empty victory if there was no one left to enjoy it. You wouldn't number enough among the living to bury the dead."

A moment before Tui Navatulevu had been proud and confident; now, as reality sank in he seemed to wither until he was again a very old man. "What would you have me do?" he asked finally. "If I surrender now, Ma'afu will not be content with baskets of earth and the other traditional symbols of atonement, he will kill off all my young men in repayment for the warriors you have killed. The people of Vatulevu will vanish as a tribe."

"I don't want you to surrender, Turaga, nor do I want you to show weakness.

The smallest sign of submission would be the signal for the Tongans to snap us up like hungry sharks. If you will follow my advice we can still defeat him, but we must use cunning, not brute force."

By this time the old chief was thoroughly weary of war: "Jasoni, I have told you before that in this you are both my head and the arm which wields my club. Whoever heard of a chief throwing away both his head and his club in the heat of battle? That is the surest way to lose both permanently. Tell me what you want and we shall obey"

The schooner was standing off, firing her cannon at the village. Balls whirred over their heads and crashed into the coconut groves behind them. They could see the remainder of the Tongan fleet assembling ready for the dash towards land.

"Whatever it is Cotterel, you'd better be damned quick about it," growled Gunning, who was beginning to doubt the wisdom of his ever coming to Vatulevu.

"Here it is then," said Jason, "We meet their first charge with everything we've got. They're not used to coming up against disciplined volleys and it should throw them into complete confusion."

"Not for long," snapped Gunning.

"Long enough. It will show them we still mean business and we won't be waiting for them to get over the first shock. After that first volley we take off into the jungle. We regroup at the mission compound and then divide into small groups which will creep back and ambush and snipe at everything which moves, making sure that there is always an avenue of escape. We can make life such hell it will be impossible for Ma'afu to stay. As soon as it gets dark Ratu Seru and his men will play havoc with their ships."

Then came the objections, which Jason had been expecting. The chief almost exploded: "But they will burn Lomanikaya to the ground!"

Jason asked coldly. "Which would you prefer, Turaga, your village burnt down or your men butchered? Do you have any alternative?"

Tui Navatulevu pointed a trembling hand at the tall pagoda-shaped temples and the sacred grove of ivi trees. "There are my gods; would you have me leave them to the mercy of the Tongans?"

Jason turned to Elija, he needed the Fijian's help as never before and he could only hope the man's eloquence had not deserted him at the moment it was most required.

"Turaga na Tui," Elija's voice was respectful but firm, "The white man is right. It is your duty to lead and protect your people. The plan is a good one. We have spoken much of gods these last months, you and I; I have told you of the only true God and His Son, our blessed Saviour, Jisu Karisito. You have listened closely to what I have said and I have answered your questions to the best of my poor knowledge."

"The time has come for you to make your choice of gods. Are you for the true God? If so, save your people. Or do you choose the old pagan gods who mean nothing and demand the sacrifice of all your young men? If you stand out in favour of Degei and the false deities, I prophesy the kai-Vatulevu will disappear from these islands forever."

The old man, faced with the most momentous decision of his life, looked from Elija to Gunning, then to Jason. He gazed at the temples and the sacred grove which had been the key to his existence ever since he could remember. He had been a loyal ally to Bau, yet the Vunivalu had insisted that the missionaries come and they had thrown his mind into a state of confusion. Now he was uncertain what he believed. In this new era of white men, only their God seemed to have any power. The traditions of his forefathers were passing away and the new men were demanding that their gods go with them. New weapons, new gods.

He looked at Gunning, a soldier and recognised leader from the ranks of the whites; his was an opinion, which he as a chief could respect.

"Are you a Christian, Turaga?"

This had to be translated for Gunning's benefit and when he got the full meaning he was shaken. It was the first time that his religious beliefs had been a crucial factor in the determination of a battle plan. With a good chance that he might be dead himself before the sun set, it was not a question he could answer flippantly. "Yes, Chief, I am a Christian," he answered solemnly and the conviction in his voice surprised even himself.

Tui Navatulevu turned to Jason and asked the same question. "What of you Jasoni, my son, husband to my dead daughter and my chief counsellor, are you a Christian?"

Jason felt his mouth go dry. Since he was 18 years old he had denied God and His Son, yet out on the reef in the very teeth of the Tongan onslaught, he had felt the presence of God as a real thing. For years he had confused God with the image of his own father and by renouncing God he had really been renouncing his father's control. It was only now, facing death, that he was able to distinguish the difference between the two.

The others were looking at him anxiously; everything hung upon his answer.

"Turaga," he said hoarsely, his tongue cleaving to the roof of his mouth as if physically unable to deny the past 15 years. "I do believe in God." He finally got it out and it was as if a great load had been lifted from his shoulders. The chief was looking straight into his eyes to judge the sincerity of his words.

"You have heard what I have said before on this subject, but I now say that I believe in God and His Son even if I cannot believe in the church!" Jason turned to look at Elija; he wanted him to be under no illusions that this meant a truce with the church.

"It is enough," said the chief, his mind made up. "We follow Jasoni's plan. The Tongans may burn the village and the old gods. From this day forth the chief and people of Vatulevu are children of the Lotu na Karisito.

*****

The decision made, they sprinted for the lines of troops. There was barely time to explain what they wanted, check the muskets and set the lines, before the enemy were dropping over the sides of their ships. The Tongans and their Fijian allies came, wave after wave of them; there were so many it hardly seemed credible that any had been killed. They splashed through the shallows kicking up great fountains of water, the air shattered by their screams and war cries. The tide was out and they had 300 yards of water, sand and coral to cross yet the enemy army seemed to fill the whole space.

Jason, Basil Gunning and the old chief stood at the centre of the Vatulevu line with Elija standing tall beside them. There were three long but pitifully thin lines — the front men kneeling with spears held like a bristling hedge of pikes; next, all that remained of the musketeers and riflemen; and behind them the traditional warriors with knobbed clubs, bows and arrows and broad-bladed axes. They waited trembling with fear, their eyes round with horror and anticipation. It was only the coolness and unconcern shown by their leaders which held them in place while the enemy horde descended on them.

Jason waited, his revolvers held loosely at his sides. All around him he could feel the men shifting and murmuring nervously. His own insides were tightly knotted with fear every bit as great as their own but he knew that the slightest sign of nervousness on his part and they would all break and bolt.

"Aim!" he roared.

The rifles and muskets came up, each man picking his target. Spears were landing in the ranks and the leading Tongans, their faces set in a rictus of hate, were almost on top of them.

"Fire!"

The guns belched an avalanche of death, shattering the enemy like a mighty fist. The forward rush stopped dead as if smashed against an impregnable wall. The Vatulevu spearmen rose and threw; it was impossible to miss and those Tongans who managed to stagger the last few yards fell beneath the clubs and axes. Using one revolver at a time and aiming each shot carefully, Jason fired twelve times, each time selecting the most heavily armed and ornately dressed warrior as his target. The clean white sand was soaked with blood and the shallows rinsed the gore. Bodies lay everywhere. The enemy reeled, broke, and ran for the safety of their ships.

"Retire!" yelled Jason in a stentorian voice, which was all but drowned by the screams of the dying.

The Vatulevu forces started forward in a charge, intoxicated by their success. "Run, you bloody fools," Jason roared, laying about him with his pistols. He used the butt to beat the bloodlust from the eyes of one crazed warrior, then he turned and ran for the jungle himself. When the others saw Jason and the chief turn, they remembered their orders and, after a moment's hesitation, followed. Once started for the safety of the trees, fear returned and they ran for their lives.

Gunning ran as fast as anyone else, but was laughing as he went at the thought of one of Her Britannic Majesty's officers bolting like a startled deer; it was damned sensible for all that. Even so he could not keep up with the pace set by Cotterel's long legs. The man might be an American and a beachcomber, but his guerrilla tactics had the mark of a seasoned general.

He staggered into the trees, his chest heaving and his sides aching from laughter. He kept on for another quarter of a mile before he dared slow down and even then Fijians streamed past him still travelling at top speed, as if Ma'afu was right behind them.

He slowed to a walk and searched around until he found the track and there he straightened his clothes and recovered his composure. As he marched towards the mission he could still hear shouts and screams behind him and the yelling of the defenders ahead. Before he came up with the others again he wanted time to collect his thoughts and rearrange his own plans.

If ever he became so old and decrepit that intrigue and battle lost their savour, he would vegetate and write his memoirs. He had led a full life but nonetheless Vatulevu would rate a full chapter. Warships the size of dinghies; three successful actions; and to top it all the conversion to Christianity of a tribe of hardened cannibals minutes before the final onslaught — it had all the elements of a fairy tale, or maybe a nightmare.

On second thoughts it might be better if he omitted the whole interlude. At the Artillery Club they would think poor old Basil Gunning had gone right off his rocker. He even knew what they would say: "Missed too many boats, old boy." Basil Gunning was determined to have more than that as an epitaph.

*****

It took two days and two nights to convince the Tovata Confederacy army that not only was Vatulevu not worth holding but, unless they retired quickly they would have neither ships left to sail home in nor men to sail them. They were never able to come to grips with the defenders nor were they ever free of them. Malevolent eyes followed their every movement and the slightest relaxation meant immediate death.

Their jubilation as they saw the defenders fleeing was overshadowed by the fact that they themselves were in no condition to follow up the rout. The venomous cracking of rifles from the hillside overlooking the village offset the discovery that the village was theirs without further loss; three men fell and the rest had to scatter for cover. The snipers were hidden by the jungle. A party of 50 men sent to scour them out found no trace but five stragglers never returned, and no sooner were the main body back in the village than the rifles opened up again. They fired at anything that moved and, what was unusual for island marksman, they were uncomfortably accurate.

The village had fallen but the Tovata army were without a single prisoner to show for the blood that they had shed. Not a single woman to ease the hungry loins, not even a child to beat to death with their gun butts. Spoils were the just reward of the victors but with every hour that passed, it became more and more doubtful if the Tongans were indeed the victors.

When Ma'afu himself came ashore from his flagship, he found his victorious army cowering in corners for protection, not daring to move. His dress, height and narrow evil face were unmistakable but the snipers left him strictly alone; he could wander wherever he wished without a single shot being fired. But let one of his men try to accompany him and the peace of the afternoon was split by the sharp 'crack! crack!' of the rifles.

When night fell it was worse. In the darkness it was impossible to tell friend from foe. The sentries set at the edge of the village were beset with shadows, some of their own imagining but others that suddenly resolved into a blazing musket or the sibilant hiss of a well-aimed arrow. The constant shouting and screaming, both real and illusory, allowed no one to sleep. Injured men lay groaning in the night with none to tend them. They were even denied water; a trip to the river to fill the clay pots was certain death either from a bullet or the poison drifting downstream. The kai-Vatulevu were steeping the water with leaves and vines that in times of peace were used to poison fish.

Before the night had ended, more than half of the army had crept back to the safety of the ships. Even there they were not safe for the moon rose to reveal canoes encircling them. The beleaguers were beleaguered. The takia were beyond the range of the guns and shifted position often. Any attempt at retaliation was a waste of powder and shot. The constant surveillance was unnerving.

The invaders were not even left the honour of burning the village to the ground themselves. Just before dawn, a fire arrow came whirring out of the jungle in an arc which ended in the thatch of the house sheltering those still ashore. The tinder dry reeds exploded into flames, illuminating the whole village.

Men spilled out running for their lives and, as they entered the light, gunfire came from the jungle. The fire, caught and fanned by pre-dawn breeze, leapt from house to house until the whole of Lomanikaya was one enormous pyre consuming Ma'afu's hopes and the will of his men to fight. Sparks shot high into the sky, and gunpowder brought ashore exploded, adding to the confusion. Men wounded in the previous days battles and too weak to escape with the others, burned to death where they lay.

Tui Navatulevu, his captains, Jason Cotterel and Basil Gunning, and his chaplain, Elija Codrokadroka, watched from the hillside with grim satisfaction. The preacher's lips moved in a silent prayer of compassion for the dying but he made no move to stop or even moderate the tactics used against the enemy.

*****

Elija was almost dropping with weariness. He had escorted some 30 kai-Vatulevu wounded up the mountain, some walking others carried on rough litters. It had been a slow and painful progress, the worst cases dying on the way. With the outcome still in doubt, it was essential that those with any chance at all be removed from the vicinity of the fighting where they might have fallen into enemy hands. Kate and the women, who had the older children on the watch for them, met the party half-way up the mountain.

It had taken Elija and the English girl all their persuasive talent to stop the women screaming and flapping about like useless hens. They had virtually no medical knowledge and even less in the way of medicaments; but using the torn up sheets from the mission as bandages, cleaning and binding up wherever they could, the majority of the wounded were now as comfortable as could be expected in the caves.

Kate had been a tower of strength. She refused to allow the sight of blood or the ghastly wounds to put her off; the only thing which had depressed her was her inability to help the more serious cases. "I have never before felt so helpless and incompetent," she had told Elija despairingly. "At my ladies' seminary they taught me French and the pianoforte — if they had thought to teach me how to dig a musket ball out of a wounded man's shoulder I might be of more use to these poor men"

"But you are doing marvellously, Kate," Elija had encouraged her. "Most of them would be dead by now if it wasn't for your work. Left to the mercies of their own womenfolk, they would have got a flood of tears to help them die but never sense enough to keep them alive."

"If I'd only thought to stock our medicine chest with gunshot wounds in mind, but in London in didn't occur to me that a mission compound would be involved in a war."

"Tomorrow I shall have some of our local herbs sent up to you, with a note on their use. Certain leaves bound on top of wounds can help them heal; they must take the place of the salves you lack."

"But what about that boy with the terrible hole in his chest and the other with the spear wound in his stomach?" Kate asked despondently. "If only we might save them too."

Elija took her by the shoulders and shook her gently. "You mustn't blame yourself, Kate. I doubt whether the best white doctor in the world could do much for those two," his voice was deliberately stern. "Hundreds have died today, you couldn't save them and you won't be able to save these. God has ordained that their time has come, we can only pray that he will have compassion on their souls. But there are others here who can be helped to live and you are their hope. If you give up, the women will relapse into hysterics again and they will all die."

He told her all he had seen and explained Jason's plan to rid the island of the Tongans. Although he was a man of peace he could not keep from his voice the admiration he felt for Jason Cotterel and Kate warmed with pride at what he told her.

"Our men will win, then. You are sure, Elija?"

"We shall win, have no fear of that," said Elija solemnly, "I only hope that it will be soon; the longer it goes on the more men die on both sides."

"Has Jason taken any hurt?" asked Kate, trying to keep the anxiety from her voice, as if he was no more to her than anyone else in the Vatulevu forces.

Elija looked at her amused; he was not fooled in the slightest. She had been wanting to ask this question from the moment they had met.

"He has not been touched, so you can stop worrying, Kate," he laughed. "It would seem that God is protecting him so that he can protect the island from the Tongans."

"The last thing Jason would like to be thought of is as one of God's servants," said Kate wistfully.

"Both good and evil can come out of war, Kate," he said quietly. "This island will never be the same again but it is my hope that it may be a better place. I think that Jason Cotterel has also been changed, but I leave you to discover that for yourself."

"I don't understand," said Kate. "In what way has Jason changed?"

"Jason will explain" he said; "I think this is something which has been worrying you both and I am sure he will want to do the telling."

"Elija, did you know that I am going to marry Jason?"

"With the possible exception of your father, there is no one on Vatulevu who doesn't know it, Kate," he answered. "For what it is worth you have my blessing."

*****

Remembering his duties elsewhere, Elija stumbled off down the track, now made more difficult by the darkness. It was after midnight before he rejoined Tui Vatulevu and Jason. He was scratched and bruised from falls he had taken but he refused to rest; there was far too much to be done.

The burning of the village was appalling even if necessary; nothing he might have said could have stopped it; but at his insistence it was the last action of the night. As he pointed out to Jason, the enemy would be expecting further attacks even if none materialised. The mental strain would be there even if their own men did not fire another shot and they would be achieving their purpose without unnecessary killing.

Dawn broke as they reached the mission compound. Men were sleeping in small huddled groups all over the place. Jason, worrying that Ma'afu might push inland at first light and find them unprepared, had them woken and sent off into the bush where they could sleep safely until needed.

Elija went to the church and the two Europeans settled down with a bottle of brandy at a table in John Denison's sleeping house to work out their next move. Later, Elija joined them. Clearly he was almost dropping with fatigue.

"For God's sake, man," said Jason angrily, "get off into the bush with the others and have a rest."

"I'm alright," Elija protested weakly.

"Here, drink this," said Basil Gunning half-filling a glass with brandy. Elija began to refuse but Gunning impatiently pushed the glass into this hand. "Go on drink the stuff. I'm not asking you to get drunk, this is purely medicinal." Elija dutifully swallowed it only to start coughing violently.

"How was Kate?" Jason asked when he settled down again.

It was Elija's chance to retaliate. "She still loves you dearly and can hardly wait for war to end so that you can get married."

Caught completely off balance Jason had the honesty to blush beneath his dark tan, much to Gunning's amusement.

"So that's the way the wind lies eh! You're a damned lucky dog, Cotterel," he said enviously. "Congratulations are in order if Kate Denison has accepted you."

"Premature I'm afraid; Denison and that son of his think I'm poison. Can you see John Denison agreeing?"

"What objections can he have? If he will bring his daughter to a place like Fiji, she's not going to marry into the titled aristocracy. She'll contract no better alliance here."

"That sounds like damning with faint praise," said Jason, looking at the Englishman quizzically.

"You know exactly what I mean. You are not without money and that plantation of yours is the best I've seen in the islands. Dammit man, you are a gentleman, which is more than Denison is at times. While he and his son are skulking up in the hills you are down here fighting for the safety of his family. Apart from anything else, the man is a professional drunkard."

What he had seen of Cotterel and his coolness under fire were enough to win his approval as a soldier. He was shrewd enough however to recognise the man as a possible threat to his own political ambitions. Marriage might be just the thing to neutralise him.

"Colonel Gunning" Elija chimed in, "can help to convince Reverend Denison that you are well matched."

"I'll thank you both to mind your own business. I'll do my own courting and if her father won't give us his blessing then I'll marry her without it. You see, Gunning, others may not share your perception. Ask Elija what the Methodists think of me; for all their calling, I'm willing to bet it's not printable."

Gunning glanced across at Cotterel as he lounged, long legs thrust out before him, filthy, unshaven and with a half-empty glass of brandy in his hand, and had to confess he did not present the conventional picture of a gentleman. But then he himself looked little different and he had no doubts as to his own status as an officer and gentleman.

"The others don't know you as I do," argued Elija, "and for that matter you don't know them either. I don't like to speak ill of my superiors but you could hardly put the Reverend Denison in the same class as Doctor Matthews. After what you said to Tui Navatulevu today I should think your differences could soon be settled."

Jason reached for the bottle and refilled his glass before answering.

"Listen closely, friend Elija," he said, a brittle edge to his voice. "I'm not going back on what I told the chief, but don't think I have suddenly become a docile lamb for the church to lead by the nose. What I said hasn't made me a member of the Methodist church: it hasn't made me a member of any church. I can just imagine what Doctor Matthews would say if I became a Roman Catholic — he probably thinks the papists are inferior to the worst cannibals."

Elija was unable to answer; like most Fijians he found the bitter infighting between the Christian sects difficult to comprehend and confusing. He just assumed that those who taught him must be right.

"It's true isn't it?" said Jason pushing him unmercifully. "Look at Vatulevu! You have done all the work yet that drunken old fool Denison is the one who'll receive any credit that's going."

Gunning's memory stirred. He recalled the time he had stood on the deck of the *Elizabeth* and told Captain Bex that the name Cotterel rang a bell with him.

Boston! That was it, Boston — and a Dr Cotterel of Harvard University. As he let the argument continue, he smiled delightedly, it was always helpful to know more of the other man than he thought you did. It was also of some personal satisfaction to know that his memory had not deserted him. It was his memory he had to thank for his reputation for omnipotence.

"That attitude is not going to help when it comes to asking Denison for his daughter's hand," Gunning interjected. "You know, Cotterel, you have such an easy way of solving all your problems. Not only is Denison a snob but he is bound to have a profound respect for a leading theologian like your father.

Jason's eyes narrowed with surprise and suspicion. This languid Englishman was not only a good soldier, he was also a subtle, cunning and dangerous man. "Take care, Gunning," he said with quiet menace, "you are such a knowing dog it will get you killed one of these days. You appear to have made a study of me. Why, I wouldn't know. But I warn you, if my private affairs should suddenly become common knowledge throughout the islands I might just do humanity a service by performing that duty myself."

Elija looked from one to the other, bewildered.

"Come off it, old boy," Gunning seemed quite unconcerned by the threat. "You seem to imagine I've been spying on you or reading your mail or something, when all I have done is make an intelligent guess. When I was in your country I was interviewed by a newspaper interested in my travels. The article stated where I had been and where I was going. I was subsequently visited by a certain Dr William Cotterel who asked me to let him know if I ever ran across his son and heir. It's as simple and innocent as that, I assure you."

"Why haven't you mentioned it before?" asked Jason, angry and unconvinced. Even on the day he had thought himself finally free of his father's shadow it was suddenly there looming over him again.

"To be honest I completely forgot about it until a moment ago," answered Gunning, telling the unvarnished truth for once.

"A theologian, Jason?" asked Elija incredulously.

"Yes," said Jason, cursing Gunning under his breath. Six months ago not a soul in Fiji knew where he had come from or why. Now, it seemed everyone must soon know.

Gunning continued: "You see, Elija, he has nothing to worry about. Doctor Cotterel is a leading member of your church and a very wealthy man to boot. If John Denison knew that, he would fall over himself welcoming Jason into his family."

"I have not seen my father for 15 years and I shall be more than happy if I never see him again. The last thing I would do is use his name for anything. I reckon he feels much the same way about me, only more so."

"That was not the impression I got. He seemed most anxious to find his son again."

"Well his son doesn't feel the same," snapped Jason. "You will be doing me a personal favour if you forget the whole thing. You too, Elija."

"But he's your father, Jason."

"Fifteen years ago that was something he decided to forget. He may have changed but I haven't; it still suits me to forget." Jason looked out of the door. The sun was now quite high in the sky and yet there they were discussing his personal problems when they should have been out hunting the enemy.

He stood. "If we don't start moving, Ma'afu is going to catch us with our pants down. Elija you've done more than enough for a while, go off and sleep somewhere. When you have rested, join us on the ridge opposite Makaluva. Make sure you don't run into any of Ma'afu's men on the way."

Elija nodded sleepily. He would have liked to go with them, but he could hardly keep his eyes open. The mountain had taken more out of him than he cared to admit.

Gunning finished his brandy at a swallow and, corking the bottle with the heel of his hand, pushed what was left into an ammunition bag. He stood, yawned cavernously, and stretched to get the stiffness out of his bones. Then he slung the bag over his shoulder and picked up a rifle from the corner. Jason, waiting for him in the doorway, watched him speculatively.

Gunning gave him a tired but cheerful smile. "Fear not, friend Cotterel" he said. "I may have given my promise to your father but then I am one Englishman who only keeps promises which afford him profit. Your dreadful secret is quite safe with me."

*****

The Tongan delegation which had visited Vatulevu eighteen months previously, failed to suborn Tui Navatulevu's loyalties. Moreover, they had underestimated Jason Cotterel's importance. On the other hand they had spied out the land with efficiency and knew their geography. As the Vatulevu forces drifted deeper into the jungle, strong Tovata columns pushed out from Lomanikaya determined to come to grips with the elusive defenders.

Ma'afu and a third of the able-bodied men stayed to guard the ships and the wounded; 200 more set off across the island towards Korovou while a similar number headed towards Qaraniqio.

The prince realised his position was becoming more untenable by the hour. It seemed impossible that this speck in the middle of the sea had managed to bring him to his knees when far greater armies had disintegrated at the mere sound of his war drums. His men had been decimated, with only a handful of local dead to show for their loss. At each turn he was baffled and humiliated. The kai-Vatulevu were like a wisp of smoke, curling all around, almost asphyxiating him. He advanced and they disappeared, only to return when his back was turned, thicker and stronger than ever, choking the life out of his army.

He had contempt for Fijians and was certain that they were not directing the defence. The white man Cotterel must be the tevoro behind it all. If he ever managed to get his hands on him, the manner of his death would become a legend never to be forgotten.

The homestead, outbuildings, jetty and bridge at Qaraniqio were all left smouldering ruins. Had the Tongans dared take the time, they would have chopped down every coconut palm on the plantation; instead they had to be satisfied with the destruction of a token few nearest to the homestead and burning off the cotton crop. Jason's livestock were saved as they had been driven deep into the jungle at the first sign of the enemy fleet. The Tongan mark would remain for many years but it was only a fraction of what they would have liked to do.

The second column marched through the deserted mission compound on their way to the other side of the island. The mission buildings might have been destroyed had not more sober heads recognised the significance of the cross on top of the church. They burned Korovou village to the ground but, like Lomanikaya, it was an empty gesture. Neither honour nor glory could be gained from the destruction of an empty shell whose owners had fled taking everything of value with them.

The Tongans crossed the island untouched though they knew full well hostile eyes were watching their every step. But the return march was very different. The burning village was the signal for the defenders to close in and the column was sniped at every yard of the way. The marksmen and bowmen were always invisible and sorties into the jungle on either side of the path proved suicidal; no sooner was the punitive group separated from the main war party than dozens of spears and axes sprang up out of the alien soil and the invaders never saw their friends again.

What began as an orderly disciplined withdrawal deteriorated into a rout. None stopped to help the wounded or those too exhausted to move a step further, but those unfortunates did not have long to wait before their worries were over for all time. Their path was lined with invisible and implacable enemies and panic in the fleeing column seemed to sap its strength and will to defend itself. Bullets, spears and arrows spurred them to run the faster.

Between Korovou and the mission 60 men must have fallen. The remainder regrouped near the church but it seemed to them the cross mocked their failure and in frustration and anger they set every building blazing. While they stayed in the mission compound no move was made against them but it needed little imagination to know what awaited them once they moved into the jungle again.

Some wanted to make a stand where they were. But their greater fear was that the remainder of the fleet might sail without them leaving them at the mercy of the kai-Vatulevu and that fear scourged them on again. They pushed scouts ahead and to the sides and tried to give as good as they got but it still took three hours to reach Lomanikaya and their losses were almost as heavy as before.

*****

Had Ma'afu dared brave the reef passages in the dark he would have pulled out there and then. But a heavy wind had sprung up making sailing conditions dangerous, and he could not afford to lose another man or ship. Men in the peak of condition might have managed but he was left with no more than half of the force that had sailed jubilantly from Lakeba and most of those were wounded, exhausted, or with their morale shattered.

Sleep was impossible. The sun no sooner disappeared than a cannon barked in the night and a shot splashed into the sea less than a cable's length from the schooner. Scared that an attack was imminent, the chiefs shook their drugged men awake. Both of the bigger ships blazed off shots in the dark but to no effect for the defenders fired again 15 minutes later from a different position. Ma'afu guessed that they were trying to goad him to the point where he would send a ship after them but he was not to be drawn; he knew that those accursed canoes were sitting out there waiting for such a move.

Torches were lit on the Tovata ships so that their crews could spot any attack. As the never-ending night drew on, the moon came up and revealed a ring of Vatulevu craft sitting like avenging angels on the silvered surface of the lagoon. The moonlight meant they were better targets for the guns on the schooner and sloop but now that they could be seen they kept well out of range.

Just after midnight two canoes detached themselves from the others and sailed straight for the fleet anchored off what was left of the village. In the bows of each a large barrel was strapped to the deck, and a man holding a lighted torch could be seen sitting on the outrigger.

They approached Ma'afu's fleet with the phenomenal speed which only a South Sea outrigger in a strong wind can achieve. Every gun that could be brought to bear opened up but with little effect — they seemed to bear a charmed existence. Then, when they were no more than 50 yards away, their crews suddenly dived overboard and swam out to sea again for all they were worth.

On the canoes came, hundreds of eyes hypnotised by their silent progress. The first exploded in the middle of the fleet with a deafening roar as a hundredweight of gunpowder ignited, though it missed the closest ship. As the second came on every man in the Tovata army sucked in his breath, heart pounding. It passed the schooner, the sloop, one drua then the next, until it was obvious it must collide with the third. Men sprang screaming into the sea and swam madly away from the sailing death machine.

It exploded at the moment of impact with a boom which echoed off the mountainside and on to the farthest horizon. Both hulls of the drua surged out of the water exposing the underneath of the platform for a long moment before it broke in half with a crash of splintering timbers. Men were crushed, others brained by flying timbers, while some died in the water killed by the percussion of the explosion.

Then the gun out on the lagoon fired again, then again, and again. As survivors from the stricken war canoe staggered up the beach the hillside rifles cracked, adding the final diabolical touch to a night they would remember until their dying day.

The defenders' hatred hung over the heads of the Tovata fleet like a thundercloud. Christians prayed to the Lord for deliverance; pagans prayed to the old gods, convinced that their defeat was retribution for the conversion of their leaders to the new faith. In later years, when Ma'afu again tried to raise a force against Vatulevu, none who had endured this night could be induced to return.

With the first faint glimmer of dawn Ma'afu, his face haggard with the bitterness of defeat, gave the orders. All sail was set and the remnants of the once powerful fleet made for the main passage. For the first time in two days no one disputed their progress. And no one saw the Tongan prince again until they reached Lakeba.

*****

Only a handful of defenders, Jason Cotterel among them, remained on the beach to see the enemy retreat like a dog with its tail between its legs. The rest raced madly up the mountainside for vantage points from which they could watch and gloat. Tui Navatulevu was carried shoulder-high by shouting, cheering warriors soon joined by a crowd of deliriously happy women and children.

At Toby Denison's lookout eyrie an impromptu victory feast was under way even before the enemy had cleared the reef. Bonfires were lit, pigs materialised from nowhere to be slaughtered and set cooking. The women, improvising a victory chant and vivid action dance, weaved in and out of their men whose weariness had miraculously evaporated in this intoxicating hour of glory.

Basil Gunning and Toby Denison were set in places of honour beside the chief to drink the ceremonial yaqona of triumph. Gunning wanted nothing more than 12 hours in a comfortable bed; but for all his weariness this was not a moment he would have missed.

For him it was a double victory for his plan had succeeded perfectly: Ma'afu was well and truly defeated. His tremendous loss of face virtually removed him as a serious contender for the throne of Fiji, but he was not so completely destroyed that he would not cause trouble for Cakobau. More Gunning could not ask. If Twyford was doing half so well stirring up the hill tribes of Viti Levu, Fiji would be a British possession before another year was out.

Toby Denison looked about him with a feeling of satisfaction and profound relief. There had been occasions, especially when he watched the villages and the mission go up in flames, when he had known torments of fear. Once he had served his purpose Cotterel had forgotten him and this was something which Toby himself would neither forget nor forgive. It was only at dawn when the kai-Vatulevu came screaming up the mountain that he learnt of the victory — for one hellish moment he had even thought the roaring crowd was Ma'afu's army.

He felt quite heady from the yaqona. He beat his hands to the rhythm of the dance and openly leered at the girls. He had been up on that damned mountain for a whole celibate week but tonight he meant to be huddled up to eager flesh.

As Denison watched the dancers' bodies, Gunning watched him. Toby Denison was a fish out of water in the islands and sooner or later was bound to be up to his neck in trouble. He was the type of person who always blamed others for his misfortunes. When the time came the Colonel would be ready and waiting to take him in hand. He would forge him into a weapon which would strike where he so directed.

But the one person with most justification to rejoice was notable for his absence. Jason stayed on the beach with a handful of others. He could not be fully satisfied that his task was done until the enemy ships were hull-down on the horizon. Only then did he turn from the sea to the hills and an appointment which superseded any celebration.

He walked slowly through the still-smoking mounds of what had once been Lomanikaya village. He knew Qaraniqio must look just as desolate and forlorn. He had seen the smoke and knew that his home was now a charred ruin. In some ways this was a good thing. About to start a new life and a new love it was better that he brought Kate back to a house of her own, a monument to the years of happiness ahead of them, rather than a memorial to the past.

He would build a new and finer house on the ashes of the old. He already had a clear picture in his mind of its long low lines, the deep cool verandahs and the spacious rooms. He would bring stone from the mountain, hardwood from the forest, and furnishings from every corner of the globe. He would build for a dynasty of Cotterels — the Cotterels of Vatulevu.

As Jason slowly climbed the track up into the hills he worked it all out in his mind. Kate's father had to be convinced, not only of the inevitability of their marriage but that he should perform the ceremony as his final act before retiring from the ministry. Otherwise the man would always be an embarrassment to his colleagues and a constant worry for his daughter.

Jason could offer him a comfortable and honourable old age. He would be with his daughter and later his grandchildren; he need never utter a word of Fijian; and if he wanted to drink himself to death he could at least do it in the company of people who understood and who would see to it that he preserved some semblance of pride.

Toby posed a more difficult problem. Jason was sure Kate didn't know her brother was sleeping with her Fijian maids, though everyone else on the island knew. The two girls openly boasted about it in the village and on one occasion they had even come to blows in public on his account.

It was doubtful if Toby realised that the easy love of the islands would soon be a thing of the past — Elija was preaching a new morality, which would sweep innocence away and replace it with the uncompromising ethics of Methodism. If Denison wanted to continue as a libertine he must sail away and find an island free of missionaries.

*****

Ulamila and Aporosa had gone on down the mountain with Lala and any of the wounded who could so much as hobble. All that remained in the caves were the hopeless cases and John Denison sitting alone on a box communing with a fast emptying bottle of his 'heart mixture'. Knowing that sooner or later Jason would come, Kate had no wish to follow the others. When he arrived she wanted to be waiting for him.

Kate saw him before he saw her. He was obviously lost in his own thoughts. Her heart went out to him. She had never believed it possible to love anyone the way she loved Jason. With him beside her, life would be a paradise; had anything happened to him in the fighting she would have been condemned to an eternal death in life.

Jason looked up and saw her. His stride quickened and his face lit up. Kate ran towards him, her arms outstretched. Much later she heard him say, "No more arguments, Kate. I'm going to see your father and we'll be married just as soon as I have a roof over our heads."

"I love you so much, Jason," Kate whispered, pulling his lips down to meet hers. She had no intention of arguing.

Part II

A new flag

19

Long may he reign

THE INTERIOR OF THE CHURCH had been festooned with coloured leaves and coconut fronds; it smacked more of a bazaar than a solemn coronation.

It had annoyed Jason that the traditional Fijian ceremonies to install and consecrate a paramount chief had been dispensed with. He had once attended the installation of the Ka Levu, the paramount chief of the Nadroga people, and had been deeply stirred by the simplicity and profound sincerity of the ritual. Here, the Vunivalu's matanivanua, had been replaced with a European master of ceremonies and the arrangements had taken on a shoddy look because of it.

Outside the church door a flagpole had been erected. At the appropriate moment, to the accompaniment of a 21 gun salute from two signalling guns, the new flag was to be hoisted to mark Fiji's entry into a new era. The flag, a rising sun on a blue background with a golden crown in the top left-hand corner, was the most garish rag Jason had ever clapped eyes on.

There was a guard of honour of Fijians, none of whom were under six foot in height, with polished rifles and shining bayonets.

They looked impressive, or might have had their founder been prepared to leave matters there. But some bright spark had decided they needed military headgear and the same advisor was a Levuka merchant who also happened to have just the thing in stock — a job lot of peaked shakos which once adorned the heads of a British regiment serving in New Zealand. The battered military relics, which had seen every battle since Waterloo, were crammed down on huge mops of Fijian hair which projected around the edges like ridiculous black ruffs. A polished brass plaque on the front of each proclaimed the wearer to be a soldier of Her Majesty's 65th Foot, the Yorkshire (North Riding) Regiment. Was it any wonder they had brought broad grins to the faces of the Europeans present?

The bugler engaged to play the royal fanfare had provided the final touch of farce. Once he had graced a well-known cavalry regiment, but had opted to desert rather than face a charge of robbery with violence. In Levuka he was known simply as 'Drunken Charlie'. Any time of the day or night he was to be found sodden with rum in a back room of the Polynesian Bar. For the price of a bottle of rum, provided you could wake him up in the first place, he would liven up a party with a variety of British army bugle calls.

Fellow planter John Thurston had nudged Jason in the ribs. "Who's the dandy? From the cut of his jib, he looks a trifle out of place among the rest of those pirates."

Jason's eyes widened with surprise. There on the stage, resplendent in dove-grey top hat, beautifully cut coat and matching pantaloons was Basil Gunning! Jason had not seen him since he had left Vatulevu several months before, though he had heard odd rumours of his movements in Victoria, New South Wales, and New Zealand. But there he was, as large as life, surveying the assembly with his usual enigmatic smile and suave charm.

"That's Basil Gunning," Jason replied, "late Colonel, Royal Artillery. I wonder what he's doing with that lot?"

"Trying to add tone to what will undoubtedly soon degenerate into a vulgar brawl," Thurston had suggested acidly.

"Nothing quite so simple, I'm certain of that. Gunning baffles me; deep down there is something he wants out of Fiji. It isn't land and it isn't money, I'm damned if I know what it is. But believe me he needs watching. Behind that smile he is hatching something and I'd dearly love to know what it is."

"You don't sound as if you have much love for the man?"

"I've no reason not to like him, he helped us out when the Tongans invaded Vatulevu."

"Was Gunning there? I never heard that."

"He asked that his name not be mentioned. At the time it seemed reasonable; he wanted to travel around the islands and, if it was known that he had manned the guns at Vatulevu, then the first time he entered Ma'afu's territory he would have faced a death sentence. It was the least we could do. Tui Navatulevu put a tabu on the very mention of his name, that's why you have heard no mention of him."

John Thurston had whistled softly, "Could he make this thing work?"

"I don't know. He is clever and ruthless enough, but if he has some secret motive of his own he could also be damned dangerous."

They had no time for more; the lali had begun to boom proclaiming the approach of the Vunivalu. Someone stood Charlie upright for the fanfare but it was soon obvious that they hadn't sobered him up enough. He began with the call to charge, which ran on into a wavering mess-call and, once started, it had taken a well-placed fist to stop him.

Ratu Cakobau, preceded by a Fijian bearing his war club mace-like, had entered the church. He wore the full dress uniform of a British admiral; in his right hand he held a naked sword and in his left he carried a large Bible.

The snigger, begun by the ridiculous fanfare had been chopped off by the sheer presence of the man. He had stalked through the crowd, up the steps, to the dais and the throne. The sun streaming in through the windows had glinted wickedly on the naked sword and reminded those who wished to laugh that they were about to invest him with temporal powers of life and death over them all.

Nor had Cakobau missed that snigger. There had been a hard look about his eyes which had seemed to say, "You white men think to mock my majesty but remember I only endure this farce to reach the throne. Once I am firmly seated, beware!"

Ratu Cakobau's secretary, Samuel St John, an American trader, advanced with the crown set on a velvet pillow. In front of Jason there had been an angry buzz from the assembled Fijian chiefs on seeing the European stand beside the throne with his head higher than that of the King. By Fijian custom it had been a terrible breach of respect.

It had not been St John's behaviour that appalled Jason, but the crown itself. The settlers had been passing it from one to the other, laughing and joking about it and he and Thurston had examined it closely before the ceremony commenced. It had a rough wooden frame wrapped with gold paper and was studded with pieces of coloured glass from the penny jewellery sold by the traders. The carpenter commissioned to make it had charged the noble sum of £4 for his masterpiece.

A Methodist minister, not Matthews who had refused to take part, led the congregation in a long-winded prayer for the prosperity of the realm and the safety of the monarch. Next, St John took over and read a preamble and oath of allegiance, the people to the King and the King to the constitution. As the ceremony dragged on and on the Europeans shuffled and fidgeted. It had been stifling hot and sweaty in the crammed church. A few had openly pulled out flasks for a quick nip and no one made a move to stop them.

Ratu Cakobau made no formal assent to the oath, he merely nodded curtly at his minister. St John stepped forward and without further ado the Vunivalu grasped the tawdry crown in both hands and set it firmly on his head. If anything, it looked more ridiculous than the guards' shakos.

The lali sounded, the guns began to fire the salute; Drunken Charlie sounded the reveille; the flag broke at the top of the mast; and then, to Jason's horror, the crowd had tittered. It began not in the audience but among the Ministers of State; from the grin on Gunning's face he appeared to have been the one responsible. Infectious, it had caught and spread, threatening to break into unrestrained laughter.

The King — he now had some claim to the title — had heaved himself to his feet. Again, his immense dignity and genuinely regal presence had transcended the farce and his subjects were hushed into silence. For once in his life, St John did the right thing at the right time; he jumped to the dais steps and waving his hat in the air, he shouted, "God save your Majesty! Long live your Majesty!"

The crowd had gone wild. Against a background of the booming guns and lali they had laughed, shouted and cheered till the rafters shook with the noise. Cakobau had been crowned King of Fiji.

*****

Jason had been choked by the most terrible anger. Those buffoons and ignorant scum had turned a noble concept into a coarse joke. Through the waving hats and arms he had seen the King making ready to leave, the cold expression on his face unaltered. It was as if he had been apart from and oblivious to all that had happened. So long as that calculating mind had lost none of its subtlety and cunning, the fawning, jeering white men might well find they had caught a tiger by the tail.

All the way back from Bau to Levuka Jason had seethed. He had been in no mood to face either Kate or the prosy Mrs Matthews. Instead he had made straight for MacDonald's Hotel. There, sitting alone at a table, Jason had proceeded to dull the memory of the day with rum. The look on his face had been sufficient to deter any from joining him. The few who did throw a greeting in his direction had been rewarded with a noncommittal grunt or an appraisal full of such contempt and challenge that they had wisely decided to take their custom to a more convivial corner of the verandah.

From the laughter at other tables it seemed the farcical coronation would be a source of amusement for Levukaites for months to come. There had been nothing funny about it; the whole fiasco had been nauseating. Was this company of drunken fools representative of the white man's world, the same world that he was throwing his son into head-first? Even if he had been blind to it before, the coronation on Bau had demonstrated what his fellow white men thought of Fijians.

Would the boy be humiliated and treated as an untouchable or, because he had money, would the tricksters fawn upon him and pervert him with the vices of their world? As drink followed drink he had come to the unpalatable decision that Aporosa would be better off if he remained on Vatulevu where his family would love him and his people accord him the respect that was his due.

His bottle of rum emptied, Jason had got to his feet determined to seek Kate and tell her of his decision to cancel the Sydney arrangements. There had been hardly a sway in his gait and he had said goodnight to MacDonald without the faintest slur to his speech.

Those who did not know him would have said Jason Cotterel was stone-cold sober, but his old cronies of the whaling days would have made a very different assessment. Jason realised he was drunk and in a fighting mood.

Then, just as he had been about to step out on to the muddy street, a party of Europeans entered laughing uproariously. "I'll never forget when he put that bloody crown on his head," a big burly German chortled. "Funniest thing I ever see. I think I die laughing." He was brushing past Jason when he was stopped in his tracks by iron fingers, which gripped and dug into his shoulder. He was swung around and thrown with a crash against the door.

"Who are you talking about, fat-face?" Jason had snarled in quiet, but savage tones.

"Here lay off, Cotterel!" said another of the group. "What do you think you're doing? Leave Schwartz alone, he's done nothing to you."

Jason had looked at the speaker and his companions, as if he had suddenly been forced to notice slime beneath a stone. "Done nothing to me! The scum in this town have done more damage to me and Fiji today than your pea-sized brains will ever comprehend."

"Oh, come off it," the man responded. "We were just laughing about old Cackaboo acting the part of the prince. You were there, you saw …" With that, Jason's fist had smashed his lips against his teeth knocking him backwards into the stinking mud of the street.

Jason had stood waiting for the rush of the others. But though he was outnumbered three to one, his face had held such menace that they backed off. "But gentlemen, don't say you are scared," he challenged. The man on the ground slowly sat up, shaking his head and feeling his jaw. Blood was running down his face and he spat out two broken teeth.

"Have any of you anything else you want to say about King Cakobau?" He turned to the German, "What about you, Schwartz?"

That worthy shook his head, the fat of his jowls wobbling with fierce denial. "You'll pay for this, Cotterel, Goddamn you."

"Why not now? Shall I fight you all with one hand tied behind my back?" Jason wanted to work off his spleen in a brawl, but they made no move. He had stared them down contemptuously and then with a scornful and somewhat disappointed laugh he had brushed past them.

*****

As he and Kate watched the *Elizabeth* grow smaller and smaller in the distance, Jason, recalled the scene at MacDonald's on the night of Ratu Cakobau's coronation and felt rather ashamed of himself. He had acted like a loud-mouthed bully. He could hardly point a finger at others if he could behave no better.

Kate Cotterel's thoughts mirrored those of her husband. She would never forget Mavis Matthew's outraged dignity when Jason arrived home in an advanced state of intoxication. The very idea of drunkenness in the mission house was scandalous.

As if that had not been enough, Jason had tried to start an argument about Aporosa. Kate had sensed this building up for several days — since they had arrived in Levuka to be exact. She did not intend her son's education to be placed in jeopardy because of the questionable activities of European blackguards. Kate had sympathy for Jason's attitude, but having looked after an alcoholic father she also knew there could be no profit gained by arguing with him when he was in his cups. She had bundled him unceremoniously off to bed.

Dear Dr Matthews! When Mavis would have read Kate a homily on the terrible dangers of the demon drink, he had looked up from his book, marking his place with one finger. "Will you kindly shut up, woman!" he had snapped sharply. "You don't know what you are talking about." This, from a husband who in 20 years of marriage had never spoken a cross word, left the well-meaning lady speechless.

The next morning, when a pale and somewhat chastened Jason had suggested that they drop their plan to send Aporosa to Sydney and instead take him back to the island with them, Kate had flown into a well-rehearsed rage. Her husband had been completely taken aback by the hurricane he had unleashed.

"Stop talking nonsense," she had stormed at him in the privacy of their bedroom. "Have you no faith in yourself as a father or are you deliberately trying to insult me? Have I been so poor a mother to your son! Is he so lacking in character that Sydney will transform him into one of those layabouts from MacDonald's whose company you appear to prefer to my own?"

The last was a blow below the belt. The astonished Jason had gestured frantically at the wall, an eggshell-like partition separating their bedroom from that of their hosts. "Keep your voice down, Kate," he had implored her.

"I will not be silenced."

"Well if you will only listen for a moment ..."

"Listen? I have been listening and I have heard nothing but nonsense. Aporosa has been brought up in a good home, he is a fine boy and will make a fine man, every bit as fine as his father. You seem to think that he doesn't know the difference between right and wrong. What sort of man will you make of him if he is hidden away on Vatulevu for the rest of his life? I will not let you deprive him of the opportunities to which his intelligence entitles him."

"For God's sake be reasonable, Kate ..." Jason began again, but Kate who had put a great deal of thought into this, the first real argument of their married life, had refused to let him say another word.

"Don't use blasphemous language in front of me," she scolded. "And as for me being reasonable, you are the one who should be reasonable, Jason Cotterel. Aporosa is still a child. He will be in a boarding school which caters specifically for the sons of gentlemen, the best school in New South Wales. Do you imagine his schoolmasters will allow him to roam the Sydney wharves? If you had your way he would spend his learning years fishing on the reef with his Fijian cousins. Is that how you would educate him to carry out his duties as their chief."

"Well ..." Jason's resistance had begun to crumble and Kate had swiftly followed up her advantage.

"It is all settled, Jason, and we are not going to change our plans now," she said, making the decision for them both. "When Peter Bex sails he is to take Aporosa with him. I am not prepared to discuss the matter further."

Poor, dazed Jason had succumbed. Now, as the *Elizabeth* showed hull-down on the horizon, she was the one who was crying. Jason held her in the circle of his arms his lips against her hair.

"Come on, darling, no more crying. It's time for us to go home."

He took out his own handkerchief and dried her tears and kissed her. Kate was a tall woman, but she was dwarfed by her giant of a husband. She raised her hand to his cheek and when he smiled she drew comfort from his strength.

"Let's go home quickly," she urged. "I am sick of Levuka."

Jason called to the two kai-Vatulevu crewmen in the bows to get the anchor aboard and began to unfurl the sails himself.

"It wouldn't worry me if I never saw the place again," he said.

"We have been away from home far too long," Kate agreed. She pictured her beautiful home on its promontory overlooking the sea and was eager to rid her nostrils of the noisome smells of Levuka and once again feel clean and wholesome. "I am sure Lala will have spoilt Ulamila terribly while we have been gone"

"'Mila is the least of my worries," laughed Jason. It was the first time Kate had heard him laugh naturally for days and she gave a great sigh of relief — her world was returning to normal. "What worries me is that your father will have finished off all my brandy and that wayward brother of yours sold the plantation to a passing trader."

*****

King Cakobau had been on the throne for three months when the hill tribes raided along the Ba River. Four plantations were burnt out, the European owners their wives and families and all of their labourers massacred. No survivors were ever found but there was ample evidence that the bodies of the victims had been eaten. Fijian villages friendly to the white men were devastated, the men butchered and the women raped and herded off into the hills.

Scouts entering the area in the wake of the raiding parties, found a few women and children who had miraculously escaped but they were too crazed with terror to tell a coherent story.

From the other side of Viti Levu a party, headed by a young English missionary, the Reverend Thomas Baker, made its way up the Rewa and Wainimala rivers and into the hills from which the Sigatoka river sprang. Their task was to ascertain whether the hill tribes were ready for evangelism; but had they known what was happening in Ba they might have come to a conclusion without bothering to leave the coast.

Baker was an unassuming, rather colourless young man, but he fervently believed in his calling and had a genuine affection for the people of Fiji. He went quietly and innocently about his investigations, each day moving deeper and deeper into the hills, never dreaming that he was about to upset a cauldron which would scald the country for a decade to come.

In Nabutautau, chief village of the fierce Navatusila people he was attacked from behind, the pineapple-club smashing the bones of his head into a hundred splinters and killing him instantly. Mercifully, he went to join the long list of Christian martyrs without time enough to know what had happened.

Baker's body was dismembered, sharp bamboo knives being used to cut through the sinews and bone. Each part was wrapped in special leaves, tabu for all but human flesh, and then steamed slowly in an oven dug in the ground. Afterwards, parcels of the hot meat were dispatched to each of the villages in the unholy alliance of hill tribes which was scourging the coastal plains. With every morsel of white missionary flesh they ate the guilt was spread and the alliance welded more strongly together.

When the news reached the coast, the tribal bards composed a lament, which was sung to a slow solemn chant.

Oh dead is Misiveka,
They killed him on the road
And then they ate him, boots and all.

20

Shangri-La

Vatulevu came through the 1867–1868 hurricane season relatively unscathed though storms battered many parts of the island group. The kai-Vatulevu maintained that their history, which was handed down from father to son in the form of chants, contained no record of a hurricane ever striking the island. Before the missionaries came this was considered to be a particular blessing bestowed upon the island by Degei, the supreme god of wind and weather; now they gave special thanks to Jehovah for their immunity.

When Tui Navatulevu saw the plans for the new plantation house at Qaraniqio with its 18 inch thick walls he scoffed at his friend, but that did not make Jason alter his specifications. The thick walls gave a wonderful coolness to the house and, as Jason told Kate, it was pure good luck that Vatulevu had never been hit by a hurricane when other islands were regularly lashed. "One of these days we shall get our share and when it's over this house will be standing and the Cotterels will be safe and sound inside."

Rumours of the troubles on Viti Levu drifted in but Jason refused to listen. He was so busy; he could submerge himself in his work and his family and forget that the rest of Fiji existed. He took tremendous pleasure out of anything he created with his own sweat and the skill of his hands. Part of himself went into everything he did.

The house was his pride and joy. The sight of it welcoming him home each evening gave him a special feeling of warmth and contentment. The bridge and the jetty destroyed by the Tongans had been rebuilt stronger than before. Jason was no longer building to serve immediate needs, he was building for endurance and where possible for beauty. The finished products would have done credit to skilled craftsmen, let alone one untrained man and his raw helpers.

Kate pulled her husband's leg unmercifully about the way he would stand for hours in the evening admiring his own handiwork. "You'll have to rename the plantation, 'Cotterel's Pride'," she laughed. But equally she could have renamed Jason, 'Kate's Pride', she was as proud of her husband as he was of his creations.

She had her own place in the scheme of things. In her evening prayers Kate never forgot to thank the Lord for the happiness and deep sense of reward and satisfaction which each day brought. On the one occasion Kate had seen the old house before the Tongans razed it to the ground she had thought it comfortable if perhaps a little too spartan and masculine. But the phoenix, which had risen from the ashes was a real family home, softened by extra touches which only a woman could add.

The gardens were her special preserve. Apart from the heavy digging, everything was the result of her own efforts. Lala and the other Fijian girls also liked gardening but their ideas seldom coincided with those of their mistress. One of Kate's few complaints was that she no sooner took on a new trainee than the girl tired of the work and returned to the village. The two girls who had come to her when she first she arrived in Vatulevu were both mothers now, their children bearing an uncomfortable likeness to her brother Toby. She now made sure that any girl working on Qaraniqio was kept well away from him.

Peter Bex brought her flower and vegetable seed from New South Wales. Most were disappointing failures but with tender nurturing she produced carrots and cabbage to augment the local vegetables, most of which were starchy and to Kate's taste rather uninteresting.

English flowers were out of the question and her garden consisted mainly of plants with multicoloured leaves. With Peter Bex's help, even this problem was well in hand. Other captains who were friends of his had promised to bring tropical flowers, especially orchids, back from their voyages to the Dutch Indies, the Malays and the Philippines. If half of what had been promised actually arrived, Kate would one day have a garden to rival any in the South Pacific.

Whenever work permitted, Kate rode out to see what Jason and the others were doing on the plantation. Apart from the stumps of a few felled coconut palms, hardly a trace remained of the Tongan damage. Young replacement palms were shooting forth strong healthy fronds; five more years and Ma'afu would be but an unpleasant memory.

Most of the palms were now in full production and it took Jason and his men all their time to keep up, collecting the nuts, pressing the kernels for oil, and making barrels ready for the next visit of the *Elizabeth*.

Jason had heard of a new drying process being used by the Godeffroy Company in islands to the north of Fiji. They shipped dried kernel, which they called copra, and in this way did away with the expense, labour and time wasted in processing and shipping oil. As soon as he had time to investigate the matter properly he hoped to convert his own production to this method.

The long staple, 'Sea Island' cotton they grew was good quality and still their main cash crop, but the market fluctuated so sharply that Jason never knew from one cargo to the next what price he would receive. He knew too it was only a matter of time before the Southern States recovered from the Civil War and flooded the market with a cheap product against which the Fiji planter could never complete.

And so he was seeking alternative crops. He had trial areas of both coffee and tea but they needed a cheap and plentiful labour supply. Sugarcane was another possibility. Some said the syrup from Fiji cane would not crystallise properly; but Jason was sure it would if handled properly. Even so, the local canes were not the best varieties and he had asked Bex to bring him as many overseas canes as he and his friends could find. He also needed a crushing-mill, but that would have to wait until he had sufficient capital.

By using Qaraniqio as security, Jason could have raised a loan in Levuka or Sydney, but as he had built the place up with nothing more than sweat and friendship he saw no merit in changing. Other planters, some of them good hard-working men, could have been in the same position as himself but for crippling burdens of debt. As soon as the first hurricane, crop failure or fall in price came along they collapsed, whereas he could ride out anything.

One of Jason's hobbyhorses was self-sufficiency — if it had not been for Kate, who quickly brought him down to earth, he could have been a real bore on the subject. He wanted Qaraniqio to be a whole world unto itself.

It produced the vegetables for his house and root vegetables to feed the labour. Soon they would have sugar and tea. The sea provided fish and turtles, Kate ran poultry and he was building a piggery in which he hoped to cross the local bush animals with imported breeding stock. His cattle were increasing, goats roamed under the coconut palms, and a mare Bex had given Kate as a wedding present had foaled. There were times when he felt like an Old Testament patriarch watching his flocks increase.

He also stuck rigidly to his principle that everything done on his own property should be duplicated in the communal plantations of the Fijians. That meant he had to be everywhere at once, leading, instructing, teaching and working harder than any other man on the island.

The people were happy to work for him, both at Qaraniqio and in their own fields, but often their idea of work and Jason's did not coincide. For short, sharp efforts Fijians had no equal; they would have moved mountains had Jason asked it of them. But when it came to a sustained and rather boring job, such as keeping a crop free of weeds, they were inclined to wander off and sleep in the shade of a tree. It was only Jason's persuasive tongue and personal example which lured them back again; even so he rarely got anyone to work for more than three days out of the week. As he explained to his father-in-law, it was understandable when you considered that the men had to go fishing or had other housebuilding chores to attend to.

In the new missionary era Sunday was Na Siga Tabu, the day of rest when no work was done. Kate normally rode over to the mission with Ulamila up before her, for the morning service, while Jason's sabbath observance consisted of pottering around the house or sitting back with his feet up, smoking his pipe and reading a book.

Tui Navatulevu berated Jason for being too easy with the people. He favoured more direct methods. Having been given an order that a job should be done his men either obeyed or suffered the kuita. They smiled behind their hands knowing full well that their chief was usually the first to become bored, and would more likely than not order the cessation of work in favour of more amusing pastimes such as yaqona drinking, dancing, or singing.

Even so, had Jason asked that the kuita be used it would have been, but he never used threats as a goad. For this reason, and to show that the Fijians could keep pace with any white man, the kai-Vatulevu, working at their own pace and using their own methods, usually did what Jason required of them.

*****

Jason had given strict instructions that he was to be informed the first moment Kate thought herself pregnant. Having lost one wife in childbirth he did not intend to have it happen again.

Nevertheless, Kate kept the news from him for she knew how he would react. Lala knew — it was impossible to hide anything from her — especially something like morning sickness. For a while the two of them kept Kate's pregnancy a secret, but eventually the other housegirls put two and two together and then the news was right around the island. Jason's first knowledge of his own wife's pregnancy came when Ratu Seru, the Tui's brother, congratulated him. Jason almost exploded.

Qaraniqio rocked with the most fearful arguments. Jason forbade Kate the use of her mare and, when she rebelled, had it taken to the southern tip of the island beyond her reach. After three days of her stony silence, he brought the horse back again.

Had Jason had his way, Kate would have been confined to her bed for the next seven months and it was only when Lala and a delegation of the other women talked some sense into him that he agreed that exercise might not be such a bad idea.

He foresaw Kate promising to do as he told her and then gallivanting around behind his back, so when Jason went to work her father took over and proved an even stricter watchdog than her husband. Apart from light jobs in the house or about the garden, the most exercise he would allow was a gentle walk down to the jetty and back.

It was about this time that Kate's brother, Toby, decided to shake the sands of Vatulevu from his shoes. It was Jason who brought the news.

"*Albatross* is back from Levuka, Kate," he said with such a worried look on his face that Kate immediately imagined that there must have been a severe drop in the price of coconut oil. "It was Ratu Seru who brought her back. Toby refused to come. He told Ratu Seru that he is never coming back."

To his surprise Kate only laughed. "Oh! Is that all? From your face I thought something terrible had happened."

"Well I'm not worried if you're not," Jason, who had never had much of an opinion of Toby, confessed. "I must say you take his disappearance very calmly."

"It is high time he struck out on his own. I've told him any number of times that he should get a plantation on one of the islands or try his luck in New Zealand or one of the colonies in Australia. Here he clings to your coat-tails and, if I know my brother, your success makes him jealous and envious. He has to fend for himself sooner or later."

"What will he do for money?"

"I presume father must have given him some. He's not likely to have left with empty pockets."

It was true that Toby Denison had not left with empty pockets, but it was not money given to him by his father. He had stolen Denison senior's cash box with more than £300-worth of Maria Theresa dollars in it. John Denison was furious; forgetting his missionary training he cursed his son roundly in highly unclerical language and swore that as of that day he disowned him completely. Both Kate and Jason tried to soften the shock and encourage him to take a more forgiving attitude, but he was adamant.

"May I suffer everlasting damnation if that misbegotten whelp sees another penny from me, either during my lifetime or after my death. And I'll thank you, Katherine, not to mention his name in my hearing again. I no longer have a son."

*****

Having disinherited his own son, John Denison took a sudden interest in Kate's unborn child. He was certain that it would be a boy — he petitioned the Lord on that subject daily — and Kate and Jason promised that if it should be a son, it would be named after him, John Denison Cotterel.

He had taken only a perfunctory interest in his own children, but this grandchild, his namesake, suddenly became the very centre of his conversation, his hopes and his dreams. Kate had only to exert herself and she was immediately execrated as an oath-breaker and an infanticide. It got so far beyond a joke that Kate finally had to implore Jason to talk to her father; he tried but to little effect.

John Denison was not the man he was when he arrived in Fiji. He had discovered he was a fish out of water as a missionary. He had found his escape in a brandy bottle and was only rescued from inevitable discovery and disgrace by his daughter's marriage to Jason Cotterel and her demand that he retire from the ministry.

Now, for the first time since his wife had run away, he felt a measure of contentment. He lived in a comfortable, civilised home and he had servants to attend to his needs; his daughter to fuss over him should he be ill; and, although deliveries from Auckland or Sydney were few and far between, sufficient funds to buy anything he wanted.

He was no longer enslaved by his own woes and worries, his scapegrace son was off his hands — for good and all, he hoped. He even had time to think of other people for a change. He no longer drank as much even though, now that he had retired from the ministry, he could have drunk himself insensible every day without the slightest sense of guilt had he wanted to. He could afford it, and in any event his son-in-law kept a stock of drink which was always open to him.

Kate had wanted to lock the liquor away, but Jason had warned her off convinced that Denison would sort himself out in his own good time. Sure enough, the absence of restriction somehow lessened his need for the bottle. He still drank, most likely more than was really good for him, but he no longer finished each day in an alcoholic haze.

He complained occasionally about his heart to draw attention to himself when he felt neglected and as an excuse for the fact that 'he toiled not, neither did he spin.' Most days he just sat in a shady spot, dreaming and awaiting the advent of his grandson.

John Denison did not put it into words, but he was proud of his son-in-law. He had only to look about him, or listen to Kate and Jason discussing progress and future plans over their evening drink, to realise how able the man was.

He entirely discounted Jason's children by his Fijian wife, they were nice enough but, unfortunately, they were of mixed race. The only child who mattered was being carried in Kate's womb. That child would one day inherit a fine estate that was all his father's making.

Denison would have liked to see Jason take office in Cakobau's Cabinet, not merely because he would have liked John Denison Cotterel to have a cabinet minister for a father, but because he genuinely believed Jason to be the ablest man in Fiji. He raised the matter once but was abruptly choked off by Jason. That alone would not have stopped him pursuing the matter further had Kate not warned him that one more word on that subject would cause her to change the name of the baby.

He tried to banish his own son from his mind. Twice, letters came begging for money. It seemed that Toby was always on the brink of becoming a millionaire;

the only factor restraining him being the lack of £1,000 or so in cold cash. John Denison answered his son's letters, but instead of sending a draft on his Sydney banker he enclosed a demand for the immediate return of the money stolen from his strongbox. Whatever money he had (and he never disclosed just how much he was worth) was going to his grandson.

*****

For all Jason and John Denison's fears, Kate's pregnancy followed a normal course. At one stage the baby seemed never to be coming; then — it annoyed Kate that it should be on a day when she had decided that she and the servants would spring-clean the house from top to bottom — it started, a sharp stiletto-like pain which made her clutch her side and stand paralysed with surprise. Lala, who had been hovering all morning waiting for just such a sign, helped her into a chair and sent one of the girls flying for Jason.

"There now, Marama, you will be alright," she said soothingly. "There is nothing to worry about. It is just your son telling you that the time has come for him to take his place in the world. We will get you to bed and before you know what has happened it will be over." The old Fijian woman's unconcern and air of competence stilled any qualms Kate might have had.

The housegirls, all unmarried and supposedly virgins, did not take things as calmly. Nor did John Denison who came hurrying in to find out what the uproar was about. He only added to the excited babble until Lala and Kate exploded in unison and sent him packing to his own quarters with instructions not to appear again until Jason arrived. They did not have to wait long; the lathered flanks and heaving chest of his horse were proof of a frantic gallop from the fields to the house. But he was no more help than his father-in-law had been.

"Jason, stop panicking and being silly," said Kate. "It only makes me feel worse with you and father going on the way you are. I wish Lala hadn't sent for you at all. Lala and I shall get on very well; we don't need any interference from men."

"But I can't just stand around doing nothing, Kate!" he wailed helplessly. At that moment Kate had a pain harder and longer than any before it. Jason might have faced the charging Tongans coolly but he went deathly pale at the sight of his wife in the agony of birth. "Good God above, Kate," he whispered anxiously.

"Turaga, this is no place for you," said Lala pushing him ahead of her out of the bedroom. "The Marama doesn't want you in here with her. If she sees you are worried she will worry herself."

"Is there anything she should worry about?"

"Nothing at all. You men are all lialia, stupid. The Marama is a fine healthy woman. You do not worry when a healthy bulumakau gives birth to a young one, nor should you worry now. If you want something to do, ride to the mission and bring that kai-valagi woman back with you. She has had plenty of children and so she may be able to help. Anyway, when the pains really come the Marama will want another white face near her."

"But we haven't got time for that," argued Jason. "It will be late before I get back with the missionary's wife."

"Ah you men! You think you know everything when in truth you haven't the brains of a crab. This is her first baby; it takes a long time the first one. We shall be lucky if it is born before tomorrows sun rises."

"Go on, Jason," Kate called from the bedroom. The pain had passed away and she felt alright again. "Do as Lala says. But I shall be furious if I hear you made Helen Simpson rush."

Jason poked his head into the bedroom again. Kate was lying comfortably back on the pillows as if having a baby was an every day matter for her.

"Are you sure you'll be alright, darling?"

"Of course I will," said Kate reassuringly, though, having overheard Lala say that the pains might go on until dawn the next day had made her feel a lot less assured than she made out. "You get Helen and, before you go see father and impress on him that he is not allowed inside this room until you get back. If he does, I'll name our son after the first Roman Catholic saint I can think of."

Jason accepted his banishment with bad grace. The following 12 hours were a nightmare he would not forget. It began with an attempt to teach a straight-laced Methodist preacher's wife how to straddle a horse, and finished with a night-long drinking session with his father-in-law enlivened by Kate's screams from the bedroom and violent rows between himself and John Denison.

The housegirls came and went with linen and hot water; Lala and Helen Simpson were never seen at all; but every time an involuntary cry or low groan was heard through the intervening wall Jason could only pray that they knew what they were about.

The labour was long though not unreasonably so, and Kate was young and strong; she would have bitten back her cries but the two women in attendance insisted she scream her head off if she felt so inclined. She was in no condition to argue with her mentors; she pushed when they said push and when the terrible pains came she found relief in her yells. As Helen Simpson said, it might be raising the hair on the back of the men's necks, but then it never hurt to let men know just what a woman had to go through at such a time. For Kate anything was justified, so long as it would provide Jason with a son.

At around three o'clock in the morning, John Denison was accusing Jason of murdering his daughter and it was on the tip of Jason's tongue to tell his father-in-law that he was nothing but a brandy-sodden, useless old Limey, when there was a long thin wail from the bedroom followed by women's excited laughter. The cry came again. It was not Kate, it had to be the baby. Both men were on their feet tense and waiting.

After what seemed an age the door opened and Lala emerged carrying a small bundle in her arms. "Turaga, here is your son," she announced proudly.

"To hell with my son, how is my wife?" thundered Jason. Without even pausing to look at the baby, he barged past into the bedroom to where Kate lay, pale and tired with dark shadows beneath her eyes but for all that very pleased with herself.

The grandfather could think of nothing but the boy. Breathing brandy fumes over the little red bundle, he kept saying over and over again. "John Denison Cotterel! John Denison Cotterel! Now there's a name to conjure with eh? John Denison Cotterel!"

21

The finger writes …

HORACE TWYFORD WAS WRITING his annual report to Lord Kimberly, head of the Foreign Office. It was a hot sticky day, but as he was working at something which gave him satisfaction, he was unconscious of the fact that his shirt stuck to his back and his prickly heat rash itched. Writing reports allowed him to feel that he was not just a forgotten cog in the world's largest diplomatic machine. Lost in the beauty of his own copperplate flourishes he could fool himself that Lord Kimberly read every word with insatiable interest.

Once the report was on its way, he would again admit to himself that he was just Horace Twyford, a rather poor tool manipulated by some junior clerk in London. But for the moment he was the Ambassador reporting to his chief on the affairs of a foreign country.

Her Britannic Majesty's Consulate,
Levuka,
Fiji Islands. 1st. January 1869

My Lord,

I have the honour to submit for your approval my report on affairs in these Fiji Islands for the period covering the year 1868.

Generally speaking it has been an eventful year and much has happened which may have a lasting affect on the future stability and prosperity of the whole Group. The first attempt at constitutional government has collapsed. Cakobau, self-styled King of Fiji, led a campaign against rebellious hill tribes which ended in a complete debacle. White settlers continue to arrive by the shipload, creating problems for which there is no local machinery to provide a solution. Levuka, the principal town, continues to be a den of unrelieved iniquity and vice and is now become the centre of an extensive labour traffic which amounts to little more than a slave trade. I am more than ever convinced that unless the islands are swiftly annexed to the British Empire chaos and anarchy will result.

1 European Settlers: There are now more than 1,200 persons of

European blood in the Fiji Group, of whom almost ninety percent are British subjects. Of these over 600 live in Levuka.

For the most part they are men and women of the very worst types, fugitives from justice, confidence tricksters, army deserters and prostitutes. Levuka abounds with brothels and what honest women there are dare not walk abroad alone by day or night. Every second building is a rum shop and men are openly pistoled to death in drunken quarrels. The whole population is contemptuous of Cakobau's police officers, who will ignore the most heinous crimes for the price of a bottle of rum. The defeat of the so-called royal forces by the hill tribes has done nothing to improve their standing.

The planters have withdrawn all support from the Government, refusing to pay taxes or recognise the authority of Cakobau's officials. This attitude is particularly widespread in the settlements bordering the Nadi and Ba Rivers on Viti Levu which have felt the full impact of the raiding tribesmen. I myself, as Her Majesty's Consul, have encouraged them in this stand, pointing out that the so-called King of Fiji and his ministers have not been recognised by Her Majesty's Government, and also that by supporting Cakobau they endanger their British citizenship and any rights they may have to British protection. I have effectively put a stop to British subjects joining Cakobau's army by bringing the provisions of the Foreign Enlistment Act to their notice.

2 Fijian Affairs: Cakobau has dismissed all of his ministers for their failure to win the backing of the Europeans and now rules as an absolute despot. After his defeat by the hill tribes he has even lost many of his Fijian allies.

The campaign in the hills was mounted as a two column affair, one coming in from the north led by Cakobau himself and the other by one of his European advisors, Colonel BS Gunning, striking from the south. The rebels appear to have been well-armed and well-informed as to Cakobau's movements. The Government forces were ambushed at a place called Nabutautau and suffered heavy losses — thirteen of the chiefs allied to Cakobau were killed, plus an unknown number of rank and file, most likely going into hundreds. Cakobau was forced to retire, his forces being harried by marksmen and skirmishing parties all the way. The attack from the south had some initial success, but at the crucial moment the Namosi tribesmen deserted and went over to the enemy. This column suffered casualties amounting to 61 men killed and 15 wounded in the main engagement and these numbers were further increased by skirmishing during the retreat.

> The whole campaign was shamefully conducted and has done much damage to Cakobau's reputation and has shown up his inherent weakness to those who might have joined him. This man who purports to be King is really no more than a petty chieftain, and an inept one at that.

Twyford laid down his pen for a moment and gazed out on to the verandah. He could have written that last part of his report 18 months before, when he and Gunning had planned it on that very same verandah. Gunning had smuggled in the guns and he, the British Consul, had seen to it that a tame chieftain was versed in the guerrilla tactics he should employ against the columns.

Gunning had insisted that the rebels follow the same pattern as had defeated the Tongans in their attempt on Vatulevu; and in the maze of razorbacked ridges and narrow jungle tracks it had proved perfect. With Gunning as his military advisor Cakobau did not stand a chance. The English soldier was meticulous about covering his tracks, but a thorough investigation would have found his imprint on every mishap right down to the final humiliating defeat.

What amazed Twyford was Gunning's patience and terrible tenacity. Pushing Fiji into the British Empire was a long drawn out process of which he himself was heartily sick and tired, but Gunning seemed to have lost none of his determination to play the role of Stamford Raffles to the South Seas.

Since Baker's ghastly murder and the massacre of European families along the Ba River, the Consul could no longer sleep at night. He still wanted to see Fiji painted British red on the maps, but he no longer wished to be the instrument which brought it about. The day he had sent his messengers into the hills he had issued death warrants for hundreds of people. The more his mind dwelt on his own part in it, the less the end seemed to justify the means. He had tried to extricate himself but it was too late; the colonel had made that painfully clear.

"I am beset by fools and cowards, I see." His tone had been soft, but it carried an explicit threat. "You sit and weep over a few miserable worms who have been killed as if you never realised it was bound to happen. At least be an honest rogue, Twyford. Do you imagine an omelette such as ours can be made without breaking eggs? Who were these people anyhow? A pious ninny, and a bunch of fugitives from justice who would have been hanged when we take over, or savages every bit as vicious and primitive as those who killed them."

"The only useful thing they ever did was die. The London news-sheets loved it: 'Missionary Murdered and Eaten by Cannibals in the Fiji Islands'. This place has never had so much attention. Meetings called by bishops, pamphlets by the dozen, questions asked in both Houses of Parliament. When this place becomes a British possession a memorial should be erected to Baker, the man whose succulent bones made the whole thing possible."

The Consul had felt physically ill; the memory made his hand tremble. As always, Gunning had the answers and they had been telling and humiliating.

"You have a short memory, Horace," he said in his silky voice. "Whose influence and money got your younger son a commission in a line regiment? My friends gave it, but they could just as easily take it away again. Would you tell your son up at Oxford, the pious one, that your lucky investments on the Exchange have suddenly turned unlucky again; the way they were before you met me? Will you tell your wife and daughters they may no longer trick themselves out in satins and lace furbelows just because you have decided to develop a conscience. I can assure you women don't look at these things the way we men do."

Gunning was so right. He might have decency enough for his conscience to suffer but he did not have the moral courage to break free. Even if he had, it would not wash away the memory. He had no option but to go ahead; there could be no turning back.

*****

Horace Twyford sighed and picked up his pen again. The pleasure of report-writing had somehow soured but it had to be completed in time to catch the packet leaving on the evening tide.

> **3 Tongan Confederation:** Since their defeat at Vatulevu the Tovata Confederacy have been relatively quiet, but following the commencement of trouble in the hills and Cakobau's preoccupation with his campaign, Prince Ma'afu and his allies, Tui Cakau and Tui Bua, have taken to the field again. They have attacked Cakobau's friends on the Macuata coast of Vanua Levu. Information received tells of complete victory for the Tongan forces — there are also reports of numerous atrocities committed by Ma'afu's lieutenants.
>
> For a native, Ma'afu has ability as an administrator and his government functions relatively smoothly in the restricted areas of Lau, Cakaudrove and Bua. Outside of these places he has little or no influence. There would appear to be no connection between him and the rebellious hill tribes, nor does he seem to have followers of any consequence on the main island of Viti Levu.
>
> **4 Labour recruitment:** The slave trade is carried on in these islands under the guise of legitimate labour recruitment. The need for outside labour has arisen due to the refusal of the Fijians to work. In most cases, living conditions for plantation labour are subhuman and their treatment by the planters harsh, but this is not the sole reason for their refusal. The Fijians themselves are an arrogant, indolent, good-for-nothing people who consider working for a white man to be degrading.

The importation of labour from other Pacific Islands, mainly Tanna, Santa Cruz, and the Gilbert, Kingsmills, Ellice and Tokelau Groups, is increasing every year. From the figures available to me at the Consulate, the first natives were imported in 1864 when 35 arrived. In 1865 a further 145 were brought in. The trade has since gone from strength to strength until in 1868 the number passed the 500 mark.

This black labour is sold to the planters on the basis of transport costs, which can range anywhere from £6.0.0 per head, plus food and clothing, both of which are supposed to be given to the labourers but seldom are. Contracts are made out for three years after which the labourer is entitled to repatriation to his place of origin — the planters never honour these contracts. The very cheapness of these slaves, I cannot deem them other than that, shows that supply is meeting demand.

Abuses on plantations are too plentiful to chronicle, but they are as nothing compared to the vicious recruiting, or rather kidnapping, methods employed by those men who bring labour to Fiji. They are known locally as 'blackbirders'. More and more of the gaolbirds and pirates who these days abound in the Pacific are entering the trade, with ships ranging from small cutters to large three-masted schooners. They are all heavily armed. Ostensibly they are legitimate recruiters who fully explain the terms of the labour contracts and only take those men who freely offer their services. In fact the natives are either enslaved by their own local chief or are hustled aboard at the point of a musket.

One of the worst blackbirders is an American, Jack O'Hara, whose armed schooner, the *Philomena* has been specially fitted out to carry human cargo. In April he landed 70 natives from Tanna on Taveuni. Rumour has it that a further 30 died or were killed on the voyage to Fiji, the dead bodies being tossed overboard to the sharks. These rumours may well be true for the master of the *Elizabeth*, which belongs to a reputable New South Wales Company, reported sighting several bodies floating in the sea not far from Fiji.

O'Hara is an incorrigible rogue. He is wanted for piracy, barratry and murder in both New South Wales and New Zealand, yet he comes openly to Levuka and no one dares touch him. In that I lack magisterial powers, I am helpless.

It is of interest that O'Hara's supercargo is an Englishman, Tobias Denison whose father, a missionary now retired, lives on Vatulevu with his daughter who is married to a planter, Jason Cotterel. Previous mention of Cotterel will be found in my report on the Tongan defeat at Vatulevu in 1866. There is nothing to suggest that either Denison senior or Cotterel is in any way involved in this slave trade, in fact the latter uses only local Fijian labour and has been extremely vocal in his denunciation of labour recruitment methods and of the Cakobau Government for condoning it.

This trade should not be stopped — the plantations would die if insufficient labour were available — but it needs regulating and strict policing to remove abuses. I would suggest that the only way this can be done is by posting several of Her Majesty's warships to cruise the area.

5 Trade: Cotton prices have declined somewhat and will undoubtedly fall further. In spite of this, cotton still heads the list of products exported from the islands in 1868. Coconut oil exports are down as a result of damage to groves during the hurricane last year followed by a period of prolonged drought. Many planters are in extreme financial straits and, as merchants are unable to enforce the repayment of loans, I foresee some Levuka Houses declaring themselves bankrupt.

6 American Claims: The war between the United States Federal Government and the Confederate States has for a number of years overshadowed the American claim that Cakobau owes $45,000 compensation for damage done to American property by Fijians some years ago. The last demands being previously reported by my predecessor on the occasion of the visit of Commander Sinclair of the USS *Vandalia*. 1868 however saw the claims renewed much to Cakobau's embarrassment. The USS *Tuscaroa* arrived in Fiji waters and her Commander demanded payment on pain of the bombardment of the Town of Levuka. Our would-be King was unable to raise even one percent of such a sum but by cunning negotiation managed to extricate himself, pledging several islands against his promise to pay the debt over the next four years. He will never be able to pay these debts and by themselves they constitute a permanent obstacle to the formation of stable government.

The great danger is that the Government of the United States may become so exasperated with Cakobau, that in order to recover, they will annex the Group as an American possession. As New South Wales, Victoria, and New Zealand make the South Pacific a sphere of British influence, an American enclave in our midst could be detrimental to our own interests.

In conclusion I beg to emphasise, yet again, the chaos and anarchy which prevails in Fiji. The attempt at a constitutional monarchy was short-lived and ludicrous; none of the problems of lawlessness and tribal warfare were solved, in fact the experiment only served to increase their magnitude. The people of these islands are unable to sleep at night for fear that they may be murdered in their beds. Nor will the considerable potential of Fiji be realised until Her Majesty's Government consents to confer on these dark islands the light and blessings of British rule.

I have the Honour
To be Your Lordship's Humble and Obedient Servant

Horace Twyford
Her Britannic Majesty's Consul
Fiji Islands.

22

In smokefilled rooms

Jason Cotterel steadfastly refused to be drawn into the cauldron of island affairs but was kept well-informed, gleaning news either from visitors to Vatulevu or when circumstances forced him to visit Levuka.

Both he and Kate knew that her brother was up to his ears in the labour trade, though they made sure her father was kept ignorant of the fact. Apart from an initial shocked discussion when the news broke, it was a subject they avoided; Kate from a deep sense of shame, and Jason because anything to do with blackbirding was anathema to him. Toby Denison was like a black storm cloud hovering just below the horizon, and which might at any moment drift to Vatulevu shattering their peace and harmony.

It was impossible to have been ignorant of the war against the hill tribes, for Vatulevu had contributed over 100 of its best warriors to the King's army. Jason and Kate shared the deep grief of the island when the remnant returned bearing their leader, Ratu Seru, wrapped in ceremonial masi ready for burial in the cave reserved for chiefs.

Jason and Seru had swum, fished, laughed and joked together; Seru had helped him build the ketches and establish Qaraniqio plantation. They had fought side by side against the Tongans. Yet when Ratu Saru's last battle had come Jason was elsewhere. Along with his sense of loss and bereavement, Jason felt he had deserted his friend in his hour of need.

*****

Kate saw to it that he did not brood. Plantation and family life filled his time and left little time for introspection. With Ulamila demanding help with her schooling, baby John crawling and gurgling at his knees, and a wife demanding that he attend to chores about the house, self-indulgence was nigh impossible.

Between Qaraniqio plantation and the communal Fijian areas, the best part of 250 acres of cotton were planted. Clearing the bush, preparing the land, and planting was one long picnic with everyone joining in. As usual, however, the tending of the plants and the monotonous maintenance required to bring the cotton to maturity were a different kettle of fish. Because Jason felt responsible and concerned that the Fijians should not suffer if the crop was a failure, he was in the saddle from dawn to dusk, rooting out the workers at first light, and swinging a hoe beside them harder and faster than the strongest. When he arrived home each night after dark it was all he could do to get down from his horse.

Kate was waiting, anticipating his every need. Clean cool clothes were laid out for him to slip into once he had sluiced away the dirt. Then, with a tall glass of rum and cold water in his hand, Jason would lie back in his favourite chair exchanging Kate's household crises for his own stories of progress, frustrations and hopes. John Denison would join them, very properly dressed even on the hottest evening. After a further drink, the three, in perfect harmony with one another, would move from the verandah to the candlelit dining room for their evening meal served by the housegirls under the supervision of the ageless Lala.

Coffee, a cigar, and a few moments with a book until heads began to nod, whereupon Kate would bundle her father off to his own quarters and take her weary husband to their bed and the solace of her arms. Life had taken on a rich and satisfying pattern and Jason would not have changed a single thing, not even to be King of Fiji.

The weather stayed dry and clear and everyone turned out to harvest the cotton. The whole island worked in holiday mood; huge meals were prepared by the women and eaten at the side of the fields; aching backs were eased by laughter and a sense of mutual achievement.

Almost 20 tons of top quality cotton were ginned and bailed and taken to Levuka by Jason. The price, which had been four shillings and fourpence per pound, was falling but he was still able to clear nearly three shillings per pound overall and was more than satisfied. The total value of the crop was £6000 of which his share, even after covering his labour costs, was almost £2000. Enough to place an order through Bex for the sugar mill rollers plus something special for Kate and the children.

Once the deal was concluded and the Sydney bank draft was in his hands, Jason had intended to head straight back for the island but it was already late in the day. He decided instead to stay the night at in Levuka and catch up with the gossip.

*****

Shaved and dressed, Jason came out on to MacDonald's upstairs verandah. It was packed with people shouting and drinking, but they were all strange faces. It brought home to him how cut off from the world Vatulevu was. Tucked away as they were one forgot just how Fiji as a whole was booming.

He did not recognise them nor did they know him. From their dress, the majority looked as if they might have been more at home in San Francisco or

Sydney than Levuka. At one table were a couple of men wearing broadbrimmed hats and the red puggarees affected by planters — 'Nadi swells' from along the Nadi River. They were newcomers too.

At least ten ocean-going vessels were at anchor in the harbour and, even though it was quite dark outside, Jason could hear the hammering of carpenters working by the light of oil lamps as they hurried to complete yet another of the flimsy buildings mushrooming up along the beach front.

Jason was about to turn back towards his room when he heard "Cotterel! Jason Cotterel!" Looking in the direction of the voice he saw William Drew beckoning to him.

The last time Jason had seen Drew was at Cakobau's farcical coronation and he had no love for the man, a prime mover in that disgraceful affair. The other men at Drew's table looked more like bankers than settlers but, as Jason had seen no one else he knew and as his object was to find out what was happening, he shrugged his shoulders and pushed through the crowd towards Drew's table.

"Hello, Jason, you're an absolute stranger these days. Sit down and have a drink with me and my friends." Drew, full of bonhomie and MacDonald's rum, pulled out a chair and sent a boy scurrying for another bottle and a fresh glass.

He introduced his friends. "I'd like you to meet three new arrivals from Victoria: Mr Butters from Melbourne and his associates Messrs Brewer and Evans. These are the gentlemen who will really make Fiji tick. Gentlemen," he said, beaming at the others as if in Jason he had captured a prize exhibit in a carnival sideshow, "I'd like you to meet Jason Cotterel. Jason's the best bloody planter in the whole damned South Pacific. If you want advice about your project ask him; he's forgotten more about planting and the Fijians than I'll ever know."

That at least was true, thought Jason, as he shook hands with the three strangers; Drew had never planted a thing in his life. "And what is this project of yours, gentlemen?" asked Jason as he lit a cigar.

"Where have you been hiding yourself, Jason?" laughed Drew tipsily. "Mr Butters and his friends are the main promoters of the Polynesia Company. The Polynesia Company is going to make something of this godforsaken place."

Jason had heard others claim the same thing but he had yet to see any of them make good their boasts. If they were friends of Drew's, what they could make for themselves would be bound to take precedence over what they could make of Fiji. He prudently decided to keep such thoughts to himself.

"You must excuse me, I get so tied up with my own plantation affairs that the rest of the world passes by unnoticed. I'm ashamed to say that this is the first time I've heard tell of your company. What are you aiming to do?"

Butters, a stout red-faced man, puffed up with self-importance, was obviously used to his fellows agreeing to anything he proposed. "The Polynesia Company has been established," he pontificated, "to relieve His Majesty, King Cakobau, of his American debts and to join in partnership with the Fijian people to develop these beautiful islands."

Jason whistled appreciatively, "Those debts amount to more than $40,000," he drawled, his American accent even more noticeable than normal. He leant back in his chair and pulled contentedly on his cigar as he surveyed the three well-fed Victorian business sharks.

"$45,000 to be exact," said Butters.

"And you intend to pay the whole $45,000? I take it you gentlemen aren't doing this purely for the good of your health. What's in it for your company? I've just sold some cotton, you never know I could be a potential investor." This Jason said with his tongue in his cheek, but he hoped it would be enough to make them disclose the details of their plans.

"You couldn't do better, Jason," said Drew eagerly. "Take it from an old friend, you couldn't do better."

"We're businessmen, Cotterel, the same as yourself," Brewer chipped in. "We hope to make a profit from our investment in the same way as you profit from your plantation. On the other hand the Polynesia Company is no one-sided affair, it will be mutually advantageous to all concerned."

Jason could see no comparison between a fat financier who earned his money from the sweat of others, and a planter who was only paid by the weight of calluses on his hands and the intensity of the ache in his back. Outwardly he smiled politely and sipped at his drink. "Go on, Mr Brewer. You interest me tremendously."

Drew looked at Jason a little suspiciously, as if guessing what was going through his mind. Jason had a reputation for being difficult.

"Let me tell it, Brewer," snapped Butters, unwilling to yield the stage. "As I started to say, we on our side pay off the King's pressing debts and, even though they amount to a considerable sum, that is not the whole of what we shall do. King Cakobau will receive a gunboat and an annuity of £200 per annum."

That will keep him in real luxury, thought Jason, the smile beginning to stiffen on his face as he listened.

"In return, the King is to give us land, mining and mineral rights to 80,000 acres in Viti Levu Bay, 10,000 acres in Natewa Bay, 23,000 acres in the Suva area, and the two islands of Beqa and Yanuca. In addition the company has been given certain privileges. In the first place, we are forever exempt from all forms of taxation, customs and excise duties. The King has also granted us a 21 year monopoly of banking facilities in Fiji and has promised the company and its settlers his full support and protection." Butters account sounded more like a religious litany than a company prospectus.

"Well, Mr Cotterel, what do you think? Do you want to be one of the fortunate investors in this noble and, I think I may say, lucrative enterprise?"

The four men looked at him, waiting for his acclamation. All Jason could do was stare back incredulously. Slowly the ridiculous, absolutely ludicrous, aspect of the deal dawned on him. These European sharks, who thought they had hoodwinked the Vunivalu into handing the country over to them, were being taken for the biggest ride of their lives.

Much to Butter's annoyance he chuckled openly. That old devil on Bau had lost none of his cunning, thought Jason delightedly, not an ounce of it. The sight of their self-satisfied faces was too much for his self-control. He lay back in his chair and hooted from pure enjoyment until the tears streamed down his cheeks.

"This is no matter for hilarity!" spluttered Butters indignantly. He pushed back his chair and stood, whilst Brewer and Evans like dutiful shadows scrambled from their seats to stand beside him. "I see nothing about the Polynesia Company which is funny, Mr Cotterel."

"You will … you will," gasped Jason weakly, only to collapse again at the sight of the three facing him. They were like indignant old maids who had suddenly been propositioned. He had not seen so much outraged virtue in years.

"Here, Cotterel …" began Drew apprehensively.

"Leave your friend alone, Mr Drew," interjected Butters stonily. "We have no intention of staying here to be insulted by this yokel. Evans, Brewer, come!" At his signal they stalked off majestic in their anger.

*****

Drew was torn between the need to keep his associates sweet and two hardly-touched bottles of rum on the table. The latter won; he sank back in his chair and, pouring out a stiff drink, finished it at a single swallow.

"It's alright for you, Cotterel," he complained bitterly as he refilled both of their glasses, "but if anything happens to put them off this deal, Cakobau will have my head."

Jason pulled himself together and wiped his eyes with a handkerchief. He took a steadying pull at his rum. "It was just the look on the fat chap's face. He was so pleased with himself. 80,000 acres in Viti Levu Bay? Why, the land doesn't even belong to the Vunivalu to give away. I'd love to be a fly on a rock watching when Butters and his merry men try to take it away from those Ra people. They're the most bloodthirsty, cannibalistic bunch in the whole Group. Go on, Drew, admit it, they haven't a chance in hell of collecting."

This time even Drew allowed himself a rueful grin. "Well, we did promise protection," he said in vindication.

"Protect them!" said Jason astonished. "Yours is a fine government, I must say. You intend to give protection to people while they snatch land away from its rightful owners. At the moment I doubt if you can protect yourselves let alone anyone else. The Vunivalu's just lost one war against the kai-colo; the last thing he needs at the moment is a second war against the kai-Ra."

"We both know the kai-Ra: this company has as much chance of taking up their 80,000 acres as I have of climbing to the moon. The same thing goes for the 10,000 acres up in Natewa Bay. Christ alive, man, be sensible! That lot's slap bang in the middle of Tui Cakau's stamping grounds and if he has nothing to say about Cakobau giving away his land, as sure as hell is hot Ma'afu will. Anyone who throws money into this Polynesia Company either knows nothing about Fiji, or is stark staring mad.

People at nearby tables were listening and Jason made no attempt to lower his voice. His last comments caused an excited buzz of conversation.

"For God's sake keep your voice down," said Drew anxiously. The idea came from them not us. I thought you were supposed to be one of the King's friends. If you can think of a better way to rid ourselves of the American debt why not let us know, instead of hiding yourself away on Vatulevu. Those damned dollars bedevil everything we do."

"So you were the one who advised acceptance of this deal?" asked Jason, his voice obediently lowered.

"Certainly, I advised acceptance," answered Drew, looking Jason straight in the eye. "I reckon they're the finest gift horse Fiji will ever be offered. They heard about the debt from the American Consul-General in Sydney, General Lambert, in fact he's in it himself. Half the nobs of Sydney and Melbourne are among the shareholders. Butters, that fat chap you were laughing at, was Mayor of Melbourne at one time. He's now speaker of the Victorian Legislative Assembly."

"I do believe Fiji is becoming too respectable for me," laughed Jason, still refusing to take Drew seriously. "Instead of fugitives and renegades we are now become a dumping ground for financiers and politicians. But tell me, what will you do when they discover that their share certificates aren't worth the paper they're printed on? These are influential people. They can make plenty of trouble, and if you are still trying to get international recognition floating bogus companies doesn't seem a very sound way of going about it."

"Who cares? That's in the future. They've already handed over $9,375 and by June they'll have settled the whole debt. When that happens the King can sit back and stop worrying that an American gunboat will pop up over the horizon and cart him off to the States. He's been on tenterhooks for the last 14 years. Can you blame him, or us, for refusing to pass up a chance like this?"

"The debts were trumped up in the first place. With proper representations in the right place, the slate could have been wiped clean without ruining his name," argued Jason. "Still, I suppose there is some justice in one piece of chicanery cancelling out another. At least it will wipe the self-satisfied smiles from the faces of Butters and his friends, which may not be a bad thing in itself."

"This is no confidence trick either," Drew objected vehemently. "Maybe they won't get all they think, but they'll get some of it. That land around Suva is worth $40,000 by itself."

"Alright Drew, alright, I give in," said Jason holding up a hand submissively. "Your motives are as pure as driven snow. I'll even refrain from asking how much you are making for yourself on the side."

Jason's words were far from how he felt. He was no longer in any mood for laughter. The man seemed to have no conception of the long-term damage he was doing.

Drew just grinned at the implication that he had been accepting bribes. "You're not asking and I'm not telling," he said. "Suffice it to say that the services of the Secretary of State are not to be had cheaply in any country and in Fiji it is more expensive than most."

"Secretary of State? I thought the King no longer had any white Ministers of State. I was given to understand he had sacked the whole lot of you. If you are Secretary of State, what happened to St John?"

"Oh, St John's gone and good riddance," answered Drew in a satisfied tone. "The King did fire us all, but then we had another meeting with him at Bau and got him to accept another constitution."

"This one gives the whites complete equality with the locals. We are to have a main house of the Legislature made up of members elected by the planters, and a majority on the Executive Council. Two out of the three judges will be white; and if a white man commits any offence up-country, a white magistrate'll try him. My title is Chief Secretary and I'm in charge of the general welfare of the state. All negotiations with foreign states come under me and I also handle all prosecutions."

"You have it very nicely sewn up, haven't you?" said Jason sarcastically.

"I think so," Drew answered smugly, the sarcasm completely lost on him.

"I suppose you have made some provisions for the Fijians, after all it is their country. But perhaps that is one of the things you'll soon be changing too."

This time even someone as thick skinned as Drew could sense the bitterness in Jason's voice. A moment before, the American had been laughing at Butters, now his expression was hard and angry.

"What's got into you?" Drew asked nervously. "Of course there's provision. The King's a Fijian, isn't he? And there'll be an Upper House of the Legislature made up of chiefs."

"And those two-to-one white judges and white magistrates?"

"Whose side are you on, Cotterel?" asked Drew angrily. "We run our affairs and they run theirs. The governor of each province will be the local chief and he'll have his own officers to run native affairs. We won't interfere with him, and we'll see to it that he doesn't shove his bloody nose into our business. I can't understand you at all. You're one of the biggest planters in Fiji; you've got everything to gain and nothing to lose by our set up. In fact we hope you'll join us as a minister; the King gives a lot of weight to what you say."

"Answer three questions for me," demanded Jason. "First of all, who will be collecting the revenue from the Fijians?"

"Why, the white district magistrates of course?"

"I thought as much, and this is your idea of not interfering in Fijian affairs." Jason waved aside Drew's immediate protests. "Secondly, I want to know if Basil Gunning is mixed up in all this."

"Sure, he's the Minister for War and Police. Why?"

"Hold on. My last question is whether or not the British Consul here in Levuka has recognised your government?"

"No he hasn't, the bastard!" said Drew irately, for this was a very sore point. "He's done everything possible to put obstacles in our way. He's even threatened to revoke the citizenship of any British subject who pays taxes to us. But just you wait and see. We'll get even with Mister high-and-bloody-mighty Twyford yet."

"And I suppose you have been using Gunning as the go-between in your negotiations with him," said Jason. He could never prove it but instinct told him that the colonel's interests in Fiji were to be found in some intrigue between himself and the Consul. Peter Bex had told Jason that the two were as thick as thieves which was hardly reconcilable with their being in diametrically opposed camps.

Gunning, a colonel in the Queen's army, had fought in Cakobau's army and had been one of his ministers, yet the Consul had never taken action against him, in spite of his dire threats directed against other innocent British subjects.

The remnants of the Vatulevu contingent had told Jason that Gunning was more a hindrance than a help in the hill campaign. In contrast to what they had seen of him on Vatulevu, Gunning could never make up his mind and even when he did his advice had invariably been disastrous. The supply system, which came directly under his control, was chaotic even by Fijian standards.

Jason had wondered if there might be method in the Englishman's madness. He was sure that Gunning's ineptitude had been deliberate; just as he was sure that Gunning and Twyford were in cahoots. They either wanted to take over Fiji themselves, or they wanted to get the country into such a chaotic shambles that Britain would be forced to take it over.

Drew was not brilliant, but he was not stupid either. He could see where Jason's questions were leading and the implication of treachery in high places. He refused to believe it.

"You're mad, Jason. Sure, Gunning and Twyford are old friends, but that doesn't mean they necessarily work together."

"Have it your own way. You seem to know best," said Jason equably. "But I'm willing to bet my last dollar that even if you get the American debt out of your hair this government will be as great a failure as the last. It will fail from lack of European support and from dissension within your own cabinet. When you and your friends start fighting, remember what I have said and see if Basil Gunning isn't somewhere behind it all."

Jason could see that Drew was listening intently and also thinking back to some of the quarrels and bickering which had already taken place. "You might just have something," Drew said softly. He looked worried and poured four fingers of neat rum which disappeared down his gullet as if by sleight of hand.

"What about yourself, Jason? If you came in with us we could sort it out. If Gunning is playing a double game, between the two of us we can get the King to toss him out on his ear."

Jason laughed sardonically. "Come in with you lot? With a set-up like that? No thank you. I have more respect for my good name than to associate myself with your half-baked government. You have deliberately set out to make the Europeans independent and to hell with the Fijians. My conscience wouldn't allow me to be part of such a fraud."

The whole of MacDonald's upper verandah now had their ears cocked to their conversation. "This is the Fijians' country. We are the foreigners and outnumbered 200 to one. Yet instead of them ruling us, you reckon we should rule them?"

"They're a bunch of murdering black savages," exploded Drew, furious that Cotterel should denounce him in public. "Without us to lead them this place would be bloody turmoil. Where would you and the other planters be then?"

Jason got up, preparing to leave. He knew that every European on MacDonald's verandah thought as Drew did. They saw nothing dishonest in exploiting Fijians. They would never agree with him but at least they had heard, perhaps for the first time, a genuinely honest point of view.

"My dear Drew," Jason drawled, "I was here ten years before you ever saw these islands and did quite well without your help. In fact I am sure Fiji would be much better off without you or your friends. There is a profound difference between the help and advice I give Fijians and what you and this bogus company are offering. Why not be honest and admit that you intend to strip the country bare and make the Fijians your slaves?"

Jason was not the only one standing. Men were shouting angrily. "Renegade" and "Bloody, native-loving bastard," were two of the least virulent phrases flung at him, but they were a mob without a leader. Jason's commanding height and his air of strength and power stopped any from challenging him physically.

"I'd rather be a renegade and a native-loving bastard than a carpet-bagging exploiter which is what you lot are." He flung back.

Turning to Drew he said, "Tell the King from me that I shall always be ready to support a stable government which is in the true interests of the Fijians. Until then I want nothing to do with you or your sordid farce. Tell His Majesty that, for the moment, I am in absolute harmony with the Consul and his Minister of War. I hope your government collapses as quickly and as completely as possible."

In the shocked silence which followed he bowed to Drew and the room at large, then, turning his back as if daring someone to attack him, he walked casually off the verandah. The last word was his and no one dared dispute Jason Cotterel's exit.

23

The wild card

TOBY DENISON LAY NAKED on his bunk in the supercargo's cabin on the *Philomena*, a six-by-four box stinking of stale sweat, alcohol and rancid coconut oil. Here, 400 miles to the north of Fiji and that much nearer the Equator, the cabin was like an oven. Huddled on the floor was a young Gilbertese woman. She was as naked as her master, battered and bruised, but too terrified to weep in case it attracted his attention. She crouched against the wall, her scared brown eyes fixed on the man, dreading the moment when he would want to make use of her body again.

But for the meantime Denison was sated with flesh. It was too hot to sleep and instead he let his mind range unfettered. He was a very different creature to the callow youth who had stolen his father's cash box and decamped from Vatulevu in 1867.

Two years had added inches to his height, his frame had filled out, and he was harder and tougher. His face was almost hidden under a full beard and his profile had undergone a further change on the night it came in contact with a flying bottle which broke his nose and left an ugly scar across his forehead. It was doubtful whether his own sister would have recognised him after that fight. Since then he had learnt the art of self-defence in a rough school, as a number of people, both men and women, had discovered to their regret.

Yet in some ways he was the same. He still paid the finicky attention of a dandy to details of dress, and although his vocabulary had been considerably enhanced, he still affected the languid, bored tones of the London man-about-town. His style of delivery imparted such an added virulence to his cursing that many a barfly and pimp spoke with awe of Toby Denison's profane eloquence.

He no longer pined for London. There, a man's pockets must be well-lined if he wanted to enjoy its fleshpots and yet keep the law off his neck, whereas in the islands he could live like the Maquis de Sade and not have a penny with which to bless himself.

Denison had no intention of remaining poor. As he lay sprawled in the disorder of his bunk he calculated what his cut would be from the 200 head of human cattle crammed below the *Philomena*'s hatches. On some ships the supercargo got a miserable five shillings, but O'Hara's methods were more efficient and, granted luck and a seller's market, his share would amount to £2 a head or even more.

It was a matter of overheads. If, when you signed on labour, you had to hand out a lot of expensive axes, muskets and powder, there was nothing in it. O'Hara had cut all that out: when he sailed into the middle of a fishing fleet, he dropped pigiron through the bottom of the canoes and hauled out of the sea those he wanted. With a crew as heavily armed as theirs, a quick raid on a lonely island was more effective than negotiating for labour.

In Fiji and Queensland planters were screaming out for labour, cash on the barrel and no questions asked. It was no trade for the squeamish but Toby had never felt the slightest qualm; kanaka labour were animals not human beings.

With a share of around £400, and possibly like amounts squeezed out of his father and another investor he knew, he would be able to set up on his own. In the beginning it might pay to sail with O'Hara, working two ships in tandem. He would get a master's share which at six trips a year would bring in an income of close to £8,000. Five years, and he could sail back to England and set up as a nabob.

That assumed no mishaps — experience had shown him that plenty could happen to ruin the best of plans. On the last trip they had caught the edge of a hurricane and for three days they had taken a battering which still made Toby go cold whenever he thought of it.

They had lost 30 head in that storm. With the hatches battened down tight most died from suffocation, but a few had been trampled to death when the savages panicked in the plunging darkness. The dead were tossed over the side and the numbers made up from the next island they passed. But it had meant delays, and planters depended on them to meet their delivery dates. Even blackbirders had a business reputation to maintain.

The worst thing which could happen was to meet up with a naval vessel. So far the *Philomena* had avoided them, but even if she did, O'Hara had a glib tongue and a stack of forged contracts to meet just such an emergency. Under the slavery laws, it was up to the navy to prove the kanaka labour aboard were slaves and not legitimate labour. With the kai-loma members of *Philomena*'s crew stripped to the buff and put in with the cargo as decoys, Toby was satisfied they could fool any naval officer fresh out from England.

Sometimes there was fighting among the cargo. He had once put 10 Santa Cruz men with 40 from Tanna, only to find out later that they were hereditary enemies. Four were killed before the crew got it sorted out. One of these days, thought Toby, it will be just my blasted luck to be throwing evidence over the side when the navy came along. If that should ever happen everyone concerned would swing at the end of a rope. He discarded the thought; O'Hara and his crew might end up that way, but he never doubted his own ability to talk his way out of even the worst predicament.

He looked at the girl in the corner and she cringed away. He decided that he was too hot and tired even for sex — she could wait till morning — and fell asleep, not bothering to dowse the light. The girl's dark eyes watched every breath he took, every movement he made, like a rabbit mesmerised by a snake. If thoughts could have killed, Denison would have died a thousand deaths that night. As it was, her legs were so paralysed with fear they were incapable of carrying her even as far as the revolver which hung in a holster by Denison's head.

*****

The *Philomena* was running among islands of the Fiji Group, her journey almost over, when trouble broke out. The cargo were fighting among themselves, just as they had done on that previous trip; no one knew why. Some had managed to prise long splinters of wood from the bulkheads and, using them as rudimentary spears, created havoc in the packed holds. Once started there was absolute panic — in the darkness it was impossible to tell friend from foe — the hold was a heaving shambles of men fighting for their lives, lashing out at anything which moved.

The pandemonium brought O'Hara and every member of the crew on the run, armed with the first weapons they could lay hands on. Through chinks in the hatch covers they could dimly see the 200 or so islanders battling for the right to live. It would have been suicidal to open the hatches. Once the maddened kanaka labourers swarmed up on deck not even artillery could have stopped them.

O'Hara was furious at the sight of so much valuable merchandise being damaged. "Put a few shots into the bastards," he roared.

His crew needed no further urging. Poking rifle and revolver barrels through gaps in the hatch covers they fired point-blank into the screaming mass of bodies. Far from quelling the riot, this only intensified the frenzy and terror of the imprisoned men. They tore at the bulkheads and hatches with bloody fingers in a desperate effort to avoid the bullets above and the stabbing slivers of wood below.

It was the turn of O'Hara and his crew to panic. The slaves were crazed beyond the point where they felt the searing pain of hot lead. Every gun on the *Philomena* was turned on the erupting cargo and fired and fired till barrels were red hot to the touch, and the smoke and acrid smell of gunpowder hung over the whole ship.

It seemed never-ending. The islanders screamed and tried to claw their way out; they were slaughtered by the score, but still they came on. O'Hara and his men knew that if just one got free it would be the beginning of a tale the ending of which they would never live to hear — other blackbirders, faced with the same situation, had found this out all too late.

Toby Denison was not squeamish, he had shot blacks before. But that had been on remote islands where detection was unlikely. Here in Fiji the circumstances were entirely different; at any moment a man-of-war, English, French, American or even Russian might come upon them; for that matter any ship would be as bad. It needed just one person to see what was happening on the *Philomena* and report it to the appropriate authorities, or act as a witness against them, and they were all dead men.

Knowing that his skin depended on it, for once in his life Toby Denison did the sensible thing. Someone had to con the schooner, especially as they were so close to land and coral reefs. He ran to the helmsman, and handing him his revolver, ordered him down to help O'Hara and took over the wheel himself. One eye to the wind, the other on the smoke-masked men at the hatches, Toby Denison kept the *Philomena* on course.

The shooting lasted for more than half an hour before the fear-crazed wretches ceased their futile attack on the hatch covers. Screaming was replaced by the weeping and pitiful moaning of the wounded. Even so, O'Hara was taking no chances; for another four hours the covers were kept on and armed men stood guard ready for any renewal of activity below.

Only when O'Hara was sure that the cargo were well and truly incapable of further violence were the dead and wounded lifted up on to the deck. Even then, loaded guns threatened instant death to anyone making a suspicious movement. They found 53 dead and another 25 badly wounded.

With attention, some might have had a chance of recovery, but O'Hara wanted no one left alive with wounds as evidence of what had happened. From his place at the wheel, Denison watched as 78 bodies were unceremoniously thrown overboard to feed the sharks and barracuda which swarmed about the ship, attracted by the smell of blood and bodies. It was difficult to see the fish in the bloodied water, but the twitching and jerking of the bodies told when they struck. The spine-chilling shrieks of the wounded told their own story.

Denison's fascination was tempered with the terrible fear that he might be involved in the consequences which were bound to follow such a slaughter. Somewhere, somehow, someday, news of this would leak out to the rest of the world and woe betide the man who could not prove his innocence.

"Why are you here?" O'Hara was standing beside Denison, his matted beard jutting forward truculently. "Where in bloody hell were you when the shooting was on?" O'Hara was a striking looking man. On a smaller man his long blond hair would have been effeminate, but it only added to his whole swashbuckling air. The story went that he kept his hair long to hide a missing right ear which had been bitten off one night in a barroom fight; Toby had never dared ask whether the story was true.

"Someone had to con the ship or we'd have finished high and dry on that reef over there," replied Toby indicating the white foam ringing an island only half a mile off their stern. "The helmsman was useless, he couldn't keep his eyes off the shooting. We were all over the place. I could see you had everything well under control down there, so I took over here. If I hadn't, we'd all be swimming along with the kanaka labourers."

"For a supercargo, Denison, you show damned little interest in the cargo." Under Denison's tough exterior, O'Hara knew him to be yellow through and through. If the truth were known, the man had been scared rigid that the blacks would break free. "That's your head money we've been pushing over the side, you lily-livered son-of-a-bitch, not just mine and the crew's."

"At least they won't be around to tell tales, Captain," laughed Toby with exaggerated heartiness. "The sharks are seeing to that for us."

"Don't laugh too bloody soon," growled O'Hara, "we've still a 120 of those black bastards down below and they're more than enough to send both you and me to the gallows."

Toby realised that his own neck was still in horrible danger. Levuka was the only place large enough to take so many kanaka labourers off their hands and these days there was always a visiting warship of some description at anchor in the harbour.

"What do you say we turn and run for Sydney?" he asked, trying to keep the nervousness cramping his stomach from appearing in his voice.

"And risk a second outbreak? You must be crazy. Anyway the British are on the lookout for the *Philomena* after our last trip. We're going to get rid of these blacks in Fiji fast, then off out of the place. We might even try trading somewhere else for a while; have a crack at Valparaiso. They need labour for the coppermines."

*****

The crew tried to scour away all signs of the massacre while O'Hara, Denison and Wilson, the mate, drank rum in the captain's cabin as they worked out a plan of action which would keep them out of the hands of the navy.

Instead of sailing straight into Levuka, it was decided to anchor on the opposite side of Ovalau, near a smaller island called Moturiki. Then the ship's whaler would be sent to spy out the land. If there was any sign of a man-of-war, the *Philomena* would run for Taveuni and Vanua Levu, selling the blacks in small lots to the planters over there. This they wanted to avoid if possible for with the numbers depleted by 78 the prices offered on the plantations, as against Levuka, would hardly cover the costs of the voyage.

Denison volunteered to do the scouting. He was not only to report on any ships at anchor, but go ashore and enquire as to all known shipping movements.

Not that Toby Denison had any intention of returning aboard the *Philomena*. What money he possessed was strapped next to his skin in a money belt. He had a revolver and the clothes he stood up in; everything else, including the girl, he was prepared to write off to experience.

It had not been a weak stomach which had stopped him firing on the cargo; nor would he suffer nightmares from the thought of his shipmates swinging at the end of a yardarm. But sooner or later the whole thing was going to come out in the open and he was determined to escape retribution even if it meant delivering up his shipmates to the hangman.

Even before the whaler entered Levuka harbour, Toby and his crew of three could see the tall masts and the white ensign of a Royal Navy vessel. As they neared, Toby recognised HMS *Rosario*, a fast corvette he had seen previously in Sydney.

Toby's companions were all for turning back there and then; nor would they listen when he argued that the main part of their mission was to discover what the corvette's movements were to be. Finally he belted one of the men across the side of the head with his revolver barrel, knocking him senseless into the bilges, and threatened to shoot the others on the spot unless they did as he ordered.

Then he tried reason: "If you go back to the ship, you'll be aboard when that man-of-war catches up with them," he pointed out, dropping any further pretence. "Sooner or later it's going to get out and you'll all hang. Put me on the beach and you are free to take off yourselves. Make for Viti Levu, abandon the whaler, and hide up in the hills and you'll get clean away."

Loyalty to captain and ship played little part in the blackbirding trade and their every instinct urged them to grab at the opportunity offered. The one thing they could not understand was why Denison refused to flee with them.

"You've all got some native blood, you can hide in the hills," he explained glibly. "I'm white, how long would I last? You only have to strip off your clothes and no one will know you were ever part of the *Philomena* but word will soon get around if a white man tries the same thing." The more he thought about it, the more Toby would willingly have traded his white skin for a less conspicuous brown one, had it been possible.

"I have friends ashore who will hide me till I can get away." It would not pay to tip his hand completely. If they were not prepared to go back and fight side by side with their shipmates, they were equally unreliable as repositories for his own secrets.

Without further argument they sailed the whaler through the reef passage into the harbour. As they passed within a hundred yards of *Rosario*'s bows, Toby's skin crawled at the thought of the gamble he was taking. His throat was so dry he couldn't swallow, but when he saw some sailors leaning over the side watching them slip by he managed to summon up enough courage to wave a casual hand in their direction.

The moment they touched bottom, Toby was over the side wading ashore while his erstwhile companions took off towards the harbour entrance with every ounce of speed they could muster.

*****

For a moment Toby stood on the rubbish-littered beach watching them; was he an arrant fool not to go with them and take his chance? The thought of O'Hara's reaction when the whaler failed to return stopped him. He was bound to guess the double-cross and when that moment came O'Hara would employ every means to track Toby down. O'Hara had a vivid imagination when it came to dealing with those who ran foul of him.

Toby made for the British Consul's office. Twyford was aboard the man-of-war lunching with the officers, or so the kai-loma clerk said. He waited on a hard seat in the outer office in a muck-sweat of apprehension for two nerve-wracking hours. A dozen times he got up to go convinced that he was a fool, only to plump down again petrified by the thought of the hangman's noose. All his hopes rested on the information he held swinging the Consul to his side, blackmail though it might be.

Horace Twyford arrived, stuffed with Her Majesty's provender and somewhat tipsy from the wine which had flowed liberally. His purpose was to collect a few papers from his office, then home to bed and a sound sleep prior to the reciprocal dinner party his wife was giving that evening. The man demanding to see him appeared a regular ruffian, like most of the renegade whites in the islands. But he was obviously agitated about something for his forehead was covered with perspiration though it was quite a cool afternoon by Levuka standards.

Twyford had never seen the fellow before, but in the long run it was usually easier to listen to such people rather than go through a lot of tiresome argument to evade it. "Alright, Mister," he snapped irritably as he plumped down behind his desk, "get on with it. I'm a busy man, I'm not sitting here all day."

"I won't keep you long, sir, I promise," Toby began, adopting a nervous manner. Apart from his genuine fears he wanted to simulate shame, contrition and horror. "My name is Denison ..."

"Denison!" the Consul interrupted, the name struck an immediate chord. "Are you related to the Reverend John Denison?"

"Yes, sir. I'm his son."

"Toby Denison! Then you are a stinking blackbirder and a blackguard to boot, sir, How dare you come to my office! You are an accomplice of that notorious scoundrel, O'Hara."

"But Mr Twyford, sir, when I joined him I thought he was an honest recruiter," Toby whimpered. "I had no wish to become an accomplice to blackbirding. Why do you imagine I am here now?"

"I have been forced to witness the most horrible and despicable crimes and I knew as an Englishman it was my duty to report the matter to you, Her Majesty's representative, immediately. I am innocent but O'Hara and his crew are devils who must be brought to justice. I want to turn Queen's evidence and help you catch him. Don't you want to capture Jack O'Hara red-handed?" His voice was shrill, he even managed to weep a little; trepidation made his acting professionally convincing.

Twyford was now all attention; he could hardly afford to be otherwise. If Denison, himself a thorough rogue, was willing to confess, the crimes in question must be heinous indeed. If would be a feather in his cap if he could land O'Hara, plus sufficient evidence for a conviction. With *Rosario* at anchor in Levuka harbour and he and the captain on good terms, he even had the means at his disposal to effect a capture. For all that, he would have been even better pleased if Denison was to go in the bag along with his master.

"What crime?" He asked with the sternness and dignity befitting his position as Consul.

"First, promise I won't be implicated," pleaded Toby Denison like a frightened schoolboy.

"I promise nothing. If this crime is as serious as you say and if the evidence you are offering leads to the apprehension of those involved, you yourself will be dealt with under the normal rules for those who turn Queen's evidence. Always provided you are not involved yourself."

"I did nothing, nothing at all. I was conning the ship the whole time. You must believe me."

"Well come on, man, don't beat around the bush. Get on with your story."

Toby gulped and began "Yesterday, not 50 miles from here, I saw O'Hara and his crew murder 78 kanakas ..."

The whole story tumbled out, the fighting in the hold, and then the final bloodbath. Twyford's face got harder and grimmer as the weeping, babbling man painted a picture of villainy which might have come straight out of the Dark Ages. At first he thought it might be a gigantic hoax, but Denison's desperate attempt to protect his own dirty hide left no doubt in his mind that his story was true. What Denison's own part had been he was unable to tell but he was certainly not the innocent he made out to be.

It never occurred to Twyford that he himself had killed more people than this rogue, even if it had been by indirect means. He boiled with rage that white men should have committed such an appalling atrocity. The bonhomie generated by the convivial luncheon party evaporated and now he was stone-cold sober.

"Where is O'Hara's ship now?" he demanded, his voice cold and impersonal.

Denison could see from the Consul's expression that unless he bargained swiftly he would hang with the rest, or on his own if it came to that. It was obvious that Twyford thought he had done his own share of killing even though on that particular point, for once in his life, he had been telling the whole truth.

"I'll tell you that, Consul, but only when you agree that my name will be kept right out of this business. That is the reward I must ask for such information."

"Now you listen to me, Denison, and listen closely," snapped Twyford angrily. "One of Her Majesty's warships is at anchor here. One word from me and you'll be in irons and on your way to stand trial in Sydney. You could be convicted as an accomplice on your own confession. Don't yap to me about conditions; if there are going to be conditions I shall decide what they will be, not you. If you think I believe you were pure and lily-white in the midst of all that villainy, you may think again."

"How did you come by these labourers? It would be clear to a complete idiot that you kidnapped them. I would stake my reputation you had as large a part in that as anyone. Don't spin me cock and bull stories about thinking O'Hara was an honest recruiter. You have been his supercargo for the last two years. Even if I took your word that you weren't involved in the present set of murders, we could get you 20 years hard labour."

Toby's face paled but his mouth hardened. If that was to be the Consul's line, he had no option but to play his final card and pray that it worked. "I don't think you would be advised to take such a course, Twyford." No longer was he whining and plaintive, his voice bore a definite, if yet unnamed, threat.

Twyford sat forward in his chair, jolted by the sudden change in the man's attitude. "And why not, may I ask?" he queried aggressively.

"Firstly, you would never lay hands on O'Hara and he is the one you are after; I am small game by comparison. Whether you believe me or not, I had no hand in those murders and you have no right to threaten me with punishment when I am offering you the necessary evidence to convict those who are guilty."

"You are wasting my time, Denison, I've heard all this before," Twyford barked. He had no intention of being dictated to by a blackbirder.

"As you will. My other reason is that Colonel Gunning would not like it."

"Gunning?" Twyford's face went a pasty white. It was as if an assassin had thrown a smoking bomb into the room and he was too paralysed with fright to snuff the fuse. He pulled himself together with considerable effort. "What are you talking about, Denison? What possible objection could Colonel Gunning have and why should his opinion, or any other person's opinion for that matter, affect my decision?" He was blustering desperately, but he suddenly felt ill.

From the confident smile on Denison's face it seemed obvious to Twyford that his past must come spilling out. Had he known the truth he might have rested more easily. Denison knew nothing of the operation to rouse the hill tribes; all he did know was that the colonel and the Consul were partners in a general plan to bring Fiji under the British flag. But from the effect his opening had, he guessed there were other secrets and decided to allude to more information than he actually possessed.

"Who do you think you are fooling, Twyford? I know all about your little plans, the Colonel told me so himself."

"Gunning told you? I don't believe it." The Consul was panic-stricken. If Denison knew, how many others were in on the same secrets?

Denison laughed scornfully. He held the whip-hand now and he was going to apply the scourge with the skill of an expert. "The Colonel did his own recruiting so far as I was concerned, two years ago. We met in New Zealand. He told me his plans, in fact it was he who suggested I join O'Hara. He has a quarter share in the *Philomena* himself — not in his own name of course — not even O'Hara knows that his sleeping partner is Colonel Gunning. I work for the colonel just as you do. He told me about your little games. He said that if I was ever in trouble to see you and you would sort it out. What does that make us, partners in crime?"

"How many others know?" asked Twyford hoarsely.

"Who knows who the Colonel confides in? No one knows through me, you may rest easy on that score, but unless my name is kept right out of this O'Hara business, I shall give the game away. I don't think the Foreign Office would be too pleased if they knew you were really working for someone else." It was now Twyford's turn to sweat.

"Come on, Twyford, don't be an idiot. I tell you the Colonel's name has never been mentioned aboard the *Philomena*: O'Hara thinks his partner is a Mr Robinson of New Zealand, he's never going to find out about Gunning. The Colonel will lose his investment when the schooner is seized, but he'll be tickled pink by the publicity. This is just the thing he is after; it'll be headlines right across the world. You yourself stand to collect all the kudos for the capture."

"How can I keep you out of it, damn your eyes?" stormed the Consul, not knowing how he was going to extricate himself from the quicksand into which he sank deeper and deeper by the minute. "Don't you understand? An amnesty can only be given by the judge who hears the case and your evidence. I haven't a chance of keeping your name out of it."

"If you get after O'Hara straight away, you won't need me, there'll still be enough evidence aboard the ship. It shouldn't take much to get the crew or the kanakas themselves to talk. I've given you the lead you need, now all I want is to be forgotten until this has blown over. Give me a letter which would prove that I was somewhere else. In it you can thank me in it for doing a job for you on that particular date."

Twyford sat with his head in his hands. The last nails were being driven in the coffin of his self-respect and integrity. One crime led to another until it seemed there was nothing too bad or evil they would not ask of him; nor was there any way of refusing without offering up himself and his family as a sacrifice to his conscience.

He looked up at Denison with absolute loathing. "Where is the *Philomena*?" he asked wearily.

Poor Horace was not going to see his bed, nor would his wife have her dinner party. Giving details of the *Philomena*'s anchorage, Denison stressed the speed with which the navy must strike if they wanted to capture O'Hara. The Consul knew the spot Denison described and, after an interminable amount of dithering, during which he was cruelly goaded by his informer, he heaved his bulk from behind his desk and prepared to leave once more for *Rosario*.

"Are you coming with us, Denison?"

"You must be joking," laughed Toby. "O'Hara would only have to clap eyes on me and, even were I to be guarded by the whole Royal Navy, my life would not be worth a brass farthing. I have decided to drop out of sight for a while. I think the time has come for me to pay a call upon my kith and kin at Vatulevu." His tone of voice left no illusions as to his opinion of his family. "You might call it the return of the prodigal son."

24

The prodigal returns

TOBY DENISON'S RECEPTION was better than he deserved. His father gave him an initial apoplectic outburst which he endured with becoming silence; if all was not forgotten at least it seemed to have been forgiven.

Kate had raised Toby in the absence of their mother and it was only natural that she should be glad to see him return to the fold. In private she scolded him for his part in the labour traffic, but being ignorant of the full enormity of his crimes she was prepared to forgive so long as he promised to mend his ways. Toby would have promised the world in exchange for sanctuary until O'Hara had gone to the gallows.

Jason said as little as possible. He despised Toby Denison intensely and hoped he would quickly become bored with Vatulevu and move on. However, as long as Kate was happy to have him around, he was prepared to keep his opinions to himself. And so there was an initial honeymoon period when Toby went out of his way to be pleasant and his hosts tried to reciprocate.

Had they known he was on the *Philomena* at the time of the massacre it might have been a different story. Levuka now had its own newspaper, the *Fiji Times*, which covered the event in gory detail. Toby expressed as much horror as anyone when O'Hara and his murderous crew were discussed. He had the Consul's letter to prove he was nowhere near the *Philomena* on that voyage yet he was able to tell the others more about O'Hara than the paper knew. It was only when he noticed Jason eyeing him suspiciously that he thought he might have overdone the detail.

Three weeks after his arrival on Vatulevu a week-old copy of the *Fiji Times* told them that HMS *Rosario* had hauled O'Hara and his crew off to New South Wales. From that moment Toby was able to relax and return to his natural self.

He began by making his father's life a misery. Whenever Kate and Jason were not about, he taunted him with being a drunkard and a failure as a missionary. He even threw in his father's face the fact that his wife had been so sickened by her husband she had run off with another man. John Denison hadn't realised that his children knew all about their mother. He no longer needed to lie, but it hurt the him to learn that Kate knew and had known for years.

Toby encouraged him to drink until the old man was incapable. His purpose was to make it worthwhile for his father to pay for peace. Toby had cleaned out the cash box previously, but this time he intended to clear the vault.

Within a month John Denison was drinking as heavily as he had ever done. He would stagger into dinner only to fall asleep over the soup, much to his daughter's disgust. Toby, on the other hand, would remain meticulously sober.

Toby told Kate that educating a kai-loma child in Sydney was a waste. The money should be kept in trust for her own children. Kate exploded and called her brother names he had never realised she knew existed; she even threatened to tell Jason what he had said. It had taken every ounce of blandishment he could summon to smooth her ruffled feathers.

The longer he stayed the less he tried to be a satisfactory guest. He abused Lala, was filthy in his habits, and began to lie around unshaven and unwashed. Had he a conscience at all he would have earned his keep by helping Jason who was grossly overworked. But in spite of Kate's scarcely veiled hints that he should earn her husband's hospitality, he evaded the issue on the grounds that he knew nothing about farming.

A few miles away two fat healthy kai-loma youngsters romped in the dust of Lomanikaya village. But it never occurred to Toby Denison to enquire after his children. By his lights they were no responsibility of his — for all he knew, there could be another dozen like them scattered around the Pacific.

*****

It was his insatiable appetite for women which was his final undoing. Of recent years he had always had a woman at his beck and call. In port it was the best that the dockside brothels could supply, and at sea the pick of the cargo.

Although the whores were accommodating, they never set a price in advance for 'Gentleman Toby'; instead they would negotiate after the event, when the degree of his perversion was revealed. Most made sure they had friends near at hand when it came to settlement time, to make sure he did not welsh on the payment. The waifs torn by O'Hara from homes on isolated islands had no such protectors to safeguard their interests.

Toby had no idea of the emotions his presence on Vatulevu stirred up in the hearts of the Fijians. Had he tossed the smallest gift to the mothers of his children, he might have placated local feelings, but his consistent indifference made the mothers implacable enemies and they saw to it that every relative and friend regarded him in the same light. It was only the protective cloak of Jason's patronage which kept them from taking action against him.

It was surprising that Toby managed to hold himself in check for so long. In their first heart-to-heart talk Kate had warned him that he had but to lay a finger on one of the girls at Qaraniqio and she would ask Jason to ship him off to Levuka the same day. Kate's warning on the one hand and the looming presence of O'Hara on the other was enough to keep anyone celibate.

By the end of the second month however the spectre of O'Hara had disappeared and his continence preyed on his mind. Every woman who crossed his path was mentally stripped and assessed as to her bedworthiness. It incensed Toby that the mission had ordained that the body must always be properly shrouded from view. The kai-Vatulevu women had obediently covered themselves from head to foot in long shapeless bags. Helen Simpson, the parson's wife, and Kate were slowly teaching dressmaking, but it took time to make seamstresses out of women who had never needed more than an 18 inch liku around their waists.

Lacking underclothes, buttocks and breasts bounced freely and to Toby, starved of the feel of female flesh, were made the more provocative by the prohibition imposed upon him. The Fijian women kept away from him unless it was absolutely unavoidable; they could feel his eyes on them and for all that he might fool the Marama, they had no difficulty reading his thoughts.

The islanders who had once regarded free love as natural, were now taught by the church to regard it as major sin. Any woman who agreed to share Toby's bed would have been hauled before the minister and elders and whipped for fornication. She would have been shamed before her sisters and suspended from membership of the church, which in effect meant ejection from the community.

Toby became so ravenous he propositioned one woman openly and, to his surprise and indignation, was turned down flat. Toby didn't know it but the story was all over the island within 24 hours and, though the women laughed about it, they were warned in no uncertain terms by their menfolk of the repercussions should any succumb to Denison's blandishments.

With a man like Toby Denison the end was written before the beginning. One night, a 13 year old girl staggered naked into Korovou Village in the darkness — both her eyes were swollen and rapidly closing and she had dozens of scratches, cuts and bruises all over her breasts and legs. Initially she was incoherent from shock but they finally got her story from her.

That afternoon, returning from her father's food gardens, she had met the young kai-valagi on a lonely part of the track. He had asked her straight out to come with him into the jungle and make love. She had refused and tried to run away and had yelled, but there was no one to hear her. He chased and caught her when she tripped on a tree root.

He punched her in the face again and again, calling her the filthiest things in the Fijian language as he dragged her off the track into the bush. He threw her on the ground and beat her till she was semiconscious and no longer had the strength to keep her legs together. The rape and the heaving buttocks above her, were only vague horrible pictures in her mind and she must have passed out again, for the first thing she really remembered was lying alone, her body one massive pain. The white man had gone.

Before she was halfway through her tale, her father and brothers were hunting out clubs, spears and muskets laid aside since the time of the Tongan invasion. By the time she finished, she was only talking to her mother and the other women, the male population of Korovou was streaming down the track which led south to Qaraniqio.

*****

Toby realised that the Fijians were bound to come for him. He had something like a three hours start, depending on when that stupid bitch woke up and ran home to tell tales. He cursed himself for having been unable to keep his hands off her dirty black hide. What was even worse, he had left her alive when he should have killed and buried her on the spot where they had lain.

The time had come for him to leave Vatulevu. Not that he was worried about that, he had had all he could stomach of his prudish sister and her self-righteous husband. So long as he could clear up certain outstanding differences between himself and his father, he would be happy to go.

He made for his father's detached quarters; the old man was asleep a half-empty bottle on the floor beside his armchair. Toby grabbed him by the shoulders and shook him backwards and forwards. "Come on, wake up!" he snarled, his voice low so that others in the main house would not hear him.

"Whatsa...whatsamarrer?" slurred John Denison slowly coming out of his stupor. His eyes began to focus and a glass of water thrown unceremoniously in his face had him spluttering and wide awake. His son was standing over him, wild-eyed and dishevelled, with two long scratches on his cheek. "Oh God is it you again. For pity's sake can't you leave me alone?"

"Wake up, you drunken old bastard," Toby shook him again. "I want to talk business with you."

"What on earth do you think you're doing?" wailed his father, suddenly scared by the vicious shaking and the look on his son's face. "How dare you assault me. Touch me again and I'll call Jason."

"Just try it and I'll smash your face in," warned Toby. He held the brandy bottle by the neck: "Don't think I don't mean what I say."

John Denison had more sense than to put him to the test. He cowered in his chair; his only hope was that someone from the main house would come. "What is it you want? You're in trouble again, aren't you?"

"Mind your own business. You want to be rid of me I know, and I'm going. But it's going to cost you or I'll be back again, just as soon as this present business has blown over."

John Denison wondered, not for the first time, what species of animal he had sired. He was willing to pay anything if money would guarantee the removal of his son's evil presence. But he was shrewd enough not to take everything Toby said at face value. "Even if I give you money, how do I know you won't come back wanting more?"

"You'll have to take my word for it won't you?" sneered Toby. "You needn't worry. After tonight this bloody place is going to be none too healthy for me for years to come. But I can still make your life miserable from a distance, and I can shove a few spokes in Jason Cotterel's wheel too, if I want to. I've friends who will help me see to that."

"You leave Jason and Kate alone," said his father sharply, frightened now for people other than himself. This in itself was a novel feeling for John Denison, but his daughter and her husband had provided him with love and the security of a home. They had brought him back from the brink of insanity and he could hardly reward them by turning a mad dog loose on their heels. "I'll pay you; how much do you want?"

"I want an irrevocable letter of credit on your Sydney agents for £5,000," said Toby bluntly.

"£5,000? You're mad, boy. That would take every penny I have." This was not the strict truth, but Toby was not to know that.

"I haven't time to waste arguing with you," snapped Toby. He snatched paper, pen and ink from a desk and set them down before his father. "I won't take a penny less than £5,000 and don't try telling me you can't afford it. Get a move on! If I know those bloody Fijians there'll be a gang of them on their way right now. If you hem and haw, you'll see my brains splattered all over your walls. Perhaps that's what you would like to see? You'd like to see me dead wouldn't you?

"What have you done, Toby?"

"Shut up and sign that letter," snapped his son.

*****

Before the old man could set pen to paper there was a knock at the door and both men looked up to see Jason step unceremoniously into the room. "Are you coming to dinner, father?" he asked, "Kate's waiting, the gong has gone twice already." Jason noticed Toby standing over his father. "Oh you're here, Denison. Well, are we eating tonight or not?"

The oil lamp threw a poor light, but as he came further into the room Jason could see that Denison's clothes were torn and dirty and his face looked as if he had tangled with a wildcat. "What's happened to your face?"

"What business is it of yours," barked Toby recklessly. He had to get his father's signature and get away from Vatulevu; everything else was secondary and nothing must be allowed to stand in his way. "Come on, sign that letter. Remember what I said." He turned his back on Jason and glared down at his father.

"Sign what? What's going on here?" Jason had no intention of being spoken to in such a manner.

"He's in some sort of trouble, Jason," said John Denison getting unsteadily to his feet. He tried to get past his son to Jason but was grabbed by the shirt and thrust back into the chair.

"Are you crazy, Denison? What on earth do you think you are doing to your father?" Jason stepped forward to help the old man.

Toby barred his way, a desperate look in his eyes. "I told you to mind your own bloody business, Cotterel. This is between father and son, family business which has nothing to do with you, so you can keep your bloody nose right out of it, do you hear?"

"He's running away, Jason. He's forcing me to give him £5,000," piped John Denison shrilly, "He says he'll make our lives hell if I don't."

"Shut your mouth, you old fool," yelled his son, livid with anger. His father had called him mad, Jason had said he was crazy, and at that moment both were right. Toby raised his fist to strike his father who shouted for help. Jason sprang forward, grabbed the descending arm and swung Denison away from his father. The two men stood there in the dim light breathing heavily and hoarsely.

"For Christ's sake, Denison, what has got into you? Do you think I'm going to stand by while you extort money and beat your father."

Denison's eyes sped around the room looking for a weapon. He snatched up the brandy bottle; a quick flick of the wrist and he smashed the bottom on the edge of the desk.

"You've interfered in my life once too often, Cotterel," he was laughing now, certain he could kill his brother-in-law. He crouched facing Jason, the flickering light from the oil lamp glinting on the jagged edges of his improvised dagger.

He lunged forward and Jason jumped back, the murderous points flashing just before his eyes. There could no longer be any doubt, Denison was out of his mind and meant to kill him if he could. He snatched up a small Indian coffee table just in time to fend off another lunge. The two men edged around John Denison's small sitting room, watching each other's eyes, waiting for the slightest move, kicking aside anything which impeded free movement. Jason circled until his father-in-law was behind him.

"Blow out the light, father," he ordered calmly, his eyes never leaving Toby's.

Toby, not relishing the thought of a fight in the dark, came in fast feinting one way then striking hard in the other. The table in Jason's hand crashed down on his wrist and the bottle dropped and shattered on the floor just as the room was plunged into darkness.

For a second Toby was silhouetted against the door and Jason, seizing his opportunity, waded in. He had the intense satisfaction of feeling the skin over his knuckles split against his brother-in-law's teeth. The next blow broke Toby's nose for the second time.

Denison was also swinging and he was no weakling; one blow made Jason's head ring. The two men charged and crashed together in the dark. Toby's knee just missed Jason's groin and his thumbs gouged for the eyes. Denison knew every dirty trick in the game and it was only Jason's long-unused but similar schooling on Nantucket whalers which saved him.

John Denison's terrified yelling and the sound of smashing furniture brought people running from the main house, Kate at their head. "Jason! Jason!" she screamed.

Her lamp showed the two men fighting for their lives on the floor. John Denison ducked past their flailing arms and legs and escaped through the door. He stopped Kate. "Don't go in there you'll be killed" he cried.

"Let go of me, father. What is happening?"

"Toby's mad!" her father exclaimed. "He tried to get money from me, then he tried to hit me and now he's killing Jason!"

"Toby and Jason!" said Kate stupefied. "Let me go, I tell you! Lala, girls, take my father," she ordered. The maids pulled at John Denison and Kate ran into the room the light held high. It was an absolute shambles of broken furniture and scattered books. Both men were on the floor; her brother had his hands locked on Jason's throat trying to choke him and force his head back onto the floor which was covered with shattered glass. Jason was trying to buck his adversary off and tear the hands away but was not succeeding.

"Jason!" Kate screamed, her heart in her throat. She set down the lamp and looked for something with which to help her husband. That the other man was her brother didn't register — he was trying to kill her husband, the father of her children. She picked up the lamp previously extinguished by her father; it had a heavy brass base which she brought down on Toby's head with all her strength. He sprawled forward as if pole-axed and at that moment it would not have worried Kate had she killed him. She was down on her knees near Jason who was coughing and rubbing his throat.

"Are you alright, darling?" she asked anxiously.

"I am now, thanks to you," he said hoarsely, trying to smile. "I made a mistake when I told your father to blow that lamp out. If you hadn't come he would have killed me."

She helped him up to his feet, blood dripping from his shoulder where he had cut it on glass. "But what happened?" Kate asked.

"I hardly know myself," he answered.

"Toby was trying to get £5,000 from me." It was her father, having broken free from the maids, who answered. "He's done something terrible and he says the Fijians are pursuing him."

Jason knelt by the motionless form on the floor and felt for a heartbeat. "He's still breathing. My God, Kate, you could have killed him."

Toby's head was covered with blood and lamp oil and he showed no signs of regaining consciousness but his sister was quite unrepentant. "When I hit him, I think I meant to kill him." She shuddered, suddenly cold, trembling and remorseful. Jason put his arm around her and led her to the doorway crowded with inquisitive Fijian faces.

"All of you, out of here," he ordered in Fijian. "Lala, take the Marama and her father to the house. I'll get Mr Toby into bed and cleaned up, then I'll come myself. Go on Kate, don't hang around here. Have a stiff brandy and give father one at the same time. Toby will be alright; what he needs now is time to sleep off that crack on the head. We'll find out what it's all about later."

Half an hour later, with most of the evidence of the fight washed away, Jason joined Kate and her father on the verandah of the main house. His head still ached and livid bruises were beginning to show on his throat, but there were no worse after-effects.

"Do you want dinner now, Jason?" Kate asked.

"Just give me a few minutes to collect my thoughts," he answered smiling. "What would I have done without you tonight, I wonder?" his voice was a low caress. "It goes to show that English girls still have a lot of the old Boadicea flowing in their veins."

"But I cannot understand why Toby should have gone off his head like that."

"He's in trouble, daughter," said her father, still looking pale and shaken from his experience. "If I know Toby it will be something to do with a woman."

"What do you think, Jason?" asked Kate anxiously.

"That could be it. Toby's not the sort of man who can be without a woman for very long. Whatever it was, it certainly turned him wild. He's as strong as a bull, and with the fear of some sort of retribution on his tail to give him a little extra, he was more than I could handle."

Kate led them into the dining room where a place for Toby was still laid.

*****

They were to find out about Toby's crime before they finished their meal. Lala came bustling into the room looking very worried. "Turaga, there are lights coming through the coconut groves. There are many men and they are running," she said excitedly.

"I have been expecting something like this," said Jason, pushing back his chair and getting to his feet. "Bring the girls and the children here, Lala, and stay with the Marama. I shall find out what they want."

"They're after that cursed son of mine," John Denison insisted. He's going to bring trouble down on all of us."

"Jason be careful," Kate called after him as he left the room. They could soon hear shouting in Fijian and Jason's calm tones trying to bring order into what was evidently utter confusion. He returned white-faced and very grim about the eyes and mouth. At his back a crowd of angry Fijians, all armed, jostled to get into the room.

"This afternoon Toby got hold of a young girl," said Jason, his voice very bitter and cold. "You know her, Kate, Epi's daughter, she's only a child. He beat her half to death and raped her."

"Oh dear God!" exclaimed Kate horrified.

"They want him, Kate. They've come from Korovou to make him answer for it."

"What … what will they do to him?"

"In their present mood they'll club him to death. For once they won't even listen to me. They demand we hand him over."

As much as Kate disliked her brother, she could not bring herself to hand him over to an angry mob for summary execution.

"But we can't do that, Jason … talk to them again … He's nothing but a primitive beast, but he is my brother, you can't let them kill him."

"But nothing, Kate! There are more than a hundred of them out there. How can I stop them? I'm not even sure I want to. From what the girl's father says, she's lucky to be alive after the terrible beating he gave her. Whether he's your brother or not, why should he get away with it? He should have thought of the consequences before he attacked her."

The raped girl's father, irritated by the delay and not understanding a word of the conversation which had passed between Jason and his wife, stepped forward. "Where is the young Turaga?" he asked menacingly. "We have no argument with you or yours but your wife's brother is lower than the filthiest kai-si. He must be punished for what he has done to my daughter."

Epi was well-known to Jason. He and his sons often worked at Qaraniqio and it cut Jason to the quick to know that anyone associated with his own family should have harmed him or his children. Jason was the man in the middle. His duty to the Fijians and an acute sense of justice pulled from one side, and his love for Kate pulled from the other. It would be a frightful experience for Kate if they did execute Toby Denison.

"Epi, listen to me," begged Jason. "You must listen to what I say. My wife's brother is sick in the head, lialia. Not only did he attack your daughter, he struck his father and not more than an hour ago he tried to kill me."

There was an excited outburst from among the Fijians on receipt of this new information. Knowing Jason's capabilities as a fighter they thought anyone would have had to be lialia to even try such a thing.

"I have never told you lies," continued Jason, "if you don't believe me, come closer so that you may see the fingermarks on my throat where he tried to strangle me. It was the Marama who saved me," said Jason, pointing dramatically in the direction of his wife. "She clubbed him over the head with a heavy weight. He has still not recovered consciousness after the blow, it was so hard. If you take him out and kill him now, Epi, what revenge will that be for you and your sons? He is unconscious, he would not feel a thing, he would not even know why he died."

As the truth of Jason's words sank in, Epi's breath came out in a long shuddering gasp. He had been pent up to kill and now was deflated as he saw his chance pass. "But if he is crazy and dangerous, Turaga," Epi argued, "he must be killed so that others may be safe."

"He must be punished, Epi, I agree. But it is not for you or me to say if that punishment should be death. Denison has committed a heinous crime and he should be brought before the chief for judgement. Tui Navatulevu is the person who must pronounce sentence. Leave him here with me and tomorrow morning I shall bring him with me to Lomanikaya to answer the charges against him."

"But he is of the blood of your wife and your father-in-law. They would help him to escape in the night," answered Epi suspiciously.

"Do you doubt my word?"

"Not yours, Turaga," said the injured father apologetically, "but what of the Marama and her father?"

Jason turned to the others; it was obvious that they had understood what had been said. Kate had collapsed into a chair with her head in her hands and was weeping bitterly. John Denison stood beside her, one hand upon her head; he seemed crippled and speechless with shock.

"I'm sure you both realise," said Jason in English, "I shall have to take him before the chief. What he will do I don't know, but on the other hand if these people think for a moment that you might help him get away they will kill him out of hand."

John Denison looked his son-in-law straight in the eye and answered in a hardly audible voice. "It is hard for you Jason. You must do what is right. But don't ask me to stand in judgement on my son, I have far too much on my conscience as it is."

Kate could stand it no longer and she ran from the room sobbing. Knowing the Fijian mentality she was sure that certain death awaited her brother whichever way the decision went. The fact that Jason was now involved meant that he too would have a hand in her brother's execution.

Jason sensed exactly what she was thinking and feeling. "But what else can I do Kate?" his thoughts went after her. "He cannot be allowed to get off scot-free and at least this gives a chance for tempers to cool down."

He knew she had placed on his shoulders responsibility for saving her brother's life. If he tried to hoodwink the Fijians or broke faith with them by organising an escape, he would destroy a relationship which had taken years to build and, what was even more important, be doing those very things of which he accused the other Europeans. He had decided to live in Fiji and had undertaken to live under the law of the chief. That law applied not just to himself personally but to everyone who lived under his roof.

Jason's thoughts briefly touched on Aporosa, far away in Sydney. One day he would come into the inheritance bequeathed by his mother, and would claim the chieftainship of Vatulevu. When that day came, would the people follow him knowing that in his veins flowed the blood of Jason Cotterel, the white man they had trusted but who had betrayed them? If he followed the course that instinct and honour dictated, where would that leave his marriage?

"Enough, Turaga. We have come for him and we shall take him with us no matter whether he is conscious or not," said Epi sharply, misunderstanding the meaning of the long silence.

Jason swung around on him furiously, "You'll do no such damned thing," he said, venting his spleen on the unfortunate Fijian. "Since when were you created Tui Navatulevu? I said that the chief will decide this matter and that's what I meant. Your daughter will be able to tell everyone what Denison did; and Denison in turn will be able to say something in his defence. The chief will decide whether he is guilty. Not you or I."

"If you want to take him now, you will also have to take me and that means you will have to kill me. Do you understand?" Jason glared at the Fijians, daring anyone to make a move towards the bedroom section of the house.

"I swear, Epi, that if either you or your sons lay so much as a finger on Denison before Tui Navatulevu has pronounced judgement, your own lives will answer for it. I swear it on the soul of my son in whose body flows the blood of your chiefs."

The speech had its desired affect. Jason's prestige since the Tongan defeat and his leadership was second only to that of Tui Navatulevu. The majority began to shuffle uneasily and edge back out of the door.

"You promise you will bring Denison to Lomanikaya tomorrow?"

"Have I ever broken a promise to your people?" Jason countered.

"Sega, i'saka, you haven't."

"Do you trust me, Epi?"

"Io, i'saka, we all do," came the reply.

"Return to your homes then and tomorrow, when the sun rises out of the sea, I shall come to the village with the white man who is the brother of my wife."

Epi and his friends bowed their heads in submission and backed out of Jason's presence, with all the respect normally accorded only to high chiefs. Jason, watching them go, felt exhausted and terribly depressed. When he turned, the only other person left in the room with him was Lala. "She has gone to her room, Turaga," the old woman said.

"And the father?"

"To look on his son for the last time, Turaga," she answered, her mind already accepting the fact that Toby Denison would be sentenced to death.

Jason knew that Lala was also wondering what he would do. His own household as well as the rest of the island were testing him.

"Send a message down to the men," he ordered brusquely, "I want five up here to stand guard over Denison tonight to see that there can be no possible chance of his escaping. When you have done that, bring me a fresh bottle of rum, a jug of water and a glass. If I'm going to have to sit this out, at least I'll have the company of some liquor in case my courage fails."

Jason sat the rest of the night hunched in a chair, alone with his thoughts. He badly needed Kate, but he did not dare go into her lest the softness of her arms weaken his resolution, and he knew that it was even less possible for her to come to him. Only the thickness of a wall separated them and, although once or twice he thought he caught the sound of her sobbing, her brother's shadow lay between them.

The next morning at first light Jason rode off toward Korovou. Walking behind him, his head bandaged, came Toby Denison and his guard of Fijians. Looking back, Jason saw Kate standing alone on the headland, watching them march off to her brother's trial.

25

Fijian justice

Jason considered Denison a spineless creature, but he behaved well throughout the trial. Surrounded by over 300 men and women, whose hatred was like a wild animal poised to strike, even stronger men might have become terrified, gibbering wrecks. But Denison sat cross-legged, head down, directly in front of the wizened old chief and seemed hardly conscious of what was said.

The girl was there. Her cuts and bruises were spectacular, especially when her cotton smock was stripped off to show the full extent of Denison's brutality. But though she was obviously in considerable pain, she wouldn't die, thought Jason.

Tui Navatulevu listened to the evidence. No one really knew just how many years he had seen pass and he looked for all the world like a small, brown, graven image. Now and then his immobility was broken by a flick of his flywhisk, first to the right side of the head, then the left with an occasional double flick at a particularly persistent fly.

Finally, the girl came to the end of her tale. There was an angry buzz of noise from her kinsfolk, eager to see blood wash out the insult to their clan.

"The girl has spoken," said the chief in a brittle, dispassionate voice. "Have you anything you wish to say, Denison?"

Toby Denison did not answer. He would have liked to jump to his feet and scream a defiant denunciation of the whole proceedings. This decrepit, moth-eaten old man had no jurisdiction over the acts of a white man.

Earlier, when he took that line his thrice-cursed, misbegotten, swine of a brother-in-law had threatened to tie him hand and foot and gag him. Now that he was actually on trial it would only antagonise the Fijians further. It would be better if he kept his mouth shut and looked woebegone and penitent.

If possible he wanted to make Jason Cotterel do the talking for him — they would listen to Cotterel whereas anything he had to say would make matters worse. He could also derive satisfaction from knowing it must really gall Cotterel to have to act as his defence counsel.

Tui Navatulevu again urged him to speak. "You understand what has been said, Denison?" Toby went so far as to nod. "These people want me to sentence you to death. Your kinsman stopped them killing you last night in order that you might say something in your own defence."

Toby said nothing. He glanced towards Jason who was watching him closely. As much as he hated Cotterel's guts, he was his only hope of leaving this assembly alive.

"If you will not speak, Denison," snapped the Tui, annoyed by the white man's stubbornness when he was doing his best to treat him fairly, "then I must take it that what the girl says is true. You are guilty of the crimes you are accused of."

"Turaga na Tui Navatulevu," Jason kneeled forward." I crave the chief's permission to speak. Denison is my wife's brother and therefore my kinsman by marriage. If he will not speak I shall speak for him."

"You may speak, Jasoni," said the chief in relieved tones.

Jason faced the chief but half-turned towards the rest of the room "I have not spoken before, Turaga, because I felt that it was your duty to decide whether or not Denison was guilty. If the girl did not tell the truth, only one other person was there to know and that was Denison himself. If she lied it was for Denison to say so. I cannot; I was not there."

"He has said nothing and you have therefore found him guilty of the accusation that he assaulted, beat and raped the girl. I think that your finding is wise and just, Turaga."

Denison looked at Jason anxiously, scared that he was about to be left in the lurch. The crowd sat forward, all attention. Heads nodded in agreement with Jason's statement, but they knew he had more up his sleeve. The girl's relatives were still after blood nevertheless the majority, now that they had seen the girl, were more interested in the trial as such, rather than the question of crime and punishment.

Fijians loved to listen to a good speaker and, from experience, they knew they could depend on Jason for a lucid argument which would raise the occasion above the mere fact of assault and rape.

"Turaga na Tui, I agree that Denison is guilty, but what should be the penalty for this offence? The girl's kinsmen say death is the only punishment which will cleanse the stain from their clan, but as Denison's kinsman I say that they are wrong."

"This girl has been beaten and we see the cuts and bruises on her naked body," continued Jason. "Three weeks from now, if she is brought before this assembly and shown to us again how will she look? The bruises will have faded, the swellings will have gone down, and she will see and walk as normal. Her cuts and scratches will have healed and her skin will be as unblemished and soft as ever."

"But if you follow the wishes of the Korovou men, where will Denison be? He will be dead, rotting in the ground. He will have paid with his life for injuries that only lasted three weeks." Jason's dramatic oratory had its effect; many of the old men nodded acknowledgement of his point.

Toby Denison's mind churned. He could not have had a better defence and he knew it. Not that he had regrets so far as the girl was concerned, unless it was his original one that he was a fool not to have killed her when he had the chance. He would have been well away from Vatulevu before they connected him with her death.

Rather than give Jason credit for what he was doing, Denison was priding himself on his own cleverness for putting Cotterel in a position where he had to work for him. If it had not been for Cotterel, he would have had £5,000 out of his father and been in Levuka by now. It was Cotterel's fault that he had to put up with this travesty of a trial.

"I ask the chief to remember," Jason was saying, "that this man Denison has been away from Vatulevu for three years, and during those years life here has changed completely. The missionaries and the lotu have brought in the new ways and with it their conception of what is good and what is bad."

"In the old days if a man lay with a woman it was an act of enjoyment, a good thing for both. Today the act of love is no longer innocent; it is bad, evil, a guilty act from which the enjoyment has been stripped away."

Jason continued, "When Denison was last here Vatulevu women went willingly to his bed. I name no names, but this is fact, we all know it." There was a gasp from the rear of the room where the women sat, but Jason was not prepared to spare feelings if it meant the difference between life and death; he had the feeling that his own marriage and happiness rested on the outcome of this trial.

"Two children living in Lomanikaya village carry Denison's blood in their veins." There was scuffling and giggling from the back of the room; Tui Navatulevu scowled and two women scuttled out of the door.

"On his return to Vatulevu, Denison found everything changed. He is a man who cannot live without women yet none would look at him. None would share his bed; it was a terrible insult to his manhood. When you decide how this man should be punished, Turaga, I would beg you to bear these points in mind."

Jason knew that the loophole in his argument was that as a clergyman's son Denison should have known the difference between right and wrong better than anyone. Had he been so eager for a woman all he needed to have done was offer marriage and he would have been swamped by applicants.

He continued, "On the other hand, if you grant Denison the gift of life, Epi and his sons may say that they are the ones who are punished whereas the guilty one receives gifts at the hand of the chief. What sort of justice would that be?"

Everyone was listening to Jason closely. His hand dipped into a masi cloth bag at his side and he pulled out three large tabua, perfect specimens of the sacred whale's teeth, the Fijian repository of all honour and wealth. There was a hiss of indrawn breath as the tabua injected an entirely new element into the trial. If Tui Navatulevu accepted them, it would mean life for Denison; if they were refused — an almost unheard of thing — Denison would die.

"These tabua I offer, Turaga, as compensation to this girl and her family for their injuries," said Jason approaching the end of his speech. "These are not a presentation from Denison himself, but from my family, from the household of Qaraniqio, for Denison is our kinsman and it follows that we have a debt to pay. Accept these and show Denison clemency."

There was a tense silence as the assembly waited for the chief's verdict. Epi's sons were glaring angrily at Jason, but their father, eyes fixed covetously on the tabua, was having other thoughts.

For some time Tui Navatulevu did not move; all present held their breath expectantly; and for the first time Toby Denison was frightened. Cotterel's speech might not have been enough to swing the issue. Perspiration stood out on his forehead in large drops and the hands on his knees trembled.

Jason looked into the eyes of the old chief, the father of his first wife, and grandfather of his son. For a moment he too felt sick with apprehension. Then Tui Navatulevu slowly leaned forward and touched the tabua signifying that he accepted them on behalf of the injured family.

"Isa!" A great exclamation went up from the audience, part relief and part disappointment. The matanivanua crawled forward to take the tabua from Jason's hands. Jason was drained of all feeling. He hardly knew how he regained his place beside Denison.

Epi's sons were arguing among themselves but Epi, who was now a wealthy man by local standards, shushed them to silence.

*****

Tui Vatulevu was speaking again …

"These tabua I accept as adequate compensation to the girl's family. But that is not the end of this matter." His voice reminded Jason of the rustling and crackling of dry palm fronds. "I have decided that Jasoni is right, the crime does not merit death. But that does not mean there should not be a lesser punishment."

The smirk of victory disappeared from Toby Denison's face. He looked at Jason waiting for him to interrupt. But Jason, refusing to acknowledge his brother-in-law; was listening closely to what the Tui was saying.

"Had this man to live the rest of his life among us, I would order that he be deprived of his manhood so that this assault on a young girl might never be repeated."

Castration! Toby wondered if he was about to faint. His loins ached as if they could already feel the knife. He was so frantic with worry he missed the meaning of the next sentence completely.

"In punishment he will be taken outside and tied to a tree. Each member of the girl's family will then flog him five times with the kuita to erase the insult to their clan. When he is cut down he is to leave Vatulevu immediately, never to return. If he should ever set foot on our island, any man among you is entitled to kill him on the spot."

"Sa dina!" roared the crowd and clapped five slow beats in unison to signify that justice had been done.

"You can't let them do this to me, Cotterel," Toby yelled, as Epi and his sons advanced on him. "I'm a white man, you aren't going to let these evil bastards flog me. They'll beat me to death. You want to see me murdered?" Jason did not even look up at him. Denison would not die but he would remember this thrashing from now until the grave.

"If you speak to them again they'll listen! For Christ's sake, Jason, you've got to help me!" Toby screamed as he struggled impotently against his guards. Jason still sat unmoving on the mats. Toby's panic-stricken yells came back to him as he was hauled off. "You bloody swine, Cotterel. I'll never forget this. I'll get you, you bastard, if it's the last thing I do."

An hour later, Jason had the *Albatross* anchored off the village and Denison was brought off in a canoe and unceremoniously dumped on the deck. The man was alive, even conscious, but his back was a bloodied mess of torn flesh. For the rest of his life he would carry the marks of his humiliation at the hands of the Fijians. The scars would never allow him to forget.

But it was in Denison's brain that the deepest brands were to be found. Tied hand and foot to the tree the knotted vines exploding the screams from his lungs, his brain had become a cauldron of hatred.

It was as if every searing blow was administered by Jason Cotterel — every atom of pain, every spattering drop of blood was his doing. Every frustration, everything that had ever gone awry was Cotterel's doing. Toby Denison hated him so intensely he had to live in order that he might devote the remainder of his life to Cotterel's destruction. He was determined to repay each stroke and every particle of torn flesh a thousandfold.

During the passage to Levuka, Jason bathed and bandaged Denison's back. Neither man spoke, but in the confined space of the cabin the atmosphere was electric.

At Levuka, the ketch only paused long enough for Denison to be rowed ashore. Jason stood in the cockpit watching him go. He had read his brother-in-law's thoughts like an open book — it was plain that Denison intended to have his revenge one day.

It would be a grave mistake to write Denison off as an ineffectual enemy. Offhand, Jason could think of nothing the man could do which might affect Kate and the family, but it would pay to be careful. There were people in Levuka and other parts of the islands who would watch Denison's movements for him. As least Denison would never dare return to Vatulevu.

He had done his best for Kate's brother. By now she must know what had happened as Lala had been there throughout the trial. He relied on Kate's sense of justice to do the rest, otherwise Denison would have already got his revenge by causing irreparable damage to their marriage.

There were times when he cursed his sense of obligation to the Fijians. It would have been easy enough to engineer Denison's escape. Then at least his marriage would not stand in jeopardy as it did now. When all was boiled down, principles were only matters of pride and self-importance. They were worthless when weighed in the balance with Kate and his family.

He missed seeing her at first because he had been watching the empty headland, his heart sinking lower and lower, his hand gripping the tiller, white-knuckled.

"There's the Marama, waiting for us," the man in the bows shouted, pointing to the jetty which was just becoming visible as they swung into the river mouth.

Jason thrust the tiller into the hands of another crewman and sprang to the foredeck. Sure enough there she was, waving madly. He waved back, his eyes dimmed with tears of relief and he gave a deep sigh of satisfaction. No matter what happened in the future, for the present he was safely home.

26
On reflection

AUGUST 1870! The Prussian guns crashed and Bismark's armies smashed their way into France. The Emperor Napoleon III abdicated; Paris came under siege and finally fell; and the economy of France lay in ruins. In the Fiji Islands, 12,000 miles away, planters were bankrupted, and business houses with large sums of money out against a cotton crop which could no longer be sold to French factories, went into liquidation.

Ten years before, even five years before, a European war would have hardly raised a ripple in the conversation on MacDonald's verandah. But by 1870 Fiji was a very different country to that which Jason Cotterel first knew. The lawlessness and the cotton boom had caused a rush of outsiders to the islands.

Every river valley had its plantations and trading stations. Levuka was a thriving centre of more then 1000 Europeans, not to mention Fijians, Chinese, and human flotsam from elsewhere in the Pacific which swirled around its dusty, dirty streets. It now boasted a school, a printing press, a mail service and the *Fiji Times* which appeared, God willing, every Tuesday and Saturday.

For all that it was larger, the town was no more salubrious. The streets were dust storms in dry weather and deep sticky mud pools in the wet. The beach was a refuse dump. Had it not been for the cleansing action of each tide, Levuka would long since have been buried under its own waste.

The population both washed and defecated in the streams, hopefully drawing their drinking water from higher up — this was the main reason most people drank their spirits neat. The town remained a haven of felon, fugitive debtor and deserter. The economy was at a standstill yet impoverished settlers could still afford to sit around all day drinking themselves insensible. Drunken chiefs and brawling whites were everywhere.

In Kate Cotterel's opinion, Levuka should have been burnt to the ground. She visited the few friends she had there once in 1870, and again early in 1871 but, as she told Jason when they finally got home, it would not bother her if she never saw it again.

As Jason predicted, Drew's Government had collapsed, leaving in its wake an even worse state of anarchy and chaos than before. There was no government, no army or police, no banking system, no confidence in business, no honesty and almost no hope.

Business staggered along, but all attempts at sound commercial practice were bedevilled by the dearth of hard currency; coinage was almost impossible to come by. Nothing came into the country for which one did not have to pay in hard cash and the country itself sold virtually nothing. Bolivian half-dollars, Maria Theresa dollars and a hodgepodge of other coins drifted sluggishly from hand-to-hand but in no significant quantities. The cotton trade had been conducted on the basis of paper promises and, with the final collapse of the paper castle, business had descended to bartering.

Jason saw to it that his family and Vatulevu kept well out of the political and economic maelstrom. As Toby Denison had discovered, Vatulevu knew how to deal with criminals and this, plus the reputation they had acquired by defeating the Tongans, meant they need not worry about the security of the island.

Without cotton Jason's income was substantially reduced, but he still had resources and had lost little in the crash. He had all the currency he needed for he had ceased to deal through Levuka. When copra production from the islands coconut groves passed the 400 tons mark it paid the Southern Cross Shipping company to call at the island for the cargo.

With Peter Bex acting as the island's agent, selling and buying for them in Sydney, Jason had no need to go near the Levuka sharks. It was years since Jason had been to Sydney where his bank manager would have welcomed him. He had a substantial deposit of his own and was also trustee/manager of the even larger account belonging to the Vatulevu Fijians.

Vatulevu was not yet producing saleable quantities of sugar. Jason needed advice on sugar-making and had heard of a man among the Polynesia Company settlers at Suva reputed to have had experience in the West Indies and who might be enticed over to help him. Nurseries for coffee and tea were well established and some quite extensive areas would be planted in 1871, but it would be some years before any return could be expected. Jason still looked on both projects as very experimental.

Copra from the coconut groves was still the backbone of his enterprise. His special pride was in the increasing herds of cattle and horses. For the most part they were self-sufficient. Vatulevu might not command the luxuries of civilisation, but in contrast to the rest of the Group, it was both solvent and full of hope for the future.

*****

Having little contact with Levuka merchants, and with only the occasional boat to bring over back copies of the *Fiji Times*, the Cotterels were used to being well behind with island news. Jason didn't even know that a new government had been formed until Peter Bex told him a month after the event.

Bex, Jason, Kate and John Denison were having a pre-dinner drink at Qaraniqio and Bex was bringing them up to date. "You hide yourself away too much, Jason," complained Bex. "As the most prosperous planter in Fiji you should take a greater interest in local affairs."

"So long as you don't blame me, Peter," laughed Kate. "Jason could go to Levuka any time he wishes so long as he doesn't want me to go too. But nothing can drag him away from his precious plantation."

Jason pulled contentedly on his cigar. Levuka had nothing to offer that compared with this. Here he sat on his own verandah, drinking and talking to the only people he cared for; in the house a fine dinner was being prepared, and tucked away in their beds were his children, Ulamila, young John and the new baby Katie. If Aporosa could have been with them, his cup would have overflowed. He had not the slightest wish to be involved in politics, Fijian or any other.

"If that government was formed six weeks ago, Peter," he mocked affectionately, "your news is already too late for me to have taken part. By now it will have collapsed."

"This time I think you may be proved wrong, Jason."

"Who are you fooling?" laughed his friend.

"Maybe I'm fooling myself," Bex admitted, "but it is a sight different to those other efforts. They might just pull it off."

"There'll be no difference. It will just be new faces trying to fleece the Fijians with the least possible effort. In my opinion that was never a sound foundation for good government and never will be."

"Well at least the ministers aren't the fly-by-nights we've seen before. I know most of them and they're as solid as you, Jason. They're determined to make the thing work, the writing's on the wall for everyone if they don't. You've been able to keep your head above water because you deal direct with Sydney."

"For which we have you to thank, my friend.".

"I don't know about that," answered Bex gruffly. "These other poor devils of planters — and there are a few who are honest enough and have tried damned hard — there's no hope for them, unless some form of stable government can be created. Don't be too sarcastic about these new men. They are triers and I don't see anybody else coming forward to get Fiji out of its mess, you included, Jason."

"I stand rebuked," said Jason. He was now very interested. It was rare for Bex to take up cudgels for the local whites. "Who are these paragons?"

"George Woods is one; a half pay naval officer. He came here to do the hydrological survey of Levuka harbour for the navy and stayed on. He's got Foreign Affairs. Gus Hennings is another."

"Any relation of the Hennings in Lau?"

"A brother. He runs the Levuka branch of the trading company."

"Well, well, well," said Jason nodding his head. "The Hennings have been supporters of Ma'afu for years, but I've never heard anything else against them. They've a name for being honest businessmen, at least by Fiji standards."

"JC Smith is another Levuka merchant; and John Sagar, he's handling Trade and Commerce."

"Now I know Sagar, he's a planter and a good one. We've met on a number of occasions when we've both been in Levuka at the same time. He always struck me as a gentleman."

Bex was right, there was a difference, thought Jason. "What about Fijians? I haven't heard you mention any."

"This time they haven't been left out. Ratu Savenaca helps Woods with Foreign Affairs, and Ratu Timoci is Minister for War and Police. I don't think that's too bad; there would be no point in putting a Fijian in charge of trade, now would there?"

"Who's the Premier?"

Here Peter Bex pulled a sour face. "Sydney Burt. He's also Minister for Finance. If there's one in the whole bunch I don't trust it's Burt; he was an auctioneer in Sydney and went bankrupt. He could be the bad egg which sends the others rotten."

"Bankruptcy is certainly not the best training for a prospective Finance Minister," laughed his host. "Though I suppose you could argue the opposite."

Kate called them to dinner and in deference to her the talk over the table centred more on plantation affairs and on Aporosa in Sydney.

Over coffee and a brandy, Jason reopened the subject of government. "It will never work, Peter. They've no source of finance and the Europeans won't pay taxes. Ma'afu will do his best to wreck it, and though you didn't mention Gunning before, if he's anything to do with the government you can be sure it will fail."

"Gunning is not in it at all," said Bex. "He's in New South Wales at the moment, I understand. You're wrong about those others too, Jason. I know it's fantastic, but Ma'afu has taken an oath of allegiance to Cakobau as King and to the government."

He continued, "Woods told me about it. They were as worried about Ma'afu as you and when he turned up with Swanston to see what was going on, they expected him to denounce the whole thing. It was Hennings who brought Ma'afu and Cakobau together. There were two solid days of talk; no one seems quite sure what was said; but at the end the old fox shattered everyone by publicly pronouncing his support for the government."

"I can't believe it! Ma'afu and Cakobau running in tandem. It seems impossible." Jason's face was a picture.

"They didn't get him for nothing, Ma'afu gets the title of Viceroy and Lieutenant-Governor of Lau, £1,000 in cash and an annual income of £500 a year."

"But he had all that before and was accountable to no one," said Jason. "Why put himself below Cakobau in the scheme of things and hand over the Tovata revenues to boot? If Cakobau ever imagines he'll see those revenues he has less sense than I have given him credit for."

"The King knows that as well as you do. According to Woods all he wanted was that oath of allegiance. He would have promised anything. He can now turn round to the great powers, the British, the French and the Americans, and prove that he is the 'Supremo' here. If Ma'afu cuts up rough in future he will no longer be an independent prince, he'd be a rebel."

Jason watched as the big banana moths bounced off the glass cover of the table lamp. In the flame Jason pictured the Vunivalu as he had once known him, sitting beside a yaqona bowl, telling him of his plans for Fiji. In spite of his failures, each year seemed to bring Cakobau closer and closer to his goal. According to Bex, elections for the new legislative assembly had already started on the main islands.

"Why don't you stand, Jason?" suggested Bex enthusiastically. "You'd bolt in, they are crying out for men of your experience. There is no one who commands so much respect among the Fijians. I am sure the King would only have to hear that you were interested and you could have any ministry you wanted."

John Denison supported this suggestion. "Bex is right, Jason. It is time you took your place in national affairs. Would you want lesser men telling you what to do?"

Jason looked across the room at Kate, but she just smiled and refused to say anything which might sway him either way. He knew she would back him all the way, but the initial decision had to be his own.

"I'm sorry, but my wife married a stick-in-the-mud planter, not a politician," he said laughing. Although she had said nothing, he knew Kate was relieved to know that he would not be leaving Vatulevu. He got out of his chair and leaning over kissed her on the cheek. Kate had been a beautiful girl, now married life and the happiness of her home had made her bloom into a truly striking woman. "I take it, darling, that you have no wish to live in Levuka as the wife of a minister of state?

"I would loathe every minute of it," she said, softly touching his cheek with her hand.

"You see, Peter," said Jason, standing beside Kate's chair, "what with my plantation and a wife like this, what have politics to offer?"

"I'm afraid I was thinking more of what you had to offer politics," said Bex with a touch of sarcasm. There were few men seeing Jason, master of his own kingdom, who would not have been envious.

*****

Jason talked as he wandered around the table, refilling glasses, "I must say these men do seem different. You may be right, they may even succeed. Their problem will be to show the Europeans that they can offer concrete solutions to the present troubles and that takes money, which we haven't got. No one will pay taxes without results and there'll be no results without taxation — where does that leave them?"

"Oh they've even got an answer to that. Or at least a short-term one. The Vunivalu has gone into the blackbirding business."

"Blackbirding?" Kate was horrified.

"He wouldn't call it blackbirding himself," said Bex. "He's ridding the Levuka merchants of a menace they've been griping about for years and providing himself with some ready cash at the same time.

"The Lovoni tribe, I'll bet," said Jason.

"That's right. They've raided the outskirts of Levuka for the last time. They made the mistake of coming out in open rebellion against Cakobau. He had to put them down or it would have discredited him in the eyes of the Europeans who could then have said he hadn't the strength to enforce orders even on his own doorstep. They killed the chief of the Yarovudi, an ally of Bau, and destroyed the village of Natokolau. In return the King laid siege to the whole Lovoni valley."

"It was during this siege that he had all the talks in Levuka about the new government. Even though he had hundreds more men than the kai-Lovoni, it took him three months to get them to surrender. The *Elizabeth* was sitting at anchor in Levuka when they were brought in."

From Bex's account it might have been better had the kai-Lovoni fought to the death. The King, his new ministers and chief officers sat on a dais while his warriors drove them past. There must have been 800 — men, women and children — a long, snaking line of emaciated figures, crawling on their hands and knees, dragging behind them baskets of earth, the traditional symbol of surrender.

"It is terrible to see people who have been stripped of every vestige of personal dignity," said Bex solemnly.

"How ghastly," whispered Kate, horrified by the vivid picture he had drawn.

"When the show was over they were sold off to the highest bidders; the planters couldn't buy fast enough. I don't know how much Cakobau got, but that's the money they're using to launch the Government. The Lovoni tribe has been destroyed; they are scattered throughout the length and breadth of the islands. They can never return because their land was auctioned off at the same time as their bodies were disposed of."

"If this is how they raise the wind to sail the ship I'm glad I've nothing to do with it. I could never look myself in the face again, knowing I'd been a party to something like that," said Jason.

"I cannot understand Europeans, and the missionaries in particular, allowing it to happen at all," said John Denison indignantly.

"I don't know about that, Reverend," said Bex. "They may have tried, but I never saw a minister the whole time. As for the other whites, they were all for it." Bex pulled a large gold hunter from his pocket, flicked it open with a thumb and got up. "I'll have to be off, the mate will have the gig waiting for me near the jetty."

The others stood up with him to make their farewells. Kate thrust a fat letter into his hand for delivery to her stepson and kissed him affectionately on his weather-beaten cheek.

*****

Jason offered to walk Bex down to the jetty. "After all you've told me, Peter, I can't see myself fitting into that government. I'll sit back here on Vatulevu. I have a premonition that if I ever do get caught up in politics, I shall never be able to wash the stink of it from my hands again."

"Perhaps you're right. Woods and the others turn a blind eye. As far as they're concerned, anything which helps to give the government backbone is fully justified."

"Too Machiavellian for me," laughed Jason.

Bex stopped just before the jetty, still out of earshot of the crewman they could see waiting. "I've something else I want to tell you, Jason, which I didn't like to say in front of Kate and her father because it concerns Toby Denison."

"Yes?" said Jason warily.

"I saw him when I was last in Sydney. He was with another friend of yours, Basil Gunning. Denison was three sheets in the wind as usual but before Gunning shut him up he said a few things about you."

"It's not news if you mean to tell me that our dear Toby does not love me overmuch," said Jason, "but nor does he worry me."

"Don't take Denison lightly," warned Bex. "I hear most of the scuttlebutt which floats around the docks and your brother-in-law has a reputation which would shame Judas. I knew there was no love lost between you, so I took the liberty of warning young Aporosa's headmaster. Being so far from home the boy is one of your vulnerable points. When I talked to the headmaster, sure enough Denison had been there, he had even asked to take the boy out for a weekend."

Jason was suddenly very frightened indeed. "Surely he wouldn't harm a child like that?"

"Aporosa's older than that girl he raped here."

"If he touches a hair on my son's head I'll tear him limb from limb," snarled Jason. The expression on his face was lethal.

"I wouldn't put anything past him, but I think I managed to queer his pitch this time, whatever it was he had in mind," said Bex. "It was just as well I got there when I did for the headmaster, thinking he was the boy's uncle, was quite prepared to let him go. I told him a few home truths about friend Denison and explained that his own head would not rest long on his shoulders if anything happened to the lad."

"You know, Jason, it's more than four years since you've seen your son. He's grown into a fine strapping lad you can be proud of and he misses you all terribly. I'm only in Sydney five or six times a year and an old curmudgeon like me is no replacement for his parents. Why don't you and Kate take a trip to see him for yourselves? You've money enough. I should know, I do your banking and your spending for that matter."

"I don't know," Jason hesitated. He had thought never to leave Fiji till the day he died, but there was no denying the idea was attractive. "What about the plantation? And Kate has the younger children to think of. No, it's impossible."

"Get on with you, Jason. Why not make old Denison work for his living for a change; he couldn't do much damage in a couple of months. And as for the little 'uns and 'Mila, bring them with you. Bring Lala along to look after them. You can see Aporosa; and Kate can make her bow in Sydney society."

Bex could see his friend teetering and kept up the pressure. "You can help sell the cargo you have aboard the *Elizabeth*; you can have talks with the factors and discuss all those things I'm forever forgetting. Why, you might even choose some bloodstock to ship back with you. I've got the contacts and your banker will see to the rest."

Jason grinned and punched Bex playfully on the shoulders. "You could sell umbrellas to desert Bedouin, you old scoundrel," he said. "Alright, we'll do it. That is of course, if you can get Kate to agree. Don't think you are getting out of that side of it. I'm going to need all the big guns and arguments you can bring to bear if we are to drag her away from hearth and home."

Kate was still up when the two men got back to the house. They walked in, huge smiles on their faces, and obviously very pleased with themselves.

"Welcome back, Peter," she laughed. "What have you two been up to? You look like small boys who've just eaten a plateful of stolen tarts."

Jason grabbed her by the waist and swung her around in a wide circle and kissed her soundly. "Peter has a marvellous idea, Kate. We're all going on a holiday!"

"A holiday? But I don't want a holiday," she said, bewildered. "I'm quite happy here at Qaraniqio."

Her husband kissed her again. "You talk to Peter. He has fifty reasons why we should go and if we're to leave on tomorrow morning's tide, I've got enough work ahead of me to last the night through."

"Pack only what you need on the voyage for yourself and the children," he shouted as he left the room, "We'll buy the rest in Sydney."

"Jason!"

But he was gone and she was left with Bex who was helpless with laughter.

27

Sydney-side

Kate didn't ever want to repeat the chaos, confusion and excitement of that night. She had begun with a point-blank refusal, but when Bex told her about Toby and his fears for Aporosa, she could not pack fast enough. No one knew Toby as she did. Had Aporosa been her own son Toby might have held his hand, but the fact that his mother was Fijian would be an added incentive for Toby to do harm, especially as he knew that one day the boy would succeed Tui Navatulevu.

John Denison hated the thought of being left behind, but he regarded it as an honour that Jason should leave the plantation in his hands. He, Jason and the Fijian foreman worked right through the night drafting a work schedule so that Denison would not have to spend most of the day in the saddle as his son-in-law normally did. Each morning the foreman would come for instructions and the issue of rations; and in the evening he would report progress for John Denison to write up in the plantation diary. Denison thought he might even enjoy himself, once the first pangs of loneliness had passed.

Kate and Lala, ransacking the house for trunks and warm clothing, abused their lord and master unmercifully. The *Elizabeth* went via New Zealand where they would have several weeks of cold weather — it was all very well for Jason to talk glibly about buying everything in Sydney — men just didn't understand what was involved.

Kate added one of the housegirls to her entourage to help Lala and threatened to scalp the rest if the house wasn't clean and shining when she returned. Menus for her father; detailed instructions as to her kitchen garden; orders for the weeding and replanting of the flower gardens — the list seemed never ending. The more she did, the more Kate realised how much her home meant to her.

It seemed impossible that news could spread so fast, but when they marshalled the excited children and made their way to the beach they found half the island waiting to see them off. Tabua were presented to Jason and Peter Bex, and farewell speeches made.

Then, just before they were to step into the boat, Tui Navatulevu's matanivanua stepped forward, a large bundle wrapped in mats under one arm. "Turaga, I come with you," he told Jason bluntly. "The Tui sends me to make presentations on his behalf to his grandson, Ratu Aporosa."

"But Jason ..." began Kate who could see a thousand problems ahead. Catering for Lala and the maid would be hard enough, but the matanivanua had never lived with Europeans before.

"Quiet Kate." Jason could guess what she was thinking but knew the chief's herald was not asking them, he was telling them — the question of acceptance or refusal did not arise.

"The Tui wishes his grandson to be reminded of the responsibilities which await him on Vatulevu," the Fijian continued solemnly. "I am to take his grandfather's greetings and tell him that we all pray for his early return."

Jason stepped aside and swept his arm towards the boat waiting to row them out to the schooner. "We are deeply honoured, matanivanua." Then in an English aside to Kate. "The more the merrier. He'll be a sensation in Sydney!"

*****

Auckland, with its host of substantial buildings and hundreds of ships, many larger than the *Elizabeth*, was an absolute wonderland, especially for the children. Kate felt utterly dowdy but, assured by Bex that the ladies of Sydney were much smarter, she avoided buying anything that was not essential, saving her shopping spree until later.

Jason installed the family in the Royal Hotel, the best that Auckland offered; not that they were ever there. Through the agents of the Southern Cross Shipping Company, wives of commercial leaders were informed that Mrs Cotterel, the wife of Fiji's richest planter was in town for a brief period and, if their husbands wished to stay on good terms with the company, she was to be properly entertained.

By making contacts and sounding out markets Jason hoped to make the trip pay a handsome dividend. Auckland businessmen were at first sceptical — they had been taken for a ride on Fiji previously — but they quickly changed their attitude. Not only did Jason Cotterel have Bex, who was known and well respected, to vouch for him; but he had high quality produce in the *Elizabeth*'s holds as evidence of what he had to sell.

He told them the unvarnished truth about conditions and problems in Fiji rather than have them believe the islands were a paradise where any fool could make a fortune. While Kate was rushing from one social engagement to the next, Jason talked business and island politics in studies, offices and gentlemen's clubs, in an atmosphere of leather, brandy and good cigars.

Auckland was a great success with the Cotterels; and the Cotterels were watched wherever they went by the Aucklanders who had never seen anyone quite like them. Wherever Jason went, Tui Navatulevu's matanivanua went too.

Aucklanders were used to Maori, who were to be seen everywhere, dressed for the most part in ragged cast-off European clothing. But the Fijian, conscious of his status, refused to change one iota, no matter how cold it became, not even when Lala and the maid put on the European clothes brought for them by Kate.

Tall, muscular and arrogant, he strode along beside Jason; his hair, a long wooden comb thrust into one side, was oiled and shone in a huge mop which added six inches to his height. He wore a loin cloth of masi, long streamers floating behind him as he walked. And in case anyone thought him a comic figure, his heavy throwing-club never left his right hand.

Jason knew it would have hurt the matanivanua's feelings had he told him to stay at home because his club tended to intimidate business acquaintances. And in any event he derived great amusement from the expressions on pedestrians' faces.

Sydney was Auckland all over again but more metropolitan. Whereas the New Zealand buildings were timber-framed, many of Sydney's were of brick or stone, the most imposing having been raised by the sweat of convict labour, a permanent memorial to the time when Botany Bay was a penal settlement lost in a remote southern world.

Now, Sydney had men of great wealth who demanded the luxuries and elegance of good living; and nothing was unobtainable for those who could meet the prices. Jason was determined that before Kate retreated again to the solitude of Vatulevu she should have her chance to outshine the greatest of the society dames, even if it took his bank balance a decade to recover from the shock.

Kate's wishes were much simpler. Rather than cut any dash in Sydney society, she was more interested in making up for the years she had been separated from her stepson.

*****

Aporosa was now 15, tall and handsome like his father, and with the natural dignity and poise which was the legacy of his mother's chiefly blood. For all his education, European clothes and now perfect English, he was the same affectionate boy they had seen off from Levuka.

In the headmaster's study he solemnly shook hands with his proud father, but then he ran into Kate's open arms and everyone was laughing and weeping at once.

But it took Jason ten minutes of fervent explanation before the head would permit his hallowed study to be used for heathen ceremonies. To that point, young Cotterel had been just another boy, however bright and pleasant. But now it appeared he had a minor princeling on his hands whose subjects wished to pay their homage. This put an entirely new complexion on matters; he could see himself boasting to other headmasters that his school was patronised by the scions of royal houses.

It was important to Jason that the boy should not forget the beauty and simplicity inherent in the traditions of his own people. Before coming to Sydney he had been too young to participate in ceremonies and his father had to coach him in the correct responses while Lala dressed him in traditional masi for the occasion.

Kate sat with the headmaster, his wife and a few of Aporosa's closest friends. The boys were wide-eyed with wonder. Their school chum, who they knew as a fellow who was up to every prank in the school, had suddenly blossomed into a Fijian prince. At the head of the room, cross-legged on the floor, sat Jason and his son. Jason in the best silk and broadcloth, every inch the wealthy planter in spite of his posture; and the boy his head held high and proud, Ratu Aporosa, heir apparent to Vatulevu.

Lala and the maid, substituting for men, mixed the yaqona under the eagle eye of the matanivanua. He had carried both the yaqona and the delicate polished coconut shells all the way from Vatulevu, having been told that for some inexplicable reason they were not available in the countries across the dark sea.

Not in the slightest daunted by strange surroundings, he might have been in Lomanikaya for all the difference it made to his composure. When all was ready, he crawled forward touched the rim of the basin holding the yaqona and produced two shining tabua.

"Turaga! I bring you greetings from your grandfather, the High Chief, the noble Tui Navatulevu." Chiefly messages were not things to be whispered and his reverberating voice could have been heard a hundred yards away. "The chief sends these tabua as a mark of his love for you, as a symbol of the loyalty of his people to their future Lord who will reign when Tui Navatulevu passes to the land of Jehovah."

"In your blood flow two rivers, the white and the brown. The white is the gift of your father, our trusted friend Jasoni who has sent you to this land to learn the white man's ways and wisdom. These tabua from your grandfather are to remind you of that other river, the brown, the blood of your mother. Tui Navatulevu commands you not to forget the brown for he grows very old and, with the death of Ratu Seru, has no brothers to succeed him. You, Turaga, are the sole heir to the title of Tui."

"The Tui commands you to remember the ways of your people and never cease to love them for one day soon you must return to rule over them in your turn. Everyone on Vatulevu longs for the time when your schooling will finish and you will be free to return to us again."

"The gifts are small" — in Fijian eyes this was not true, but it was part of the tradition that the giver should deplore his gifts. "They do no honour to your greatness, but I ask that you accept them as tokens of our love; drink the yaqona to seal this ceremony."

He crawled across the carpet and passed the tabua to the boy, who took them reverently. The feel and smell of the tabua made Aporosa nostalgic for his home, the blue skies, the clear waters of the lagoon and the playmates with whom he had fought in the sand and fished the reefs. Despite the presence of his father, his stepmother and his sister, he felt suddenly alone on alien soil and he longed for the sight of Vatulevu.

In the absence of a matanivanua of his own, Jason had decided that the boy should make his own acceptance speech.

Aporosa had been worried that his Fijian, rusty from disuse, might be unable to meet the challenge of a formal speech, but once started it all came back: "Oh messenger from my noble grandfather, na Turaga bale, Tui Navatulevu," Ratu Aporosa's voice was low and almost inaudible by contrast with the matanivanua's resonant tones. His quietness and humility added to the sincerity of the moment. "I accept your tabua in the hope that Vatulevu, its chief and its people may prosper and live in peace."

"I am the poor servant of my chief and my people. I will never forget them. I hold myself ready to return to their service whenever they may call. Take this message to the Tui, my grandfather; tell him of my love for him and all on Vatulevu."

It was short and simple, but even for those who could not understand the language there was no doubting the feeling behind the words. As Kate told Jason later that night, "He looked so solemn and brave. It was like watching a young knight take his vows of chivalry."

Jason was so proud of his son he felt he might burst with the emotion welling up inside. He knew that in later years Aporosa would look back on that moment as a turning point in his life; the moment when the boy became a man.

*****

Jason left the headmaster in no doubt as to the consequences if any harm came to Aporosa from Toby Denison. He also told his son, omitting nothing so that he might understand why his uncle by marriage was no longer *persona grata* with anyone from Vatulevu. In fact the danger appeared to have passed, for Peter Bex's spies told them that Denison had already left Sydney for Fiji on an errand for Gunning.

The whole family was swept up in Sydney's social whirl which, in retrospect, made Auckland seem a dreamy, quiet backwater. Aporosa was given a holiday for the period his parents were in Sydney. Immediately, the matanivanua transferred his allegiance from Jason to his son — every step the young chief took was shadowed by his future Grand Vizier. Of one thing Jason could be sure, the ever-present club would taste the brains of any who dared lay a finger on his son's head.

Years of sending over high quality copra and cotton, plus his warm bank account, ensured that Jason was not unknown in Sydney. His banker considered him something of a novelty in that he had never asked for financial assistance; for this very reason he might have had all he wanted.

He was seen as a man who had made a success where everyone else seemed to fail, and so dozens of businessmen, many with a forlorn record of investment in the islands, wanted his opinion and advice. He talked crop projections, market fluctuations, transportation and expansion possibilities for hours on end.

It would have been easy to romanticise Fiji's potential and hoodwink even hard-headed businessmen. One mention of the islands and Sydney and Melbourne financiers forgot the enormous continent at their backs screaming out for development and became hypnotised by dreams of easy fortunes to be made on tiny atolls lost in the immensity of the Pacific Ocean.

Kate spent her time sightseeing and shopping. Not only had Jason ensured she had all the money she might require, her father had also given her a banker's draft. What Toby had tried to get by extortion she received without asking and her father would have been most hurt had she refused.

The house at Qaraniqio, never far from Kate's mind, got the lion's share of the spending. The latest model of closed stove, new curtains, a huge desk for Jason's office, a comfortable rocker for her father; parcel after parcel was sent to be loaded on the *Elizabeth.*

Nor was Kate so busy that she forgot the people of the island. For Helen Simpson, the wife of the new missionary, a handsome dress for Sunday services and, through a friend of Peter Bex, Kate commissioned a beautiful carved lectern for the minister. There were bolts and bolts of material for the women and four treadle sewing machines of the very latest model.

Jason had two major extravagances. He spent more than £100 on books to be the nucleus of a library that would serve himself, his sons, and perhaps the whole island when more Fijians could read. The other was the purchase of livestock and here he really splashed out, spending over £1,000 of his own money and an equivalent amount from island funds.

He spent two weeks viewing the great holdings of squatters like the Macarthurs, trying to absorb all he could on breeding, husbandry and pastures in the short time available. He carried with him letters of introduction to smooth his path and the squatters, recognising an outdoor man like themselves, did all they could to help. If he wanted stock, they saw to it that the animals were the best they had and this was something they would not have done for their nearest neighbour.

As Jason had more and more livestock delivered to the *Elizabeth,* Bex had pens and crates all over the deck and in the holds. He told Jason with mock ferocity that he was turning the pride of the Southern Pacific Shipping Company's fleet into 'a bloody Noah's Ark'.

28

Higher circles

JASON ARRIVED BACK in Sydney bursting with high spirits. He dashed into their suite at Sydney's most fashionable hotel eager to snatch Kate up in his arms, only to find her draped in satin, stuck with pins, tattooed with chalk marks and guarded by no less than three seamstresses. Undeterred he gave a yell and, brushing the women aside, proceeded to kiss his wife soundly to the scandalised delectation of her attendants.

"Jason stop at once!" shrieked Kate, "You are pushing pins into me and I'm sure something is tearing. If you don't let these good ladies carry on, the dress will never be finished in time."

"In time for what?" roared Jason with mock anger. One of the ladies, a little squeezed up old maid, blushed furiously as if she feared he might assault her. "Anything which stops me from kissing my wife after I've been away for more than two weeks can go to the devil!"

Kate took a large gilt-edged card from her dressing table and passed it to him. "Behave yourself, Jason. Whatever will the ladies think? Anyway, you can hardly send Lord Belmore to the devil."

Jason read the card and whistled appreciatively. "His Excellency the Governor of New South Wales and Lady Belmore request the pleasure of the company of Mr and Mrs Jason Cotterel at dinner." All three of the seamstresses beamed at him. "Well, what do you know about that then? Yankee beachcomber and renegade makes good. We dine with the nobility no less."

"And you will need proper evening dress for the occasion," laughed Kate. "I've had Sydney's best tailor waiting to measure you these last two days. Go to him this instant or he'll never be able to finish it for Saturday."

Jason caught up his hat and made for the door. "Well that's a fine welcome I must say, no sooner home than kicked out again."

*****

Punctually at seven o'clock on the Saturday evening, a hired carriage delivered the Cotterels to the front of Government House. Ahead of them on the gravelled drive were the carriages of the other guests. When their turn came to step down on to the flambeau-lit steps, one of His Excellency's aides, a handsome young man resplendent in the uniform of Her Majesty's Hussars, took Jason's card and announced them.

"Mr and Mrs Jason Cotterel from the Fiji Islands."

As they entered the reception lounge, they were a handsome enough pair to catch the eye of all present, Kate's smooth blonde hair shining like pure gold in the light from the chandeliers. Her gown of white satin was simple but striking, making the other women look like gaudy parrots in comparison. Her only jewellery was a pearl set, necklace and ear rings, once the pride of her mother but left behind perhaps as a sop to her conscience, and which Kate now wore for the first and perhaps the only time in her life.

Kate's heart swelled with pride as they walked across the polished parquet flooring to where the Governor and his lady waited to receive their guests. She knew that she was looking her best, and Jason beside her, in black, superfine broadcloth, silk and starched white linen was, to her mind, the most distinguished man present. Kate curtseyed and Jason bowed over the vice-regal hands, there were a few smiled words of welcome and they moved on to where the other guests stood talking.

It was not a particularly large party, and seemed comprised mostly of people Jason had already met since their arrival in Sydney. As Jason's banker remarked as he drew them into his circle, "This seems to be a Fiji party; all of us have some sort of interest in the islands and you seem to be the guest of honour. My bet is that the old man intends to put us all through our paces while the port passes."

"There, Kate, it's business after all," laughed Jason, winking at her, "and you thought His Excellency was another victim of your big blue eyes."

"My husband will never take anything seriously, Mrs Wharton," said Kate to the banker's wife. "If the truth were to be told, he would hate a really social evening. He likes nothing better than to talk for hours about coconut politics. My only fear is that once he has started we poor ladies shall be deserted for the remainder of the evening."

"I'm sure we would never be so ungallant, Mrs Cotterel," drawled a new but familiar voice from behind Jason and Kate. There, as smooth, suave and cat-like as ever, was Basil Gunning. "Cotterel, Mrs Cotterel, your obedient servant," he said bowing.

"You here, Gunning?" asked Jason.

"But my dear Jason, did you think I would not be as socially acceptable as yourselves?" It was all very polite and supposedly a joke, but there was an underlying trace of insult.

There had been a time when Kate had thought Colonel Gunning amusing and innocuous, but no longer. Jason had told her that her brother was under Gunning's influence; consequently she blamed him for Toby's moral degeneration and now loathed him intensely.

"Can you wonder at our surprise, Colonel?" she said, her voice hard and clear. "We are told that you only associate with rogues and blackbirders these days."

For once the smile was wiped from Gunning's face and for a fleeting moment his mouth went white and his eyes glinted, revealing the tiger beneath.

"Men such as your brother, I presume you to mean, ma'am?" he asked, setting the smile carefully back in place.

"If my brother has become a scoundrel, Colonel Gunning, then you were his mentor!"

It was most unusual for young matrons to abuse gentlemen in public and even more extraordinary on their first visit to Government House. Kate could not have cared less. She looked up at Jason who smiled his approval — his was the only opinion which mattered.

The Whartons, no friends of Gunning's, moved closer to their *protégés* from Fiji. Kate turned her back on the Colonel with calculated deliberation and Mrs Wharton followed her cue perfectly.

"And how are the children enjoying their visit to Sydney, Mrs Cotterel?" she asked as if nothing untoward had happened. Wharton himself took Jason up on his recent trip inland. Gunning was suddenly ignored and alone on the outside of a group which quite obviously found his company distasteful. For a moment he looked furious, then he pulled himself together and, ignoring the whispers of other people who had heard and seen what happened, sauntered across the room towards some new arrivals.

"Mrs Cotterel doesn't care for the gallant colonel, I see," said Wharton watching him go.

"With reason," replied Jason. He was thankful that he had left the management of the affair to Kate for his own methods were more direct. An insult and snub could be glossed over, but if he had knocked the man down their evening would have come to a very abrupt end. In many ways Kate's methods had greater bite and effect.

"Don't forget Gunning can be dangerous. I don't know his reputation in Fiji, but I have heard some unsavoury things about his doings here. He is careful to work through agents so that if anything goes awry with his plans no blame can be pinned on him. It was very courageous of your wife to be so outspoken, but be careful that he doesn't try to get his own back in some way. To be named scoundrel to his face, and in the Governor's drawing room at that, is an insult he will move heaven and earth to avenge."

*****

At that point an aide arrived to explain that, the Cotterels being their Excellencies' principal guests, Lord Belmore would escort Kate to the table and she would sit at his right hand, while Jason should offer his arm to the Governor's lady and sit at her right. In that manner they proceeded through the double doors leading into the dining salon.

Lady Belmore's chef excelled himself. Dish after dish was offered the 30 guests by impassive footmen. *Vichyssoise* chicken soup or *consommé Julienne*; cold *salmon à la mayonnaise verte*; *lobster Bisque*, *tournedos à la Béarnaise*, roast duck stuffed with apples and prunes, cold chicken in aspic, roast lamb, sirloin of beef and, if none of these suited, 'a trifle of game pie, sir?'

The wines were equally good and the major-domo, whose trained eye could detect the lowered level in a guest's glass at fifty paces, saw to it that even the ladies' delicate sipping amounted to a considerable consumption by the end of the evening. If Belmore intended to talk business after dinner, thought Jason, he must be working on the principle of *in vino veritas*.

Jason kept up a patter with his hostess, light frothy stuff mainly about Sydney, the meal, and the relative merits of various sauces — it took no great mental effort. He was sorely tempted to describe a scene he had witnessed as a young man when, after a particularly tough battle, allies of the Vunivalu had cooked and eaten the bodies of their enemies. What sauce would Lady Belmore recommend for steaming human flesh?

The light from scores of candles glowed softly on the hair and bare shoulders of the women. The dark gleaming patina of the banqueting table, the glint of crystal decanters carried by soft-footed servants, and the shining silver, could have been part of a scene from the Belmore's London home rather than in the distant Southern Hemisphere.

The British did this sort of thing well and would in all probability duplicate it in Fiji if they ever decided they wanted it as a Colony. In Jason's view, however, government was not lobster bisque and green mayonnaise, it was of the people, for the people and, most important of all, by the people.

At a signal from Lady Belmore, the ladies rose and were bowed from the room by the gentlemen. Jason caught Kate's eye and smiled wryly, as if to say, "Now to business while you run off and play."

In answer to which Kate gave the faintest suggestion of a wink that said, "Go on, you love every minute of it. You can't fool me."

*****

Decanters of port and brandy were placed on the table and the major-domo wheeled a large humidor of choice cigars from guest to guest. For a while the idle chit-chat continued, but when glasses were full and cigars were drawing properly, the Governor rapped gently on the table to attract attention. "Well gentlemen, now that the ladies have left us we may turn to the more serious things of life."

Lord Belmore was a fat, jolly sort of man, more a Mr Pickwick than the American idea of nobility. However, those who thought his looks indicated a lazy mind had often come to the contrary view on later reflection.

"I like good food and fine wines," Belmore told them, "especially when they travel in the company of intelligent men and informed discussion. We cannot forever meet in the formal atmosphere of an office and I for one find more business is done and sounder information gained when the inner man has first been satisfied."

"You will have guessed what our subject is tonight. You are leaders in your own fields and you share a common interest, Fiji. Her Majesty's Government is closely following developments in the islands. This is understandable when you consider that we have been offered possession of Fiji on two occasions, and that despite our refusal 90 percent of the white settlers, and almost all of the foreign capital invested there, is British. But I wish to say at the very outset that Britain has no plan to make Fiji a dependency or to annex it as a Crown Colony."

Jason looked down the table towards Gunning. If what Lord Belmore said was true and if his own interpretation of Gunning's aims was correct, how would that gentleman take such a statement?

"I think the truth of my words is borne out by Government's refusal to accept the offers of cession made by the Fijian chiefs in 1860. We are hopeful that an indigenous government will emerge, strong enough to bring stability, law, order and prosperity to the islands, rather than that we have to assume the costly responsibility of running the place ourselves."

The Governor continued, "What I would like you gentlemen to discuss is whether or not you think this idea of a strong Fijian government will ever become reality. Both here and in London we are under considerable pressure and organised attack on the subject. Some of you, I know, feel great sympathy for Her Majesty's Opposition on this matter and I expect you to give your views as freely as those who support the present Government. As senior representative of Her Majesty in the Pacific, it is my duty to advise her ministers and in order that I may give an informed opinion, and I need your assistance."

"Our guest of honour tonight is Mr Cotterel, without doubt Fiji's leading planter and, I am told, an expert on Fijian affairs. I hope he will give us his thoughts on the future of his adopted homeland. In fact, sir, you might like to open the discussion."

Jason bowed in acknowledgement. He was prepared to say his piece though it remained to be seen whether or not they found his opinions palatable. "I have very strong views on the subject of Fiji, your Excellency," said Jason. "But as the only Fiji resident here and a non-British subject into the bargain, I would rather the other gentlemen spoke first." Jason knew that what he said could well be vital to Fiji's future and he wanted to be able to attack the weak points of others arguments rather than be on the defensive himself.

The Governor nodded understandingly and turned to another of the guests who had been introduced to Jason earlier as one of New South Wales's leading barristers and a member of the legislature.

"I think, sir, that we should annex the islands with the least possible delay," he said, quickly showing where he stood. "Fiji is making a mockery of our legal system. Debtors and every other sort of felon fly there and are safe from retribution. We cannot touch our own criminals and I understand that they have made the chief town, Levuka, the most lawless pesthole in the Pacific. I hear that not a night goes by without a murder or violence of some sort. In my opinion it is our moral duty to stamp this out."

It only needed one person to start and everyone wanted to speak at once. As soon as the lawyer finished another took up the tale.

"Look at the labour trade, my Lord. This so-called blackbirding is nothing less than traffic in low-priced slaves. Whereas Her Majesty's Government showed the lead in stamping out the slave trade in other parts of the world, here on our very doorstep it is allowed to flourish untouched. Fiji is the centre of the whole dirty business and the only way to stop it is for Britain to annex the islands."

Jason watched Gunning toying idly with the stem of his glass. According to Bex, who knew the ins and outs of every ship which moved in the Pacific, the colonel was rumoured to have financial interests in several blackbirding ventures. Gunning looked up and their eyes met.

The Englishman's enigmatic smile broadened as he turned to Lord Belmore. "This is something Cotterel should be able to tell us more about, my Lord," he said, the benign smile disguising the menace behind his words. "After all, his brother-in-law was an associate of the notorious O'Hara."

A gasp of horror came from the other guests and Lord Belmore looked furious. Jason's hand tightened on his glass, which he longed to throw in Gunning's face. He controlled his temper with difficulty and responded, "So I understand, your Excellency, but I work on the principle, 'God gave us our relations, but thank the Lord we may pick our friends'."

There was a relieved burst of laughter from the dinner guests and his host gave him a look of appreciation. But Jason was not yet finished with Gunning and the governor's approval might be short-lived.

"There are no indentured labourers or slaves on my own plantation. I abhor this trade as much as any of you and those who know me know my publicly stated opinions on the subject. Gunning has pointed the finger at me," here he smiled sweetly at his now openly-acknowledged enemy, "but I am given to believe, Colonel, that you have found it a most fruitful field for investment."

This was throwing down the gauntlet with a vengeance. The table was tense with apprehension at what might follow. Cotterel had been deliberately provoked, but he had retaliated by publicly accusing one of Her Majesty's officers of personal complicity in the slave trade. It was only Belmore's intervention that stopped the affair going further, for the look on Gunning's face showed that he was about to call Jason a liar.

"Gentlemen, gentlemen! This has gone far enough, we shall all progress more easily if we refrain from bringing personalities into the discussion. Wharton, as a banker, give me your opinion of the situation in Fiji." Lord Belmore sat back in his chair and, for the umpteenth time, cursed the Secretary of State for sending him to a place where men did not know the basic principles of diplomacy or, even when they did know, refused to follow the rules.

"My opinion, your Excellency, is that Fiji will never realise its undoubted potential until it is adequately financed," said Wharton, taking up his burden obediently. "Both the planters and the business houses are asking for our help but we must refuse. Without a stable legal system we cannot secure our investments: mortgages and liens are not worth the paper they are written on if the financier has no legal assistance to recover from defaulters. The islands have definite potential — Mr Cotterel has proved that in no uncertain manner — but few will risk capital there. The white planters desperately need stable government but I doubt if King Cakobau will be able to provide it."

A senior naval officer pointed out the strategic importance of the islands in relation to New Zealand and the British Colonies in Australia. If Britain did not secure Fiji, one of the other powers with fewer scruples would; constituting a permanent threat to British interests in the South Seas.

Jason felt like a lost soul crying in the wilderness. The rest of the table, apart from an odd one or two who did not seem capable of forming an opinion on any subject, were unanimous that Fiji should be taken over by the British. Their views went through the whole gamut of possibility and absurdity, ranging from the repression of cannibalism and the duty of all Christians to convert the heathen, down to the view that if there existed another jewel which might be added to Queen Victoria's crown, it was the duty of every Englishman to work towards that end. If the dinner guests were a representative cross-section of British thought, Lord Belmore had not been exaggerating when he said the British Government was under pressure.

Gunning was the most scathing of the lot. He seemed to have forgotten that in two successive governments he had been one of King Cakobau's ministers. "All of these arguments in favour of annexation, my Lord, could be settled, if Fiji had stable government." Belmore gave a curt nod of agreement.

"I am prepared to stake my fortune, however, that such a government can never exist. The calibre of the people militates against it; they couldn't organise a cricket match let alone a whole country, and another feeble attempt at government is in the making even now." Gunning's tone was contemptuous, "If I had any hand in the formation of British policy, not only would I see to it that Her Majesty's

Government refused to recognise the Cakobau Government, but I would take active steps to destroy something which can only be delaying the inevitable." There was a spattering of applause as he finished speaking.

In the silence which followed no one seemed prepared to take up where Gunning left off; the Governor seemed lost in his own thoughts. There was an uncomfortable pause then, when Lord Belmore spoke, he was looking straight at Gunning. His tone was polite and quiet but his guests got the impression that he found something profoundly disquieting about the colonel.

"All that you have told us may be correct, Colonel, but Her Majesty's Government would have little sense of honour if, after refusing King Cakobau's 1860 offer of Fiji as a free gift, it then turned around and destroyed his own effort to govern."

Jason, highly impressed, listened closely as the Governor, his forehead furrowed, continued. "You also remind me of another point, though this is may not be the best time to raise it. As a member, be it only on half pay, of Her Majesty's armed forces you are subject to the Foreign Enlistment Act. The provisions of that Act state quite clearly that if any British subject enters the service of a foreign state without having first obtained permission from the Foreign Office he is liable to a heavy fine or imprisonment."

"How then, Colonel Gunning, do you account for the fact that you have served as a Minister of State and military aide to King Cakobau? Was that not the title you had on your ill-fated campaign? But no matter for the moment, this will be for you and me to discuss at a later date." This was said in the pleasantest of voices but there was no escaping the scarcely veiled threat.

"Now," said Lord Belmore heartily, "we have all had our say and it is for you, Cotterel, to either agree or show us where our thinking is at fault. You must feel free to speak with absolute candour."

Jason smiled and laid his cigar down in the crystal ashtray. He liked Belmore, both for the way he had put Gunning in his place and for what appeared to be a genuine concern that British policy should be beyond reproach. What he was about to say might well influence the framing of future policy and he would have preferred someone more adept with words, like his fellow planter John Thurston, had been in his place.

"Your Excellency, gentlemen, before I put the case for a Fijian government I had better put you in the picture as to my personal position. As most of you know, I am still technically an American citizen. Some 18 months ago a petition was got up by the Americans in Fiji, which I personally refused to sign, asking the President and Congress to annex Fiji. This may bear out what others have said this evening about Fiji being a ripe plum waiting for one of the Great Powers to pick."

"The United States, like Great Britain, did the honourable thing and refused to discuss the matter. The message that came back warned all Americans resident in Fiji that they must obey whatever government was in power. This then is my position from the legal point of view. But in addition I regard myself these days as a citizen of Fiji rather than an American.

"I live on a small island ruled by a chief and, as an outsider who has been made welcome, I feel bound by his laws. He in his turn owes allegiance to King Cakobau, so I guess I owe exactly the same sort of allegiance for as long as I remain a resident of Vatulevu."

"What I am trying to say is that I came among the Fijians as a stranger, and it is not in my code to repay kindness and hospitality by joining anything which might overthrow their government, no matter how bad I may think it, not even if I was absolutely sure I could do a better job myself."

There was a rumble of disagreement from some of the guests, but Lord Belmore was quick to intervene, "Please, gentlemen, you have had your own chance, now be courteous enough to let Mr Cotterel finish what he has to say."

"Thank you, sir. I realise that some of the gentlemen here may not agree with what I have said, but if Americans came to New South Wales in numbers and demanded that you pass to them the reins of government, I have a very good idea what your reaction would be. I know what my own feelings are when I hear white men suggesting just that with reference to Fiji."

"With the exception of your Excellency all the previous speakers have advanced the same theme: what will be best for New South Wales and the white settlers in Fiji? You wish to protect your laws and investments, to assist your missionaries, secure your defences and protect your good name against the taint of slavery. Where, may I ask, do the Fijians come into your scheme of things? After all, they were there before the whites, the land is theirs and they outnumber the whites by 200 to one."

"Unless you are willing to follow a course of open piracy you must be prepared to accept a position where the white man is a guest in the islands. You and your settler friends must recognise the fact that Fijian interests and desires, no matter if they conflict with your own, must be of paramount importance."

"The fact that you have become so prosperous would seem to indicate that your interests are well covered," interjected the barrister.

"I only excuse that remark because it was made out of ignorance," said Jason, nettled by the accusation. "For every hour I put in on my own plantation I spend three working in the Fijian plantations; not just advising, but working with my hands, hard manual labour such as none of you has ever known."

"Gunning, as you have heard, is no friend of mine but he has seen the extent of the Fijian coconut groves. Ask him, ask Wharton here, if the credits standing to the account of the people of Vatulevu are not triple my own"

Gunning sat silent, neither agreeing nor denying, but his silence was as good as proof. Wharton was not as reticent. "What Cotterel says is true. Every shipment of Vatulevu produce which is sold here is credited 75 percent to the island account and 25 percent to Cotterel. I know my bank has nothing comparable from Fiji or any other island group for that matter; nor has any other bank in this town."

The barrister had the honesty to look rather shamefaced and the others were obviously impressed. But Gunning interjected, "What you have omitted to tell His Excellency, Cotterel, is that you virtually rule that island of yours. The chief and the natives listen to everything you say as if it were God himself speaking."

Jason was ready to take him up, but Lord Belmore, who was proving to be a most effective ally, forestalled him. "There is a profound difference between the advice of a wise and trusted guest, and obedience to the commands of a tyrant. Cotterel believes in the first, whereas you would have Her Majesty's Government force themselves on the Fijians. Experience from New Zealand has shown that the governing of an unwilling people, no matter how well-intentioned, can be a damned expensive business."

As he listened to the Governor, Jason could not help but think, that if Britain had accepted when Fiji was offered to her, and if men such as Belmore had been sent to rule the islands, Fijian interests might have been protected from all encroachments by white men.

"If we accept your idea that the Fijians should govern themselves," Lord Belmore was speaking to Jason now, "how likely is it that King Cakobau will be able to form a stable government? Gunning and I disagree as to method, but he only stated a fact when he pointed out that other attempts at self-government have been ignominious failures."

"Unless the King gets honest and unstinting support," replied Jason, "he will fail again, but this time it will not be because of the low calibre of his ministers. For the first time he has men of education, men whose main desire is to help the people and make Fiji a decent place for both Fijian and European. The Fijians will support the King, but on their past record it is the European population who will try their damnedest to bring him down."

"The criminal element know that stable government will result in some sort of extradition treaty with New South Wales, and so they'll be against the King for certain. But these days there are honest merchants and some hard-working planters who desperately need good government, yet still dare not support it."

"The British Consul has issued repeated warnings that any who co-operate with the government or pay taxes will automatically be deprived of their rights as British subjects. He has publicly denounced the government as illegal and derides its authority at every opportunity. This attitude from the Queen's representative suits the criminals but the others, who under different circumstances might have been the mainstay of the government, are lost between the devil and the deep blue sea."

Lord Belmore nodded and Jason felt encouraged to finish. "I respect what your Excellency has said about Britain's attitude; on the other hand your man on the spot, who so far as Fiji is concerned speaks for Britain, refuses to recognise the King and actively undermines his efforts at government. So long as he continues in that vein, who can blame the other Europeans for thumbing their noses at the King? You want Fiji to be independent yet Britain herself creates the major stumbling block."

Jason sat back. He wanted to get back to Vatulevu and be done with politics and all of this messy arguing. Having seen what Lord Belmore must go through week after week, year after year, he would have fled to the ends of the earth rather than be a Governor.

They had been talking intensely for well over an hour; Jason was exhausted and, he had to admit, slightly tipsy, but that was excusable if it had helped loosen his tongue. It had done the same for the others, allowing him an insight into the minds of the British on both the official and the civilian side.

Lord Belmore stood. He had allowed Jason the final say and was sparing him from further argument. "Well, gentlemen," he said, beaming at his guests as if they had been swapping ribald stories rather than discussing the future of a country and a whole race. "You have given me much to think about; it has been instructive and you may be sure that your views will be passed on to London. I suggest we now join the ladies before they decide to excommunicate us."

*****

The next few days were a rush of shopping and packing. As Kate told Jason, since they left the island she had never had time to do anything at an orderly and civilised pace; she would be well pleased to be home.

It was hard to leave Aporosa behind and, to make matters even worse, they regretfully decided that Ulamila should stay. Kate found herself traipsing around schools, inspecting facilities and talking to headmistresses. She finally selected a suitable Ladies Seminary and, the day before they were to leave Sydney, saw Ulamila tearfully but safely installed.

Jason had little time to dwell on the conversation at the Governor's dinner table, apart from wondering whether he might not have laid it on too thick and made something of a fool of himself. No matter how much he had been provoked his conduct had hardly been that of a gentleman.

He had not expected to hear more from Lord Belmore and was surprised when the Governor's aide turned up at their hotel with a letter marked for Jason's eyes only.

> Dear Cotterel,
>
> I must thank you and your charming wife for attending our small dinner party. I am also sincerely indebted to you personally for what you told us about affairs in the Fiji Islands. I have taken the liberty of

incorporating most of the points you made in a report to London. I sensed that you were desirous that your opinions might spread further afield than a New South Wales salon; if so you may rest assured that your wishes have been carried out.

If and when you next see King Cakobau, I should be most grateful if you would tell him of the sincere wish Her Majesty's Government has for his success. Coming from yourself, I do not doubt that your message will carry more weight than any formal letter from me.

I have issued instructions to Her Majesty's Consul in Levuka which will, I hope, alter his attitude of hostility towards the Cakobau Government. Should my orders fail, it would be a personal favour to me if you could write apprising me of the situation.

Colonel Gunning has left on a packet for the islands. His departure was precipitate almost to the point of being unseemly, perhaps as a result of my remarks about the Foreign Enlistment Act. Knowing that I meant to take him to task, he now qualifies as a fugitive himself. Gunning is an extremely able and ambitious man, though I suspect a trifle unscrupulous. Should he cause trouble in Fiji, a word from the government there would enable me to act in their best interests. Gunning is still, in theory, a member of Her Majesty's forces and as such is subject to disciplinary action.

In conclusion, I hope you will forgive me if I point out, that unless men of honour such as yourself take a leading part in King Cakobau's experimental government, it has little hope of achieving its objects. What you have done on your own island you must now duplicate at a national level. Men of your calibre and experience are vitally needed to guide the young nation's first footsteps.

I shall be following Fiji's progress with close interest and I hope that it will not be long before you and I can meet again to discuss ways and means by which Her Majesty's government may help. I would deem it an honour if you would feel free to write to me at any time and on any subject about which you think I might be of assistance.

I have the honour to be etc.,

BELMORE

Jason's opinion of Belmore, already high, was further raised. At dinner he had shown he would stand up for principles and was prepared to help the underdog. This letter proved that he was also a man of action. After the aide had gone Jason showed the letter to Kate.

"What do you think, darling?" he asked.

"I think you must have been very persuasive indeed for Lord Belmore to write a letter such as this," said Kate keeping her voice deliberately light to hide her own doubts and worries. "On the other hand, if you are asking me whether or not you should enter polities, that is for you to decide."

She put her arms about his neck and leaned her head against his chest. "Don't ask me to talk you into politics, darling. I should hate it, you would be away the whole time and it is such a dirty business. You make up your own mind on what your conscience says you must do and I shall abide by that and help you as much as I can."

"I know that but at the moment I don't know what my decision should be."

"Well, you have two weeks aboard ship to think about it. See what Peter Bex has to say, and when we get back talk to John Thurston — you know you respect his opinion. If you are going into the government, so should he."

Jason held her tightly in his arms. Her head came up and their lips met. "What would I do without my Kate?" he whispered.

29
Skullduggery

ALMOST THE LAST BUILDING at the northern end of Levuka was a ramshackle, wooden structure set on long piles which allowed it to extend out over the beach and water. It was built as an hotel by a man named Keyse.

Now it was being used by penniless drunks as a doss-house. Year by year it became more derelict. Timbers were stolen for use elsewhere and there was no glass in the windows. Eventually the piles would rot and the whole thing would collapse into the sea, to be washed out of men's minds on the outgoing tide.

That was until Toby Denison decided Keyse's Hotel might suit his purpose, at which it took on a new lease of life. Carpenters arrived to replace rotting timbers, doors were rehung and made extra strong, window frames were thrown away and in their place went heavy shutters. The drunks had to find a new place to collapse. It was still called Keyse's Hotel but you had to be one of Toby Denison's cronies before you were allowed admittance.

Many would have liked to know what went on in Keyse's Hotel and more about its new owner. Denison had suddenly turned up in Levuka. He had made no attempt to find work or establish a business though, from the way he scattered largesse, it was obvious his pockets were well-lined.

For a man with no job he was always busy. Normally he could be found in MacDonald's upstairs bar talking in conspiratorial tones to a visiting planter or one of the town's lesser merchants. To those who made a point of analysing his movements it soon became apparent that Denison chose his associates solely from those violently opposed to the latest Cakobau government.

Nobody knew that Horace Twyford and Toby Denison were working to the same end and for the same master. Denison had returned from Sydney with clear and concise instructions for both. They were to be horses in double harness with Basil Gunning holding the reins. The colonel's plan called for the Consul's active support but Denison, as a known blackbirder, had been warned not to compromise Twyford. Meetings were therefore held late at night with Denison sneaking up to the Consul's home by little used tracks.

When Gunning himself finally returned to Fiji the time came to turn words into action. On his very first night in Levuka a meeting was held at Keyse's Hotel to weld the enemies of the government into an organised party. Gunning even had a name for his society. He chose to emulate an organisation which at that very moment was sweeping the Southern States of America, dedicated to the supremacy of the white man and the suppression of the black. Accordingly, on February 16 1872 Colonel Basil Gunning founded the Fiji branch of the Ku Klux Klan.

His audience comprised around 30 of the toughest diehards the islands could produce. They sat, some on chairs, others on the floor their backs comfortably against the wall. All had glasses or bottles in their hands, rum and gin having been supplied free by the management. Free booze would have been sufficient to draw a good attendance, but what the Englishman had to say echoed their own feelings. They only needed someone like Gunning to set those words to the music of action.

"We didn't come to Fiji to take orders from a bunch of dirty natives! If orders are needed, we'll be the ones to give them. Woods, Burt and that lot would have you kowtowing to the chiefs like a pack of ignorant baboons. I believe blacks have their own place in the scheme of things, but it isn't lording it over white men. Look in the Bible and you will discover God made blacks to work for the whites."

None of them had seen a bible in years, yet they nodded their heads in complete agreement. "The man who says that the blacks are as good as us is a traitor to his own skin — he's denying the written word of God and he should be stood against a wall and shot!"

Basil Gunning stood there, his arms outstretched like a prophet. Had those who sat beside him at Lord Belmore's dinner party seen him haranguing the assembly in Keyse's Hotel, they would never have believed it was the same man. He had dressed for the part deliberately wearing rougher clothes than he normally affected; a revolver hung at his hip and he took the occasional swig from the bottle he was holding. The dandified Colonel Gunning would never have got through to these thugs, but a hard-drinking, coarse-tongued artilleryman had no trouble at all.

His speech was greeted with shouts of drunken approval. "No black bastard is going to tell Tom Johnson what to do!": "You're the boy for us, Gunning. Lead us to 'em." Gunning smiled back, delighted by their enthusiasm. In normal circumstances he wouldn't have been seen dead with any of them but so long as they were useful they could consider themselves his bosom friends.

"What do you want us to do?" yelled Denison, seated with the bulk of the audience to feed the right questions at the right time. "You name it and you'll find we're with you all the way. Isn't that right, friends?" There was a roar of support.

"Thank you, thank you," said Gunning holding up his hands for silence. They quietened to hear what was to come. "I've told you about the Ku Klux Klan and its aims. We'll form our own Klan and elect a leader. Everyone who joins us will take a solemn oath to abide by the orders of his leader, to defend his brothers and to keep the secrets of the society. Oath breakers to be summarily executed on the orders of the leader."

"If we're to smash this government of primitives and rule Fiji ourselves, we must be strong. Cakobau's minions are selling the white man into servitude. Unless we are disciplined, unless the Klan can present a solid front to its enemies, we are lost! All of us will finish up slaves! Any who join and then turn traitor must pay the penalty of death!"

"I nominate Gunning as Leader," yelled Denison, again right on cue. There was no need to count hands, the unanimous roar was enough to drown any other nominations.

Denison himself now took the floor and read out an oath of allegiance which just happened to be in his pocket. Those present, most of whom were so far gone with liquor they hardly understood what they were doing, came forward one by one and recited exotic pledges of allegiance to their white brothers and death to any black who might dare to thwart their aims. A cutlass was held at their throats and they sealed the oath by kissing a Bible and shaking hands with their new master.

Gallons of raw spirits flowed down throats to the point that some had to be physically reminded that they were now under the directions of a leader who would say when they came and when they went. The new klansmen were so fired with liquor they would have marched on the government compound on the opposite side of town there and then. Gunning was well satisfied with their ardour but he was not going to set them off half-cocked. When he was ready he would make his move and when he did it would be decisive.

His first orders were to boycott the government by refusing to pay taxes and to coerce others by any means, fair or foul, to follow their example. They were to deny the government all rights over white men, and seek recruits so that the Klan would become an army of straight thinking white men ready and willing to take command of Fiji.

They were to carry arms at all times so that, no matter where they were when the order came, they would be ready to march. At the sound of three shots fired from a carronade, all klansmen were to drop everything and report on the double to Keyse's Hotel.

"But there's only one carronade in Levuka and it belongs to the bloody king," objected one klansman, more sober than the rest.

"That is where you are wrong, my friend," smiled Gunning. "I think you may show them now, Denison."

Denison, revelling in his moment of glory, led a procession of drunken hooligans on a tour of the old building. On the long enclosed verandah facing south into the town were no fewer than three carronades! To bombard Levuka, all they had to do was open the wooden shutters which were like gun ports on a man-of-war.

The place was a veritable arsenal. In other rooms were box after box of cartridges, stands of new rifles, bayonets, even swords for officers — Keyse's Hotel had been transformed from doss-house to fortress. There were enough arms there for the Klan to stage a *coup d'état*. The Klan had the men, the money and the munitions. All that remained was for Basil Gunning to give the word and the Cakobau regime would be at an end.

As usual, oaths of secrecy or not, the whole of Levuka knew about Keyse's Hotel and the Klan before they even had a chance to drink their morning eye-opener. But that too was just as the gallant colonel had planned it.

*****

Gunning was having to adapt his overall strategy. He still reported to his friends in London and drew on them for funds; but he was beginning to see that there was little chance of his becoming Governor of Fiji. He had powerful backing but people like Lord Belmore would discredit his work. Not even a new government in London would touch a man suspected of blackbirding.

Moreover, he was weary of waiting. Originally he had hoped it would take no more than two or three years to execute his plan. But one year dragged into the next and Fiji was still not British nor, if Belmore's attitude was indicative of British thinking, was it ever likely to be. On the other hand, the islands were in such a state of political flux that there was room for the emergence of a strong man. Brooks in Borneo had set himself up as the independent Rajah; if he could do it, so could Basil Gunning.

He kept these thoughts very much to himself. Lesser beings such as Horace Twyford had to retain the illusion that they were working for the greater glory of the British Empire. They might not have been so willing and useful had they known that they were seeking the personal aggrandisement of Basil Gunning.

The Cakobau Government were playing right into his hands. Woods, with his quarterdeck manner, was highly unpopular; and Burt was proving himself increasingly inept at handling finance. With the encouragement of the Consul and strong-arm work by klansmen, the Europeans were refusing to pay taxes and even the native poll tax and land tax were in arrears.

The government had been operating for just a year and was in debt to the tune of £20,000. A shoestring budget was needed but instead Burt was promising roads, hospitals and schools. Without a feather to fly with, those promises made him a laughing stock.

The elections, which were supposed to bring the Europeans behind the government, only served to pack the legislature with men implacably opposed to Burt and Woods. In the face of such hostility they chose to rule the country by the executive decree of cabinet. Understandably, that made them even more unpopular and produced more recruits for the Klan.

*****

One decree established a police court with the proclaimed purpose of cleaning up crime in Levuka. As most of Gunning's men were wanted for one offence or another, a court was the last thing they would tolerate. Their leader passed the order to disrupt the court and make it as much a laughing stock as the King's ministers who had fathered it.

Court was held in a wooden building; the library and reading room for Levuka's would-be intellectuals. On other occasions it was used as the assembly chamber of the legislature. Wooden forms were set out for spectators and two tables, one for counsel, the other for the magistrate.

At the first sitting, Denison and 20 klansmen turned up early enough to make sure there was no room on the public benches for government supporters. The Klan even provided the accused with counsel, a lawyer from Victoria named de Courcy Ireland. This worthy, with the armed men at his back, aimed to dictate the law to the magistrate.

But the magistrate, another lawyer from Melbourne called Tregarthen, was no fool, nor was he ignorant of the Klan's intentions; everyone in Levuka knew. And so he had made a few preparations of his own though he knew better than to show his hand too early. For his personal protection he had tucked a revolver into the waistband of his trousers and the accused were marched into the court under a guard of Bauan warriors.

The first accused, Rees, was himself a klansman. He was charged with causing extensive damage to a shop whose owner had refused him free liquor. Tregarthen gave permission for him to confer with his lawyer. He cocked his eye for any sign of unrest among the crowd but they sat quite still, not even talking. The whispered consultation dragged on until Tregarthen's temper got the better of him.

"Come on, come on," he snapped. "Your man knows the charge. What does he plead, guilty or not guilty?"

Rees smirked insolently at the magistrate. He knew he had the backing of every man in the courthouse apart from Tregarthen and his guards.

"I'm not pleading any bloody thing and you can't make me," he shouted, just as Ireland had instructed. "You can neither try me nor charge me. You're nothing but a bloody farce!"

There was a roar of approval from the klansmen and Tregarthen's gavel banging for silence could hardly be heard above the din. Denison and his men were standing and jumping up and down on their forms, brandishing weapons; at any moment they would charge the bench.

Tregarthen drew his revolver and shouted to the guard commander to close up on the prisoner to prevent an attempt at escape. The magistrate's revolver and the muskets of the guard were pointed straight at the stomachs of Denison and the lawyer. The doorways and windows were suddenly filled with muskets, backed by grim Fijians who would have liked nothing better than to fire into the packed crowd of Europeans.

There was a stunned silence. Now that the odds had evened out, neither Denison nor his cronies had the stomach for a fight. It was Tregarthen's turn to smile. He laid the revolver down beside his gavel. One shot from him and the Fijians would promptly follow suit. Once they cut loose there would be no stopping them until every klansman was stretched out dead on the courtroom floor.

"I shall enter a plea of guilty," said Tregarthen in a cold, no-nonsense voice. It was as if there had been no break in the discussion.

"Like hell you will!" yelled Rees.

"And I now add to the charge one of contempt of court," said Tregarthen, unperturbed.

"You can't do that," shouted Ireland, springing to his feet. "What is the meaning of surrounding the court with armed men? You are threatening the lives of private citizens. This is an outrage unparalleled in the annals of justice."

"Mr Ireland, this is the first sitting of this court and I have been more than patient with you. Now I warn you that unless I am accorded more respect and co-operation, you will find yourself charged with contempt along with your client. You come here with a parcel of cut-throats whose goal is to subvert the laws of this country. Watch your step, Mr Ireland, or you may find yourself on even more serious charges."

"I must protest," blustered Ireland, waving a piece of paper. "The man you are trying is a British subject. I have a letter from Her Britannic Majesty's Consul which states that your court has no authority over British subjects. It is extremely doubtful if you even have authority to try a Fijian. This court does not have the approval of the legislature."

Tregarthen was red in the face, his patience at an end. "To hell with your British Consul! I don't care if Rees is a Chinaman. I hereby find him guilty and sentence him to two months imprisonment. If you don't pipe down this minute, Ireland, the guards can cart you off with him."

There was no doubt that he meant every word and the lawyer collapsed in his seat like a punctured balloon. "Take the prisoner away," Tregarthen ordered.

Rees was led out cursing violently, but a wink from Denison as he passed told him that the Klan would see to it that he was soon freed.

From the Klan's viewpoint the next case was even more important as its outcome could affect anyone who had criminal or civil offences outstanding against them in other countries. To win support in Victoria, New South Wales, and New Zealand the government was about to try its first application for extradition.

An accountant from Melbourne named Crossley was accused of embezzling trust funds. The case was of considerable significance because if, after hearing the evidence, the magistrate decided there was a case to answer, he would be put aboard the *Elizabeth* for deportation to Victoria and trial: no escaped felon could ever regard Fiji as a safe haven again and the freedom of a large proportion of the European population would be in jeopardy.

As the bailiff from Melbourne read out the charges Crossley, a small rat of a man, kept looking back over his shoulder to the klansmen his eyes anxiously appealing for help. Denison and Ireland conferred in whispers. Though their own armed men filled the court, the Fijian guards outnumbered them by two to one. It would seem that Tregarthen and the government had already won the first round and, unless they were to lose the whole match, they urgently needed to consult their leader.

When the bailiff finished his evidence, Tregarthen laid down his pen and nodded to Ireland. "I presume you appear on behalf of the defendant, Mr Ireland?"

Ireland got to his feet and assumed a pose meant to convey disdain. "I appear for Mr Crossley, but I can only reiterate that this court has no jurisdiction over a British subject, nor has it the right to order extradition. After discussion with my friends we have decided that we may no longer associate ourselves with these irregular proceedings. We shall take this matter further in the legislature where we can debate your conduct free from armed threats. We shall be demanding your immediate dismissal and impeachment."

Ireland swung on his heel and stalked out of the courthouse followed by Denison and the klansmen. Tregarthen, not wanting to push his luck too far, let the insult pass. He was well satisfied with the morning's results. From the Cakobau government's point of view it was a resounding victory. He only hoped that when the inevitable counter-attack came, other government officers would play their part as successfully.

Later that same afternoon, the carronades at Keyse's Hotel boomed three times and every bar in town emptied as klansmen hurried to answer the summons. Levuka closed its shutters, merchants barred their doors and anxious mothers snatched children from the streets. Everyone knew of the arsenal at Keyse's Hotel and no one was taken in by Denison's story that he had set up as a gunsmith; while he certainly had the stock in trade he never sold so much as a spent bullet.

*****

The government set a strong guard around the gaol, expecting an attack. But it had not reckoned on Gunning's professional skill. He wasn't about to commit his forces to a pitched battle. The klansmen might be expert at rolling a drunk or shooting an unarmed opponent from cover, but their training had not reached the stage where they could take on King Cakobau's warriors. On the other hand, unless the Klan did something it would lose so much face that pro-Cakobau townsfolk might be encouraged to take a stand against them.

Instead, two boatloads of klansmen ambushed the Victorian bailiff that evening as he and his prisoner were being rowed out to the *Elizabeth*. The bailiff was armed and Crossley was manacled but there was no room in the small dinghy for extra guards as well as the oarsmen.

The Klan's boats waited for them in the darkness. Some 50 yards short of the schooner's side they closed in. A bullet through the temple knocked the bailiff out of the dinghy before he had a chance to reach for his pistol. The sailors, not wanting the same treatment, were overboard in a flash swimming for the shore. Crossley was whisked away and that was the last the Victorian authorities ever saw or heard of him.

Aboard the *Elizabeth*, Peter Bex, Jason and Kate Cotterel, and John Thurston were seated at dinner. Thurston, who had been elected to the legislature as a member for Taveuni, was in Levuka for the current session, whilst the Cotterels were on their way home from Sydney. They were just discussing the court cases when the flurry of shots close at hand brought them to their feet and running out onto the deck after their host.

The lamps in the rigging did not throw a large enough circle of light for them to see what was going on. They shouted at the vague cluster of boats but the only answer was a loosely aimed shot which thudded harmlessly into the rail not far from Jason.

Bex bellowed for his crew to get guns and man his gig. But by the time they pushed away from the side the attackers were well away. All they found was an empty dinghy and the murdered officer floating face downwards in the refuse-littered water. Bex, who had been expecting the bailiff and his prisoner aboard, was able to tell them who he was — there was no need to guess who the murderers were.

"Those Goddamned klansmen," spat Bex. "This is Gunning's work. Him and that blasted brother-in-law of yours, Jason." Bex hadn't noticed Kate join them until he had finished speaking and his face reddened with embarrassment. "I'm sorry Kate, I … I shouldn't have said that about your brother."

"If my brother is associated with this contemptible society, whatever it is they call themselves, and the dreadful murder of an innocent officer, I hope that he is apprehended and made to answer for his crimes," answered Kate stonily.

For years she had made excuses for Toby but her conscience could dissemble no longer. He was a criminal, the ringleader of men dedicated to the destruction of all those things that made up an ordered, law-abiding society.

"Good for you, Mrs Cotterel," said John Thurston admiringly. He turned to Jason. "Tonight's events should be enough to make up your mind. I know it is enough for me. I am standing on the sidelines no longer, I'm going to see the King and offer my services and I think you should accompany me. Woods and Burt have tried to help and this is the result. Together, we can at least bring over to the King those Europeans who haven't already been infected by Gunning and his bullies."

"I will be with you, John," said Jason sombrely, not looking at his friend but at his wife. "I won't be returning home immediately, Kate. You and the children must leave without me. You do understand, don't you?"

There were tears in Kate's eyes so that she could make out only a blurred image of his face. She had just lost a brother and now it seemed that she must sacrifice her husband. "I understand," she whispered.

30

Changes at the helm

On their way to Bau in John Thurston's cutter the following day, Jason hardly said a word. Watching the *Elizabeth* leave without him had been a terrible wrench; he would be lucky if he saw his family for three months out of every twelve and his plans for Qaraniqio must take second place. The trouble with a political life was that once you grasped the reins of power it was almost impossible to put them down again.

Rather than go straight ashore at Bau they followed Fijian custom. As soon as the anchor dropped, two of Thurston's crew went ahead with a tabua. They were to present it on behalf of their master and his friend and respectfully request an audience with the King. In response, a group of Fijian elders dressed in ceremonial masi arrived and presented tabua in their turn. The King, they said, was always ready to hear words of wisdom from such trusted advisors as Thurston and Cotterel.

On the beach they were met by more court officials and, followed by a great crowd of curious Bauans they were escorted to the huge thatched bure where the King was to receive them.

Jason Cotterel and John Thurston removed their shoes outside the door, slipped inside and crawled across the floor to sit cross-legged on the mats in a position of honour. Jason had not set eyes on the King since the day of his farcical coronation five years before. While the ceremonial yaqona was being mixed he looked at him closely and was startled by what he saw.

The King had tasted the fruits of the royal tree for the past five years and, from the deep lines etched on his forehead and at the corners of his eyes, he had found that taste bitter indeed. His beard was snow-white, and it seemed he only kept his shoulders straight and proud by conscious effort.

Cakobau had become an old man and the sight made Jason feel guilty. He had sat back on Vatulevu surrounded by love and the comfort of a good home while this man had fought unceasingly to ward off the rapacity of the white man, and the ignorant savagery of his own people, with hardly a friend to help him.

After they had drunk the yaqona and listened respectfully to the high flown phrases of the presentation speech, it was John Thurston as the elder and an elected member of the King's legislature who spoke first.

"Your Majesty, Turaga na Vunivalu, Great Chief of Bau and Kaba, I come here today with my good friend Jason Cotterel in order that we may offer our services. It is our hope that you may find some use for us in the weighty business of administering your country. We do this because we fear that Fiji is in a state where your government may collapse as it did in 1868 and 1869."

The King said nothing and his dark eyes were hooded so that it was impossible even to guess his mood.

Thurston, deciding that complete frankness was the only possible course, continued. "Your ministers, especially Mr Burt, are so unpopular that their persons constitute major obstacles to the fulfilment of your hopes for sound government. By diplomacy you managed to free Fiji from the iniquitous American debts, but prodigal spending unsupported by revenue has put the country so far into debt that, as in the old days, threats from visiting warships demanding payment may soon be expected."

"In Levuka, the white men have formed a society to organise opposition to your Majesty and your government. They flout your laws, ridicule your courts and openly speak of rebellion. The hill tribes are raiding and ravaging the western coasts of Viti Levu unchecked and I am told that Prince Ma'afu again flirts with ideas of ruling Fiji himself."

Thurston wondered if he had said too much, but as Cakobau remained impassive he decided to finish. "Lawlessness, debauchery and legalised slavery have made the name of Fiji anathema in the halls of civilised nations. Your enemies trade on this, they speak behind your back, they write to foreign governments reviling you. They now combine to topple you and your ministers from power."

Jason checked every word against the facts and knew them to be true. How the King would like such unpalatable facts thrust beneath his nose was a horse of a different colour and Jason admired Thurston's dogged courage. It was a formidable list for even a stable and wealthy government to tackle and he began to have serious doubts as to their own ability to find a solution.

"Cotterel and I are not here, Turaga, to fill our pockets from your treasury," said Thurston coming to an end. "We could make more money by staying on our plantations enjoying the peace and the love of our families. We have come at this time of crisis when others are falling away, to prove that we are still your loyal and sincere friends. The programme we would humbly suggest you follow would settle the debts, establish a rule of law, and above all reassert the supremacy of the Fijians in their own country."

When he had finished, the King looked up slowly with an expression which was anything but friendly. "What do you expect me to answer, Thurston?" he barked. His voice had lost none of its old fire.

"Would you like me to say, 'thank you very much Mr Thurston and Mr Cotterel, I hereby shower you with tabua and other honours for making such a magnificent offer?'. Do you wish me to step down and make you King in my place? Well, I shall do none of those things." Jason felt the full force of those penetrating black eyes.

"If Fiji and its people are in a desperate condition it is because men of your standing have not come forward before this. You step up at the eleventh hour offering assistance. You come when I fear it is already too late, when the ship of state has all but foundered for lack of a competent crew. It is little use giving instructions to the helmsman if the sails, mast and rudder have all gone overboard."

"You have the effrontery to tell me, the King, that Fiji's name is a filthy smell in the nostrils of other nations. Tell me who has carried these tales if not the church, the same church that said it would be my rod and would comfort me, yet whose missionaries write to Peritania blaming me for every crime which is committed. I am surprised that you do not have Matthews with you offering help."

Jason began to think that coming to Bau was a bad mistake, but there was worse to come. "I am blamed for the deeds of the white man! Show me a Fijian murderer and I shall execute him. Bring me a Fijian blackbirder and he will be condemned to a lifetime of slavery. But if the criminal is a white man, if I try to take action against any one with a white skin, a man-of-war will appear over the horizon and blast Bau to pieces."

"I counted you my friend, Cotterel, but when I needed you, you ran away and hid yourself on your plantation. You made a public laughing stock of men I sent to speak to you. I know what you said to Drew about the Polynesia Company. I am sorry that plan did not appeal to your fastidious taste, but that same company paid off the Americans, your own fellow countrymen, for me. I did not see you offering your services to go to America and argue my rights. Now you have the audacity to come here offering me your services."

"Sa dina, i'saka," said Jason, acknowledging the truth in the accusations. He hung his head, hoping they might soon escape. Beside him, he could feel Thurston fidgeting.

"You come, Thurston, when it is too late," continued the King. "How many times have I sent messengers to you begging for help? You have too exalted an opinion of yourself. You will only associate with this one and will not work with that one. You wait until the efforts of others, and honest efforts they were for the most part, are smashed into a thousand pieces and then you make your offers."

"My past experience tells me that no white man is to be trusted; why then should I trust you? You are white. Don't think I am ignorant of what is happening in Levuka. Colonel Gunning is plotting to destroy me. I think he would like to be King in my place, yet he too once said he was my friend."

"Did you know that tomorrow the British Consul will issue an order to masters of British ships ordering them not to pay harbour dues, and to British merchants threatening them with deportation on the next man-of-war if they dare to pay customs and excise taxes? Yet Mr Twyford is another white man who continually assures me he is my friend."

Jason only had to pass this piece of information on to Lord Belmore and it would be the Consul who would be deported, not the merchants. It was clear that the Fijian clerks in the consulate were acting as intelligence agents for their King.

"We Fijians are the ones who understand what the law of the club, the spear and revenge really mean. You whites came with your church and your cheap trade goods and said that we were the savages. You kai-valagi said you wanted civilisation and law and I agreed that you should have them. But immediately the laws are promulgated the people who resist them are not the Fijians but the valagi, the foreigners, who were screaming out for them."

"If the whites in Levuka want us to settle this in our old way, I am quite happy to start a war of the races. Levuka is neither too big nor too strong to withstand me. In the days before I had Christian principles I attacked towns with double the population of Levuka and today there is neither stick nor stone to tell the traveller those towns ever existed. What I did to people of my own race I can do to white men."

The King sat back; he had finished and looked spent, but relaxed. It was as if he had been wanting to get that entire tirade off his chest and now felt better for being rid of it.

Thurston was up on his knees speaking, "I deeply regret that we have taken up your Majesty's time. From what you have said I must presume that you have no use for the services we offer and I therefore beg leave for myself and my friend to depart."

"As always, Thurston, you presume too much," answered the King sourly.

"What do you expect us to presume?" said Thurston truculently. "We came here wanting to help and all we receive at your hands are insults."

Jason waited for another outburst but instead the King was smiling. "With people I have no use for I am polite; why should I waste pleasantries on such as you?" said the King, delighted by Thurston's outraged dignity and hurt pride. "On the other hand, had I blamed you personally for the latest incidents you would never have been given audience. You deserved to get the edge of my tongue and you both know it. You are now offering to help, and help you will. But it would have been better for my country had you both made your offer five years ago, when it was first needed."

The King had been uncomfortably accurate when he said John Thurston's main fault of character lay in his pride and sense of infallibility, and for once even he looked chastened.

"I acknowledge our dilatory behaviour and humbly beg your Majesty's forgiveness," he said. Jason guessed that this must have been the first time Thurston had ever begged pardon and it was a mark of the man that he was able to do so.

"If your Majesty does have a use for us," said Jason, speaking for the first time, "would you be so good as to explain what you have in mind."

"But I thought you knew, Cotterel," said the King, chuckling. "You are to be my Minister for European Affairs. I look to you to win the support of the Europeans and rid me of this ridiculous Ku Klux Klan. I can think of nothing more difficult and for the moment that will do."

"And me, sir?" asked Thurston warily.

"But what else could you be, Thurston, but Chief Secretary, the head of my government. Having told me what is wrong, I now make you personally responsible for all of my country's problems."

The astonishment on John Thurston's face was all that Cakobau could have wanted. For once the King of Fiji could forget his worries and laugh at the dumbfounded expression on the faces of his new ministers.

*****

King Cakobau's 'navy' comprised the 30 ton schooner, *Marie Douglas*, and the *Vivid*, an armed cutter under Captain Daniel O'Neil. Because keeping even this minute fleet afloat was too much for the economy; the vessels had to double as merchant vessels carrying cargoes of copra to earn enough to pay the wages.

The lack of European support was the most serious single problem facing the monarchy, and so when Jason Cotterel joined the Cabinet it was decided not to chain him to a desk but to send him around the Group explaining government aims and policy. Regardless of expense, the *Vivid* was taken off the copra run and placed at his disposal.

He was meant as a counter to the rebellious elements. As a planter himself, able to talk agriculture, understand the planters' difficulties and with 18 years of Fiji experience to back up what he said, he was more likely to get a hearing than the other ministers.

The arrangement suited Jason. While it took six months to visit all the scattered European settlements and plantations, he was able to make frequent calls at Vatulevu to see how his family and the estate were faring.

By and large he was well satisfied with his affairs there. John Denison appeared to have enjoyed his period of sole control and was helping Kate all he could, but she was pregnant again and soon would not be able to supervise the multitudinous operations which made up a busy plantation.

'Showing the flag', was an operation which O'Neil, once a Lieutenant in the British Navy, knew backwards. Nothing could rid the cutter of the strong smell of coconut oil but otherwise she and her crew were as smart and shipshape as their captain could make them.

The flag itself was no longer the rising sun abomination Jason had seen at the coronation. The new version was white, with a central motif of a dove and olive branch surmounted by an orb, a cross and the crown. Beneath this was the motto, Rerevaka na Kalou, ka Doka na Tui — Fear God and honour the King.

Each time he sailed away and the great mountain sank back beneath the horizon, Jason cursed himself for a fool to have ever got himself involved in politics. The settlers who had poured into Fiji while Jason had been hibernating on Vatulevu were a breed of men new to him. His message calling upon them to get solidly behind the Government fell on deaf and often hostile ears.

They were interested only in a government which would help the white man take over the whole country, the quicker the better. When would the Government establish a trading bank sympathetic to planters' needs? What were the ministers doing about labour for the plantations? When would the Government wipe out the pestilential hill tribes, once and for all? What about more cheap land? Who did Cotterel and his mates think they were, trying to shove around honest British subjects? Who was going to make them pay taxes?

Jason made speeches, he argued, explained, and on one occasion when a burly German referred to King Cakobau as, 'that *verdamdt schwarzhund*,' sailed in, fists flailing like hammers until the offender, lying battered and bloody in the dust, confessed to the error of his words. The occasional settler was trying to live and deal honestly with the Fijians, but the majority regarded Fijians as brainless savages to be cheated whenever the opportunity presented itself.

There were the odd flashes of success, but, as one month ran into the next Jason became depressed by the hopelessness of his task.

*****

He had only fleeting visits to Vatulevu yet even one night in Kate's arms was enough to revitalise him. He hated leaving, but there was always the thought that he was at least trying his utmost to make Fiji a better place for her and their children.

Kate was horrified by what the work was doing to her husband. Each time the cutter dropped anchor off Qaraniqio Jason would come ashore looking more weary than ever. In a few months, deep lines of depression had turned down the corners of his mouth and his hair was noticeably greyer. Her every instinct wanted to beg him to give up his thankless task, but her surrender would be the final straw; he would never give in so long as he had her to encourage him and he desperately wanted to succeed.

The other person to whom Jason could unburden himself was John Thurston. He visited Levuka regularly to report and he made sure that his old friend was given the grim and unvarnished truth.

"While the settlers maintain their present attitude, I cannot see us getting them to accept any form of government. They whine about this and demand that, but when it comes to dipping a hand in their pockets for taxes, or fighting for laws meant to safeguard their own interests, it's a very different matter. The customs duty on tobacco is bypassed by open smuggling and there isn't a single plantation that isn't making rum to avoid excise. You couldn't stop it even if you had the whole British navy behind you."

"The funny side to it is they imagine that you and I are feathering our nests in grand style and are being dog-in-the-mangerish by complaining when they do the same thing. Most are so dishonest themselves they simply cannot believe anyone would want to build an honest government. My God, if they only knew the number of times I have wanted to throw it all in their faces and let them get on with it."

"That is just what Gunning would like us both to do," warned Thurston. "So long as white men like you and me hold the reins the Fijians, through the King, are still masters in their own land. If we throw in the sponge, Gunning and his klansmen will take over and then, God help the Fijians."

"Don't worry, the Fijians know it," answered Jason "The ones I've spoken to are fed up with being kicked around and told to shut their mouths in their own country. If the settlers don't learn some manners soon they are going to find themselves up to their dirty necks in a war they'll never be able to stop.

"The planters won't listen to anything I tell them. And our friends the Klan or the 'British Subjects Mutual Protection Society and Volunteer Corps' as they've now started calling themselves because it sounds more respectable, have been shadowing me wherever I go. I try to forewarn people of my visits with messengers so that outlying settlers can come to a central point. But as soon as I let it be known where I will call, the Klan sends in a party ahead to set the planters up against me. Once I leave, in they go again to undo any good I may have achieved."

"So long as that's all they do," said Thurston anxious for his friend's safety. He had problems enough of his own in Levuka, but Jason was out on a limb by himself.

"They haven't the guts to face me man to man," scoffed Jason. "They had a shot at me the other day as we entered the estuary of the Ba River. I was standing in the stern with O'Neil when suddenly about five rifles opened up from the cover of the mangroves. They drilled the helmsman through the shoulder and O'Neil got a nasty graze, but they missed me completely. The Ba settlers blamed it on the Fijians of course. My money says that my dearly beloved brother-in-law was behind it somewhere. I wouldn't put it past him to have been one of the riflemen."

"Good God, Jason!" Thurston exclaimed. "You must be more careful."

"How can I be more careful? I've got O'Neil, his crew and an armed cutter. How can I be cosseted more than I am now?"

"If we could only get something definite on Gunning and Denison and use it as a lever for your friend Lord Belmore to deport them." Thurston had seen the Governor's letter and was seeking an opportunity to use it. "Without them the Klan would collapse and half our worries would be over. They're behind the trouble in town but I can't pin the blame firmly on them."

Jason noticed that there were few people on the streets and a number of the merchants had closed and shuttered their shops. But he had been too preoccupied with his own problems to put two and two together.

"What's up now?"

"Well there is the business of Billings and Hall for a start," Jason looked blank. "Two merchants with courage enough to sign a letter to the *Fiji Times* denouncing the Klan — both finished up dead in a back alley. We know the Klan were the killers, but it was done at night and no one will come forward to act as a witness. I can't say I blame the people too much, even the honest ones are too terrified to open their mouths.

"Secondly, there's the cutter *Volunteer* which we seized for violations of the new Labour Regulations. I know the Klan are going to try to recapture her but apart from taking routine precautions I cannot make any move until the Klan makes theirs. By then mine is liable to be too little and too damn late."

"Where does the Consul stand?"

"Where do you think?" answered Thurston irritably. "If he's not the main organiser at least he's encouraging them in every way he can. Gunning spends half of his time up at the residency cooking up new outrages against us."

"A government official can't walk along the beach these days without being abused, spat on and challenged to defend himself a dozen times over. They've even got to the stage of open defiance. There's a planter called Smith holed up over at MacDonald's. He openly boasts of shooting a son of Tui Yasawa. The Fijian policemen, poor devils, are too scared to go in there after him."

An idea began to germinate in Jason's mind. "I think the time has come for us to use a little intimidation of our own," he said thoughtfully.

"What do you mean?" asked Thurston, worried by the look on his friend's face. "You of all people must be careful around them, Jason. They're not playing games. You should know that from what you've just told me about the Ba ambush. It would be a tremendous feather in their caps if they killed you."

Jason smiled reassuringly. "As Chief Secretary, the less you know the better. I think I have a plan which will force them out into the open and bring about a showdown. Leave the details to me, all you have to do is tell the King to marshal what troops and guns we have, just in case I pull it off."

"But HMS *Cossack* is in port. For all I know her captain might take the side of the Klan and then where would we be?"

"If the British navy wants to protect a bunch of rogues and murderers, let them. But they will also have to take over responsibility for the whole country. If the captain starts to complain threaten to toss the whole government in his lap, then watch him jump out from under. England has refused to take on Fiji and no mere captain with his eye on the promotion list is going to stick his neck out that far. If he did, the Admiralty would have no hesitation in chopping it off for him."

"What is it you intend to do? You cannot take the whole lot on single-handed!"

"Stop worrying, John, I shall only provoke them a little," said Jason cramming his broadbrimmed hat firmly on his head, "and maybe bring this man Smith in for you."

With the promise of some action instead of the useless talk he had endured over the past months, Jason felt quite his old self again. He got out of Thurston's office quickly, the time for argument had passed and the Minister for European Affairs had arrangements to make. If he was to put his head into the lion's den, he was going to be very sure he was ready for the roar.

31

Confrontation

GUNNING WAS HOLDING his evening *levée* on MacDonald's upstairs verandah. At his table were his lieutenants, Denison and de Courcy Ireland, plus two tame members of the legislature. At the other tables klansmen drank and gambled as if their very lives depended on it.

A year earlier, most would have been found in the dives further along the beach, the more exclusive preserves of MacDonald's verandah barred to them. Gunning's bottomless pocketbook had changed all that. MacDonald would once have been horrified by their filthy clothes, constant fighting, and the way they abused the servants, but now his cupidity had got the better of him.

A fat mountain of a man, MacDonald always sat at a small table next to the entrance corridor. From there he could see everything that went on and supervise the waiters. He never failed to greet his customers when they arrived and wish them 'Good Night' when they finally staggered off to their beds, but he never encouraged anyone to join him at his table. He preferred to sit alone and count the days until he and his wife would leave Fiji for a plush retirement in San Francisco. The way the Klan drank that day was approaching faster than he had ever hoped.

He was mentally balancing his cash box, a task he never tired of, when he noticed a pair of elegant grey trousered legs standing beside him. "Good evening, sir," he said automatically. As he looked up his eyes widened with surprise at the sight of Jason Cotterel in a suit that would have done credit to a London *soirée* rather than a sleazy South Pacific bar.

"It's good to see you, Mr Cotterel," MacDonald gushed like a widow with three marriageable daughters. "You're a stranger here these days."

Jason scrutinised the crowded verandah with contempt. As his silent surveillance was noticed, conversations broke off and people twisted in their chairs to see who was attracting so much attention. His obvious disdain soon had the whole room hushed, watching and waiting.

"Do you wonder I don't come here any more, MacDonald," his voice was loud and derisive, "when you let in scum such as these."

There was an immediate uproar from the men at the tables who had heard every word. Denison leant forward and said something to Gunning, but was stopped by an impatient shake of his leader's head.

"Now Mr Cotterel, sir, I must ask you …" began MacDonald, frightened that his hotel and his livelihood were about to be wrecked in the forthcoming riot.

Jason interrupted him: "Which is the murderer, MacDonald? They tell me you use him like a cheapjack show to attract custom."

MacDonald went white and tried to stand up, but Jason's fingers gripped his shoulder and thrust him back into his chair. There was no need for him to indicate, for at the mention of 'murderer' everyone automatically turned and looked at the big, black bearded Smith, sitting at a table near Gunning.

"Is that him?" Jason was scornful. "He doesn't look much, but I daresay he filled himself up with liquor first and then shot his victim in the back. You should be making quite a profit out of him, MacDonald, he looks a real rum-pot to me."

His audience could hardly believe their ears. The whole town walked warily around the Klan, yet here was one solitary man brazenly taunting them. It was too much for Smith. With over 30 people at his back, a fight with a dandified government minister was just his meat.

He pushed his chair over and surged through the crowd like an angered bull, his friends barracking him on. As he came, Jason sized him up. The man was blind with rage, over-confident and drunk into the bargain. This would be even easier than he had imagined.

"And what does Mr High-and-bloody-mighty Cotterel want with me, eh?" Smith bellowed, his face thrust within an inch of Jason's. The rum fumes were almost overpowering. "You want some of the treatment I dish out to kanakas?"

Jason wrinkled his nose disgustedly. "I have seen you, which is what I wanted, but I have no wish to smell you — you stink. I would be grateful if you would remove your dirty hulk from beneath my nose."

"So I offend your aristocratic bloody nose, do I?" Smith exploded. "I'll teach you a lesson, you bastard." Smith threw a punch which had it landed would have done enormous damage, but he might just as well have written a letter announcing his intentions.

Jason ducked easily and Smith never had another chance. Jason grabbed his assailant's arm by the elbow and, with the other hand in his armpit as a lever, spun Smith sideways and threw him into the corridor. The crowd, half out of their chairs, heard the thud as Smith landed though they could not actually see what happened.

Without even a glance at Smith, Jason had turned back to face the packed verandah waiting for their champion to come charging back. They heard a scuffling sound but no Smith appeared. A klansman shouted, "Come on, Smith. You aren't scared of a pansy like him surely?" But no answer came, and the satisfied look on Cotterel's face told its own story.

Realisation dawned. Surrounded by a huge guard of his friends, the police had been unable to arrest Smith. Instead, one man had cut him out with ease and delivered him to the police waiting in the corridor just out of sight. For a moment the mob was too stunned to do anything, then the leader spoke.

"And what, my dear Cotterel, do you imagine you will do with Smith?" Gunning had sat coolly through the whole episode — it was a mark of the control he had over his nerves that he had not even lost the long ash from his cigar.

"It's not what I shall do, Colonel," said Jason equally calmly, "it's what the court is going to do. He will be tried on a charge of murder and if he's guilty, he will hang."

"You can't hang a white man for shooting a native!" shouted Denison.

"My esteemed brother-in-law!" said Jason with a mocking bow in his direction, "I was beginning to think the jackal had forgotten how to howl."

His tone changed and his voice crackled with anger, "Of course Smith will hang! Neither you nor your yellow bellied assassins will stop us. The man has condemned himself out of his own mouth. A trial is to be held tonight, so if you want your legal shark to help he had better get moving."

A dozen klansmen made for the corridor but stopped abruptly as Jason swept aside the tails of his long grey coat. His hands rested lightly on the butts of the two revolvers he had used fighting side by side with Gunning against the Tongans. "I said nothing about you scum, I said the lawyer could go." His voice was firm and his cold eyes said that he would not hesitate to use those guns. For a long moment the klansmen looked death in the face and tested their mettle.

"Sit down!" Gunning ordered angrily. "There's not one of you with the guts of a rabbit. Go on, Ireland, get down to the courthouse and see what can be done for Smith!"

As de Courcy Ireland scuttled past, Jason fought down the impulse to speed him on his way with a swift boot up his backside.

He jeered at the crowd: "Your Leader seems to have no more guts than the rest of you. I didn't see him coming forward, but then the long range gentlemen of the artillery only show fight when they can bring down a barrage of guns to help them. You are all wind, Gunning," taunted Jason. "You are a liar, a cheat and a murderer, and it now seems that I must add coward to the list."

No man had called Gunning half of those things without being made to erase the dishonour with his own blood. The Colonel was no longer smiling, his lips were a thin line of fury.

"You are prepared to meet me, I presume," he said in tones which suggested each word was chipped from ice.

"But of course; that is why I am here. I thought you understood that." Jason was smiling. He was enjoying himself for the first time in six months.

"You can't fight a duel on my verandah!" protested MacDonald in a shrill voice.

"Shut your mouth, MacDonald! You laid yourself open to this when you first took their dirty money."

"I do not conduct affairs of honour in barrooms," said Gunning in his haughtiest tone. "If your seconds will wait upon me this can be arranged properly."

At Jason's signal, Daniel O'Neil and Sagar, another of the ministers, materialised beside him, both with revolvers belted around their waists.

"My seconds, Colonel, Messrs O'Neil and Sagar. Now, if you have guts at all we fight right here and now."

Jason was sure Gunning would back down. From his past record, unless he was standing behind double-shotted guns, he liked others to do the killing for him. There was a world of difference between fighting as part of a general battle and coolly facing a challenger over pistols. From Jason's point of view a refusal, so long as it disgraced Gunning in the eyes of his men, would be equally satisfactory.

Looking at his three opponents, Gunning knew that if he accepted the challenge he would be dead within five minutes. It seemed impossible that his dreams of power should end in a sordid barroom brawl. He said nothing. As his men watched their leader hesitate, whispering started up among the tables.

"Don't be a fool, Colonel," said Denison loud enough for all to hear. "This is Cakobau's murder squad. The moment you stand up, if Cotterel doesn't kill you, O'Neil or Sagar will." While he spoke his hand was creeping towards a Derringer tucked into the top of his pants; but as he was about to draw and fire there came a crash and he felt the wind of a bullet fan his face. Eyes round with fear Denison brought his shaking hands out into the open, empty. His revolver clattered to the floor.

Cotterel had hardly moved, but smoke curled from the revolver in his right hand. He had fired from just above the hip in an exhibition of speed and marksmanship enough to daunt the bravest of duellists.

"I think not, Denison," he said. "My wife would not wish me to kill her brother, but she would infinitely prefer that to her brother killing me." He reholstered his gun and looked back to Gunning. "Now, Colonel, I haven't all night, I want to be present when your friend Smith is sentenced to death. What is it to be? Are you a man? Or a yellow bellied coward sheltering behind the guns of your bravados?"

"I do not indulge in barroom brawls and I only fight with gentlemen; a class which hardly includes renegades like you," said Gunning, striving to maintain his usual supercilious drawl.

This evoked an outburst of protest from the klansmen. Not for one moment had they doubted that their leader would accept Cotterel's challenge. But now expressions of disgust were to be heard, especially from those Gunning had called gutless.

Jason's eyes never left Gunning's: "I must ask Lord Belmore to pass this story to his friends in London. I'm sure they will all want to know that Basil Gunning is a coward, a liar, a cheat, a murderer and a contemptible worm," said Jason trampling the man's reputation deeper into the mire.

"If I were you, Gunning, I would leave Fiji; there is nothing left for you here. From now on any man who insults or interferes with a government officer will have me to reckon with. Nor shall I be issuing challenges, I'll be sending along a few kai-Vatulevu with a bull whip!" He laughed scornfully.

His laughter was like a slap in the face. The room was silent. With slow, taunting deliberation he turned his back on the Klan and, linking arms with his two friends, walked away out of sight down the corridor.

By morning the tale of the Klan's humiliation would be all over town and a laughing population was impossible to terrorise. Jason knew it was not the end of Gunning by any means, but he had blown a wide crack in his facade which would take a lot of plastering over.

*****

"We have forced him to a show-down," Jason later told the meeting in John Thurston's office. "We've got Smith when they swore we would never take him. He's been convicted and he'll hang this evening. On top of that the Klan is the laughing stock of Levuka. Gunning must make his move now or pack up completely."

"My guess," said Sagar, "is that they will storm the gaol to rescue Smith. If the Klan can free him they'll have proved themselves to be more powerful than the government. If they fail, the Klan is broken forever."

Thurston looked at his ministers. The position was now quite clear in his mind. They were dedicated men; the deadwood had been pruned long before. Had they only been allowed to start again with a clean slate, a modicum of finance and the goodwill of the population, a team such as this could have put Fiji on the map.

But in the current situation they had little hope of success no matter how hard they tried. Even if they survived this Gunning business they were only staving off from day to day another inevitable collapse. As head of government, he felt it was his duty to the King to soldier on, holding together the remnants of the administration for as long as was humanly possible. He tried not to let his own depressing vision of failure infect the others.

"We've you to thank for this, Jason," he said warmly. "This is our chance to run Gunning out of the country. I've spoken to the King; he favours a direct attack on Keyse's Hotel, the seizure of their arms and the imprisonment of the whole lot of them."

"I agree," said Woods, the ex-naval officer. "Put carronades on top of the hill and blow Keyse's Hotel apart; then we smash them with a frontal assault." He was an honest if arrogant man. In the navy there was only one treatment for mutineers — death.

"You forget those two men-of-war," said Jason pointing through the office windows towards the harbour where a German corvette and HMS *Cossack* were moored. "Surely you don't think they will sit back and allow us to bombard white men?

"We must first make it clear to those two captains that the Klan are the aggressors. We've got to show them that we have a problem of rebellion but that we are strong enough to handle it without their interference. They will report events here to their home governments and it will help us to gain recognition if we demonstrate that we can handle a *coup d'état*, especially if we do it without bloodshed."

"What does the Minister for European Affairs suggest?" The man who asked was Fijian but he was dressed in a fine European suit, spoke English with a cultured voice and wore a clerical collar. Elija Codrokadroka, now ordained and freshly returned from England, had been immediately recruited into the Cabinet.

Jason smiled at his friend, whose use of formal titles was a private joke between them. "I would suggest to the Minister for Native Affairs, that we use a little guile of our own," he said with mock solemnity. "If the Klan want Smith, why not let them have him? He is a convicted murderer under sentence of death. By breaking into the gaol and giving him shelter at Keyse's Hotel in defiance of the King's judges they will place themselves beyond the law, which is exactly where we want them.

"I suggest we leave only a token guard at the gaol with instructions to withdraw at the first approach of the klansmen. In the meantime we assemble our own forces out of sight and get those carronades up the hill."

At that moment a gun boomed three times in the northern part of town — the klansmen were assembling. The ministers looked at Thurston, the time had come for a decision.

"Unless anyone has a better plan, we will use Cotterel's. I add just one proviso, not a single shot is to be fired at Keyse's Hotel until I give the signal.

"Jason," he said to his friend, "I think the time has come to use that letter from Lord Belmore." The others looked bewildered, but Jason's mind had been travelling on parallel lines.

"It's in my kit, sir. One of O'Neil's men can have it here in 15 minutes."

"Tell them to bring it straight over to HMS *Cossack*. You and I will pay her commander a formal visit."

32

Showdown

Between them, Sagar and Elija Codrokadroka managed the affair of the gaol beautifully. As the armed klansmen came down the road toward the wooden lockup, it appeared that at least a score of Fijian guards were in residence. But as the mob drew closer, ignoring challenge after challenge from the guard commander, Elija was reducing the guard by sneaking them out one by one through a back door where the attackers could not see them leave.

Smith was lying bound and gagged beside his bed so that he could not warn his friends. Neither of the ministers wanted anyone hurt; their plan was to provoke the klansmen into firing so that they would openly declare their state of rebellion.

Sagar, gauging the distance carefully, put his head though the window and yelled out to the advancing klansmen who were led by Toby Denison. "Denison! This is Sagar speaking." At the sound of his voice the rebels went to cover like startled deer. "Tell your men to disperse and return to their homes or wherever else they come from. If you attack this building you are rebelling against the King. As a Minister of State I must warn you, if you do not disperse you will all answer for the consequences."

He had just time enough to duck and drop to the ground before a fusillade of rifle and pistol bullets smashed into the building.

"Get under cover, Smith," he yelled to the prisoner, "or your friends will shoot you before they have a chance to rescue you." As Smith rolled under the bed Sagar sprinted for the back door just behind Elija and the guard commander.

For a good 15 minutes a storm of bullets perforated the thin walls of the building. As a display it was everything that the ministers could have wished. Smith cowered on the floor terrified that the next bullet would be the one with his name written on it.

The fusillade gradually slackened as the klansmen realised that no one was returning their fire. A few more tentative shots were fired, but still there was no reaction and it was obvious that the defenders were either dead or had fled.

Denison got slowly to his feet. "Charge!" he yelled, running for the gaol and firing as he went. Their victory cheers and *feu de joie* could be heard miles away as the klansmen dragged Smith from beneath his bed. It never occurred to Denison or his men that they were doing exactly what the government wanted.

*****

Thurston, Cotterel and Woods, dressed formally for their visit to HMS *Cossack*, waited on the other side of the town. As the shooting started, the Chief Secretary turned to the others, "That is our signal, gentlemen; the boat is waiting."

O'Neil's boat crew of Fijians, all over six feet in height, were drilled to a precision which would have done credit to any man-of-war. As the ministers were rowed smartly out to the warship, Woods gave them a running commentary on the activity aboard HMS *Cossack*.

"She's got her boats in the water, loaded with marines and armed matelots. It looks as though the captain is thinking of sending a landing party ashore."

"The moment he does," said Thurston, "Captain Douglas will find himself the new King of Fiji."

"The German commander's gig is tied up alongside. They must be having a conference of sorts," continued Woods. "Another boat is there too, it looks local."

"If I know anything, it will be our dear friend Horace Twyford, Her Majesty's Consul. He'll be telling them what a patriot Gunning is and what a pack of renegade scoundrels we are," said Jason caustically.

His eyes strayed towards the cutter *Volunteer* which had been seized by the government. "John, George! What's going on over there?" Men could be seen swarming and struggling on the decks. Several Fijians dived overboard and shots were fired.

As the *Vivid*'s boat brought them to the man-of-war, they saw the flag of Fiji on the *Volunteer* come fluttering down and a red one, emblazoned with three white K's, being run up the masthead in its place. But far from being dismayed, this fresh Klan victory was a source of satisfaction to the Chief Secretary and his colleagues.

"As long as our men are in position," said Thurston in a low voice, so that those on the decks above them might not hear, "they couldn't have made their capture at a more opportune moment. Not even Twyford can make excuses for them now."

A young midshipman met them as they came up the side on to the holystoned decks. There were no piping bo'sun's whistles, no guards and no guns, which Thurston as the chief minister of Fiji had every right to demand on a visit to a warship of a foreign power. "Very shoddy, very shoddy indeed," rumbled George Woods ashamed for his old service.

"Your business, gentlemen?" asked the midshipman. He was little more than a boy yet his tone was insolent.

George Woods had too many years of navy seniority behind him to be treated in such cavalier fashion by a junior snotty. "More civil, you ignorant young jackanapes," he barked. "You are speaking to the head of the Fiji government. We wish to see your captain immediately."

The angry voice of command snapped the boy to rigid attention. "Aye aye, sir! If your party will please follow me to the quarterdeck, sir. This way, sir."

As Jason had predicted, when the now perspiring midshipman ushered them into his captain's presence, not only was von Schumann, the German Commander, there, but so was a very self-satisfied Horace Twyford. When the introductions were over, George Woods, still bristling from their brusque reception went straight into the attack.

"Since when, Captain Douglas, has the Royal Navy done away with honours when the chief minister of a foreign country and members of his cabinet visit one of Her Majesty's men-of-war?" he demanded.

Douglas was taken aback; he was under the impression that Thurston and his friends had come to beg British assistance to put down the coup. Men about to be thrown out of office did not preface their requests with complaints. But his surprise was only momentary — no one spoke to a British captain like that, particularly on the deck of his own ship.

"On this ship, Mister," he snapped, jaws thrust forward pugnaciously, "I decide who receives honours and who does not. From what the Consul tells me, it is extremely doubtful whether there still is a government in these islands."

Thurston signalled to George Woods to hold his tongue. "So you already know of the rebellion, Captain?"

"Only what I have seen on that cutter, the shooting over in the town, and what the Consul has told me."

"As one of the main instigators he should certainly be able to tell you plenty," said Jason looking at the Consul with such meaning that Twyford dropped his eyes nervously. Getting the same signal as Woods, Jason also shut up, leaving the talking to Thurston.

"From the armed sailors and marines we see in the boats below us, I take it that you intend to put your forces at the disposal of the rebels."

This was in fact what Twyford had been urging Captain Douglas to do, though he had not used the term rebellion.

"It is my duty, sir, to protect the lives of British subjects," said Douglas truculently.

"And if I gave you my word as a gentleman, that every act of violence and every shot this morning was fired by those same British subjects as acts of rebellion against King Cakobau's government? What then?"

"Your British subjects have stormed the gaol and released a convicted murderer! Under your very nose they have seized a vessel belonging to notorious blackbirders! Are you telling me that you will give support to these scoundrels? Is the British navy now to protect and encourage atrocities such as these?"

Douglas looked to Horace Twyford for help, but he was no man to stand up to John Thurston on the rampage. Douglas was on his own. Rather feebly he answered, "With the collapse of your government, it is my duty to step into this state of anarchy and save lives. My men will ensure that law and order are maintained and lives and property are protected."

"And you, Commander?" asked Thurston swinging on the German who was amused by his English colleague's discomfiture. "What does the German navy intend to do about this rebellion?"

Von Schumann's heels clicked as he bowed. "The Imperial German Navy, Herr Thurston, vill do notting," he said in heavily accented English. "I haf order all German, stay at home and do notting. If real danger, my boats vill carry German peoples to safety on board my ship."

"Do you agree with Captain Douglas that my government has collapsed?"

"I think I vait and see, Herr Thurston." He was not going to be pushed into a position which might later rebound to his discredit and the embarrassment of his own government.

"Thank you," said Thurston curtly. He turned again to Douglas. "You, on the other hand, think we are finished. Well I do not share your opinion. I warn you, Captain Douglas, the moment you send your men ashore I will see to it that you will suffer the gravest consequences."

"Are you threatening me, Thurston?" asked Douglas, as if unable to believe his own ears.

"I am certainly threatening you! And if you push me too far you will discover to your disadvantage that I am prepared to do more than threaten." Thurston, who had trod the deck of an East Indiaman for years, was not to be intimidated by another sailor. He was fighting as head of government for Fiji's right to have its own government, free from internal rebellion or foreign intervention.

Watching from the sidelines Jason was all admiration. He had always known Thurston as a man who was prepared to stick up for what he thought were his rights, but he had never seen him in a fighting mood like this before.

"I am warning you, Douglas, that I have been empowered by the King to act on his behalf. You interfere in any way and we shall hand you, as the Queen's representative, full responsibility for the islands. Our flag will be lowered, the troops and police dismissed, all civil servants, magistrates and tax collectors will stop work and government offices and courts will close down."

"On you personally will rest responsibility for all security and order. That is what you told me a few moments ago, isn't it? You want to step into a vacuum and maintain law and order; well I suggest you make your move and discover just what it feels like to be in a real vacuum!"

"Nor shall we stop there. Through our friends we shall lodge the strongest protests with both the Imperial German Government and the United States of America. Britain may not be prepared to recognise us as the *de facto* Government of Fiji, but they are!"

Captain Douglas blanched beneath his tan. He was in the middle of what was supposed to be a routine Pacific cruise. He could vividly imagine the reaction of their Lordships at the Admiralty when it was learnt he had taken it upon himself to overthrow governments and annex whole countries in the name of the Queen, especially a country which Britain had specifically said she did not want.

"Mr Thurston ..." he began nervously.

"Now it's 'Mister' is it? Don't shilly-shally with me, Douglas. Do you intend sending those marines ashore or don't you?"

"Take no notice of him, Captain," Twyford said, trying to strengthen the captain's wavering resolution. "As Her Majesty's Consul I assure you that he hasn't the backing of a single European other than those two standing beside him. If they resign and haul down their rag of a flag it will not make the slightest difference. They can't dissolve an administration where none exists, and if they refuse to step down peaceably then Colonel Gunning and his forces will make them."

George Woods was puce with rage. He stepped forward and tried to grab Twyford by the neck. Jason and the von Schumann had to forcibly separate them.

"Are you going to stand for talk like that, Thurston?" Woods demanded.

*****

It took everyone a few moments to settle down. Thurston regretted that he had brought Woods along at all. It was easy to understand his anger, but fisticuffs on the quarterdeck of a British man-of-war did nothing to help their reputation.

"I think you might take us a little more seriously if we gave you a demonstration." Thurston nodded at Jason who took from his pocket a large white handkerchief and walked to the taffrail. Douglas and his companions watched with puzzled expressions on their faces.

"How many men does Gunning have?" Thurston asked Twyford.

"Around 100 and they're all white, well-armed and determined," snapped the Consul, rubbing his throat after Wood's assault.

"I have Keyse's Hotel surrounded by double that number and believe me they are equally determined. If Captain Douglas and Commander von Schumann will each take a telescope I shall prove that I am not lying."

When they were ready Thurston said, "Wave the handkerchief, Jason. Gentlemen, if you will watch the buildings to the south of Keyse's Hotel and the open ground to the north you will see what I mean."

Sagar and the other ministers still ashore had been waiting for the signal. Even without a spyglass the men on the warship could see the sudden movement of armed troops deploying themselves on both sides of the old hotel.

"I see them, Herr Thurston," said the German, smiling.

Douglas closed his glass with a snap and gave Twyford a look which spoke volumes. By listening to this fool of a Consul he was jeopardising his reputation and in all probability his career.

"Don't be fooled by this ridiculous display," blustered the Consul. He was using his own handkerchief, but it was to mop the perspiration from his forehead, not to signal friends. "A parcel of natives will never stop Gunning's men; they'll run at the first salvo. Look how easily they captured the gaol and don't forget they have guns mounted at Keyse's Hotel."

"Captain Douglas, if this is a sample of the advice Twyford has been giving you, I don't wonder that you are ready to blunder ahead," said Thurston. "Our men withdrew from the gaol on my instructions as we wished to avoid bloodshed. None of the shots you heard were fired by our men. They have strict orders not to fire in earnest until they get a signal from me.

"As to numbers, within 24 hours the King can have another 1000 warriors here. We can lay siege to Keyse's Hotel so closely it will only be a matter of days before they collapse from lack of food and water. Don't be misled by Twyford, the Fijians are spoiling for a fight. They have many scores to settle with the Ku Klux Klan."

"I suppose it is stupid even to ask," said Douglas bitterly. "Do you have artillery of your own?"

Thurston nodded to Jason, who waved his handkerchief again. There was an immediate puff of smoke from the top of the hill overlooking the hotel and the delayed flat booms of two pieces being fired.

One shot missed, but was close enough to splash the rebel stronghold with water as it plunged into the sea; the other ploughed spectacularly, if relatively harmlessly, through the gabled roof of the building. From the seaward side, O'Neil on the *Vivid* fired two more shots. It was a graphic illustration of the government's preparedness.

"I only have to tell Cotterel to wave that handkerchief one more time and our forces will attack in earnest," said Thurston. The echoes from his guns were still reverberating off the hills. "Those 100 white men won't live to see this evening's sunset."

"Captain Douglas!" Twyford pleaded. "*Cossack*'s guns could knock out Thurston's positions with no trouble at all. You are not going to stand aside and see white men massacred?"

"Shut your mouth, Mister," snapped Douglas viciously. "It would appear that I've got myself involved in this mess because I listened to you in the first place."

"Twyford is right," said Thurston. "If you come in on the rebel side the government forces would not have a chance. Our success would then depend upon our friends. Commander von Schumann's government has already granted us recognition and in the event of an attack by a foreign power we would immediately call upon the Imperial German Navy for assistance."

"I am at your service, Herr Thurston," said the German with his bow and heel click. He was grinning from ear to ear.

Douglas was purple with near apoplexy and personal mortification. He would willingly have hung Twyford from his yardarm for putting the Royal Navy in a position where they must suffer such insults. As it was, he promised himself the satisfaction of writing a report on the Consul's perfidy and ineptitude that would blast him right off his comfortable Pacific Island perch.

Thurston and his colleagues stood silent, waiting for the outcome. It was difficult to keep a straight face with Twyford looking as if he might burst into tears, and Douglas torn between having an imminent fit and an intense desire to commit murder. Von Schumann, who intended to dine out on this story for years to come, turned away and busied himself with his telescope lest he should lose all sense of decorum and burst out laughing.

"Alright, Thurston, damn and blast you, I apologise," exploded Douglas. He turned and advanced on Twyford who retreated across the quarterdeck before the menace in the captain's face.

"You, sir, are a disgrace to the British flag. I shall see to it that you are stripped of office and never given another post north of the South Pole. If you were a sailor I'd have you flogged and keelhauled."

"And you can wipe that stupid smile off your face too, Woods," said Douglas now in full cry and prepared to do battle with any who thought to humiliate him further. "What you are doing serving with this ramshackle government when you are a half pay naval officer yourself, I do not know, but I shall certainly see that their Lordships at the Admiralty are apprised of the fact."

He turned on Thurston. "You have your apology, Thurston, but we cannot leave matters there, no matter what von Schumann may say. You have given ample proof that left to yourselves you could put this rebellion down, but I cannot sit here in the harbour and watch Fijian troops kill 100 British subjects."

"None of us want that to happen, Captain Douglas. I think that with some co-operation we can settle this to our mutual satisfaction," said Thurston. He looked at Twyford and the German commander who still had his back to them. "For this part of the discussion it might be better if we were alone. I think we can dispense with the Consul's services. As you can imagine, he is now *persona non grata* with my government."

Douglas was ready to grasp at any straw. "You may leave us, sir, at once," he ordered Twyford. "I will have words with you later."

Von Schumann also took the hint and made his apologies. There were rounds of bowing, heel clicks, salutes and hand shaking until he was finally piped over the side to his waiting gig.

*****

"Well, Mr Chief Secretary," said Douglas, acknowledging Thurston's status for the first time. "What is this solution of yours?

"Jason?" John Thurston handed over.

"One of the *Vivid*'s crew is waiting on the main deck with a letter I would like you to read, Captain. I think you will find it has a bearing on this matter." Jason beckoned and the Fijian who had been patiently waiting ran up to the quarterdeck with the letter.

"Letters!" snorted Douglas. "We want action not damned letters."

"I think you will change your mind when you read this one, Captain. It is to me from Lord Belmore."

Douglas, surprised that a planter in Fiji should be receiving letters from the Governor of New South Wales, surveyed Cotterel with new eyes. As he read it his surprise grew; it was evident that Cotterel must have made a deep impression on Belmore for him to make such promises. "You realise of course that this is a personal letter," he said gruffly as he handed the letter back to Jason. "I don't doubt for a moment that it is genuine, but on the other hand it hardly constitutes a set of orders for me."

"If either the Chief Secretary or myself asked you to carry a letter to Lord Belmore you would certainly get those orders," said Jason, "But that would not settle our immediate problem. We must resolve this Ku Klux Klan business today and if, by enlisting your help, we can do it without the loss of life it could only be to your credit."

"And strengthen yours, I presume," snapped Douglas. "What baffles me is why that idiot Twyford should have told me such a cock and bull story."

"The man is completely under Gunning's thumb," said Jason bluntly. "I cannot prove it, but I am positive that it was those two who stirred up the hill tribes and they have done everything they can to bring down the monarchy.

"Gunning suffers from delusions of grandeur. He sees himself as the Stamford Raffles of Fiji, if not the king. Maybe their idea is to force Britain to take over the islands, but in my opinion Gunning and Twyford are not pushing British interests, they are out to feather their own nests."

"You want me to arrest and deport Gunning and the Consul?"

"Yes, we do," affirmed Thurston vehemently. "The government will still have European opposition to overcome, but with Gunning and Twyford out of the way this attempt at organised rebellion will collapse like a house of cards."

"I have no authority to remove a Consul from office, gentlemen, but I can put in a report to Lord Belmore and the Admiralty which will ensure that he is removed post-haste." Douglas was won over and Thurston and his friends could heave a sign of relief. "In the meantime I shall give him such a blistering he'll be too scared to open his mouth for the remainder of the time he's here."

"What about Gunning?" asked Thurston.

Douglas had met the colonel on a couple of occasions before coming to Fiji. They came from similar service backgrounds and had mutual friends by the score. He knew only too well that Gunning had influence and connections in England. Now that he had been given a clearer picture of what was happening in Fiji however, his duty was quite clear. He only hoped that the Admiralty would back him if Gunning tried to pay him back for what he was about to do.

"Alright, I'll deport your rebel leader for you. I think it would be better if I went ashore and did it myself with none of you around. I also want to make it quite clear to any of his followers who may be British subjects just what their position is. If they choose to take up residence in a foreign country, they must either abide by the laws of that country or pack up and go home."

Thurston smiled and put out his hand to shake that of the captain. "Thank you, Captain Douglas. I shall tell King Cakobau that we have left this matter in your most capable hands. If, before you leave Fiji you have enough time, I know he would appreciate it if you could call on him at Bau. He will certainly wish to thank you himself. Now, we must go ashore and call off our troops before some hothead sounds the charge."

"Officer of the watch!" bellowed Douglas.

"Sir!"

"Bo'sun's mates and marines, man the side! The Chief Secretary of Fiji and his ministers are going ashore."

33
An untoward outcome

DOUGLAS'S ARREST OF COLONEL GUNNING was the main topic of conversation in the islands for months and hundreds of different versions of the events spread like wildfire in no time at all.

By the time Captain Douglas and his men arrived off Keyse's Hotel, the klansmen had lost the will to fight. When they stormed the gaol, well-lit with rum, they had been supremely confident; but as the glow of the spirits wore off and they saw their stronghold surrounded by Fijian troops their morale drooped. The shot which crashed through the roof showed their fortress for what it was, a dilapidated old hotel.

The majority were ready to surrender there and then and beg for mercy. It was only Gunning's constant assurances of the aid which would be coming from HMS *Cossack* which held them steady. To Gunning's watchful eye it was obvious that Denison and Ireland were as eager to desert as any. He was determined to shoot both if necessary.

More galling than the cowardice of his men was the thought that he had been manoeuvred into this untenable position against his better judgement. His plans had been progressing slowly but surely when suddenly the pace had accelerated beyond his control. From the moment Cotterel had appeared on MacDonald's verandah, everything had gone haywire. He had fully intended to have a showdown with the regime but, like the Iron Duke, he liked to be sure of his time and ground before committing his troops to battle.

The moment he heard the gaol had been taken without the slightest government resistance, he knew that he had been out-generalled. He also knew from past experience that Cotterel was to blame. The appearance of troops in force and the experience of being under fire from two angles, both impossible for his own guns to reach, made him realise that in an all-out battle the government forces could crush him like an insect.

Twyford was his last hope. The Fijians had an expression, vakararavi ki na vunikau vuca, 'don't lean on rotten trees'. After all the years of planning, everything now depended on one man and he seemed likely to collapse at the first sign of opposition. The notion of the Consul arguing down men like Thurston and Cotterel was clearly a pipe-dream.

With mixed trepidation and relief he watched the approach of Captain Douglas and his boats, packed with armed men. Knowing that the slightest show of fear on his part would send every one of his men bolting for safety, he walked out on to the jetty at the rear of the building as if to greet a deliverer.

Thirty of the more sober klansmen were drawn up as a guard of honour to welcome the naval party. Looking at them Gunning knew a moment of disgust; he wondered what could have driven him to associate with such scum.

As the boats touched, Gunning was there with his hand outstretched towards Captain Douglas and a warm smile of welcome on his face. "I was never so pleased to see anyone as I am to see you and your men, Captain Douglas," he said with more heartiness than he felt.

Douglas glared back at him and, at his signal, armed marines poured out of the boats and up the jetty steps. Their rifles formed a lethal barrier between Gunning and the klansmen.

Gunning's smile faded and the colour drained from his cheeks. His outstretched hand dropped slowly to his side. Seven years work, all of his scheming, his hopes and his personal ambitions were in ruins.

"I don't understand, Captain," he protested, "what does this mean?" He knew very well what it meant, but it seemed that he had to say something.

"What does it mean, sir?" Douglas, who had been waiting for this moment for the past 30 minutes, fairly spat the words out. "It means that you, one of Her Majesty's officers resident in a foreign country, have seen fit to foment revolution and as a result you are under close arrest. You are to be deported to New South Wales to answer for your actions. I would not be surprised if you didn't finish up on a gallows."

Gunning's face was bleak with shock as the full ramifications sank in.

"Disarm every man in the building and spike those guns!" Douglas ordered the midshipman with the landing party.

"Aye aye, sir."

As the young officer moved towards the guard, there was an uneasy shuffling and murmuring. The more courageous looked to Denison and Ireland for a lead.

"Shoot the first blackguard who disobeys orders, Mr Gregson!"

"Aye aye, sir."

Toby Denison was the first to drop his rifle — it might have been red-hot he got rid of it so fast; he also stripped the revolvers from round his waist and threw them down. The rest followed suit. Their arms, once intended to conquer Fiji for the white man, clattered onto the wooden jetty like so much useless hardware. Most were as scared as Denison, but a few had tears of shame and bitter disgust in their eyes. Their glorious revolution was over.

Gunning straightened his shoulders and, mustering a portion of the dignity expected of a Colonel of Royal Artillery, unstrapped his belt which carried not just a pistol but the sword which he had worn on more honourable occasions. Passing them to the grim faced Douglas he said, "I am entirely at your service, Captain."

*****

Gunning was not hanged as Douglas had predicted; his influential friends were able to save him from that. But he was cashiered. Ironically, the charge was not that he had incited rebellion against a foreign monarch but that he had served as military advisor to King Cakobau without having first obtained permission from his own government.

Nor did he suffer financially; he was given very adequate compensation by his principals who had no inkling of his personal ambitions and were well-satisfied with what he had done. In spite of Gunning's public disgrace the men behind him still anticipated reaping a profit from their investment in the longer term.

Seven years before, Fiji had been unknown other than in missionary circles, but that was no longer the case. Philanthropic and humanitarian societies were pouring out a veritable deluge of literature on this paradise blighted by blackbirding, cannibalism, paganism, lust, depravity and, above all, political anarchy.

The British government was held responsible by failing to take up its duty, the so-called 'white man's burden'. Delegations led by such figures as the Duke of Manchester waited upon the Secretary of State for the Colonies; leading clerics fulminated from their pulpits; and the press thundered on the subject of England's duty and honour in banner headlines.

In the House of Commons, where the issue of Fiji would finally be decided, Alderman McArthur, representing the City of London, put a motion which named King Cakobau and his ministers as 'a mongrel Government, short-sighted, penny wise and pound foolish'. His motion prayed that Her Majesty the Queen would be graciously pleased to establish a protectorate over Fiji.

Prime Minister Gladstone, who viewed colonies as an expensive and usually embarrassing luxury, managed to defeat the motion but only by a narrow margin.

It was common knowledge that it was only a matter of time before the swinging political pendulum brought Disraeli and his party, who were dedicated to Imperial expansion, back from their long sojourn in the outer darkness of opposition. When that day dawned, the sun would shine on the men who had sent Colonel Basil Gunning to Fiji in the first place.

Pressure was also being directed from Sydney and Melbourne where business interests wanted to get their hands on the islands. The New South Wales legislature went so far as to rebuke their Governor for his tacit recognition of the Cakobau regime.

Earlier, Woods had visited Melbourne and raised a loan for the government, but shareholders were now terrified that holders of Fiji debentures would see their investments disappear. They wanted Britain to take over the islands, debts and all.

*****

In Fiji, despite the best-intentioned efforts of John Thurston, Jason Cotterel, Elija Codrokadroka and their colleagues, both Fijian and European, affairs went from bad to dreadful. No matter how they tried to curb expenditure debts kept piling one on top of the other. With little or no revenue from taxes they had no chance of reducing the ominous mountain.

The Klan was broken, Gunning deported, and a new and more amenable man had replaced Horace Twyford. But the settlement of those problems brought them no closer to winning the support of the European settlers.

Six months before, John Thurston and Jason Cotterel had been respected private citizens; now they were pariahs, cast out from the company of their fellow white men.

"If we have one European left who doesn't hate our guts, Jason," said a dejected Thurston one day, "it is certainly no one I know." They had just finished listening to complaints from a delegation of Levuka businessmen and he was more bitter than ever. There had been the usual carping and moaning and, to make matters worse, several of those present were men who had originally backed them and the King.

"They were the ones who wanted security for business and protection against debtors. Today there isn't one who doesn't deride us behind our backs and they all owe money in back taxes."

Jason could have told him the main cause of their hatred was not just taxes. None of those merchants had been members of the Klan, nor had they even been friends of Gunning. However, when the Klan was broken every white man in the islands saw it as a defeat of Europeans by Fijians; the white by the black. Reason no longer entered into the debate and the fact that the klansmen were drunken thugs was forgotten.

The way their memory was venerated by the merchants and planters those who had stormed the gaol might have been Christian martyrs. Jason and the other ministers were execrated for the part they had played in the humiliation of their white brothers.

Wherever Jason had gone in the last few months, planters had asked whether it was true that Britain was about to take Fiji over as a Colony. "It is this talk of annexation which is unsettling everyone," Jason told Thurston. "Those storekeepers aren't going to give us support while they think there is even an outside chance of Britain coming in. It is the same everywhere I've been. They talk of nothing else."

"I'm not so sure they're wrong," answered Thurston gloomily. "We make no headway at all. The Europeans are as determined as ever to take over the islands and if the Fijians try to stop them one side will finish up being exterminated. It may not happen this year or even ten years from now, but eventually, when there are enough white men, the Fijians are doomed to be wiped out."

"Even now we cannot protect Fijian interests properly. I think we should seriously consider handing over the whole set-up to Britain."

"You are forgetting the King aren't you?"

"No, I'm not. He is even more fed up than I am. The novelty of wearing a crown and being called King is wearing terribly thin. All it has brought him is worry, war, and an ever-increasing millstone of debt. If he thought he could hand over to the British while still retaining a place of honour for himself, he would do it tomorrow."

Jason did not dare take the matter further. He did not even ask if the rumours that an approach had already been made to London were true. He trusted the Chief Secretary and if he did not see fit to volunteer such information, there must be a good reason for his reticence.

Even his own views had shifted. British rule was no longer the total anathema it had once been. He would rather be ruled by the Lord Belmores than the Denisons and the de Courcy Irelands who were fast becoming the only alternative. It was a choice between two evils, but so long as trustworthy administrators were appointed, at least under British rule the Fijians might have some chance of survival.

Jason was as fed up with politics as the King. He had only joined the cabinet from a sense of duty; he had never hankered after power for its own sake. He could take some pride from the fact that he had been responsible for thwarting Gunning's plans; if it had not been for him the Fijians might already have gone under. But pride was small recompense for being separated from his family. Had it not been for his respect for and admiration of John Thurston, he would have resigned his ministry long before, but he could not leave his friend in the lurch.

34

Bad to worse

FOR A WHILE AFTER the defeat of the Klan, affairs progressed quietly and it even seemed that the government might succeed, but the dream had faltered. The final straw came with a run on the bank established by Thurston. Crowds thronged outside the bank demanding that their paper money be exchanged for hard currency — hard currency when its very scarcity had been the whole reason for printing the notes in the first place!

When John Thurston and Jason Cotterel arrived to quieten the shouting, screaming mob, the significance of Denison and de Courcy Ireland being at the forefront of the demonstrators was not lost on either of the ministers.

"We'll pay out as soon as the taxes come in," shouted Thurston desperately. "If we open those doors about 20 of you will be paid and the rest will be left with nothing. Half the business houses in town will be ruined."

"Go to hell, Thurston, you lying bastard," yelled an irate planter. "You know that no one's paying taxes and even if they were they wouldn't use hard money. Anyone with sense would pay you back in your own useless paper."

"Open those doors, Thurston, or we'll break them down!"

"These notes say that the bearer will be paid hard cash on demand and we are demanding that right now." This last came from Toby Denison, a great person to talk of rights. His last clash with government ministers had taught him a lesson he was not likely to forget in a hurry. Since then he had maintained a pretence of operating within the law.

Toby prided himself that the run on the bank was his idea. If it was smashed it would bring the government into disrepute both at home in Fiji and overseas for there was Victorian and New South Wales loan money at stake. As Thurston's personal creation it would also hit the ministers where it really hurt. Starting the run had required little effort and capital on Toby's part and, once started, the government had a panic on their hands which they were incapable of stemming.

Jason, John Thurston and the bank manager conferred inside the building while the crowd hammered on the doors and rattled the window bars.

"How many people could we pay out, John?" Jason asked.

"As I told them, about 20, perhaps a few more depending on the denominations and amounts they want to change." Thurston looked ill with worry.

"What if I were to guarantee payment from my own funds in Sydney?" Jason suggested. "Those people out there know I have money and I think they would take my word if I said they would be paid just as soon as I got money across from Sydney."

John Thurston looked at his friend incredulously, a smile of real affection crossing his face. "You would do anything to make this Government a success, wouldn't you, Jason? If we only had 100 more men in Fiji like you, nobody could stop us."

"Well, what about it? Shall I go out there and tell them, or do you want to do it as Chief Secretary?"

Thurston thought it over for a long minute and then said solemnly. "I honour you for your offer Jason, but I cannot accept. Even you couldn't meet the demand once it was known someone was guaranteeing the notes. It would take £100,000."

"Whatever we do the bank is destined to fail and I don't see why you and your family should face financial ruin as well. If it must fail, let it fail right now. I meant what I told those people out there. When the taxes come in those notes will be honoured. If they want to see those notes worth what they purport to be worth, they must get behind the government and see that it collects its taxes. When the bank crashes there will be none to blame but themselves."

The bank duly failed and Denison and Ireland went shouting their triumph and the government's defeat to the four corners of the islands. Overseas financiers swore they would never invest in Fiji again. Those locals who had been paid by the government in local notes were determined never to sell Thurston so much as a bent nail in the future without first feeling and testing the weight of his money.

*****

The next crisis soon was upon them. In a matter of days news arrived of a massacre at Vunisamaloa on the Ba River. The hill tribes had attacked the plantation belonging to a William Burnes, killing Burnes, his wife, their two children and 18 of his labourers.

Not only was there an outcry from the other planters, but ministers could expect the very worst publicity in Sydney and Melbourne papers. Denison and his cronies put it about that the King was encouraging the savage kai-colo to slaughter every white in Fiji.

Thurston explained to an emergency cabinet meeting that the situation was even worse than it appeared on the surface. "We have been hoist with our own petard, gentlemen. Dr Clarkson, as Minister of Finance, visited Vunisamaloa recently and while there he warned everyone on the plantation against actions which might antagonise the people from the hills."

"In this he was following my instructions. We were trying to stop the indiscriminate killing that has been going on. As you know, in many places a strange Fijian has only to show his face and a trigger-happy European will try to shoot him. Over their rum they boast about the number of Fijians they have shot as if they were counting a bag of partridges."

Clarkson interjected, "I warned Burnes and his men that if they shot a native they would be charged with murder. I impressed upon them that the suppression of these raids was the duty of the Government and that anyone taking the law into his own hands would suffer the gravest consequences. To make sure that the labourers, most of them Tanna islanders, also understood I took a hangman's noose, put the rope around the neck of one of the labourers and slung the other end over the branch of a tree. I told them that would be the fate of anyone who took up arms against the hill tribes without proper authority."

"You can guess the rest," concluded Thurston. "It was almost as if Vunisamaloa was specifically selected because of the good Doctor's words. When the attack came, most of the labourers were without arms and those who did have guns were too terrified of the repercussion to use them."

There was a stunned silence. Jason Cotterel looked over at Clarkson, a recent addition to the Cabinet and a thoroughly decent man. The poor man looked crushed — those deaths would be on his conscience until the day he died. In the back of Jason's mind was the thought that the way the Burnes Plantation had been picked out from all the others might not be just a tragic coincidence. It all had a certain ring he had heard before.

"What will you do, sir?" Codrokadroka asked.

"As I see it," said Thurston, "we have two tasks. We must stop the settlers taking independent action. With some of the Ba hotheads leading a punitive expedition they stand a more than even chance of being wiped out themselves. On the other hand we have a duty to protect life and property."

"If we are to retain any standing with the planters we must show them that we intend to bring the instigators of this massacre to justice. It means a Government expedition. As Minister of War, Ratu Timoci should organise it, but I have already received a message saying that he is too busy with personal matters to attend this meeting."

Thurston's tone showed that he had almost reached the end of his tether with that particular minister. Jason sympathised: except for Elija it was impossible to impress a sense of urgency on most Fijians and that included the King. With all his other troubles Thurston should at least have been able to count on wholehearted Fijian support.

Even before the Chief Secretary opened his mouth, Jason knew that he was going to be landed with responsibility for the expedition. Goddamn and blast Ratu Timoci, he thought. He had been looking forward to at least two weeks at home but at this rate he would be lucky to see Kate and the children for two or perhaps three months.

"It will have to be you, Jason," said Thurston confirming his fears. "Europeans have been attacked and they are the ones kicking up the fuss, so it's really your province anyway. You will have trouble with the settlers in Ba and Ratu Timoci would be hopeless handling that sort of thing."

"Trouble in Ba? I don't need to go to Ba; these days, wherever I am trouble dogs my footsteps."

John Thurston understood Jason's annoyance but there was no one else he could send who either had the slightest idea of military tactics or could stand up to the planters. He could not afford to sympathise; all he could do was issue orders and point out pitfalls.

"This planter opposition will be highly organised, Jason, so be careful," warned Thurston. "My informant tells me that your brother-in-law and Ireland are stirring up the planters and bringing them together to form an independent punitive force. They say they will oppose any government force we send. They've already got a head start so you will have your hands full — I only hope they haven't already started off into the hills."

Jason did not argue. The last thing he wanted was to add to Thurston's difficulties. "Leave it to me," he said smiling wryly, "I will see what I can do."

*****

Jason Cotterel and a government column were landed at the mouth of the Ba River after a hectic three weeks in which Jason had never seen his bed for longer than four hours at a stretch and, in the avalanche of detail demanding his personal attention, it was usually only on alternate nights that he got that much.

Technically, the troops were under the control of two former professional soldiers, Major Fitzgerald and Captain Harding, but as the Minister of State responsible for expenditure, they came to Jason for every decision. Not only that, but invariably they made such a mess of things that the King's army would have sat in Levuka for six months had Jason not taken over. Others told him he was crazy not to delegate more responsibility, but he shrugged it off. War was far too serious a business to be left in the hands of soldiers.

The force comprised 60 trained Fijian troops, a small army of auxiliaries who were little more than camp followers, and a tiny contingent of 16 European volunteers with 200 reinforcement troops expected shortly. They were a motley collection, with all shapes and sizes of weapons and not a proper uniform between the lot, but given adequate leadership Jason hoped they would fight well enough. His immediate problem was the settlers' own army.

There were scores of Fijians to meet them at the landing but not a single European. From the Fijians, Jason learnt that 100 white men were camped up river near the Kennedy homestead right on the Government line of march towards the hills.

Jason had sufficient forces at his disposal to push them to one side, but an open conflict would also sound the death knell of the Cakobau government. Jason's task was to neutralise or, even better, get them to join forces with him against the common enemy. With Toby Denison and de Courcy Ireland at their head he did not care much for his chances.

Jason needed time for reinforcements to arrive and to provide more training before the campaign started and so he gave orders to camp where they had come ashore. Soon a nondescript town of canvas tents and brush shelters sprang up along the banks of the river. He instructed Fitzgerald and Harding to sit tight. With so many armed men in the area the kai-colo would not attempt another raid in the Ba area, for they would be too busy looking to their own defences.

The King's forces ignored the existence of the other army not ten miles away and, according to the Fijians, this caused more confusion in the settlers' ranks than a direct assault might have done. The latter held meetings day and night, argued violently, and even fought among themselves. At first their lust for vengeance had been white-hot, but the longer they hung about doing nothing the more their tempers cooled, and as the rum and food supplies ran low there was an equivalent flagging of enthusiasm.

Adding to the pressure, Jason sent out runners with pamphlets, which read:

NOTICE TO ALL SETTLERS

Government forces have been assembled in Ba for the purpose of punishing the authors of the recent atrocities committed at Vunisamaloa. Major Fitzgerald intends to attack Karawa as soon as final preparations have been made and invites anyone to accompany him.

Signed – Jason Cotterel,

Minister of State for European Affairs.

At the same time Jason instigated rumours that uprisings were likely in both Nadi and Ra. These were not altogether false, for three Bauans had been killed and eaten by the Nakorowaiwai people in Ra. In Nadi, the tribes along the Sabeto River were notorious for their hatred of the planters and, with the absence of menfolk in Ba, they might take the opportunity to raid plantations left in the care of women and children. The thought of defenceless wives and families was enough to send a considerable number scurrying home.

Jason received unexpected support when John Thurston and Swanston, once Ma'afu's secretary and now a minister himself, arrived with the reinforcements aboard HMS *Dido*. Captain Chapman did not intend to repeat Captain Douglas's mistake. As soon as he learnt of the trouble he had placed his ship and men at the government's disposal. Nevertheless he was obviously relieved when Jason explained his tactics.

"Capital, Mr Cotterel, absolutely capital. You have shown admirable restraint in your dealings with the planters. No purpose could be served by rushing headlong into a confrontation which would be bound to cause suffering and loss of life on both sides. What is your next move?"

"Just sit tight and keep up the indirect pressure," said Jason calmly. "I'm making no move to see them, but if they come to me I'm ready to talk."

"What about provisions for your men?" asked Chapman.

"It's a problem, but we are better off than they are in that respect. Their force is wholly European and it demands things unobtainable in these parts. For example, you can't keep a parcel of harum-scarums like that happy unless you have ample supplies of rum and gin to oil the moving parts. We have only a few Europeans and if it came to the point where we needed anything, I daresay I could call on you, Captain, to supply us. As for the Fijians, the local villages supply us with root vegetables and parties of our own men are out fishing in the river and on the reef."

"That doesn't mean we don't need your help, Captain Chapman," said Thurston joining in. "I agree with everything my minister has done, but it doesn't alter the fact that our forces are here to punish the hill tribes and stop this raiding once and for all. Therefore, the sooner this business with the settlers is finalised the better."

"This whole problem has been created by two men, Denison and Ireland. Their aim is to embarrass the government. Neither are residents of this area, they have come from Levuka in the hope that they can make enough political capital out of the massacre to bring my government down."

"You will recall my telling you about Gunning who was deported aboard HMS *Cossack*. Well these were his principal lieutenants and though he is now well out of the way they carry on his work."

Before coming to the islands, Chapman had been well-briefed on Douglas's near disgrace and the lessons to be learnt from it. He had no trouble in coming to a decision.

"I think a few more deportations would be in order, gentlemen," he said, smiling at the look of relief on John Thurston's face. "Well, what is to be done? Do we go to the mountain or do they come to us?"

"You won't have to budge an inch, Captain," said Jason answering for them all. "My bet is that they already know you are at anchor. If they're not aboard within the hour I'll eat my hat."

In fact they had even less time to wait, for within 30 minutes the officer of the watch reported the approach of a cutter. It was a small craft, but crammed so full of armed settlers that there was virtually no freeboard left. Captain Chapman escorted his guests from the wardroom to the quarterdeck where he intended to receive the delegation.

The planters' villainous looks were against them from the beginning. They all had beards and wore broad-brimmed Tokelau hats with red puggarees. They looked a dirty band of brigands by comparison with the neat sailors and marines of the warship. Jason now knew most by sight if not by name, and among them were decent men, genuine hard-working planters whose tempers had been inflamed by the massacre. They had become mere tools in the hands of Denison and Ireland.

Chapman watched with fastidious distaste as their muddy boots soiled his scrubbed decks and gave instructions that only six should be allowed on the quarterdeck, the rest to remain in the waist.

This resulted in a brief angry discussion as leaders were sorted out, but eventually it was done and Denison led the spokesmen up the companionway. From the angry flush on his face, Jason could tell that the captain's reception of his men, coupled with the sight of the ministers talking amicably with the ship's officers, had acted like a red rag to a bull. He and Toby seemed fated to sail on collision courses, thought Jason, but so long as Toby led the forces of anarchy and he worked for stable government it was inevitable.

"Captain Chapman we are …" began Denison. But he was allowed to get no further.

Chapman pointed with high disapproval at the revolvers at each man's hip; two even carried rifles. "I'll have you know, Mister, that captains of Her Majesty's ships are not in the habit of allowing delegations of armed men onto their quarterdecks, especially not a delegation of rebels."

"So that's what they have been saying, is it?" Denison was livid at this immediate attack. "You might at least have the courtesy to allow us to present our case. This government against which you say we are rebelling, has bankrupted the country and has ordered the natives to kill off every European in Fiji. Do you wonder that we refuse to listen to any more of their lies? If you want justice in Fiji you have to have a black skin."

Chapman's eyes bulged and his blood pressure soared dangerously.

"How dare you speak to me in that manner," he roared. He turned to the officer of the watch. "Mr Colgan! A dozen marines up here on the double!"

"Aye aye, sir."

Ireland, alarmed by the way things had got out of hand, stepped forward. "Please, Captain, excuse my friend, he doesn't know what he is saying; this affair has unhinged him. We are all British subjects and we came here to enlist your support. Believe me, sir, none of us wishes to insult you or our British flag in any way. We are most grateful that you have seen fit to receive us at all."

Trust Ireland, thought Jason, he'd smooth-talk a victim while finding a spot to thrust home the dagger if possible. This bogus lawyer annoyed him even more than his brother-in-law. All this theatrical nonsense — guns and swagger. He doubted whether he, Thurston and Swanston between them could have raised so much as a penknife.

Ireland's diplomacy mollified Captain Chapman somewhat, for he waved aside the marines who came pounding up rifles and bayonets at the ready.

Ireland followed up his advantage. "We regret the necessity for weapons, Captain. We carry them only for our own personal protection. As we passed through the lines of the native army we were fired on several times."

This was a fabrication which Ireland hoped would impress the captain and when one of the six, whom Jason knew to be an honest man, shuffled his feet uncomfortably it confirmed his suspicion.

He intervened: "Excuse me for interrupting, Captain, but that is a palpable lie." Our men have the strictest orders not to fire on anyone and even if they had we would have heard the shots from here." He looked directly at the settler who disliked Ireland's methods and, embarrassed, the man's eyes fell before his.

"Thank you, Mr Cotterel, that was just what I was thinking myself."

"This happened further up river and the wind is blowing in the opposite direction to your ship, Captain," said Ireland compounding his lie.

The planter shrugged his shoulders with disgust and stepped forward to speak. Denison tried to shush him but he refused to be silenced.

"It's as Mr Cotterel says, sir. I don't know what Ireland is trying to do. We weren't fired on at all. We have a real grievance against King Cakobau's ministers, Captain, but lying is not going to make our case any better. The natives massacred white settlers and we aim to teach those black beggars that they cannot attack us without getting the same medicine themselves."

"An honest man, I perceive," said Chapman sarcastically. "And if the liar is this Ireland, of whom I have heard so much, it logically follows that his obnoxious friend must be Denison. You two I shall be seeing again, but first I have a few things to say to the rest of you which you will pass on to your companions.

"I want it made quite clear that I will not interfere with King Cakobau's government; my interests lie purely with British subjects resident in Fiji. May I say that you are becoming an infernal nuisance so far as Her Majesty's government is concerned. Your irresponsible conduct brings all British subjects into disrepute."

"It will stop forthwith! If you wish to have a crack at these murderers, offer your services to the officer in charge of King Cakobau's troops. I'm sure he will oblige by putting you in the van of every charge." Chapman's voice brooked no argument and with the exception of Denison and Ireland, both of whom were crimson with anger, the rebels hung their heads not daring to look Chapman in the face.

"If you are not prepared to fight in the government column you will lay down your arms and return to your homes immediately. I am not asking this, I am ordering you. If you fail to comply I shall have no option but to bring you forcibly to your senses.

"You may thank your lucky stars that to this point you have had Mr Cotterel, a most patient man, to deal with. If you force me to act you will find that I am less long-suffering." He stopped and there was silence. "You understand?" barked Chapman.

The four planters looked at each other, then the one who had exposed Ireland's lie spoke again. "We understand, Captain, and we'll tell the others, but what about our grievances?"

"I think I speak for Mr Thurston and his colleagues when I say that, provided you obey my instructions immediately and the government forces are allowed to proceed on their campaign, we shall come ashore and listen to what you have to say." Chapman looked across at the Chief Secretary for confirmation.

"That is quite satisfactory, Captain Chapman, and I assure both you and these men that wherever it is humanly possible and in the interests of the country, we shall endeavour to redress these grievances," said Thurston solemnly.

Jason looked at Toby. He was taking no notice of the proceedings but was looking straight at Jason with hatred writ large on his face. There was no doubt whom he blamed for this most recent reversal of his plans.

The planters filed off as peaceably as pet lambs. Denison and Ireland turned to follow them down to the main deck when Captain Chapman's bellow halted them in their tracks. "Where are you two going? I said I wanted words with you!"

"Er…I…we want to help them explain things to the others," stammered Ireland.

"They are quite capable of doing that without the help of professional agitators and anarchists."

Toby Denison lashed back with the courage of a desperate man. "Agitators and anarchists! Who do you think you are talking to?" he exclaimed angrily. "You aren't the only one who has power, Captain. You lay a finger on either of us and we have friends who will make you regret it till your dying day."

Chapman looked him up and down as if he was some noisome slug which had just crawled out from beneath a stone. He chose to ignore the remarks and turned to Thurston, "I take it these two are British subjects?"

"Ireland is. He was practising as a barrister in Victoria."

"Then we must return him to his homeland," said Chapman acidly. "It remains to be seen on which side of the bar he will stand. And Denison?"

Thurston looked at Jason who had turned away from the group not wanting to be part of his brother-in-law's final degradation.

Denison answered the question himself. "I'm British," he snapped, "but I might just as well have been Chinese for all the good it's ever done me. Didn't they tell you, Captain, the great Jason Cotterel, the noble Minister of State and wealthy planter, is my brother-in-law." Chapman looked startled.

"It's true, ask him. He has his back turned he cannot bear to even look at me, but I'm his brother-in-law alright. Not that it ever did me any good. He turned my own father against me and even had me thrown off his precious island by his equally precious Fijians."

Jason flushed with anger; his shoulders hunched at the abuse. He knew that if he once turned and saw that spitting venomous face his control would snap and he would smash his fist into Denison's lying teeth. It seemed impossible that a creature such as Kate could have sprung from the same womb as this animal.

"I won't have that sort of talk aboard my ship," roared Chapman. "You and Ireland are coming to Sydney with me and if you don't pull yourself together you'll travel the whole distance in irons!"

"And leave that bastard lording it here? Like hell I will!" Denison's voice cracked with fury.

"Jason look out!

Don't be crazy, man!"

Jason heard Thurston's and Chapman's warning shouts and, guessing that Toby had gone for the revolver at his side, tried to spin around and leap out of the line of fire. He was not fast enough; it was as though there were lead weights on his legs and he was looking straight down the barrel of the gun. There came a crash and the beautifully holystoned decks rose to meet him.

35

Fight for life

Jason Cotterel would have been dead within hours had Captain Chapman not had his surgeon in attendance in seconds of his hitting the deck. Even so his chances of survival were marginal.

He was carried below to the officers' wardroom. The arm, a terrible mess, was pumping blood. The elbow was irreparably damaged. The surgeon only needed one glance to see what must be done. British naval surgeons were abysmally ignorant of disease treatment but no one could fault their technique when it came to amputations.

The chest was the more serious wound; at such short range the heavy bullet had gone right through. Its point of entry was a neat purple hole just above the right nipple, but its exit a fist-sized hole. The surgeon set to work, calling on all his skill and experience. The remaining nine-tenths of cure he left in the hands of the Almighty and the patient's own will to live.

Jason regained consciousness in the First Lieutenant's bed. First he could distinguish voices and then, as if out of a mist, he could put names to faces. Thurston, Chapman and another man he had never seen before were suspended above the bunk like disembodied spirits. That was rather how he felt himself. He seemed to float on a turbulent sea of pain — it was almost as if he was observing the pain of someone else.

"Toby?" he whispered.

"You must not talk, sir," the stranger said fervently. "You were shot in the lung and talking could kill you." He appealed to Thurston, "You must impress on your friend that unless he lies quite still and refrains from talking, he has no chance."

John Thurston looked down at the bloodless face of his best friend and most trusted colleague. He was amazed that Jason had lived as long as he had. He blamed himself: Jason had always been there to lean on and he had leaned too heavily. Every difficult job, every time there had been any element of danger, it was Jason who had been called. He should have been at home enjoying a well-earned rest, but instead he had sent him among people who hated him.

Thurston, who prided himself on his sense of justice, had thrown away his finest asset and if Jason died he would be the person responsible.

"Denison is dead, Jason," he said quietly. "After he shot you, the marines tried to grab him but he was too quick for them. He put his revolver in his mouth and blew the top off his own head."

So that was how it ended, thought Jason wearily, Toby dead, with himself soon to follow. It was as if it had been preordained from the moment they first met. Strange, he could not think of him as a villainous rebel leader; he was still the same boy, torn between fury and terror, who had vowed enmity years before when Jason had refused to haul him from the refuse-littered waters of Levuka harbour. His problem had been an inability to love and trust. It was as if the world, knowing it had a misfit tearing at its vitals had struck back time and again until it finally forced him to take his own life.

"Poor Toby," he whispered. He could feel himself floating into unconsciousness again.

"Jason, you mustn't talk, you heard the doctor," Thurston pleaded.

It was as if he had not heard the warning or he no longer cared. He looked up at his friend. He respected and loved Thurston as he did no other man but it was still not enough. If he had to die, he wanted it to be in his wife's arms. When he was buried his dust should mingle with the dust of the island.

"Take me home to Vatulevu, John." he whispered.

*****

With the strange and inexplicable speed with which news travels through the islands, the whole of Vatulevu knew of the shooting in Ba long before HMS *Dido* dropped anchor in the lagoon. A silent crowd of Fijians watched from the shore while Kate, who had learnt from Lala that something had happened to Jason, was waiting on their ketch ready to go aboard the moment the man-of-war came to rest.

She came over the side, pale and shaken her eyes big with anxiety. Despite her advanced pregnancy and the fact that her face was harrowed with worry, Kate Cotterel was still one of the most striking women Captain Chapman had ever seen.

"How is Jason?" Kate asked, coming straight to the point. She was obviously bracing herself for the answer.

"He's still alive, my dear," answered Thurston, "but he has been unconscious for the past two days. You must be very strong, Kate, the surgeon thinks he has little chance of pulling through. He has lost his right arm and there is a large wound in his chest which isn't healing." He put an arm about her shoulders and led her to the companionway which would take them to the cabins.

"Who did it?" she asked bitterly.

John Thurston looked at her surprised. Having seen the crowd waiting on the shore he had assumed she had learned the name of her husband's assailant. "I'm sorry Kate, I thought you knew. It was your brother."

"Toby!" She stopped short on the stairs and looked back at Thurston, horrified. The baby she carried beneath her heart kicked as it registered its mother's shock.

"He was to have been deported for his part in the rebellion and he blamed it all on Jason," Thurston explained. "I don't know what really happened, he became hysterical and then suddenly went off his head and shot Jason. Then he shot himself. Your brother is dead by his own hand, Kate."

Kate went white and swayed and Thurston leaned down to help her, but she shrugged his hand away. "I shall be alright. Toby is dead, but at least Jason lives. Take me to him at once."

It was as if a spring was coiling within her, providing the strength to go on. Lesser women would have fainted dead away on receiving such a blunt message.

The surgeon was waiting in the cabin. He stood aside to let Kate see her husband.

She hardly recognised the face on the pillow. It was drawn and haggard, the eyes deep dark sockets. "Dear God in heaven," she whispered.

"He is still alive but in a coma," the surgeon told her apologetically, as if he himself was at fault. "Your husband is fighting to live with every part of him."

Kate rounded on the men an expression of grim determination on her face. One glance had been enough for her to decide what must be done. "I wish my husband brought ashore immediately."

"But, madam," the surgeon expostulated, "he is in a highly critical condition. If we move him now it might kill him outright."

"If he stays here he will definitely die," she snapped, ready to fight every doctor in the world if necessary. She knew instinctively that if she could get him ashore to his own home she could save him. "Jason has lived this long to reach his home and family and that is where he is going. If my husband does die it will be in his own bed, in the home he built with his own hands."

In the face of such resolution the surgeon could only bow and keep his mouth shut.

"Will you please make immediate arrangements to bring him up on deck," she ordered. "Make sure he is not jolted in any way. Carry him on that mattress, I will see that it is returned later. If you will look after things here, John, I shall see that everything is ready to receive him ashore."

Kate ran from the cabin, not waiting for any argument. Her heart was beating like a hammer on an anvil but she was certain that she could save him. Her love, her care and her will-power had to be enough to keep Jason alive. Dear God Almighty, they had to be!

*****

Jason's inert body, strapped to the mattress, was carried inch by inch up the gangway and lowered into the Captain's gig. Chapman personally saw to it that an awning was rigged to protect the patient from the harsh sunlight. The davits were oiled and the ropes checked for the slightest unevenness that might cause jolting as the boat was lowered. In one operation, gig, crew and the unconscious man were set smoothly down on the water, and with slow measured strokes which hardly raised a ripple on the surface of the lagoon Jason Cotterel was brought towards the crowded shore.

As the boat reached the shallows the Fijians waded out to steady it against the movement of the small waves which swished up the beach. Men who had worked, laughed and fought beside Jason for the past 20 years carried him with anxious care up the hill to the plantation house.

Chapman, who came ashore in another boat was amazed. He had always been told that Fijians were ignorant, indolent, unfeeling savages, but these people seemed to treat Cotterel with the love and worship they might have accorded a pagan God. It was a relationship between black and white such as he had seen nowhere else in the islands.

Step by step, the cortège moved up the hill, the matanivanua supervising every movement and with soft commands directing the speed and the placing of feet so that the mattress and its precious load maintained a perfect level the whole time; across the well-trimmed lawns and up the steps to the verandah where Kate and the surgeon waited to ease the returning master of Qaraniqio into the comfort and security of his own bed.

In the main bedroom, laid out on crisp white sheets, his head on a soft pillow, Jason's eyes flickered and slowly opened as if he knew where he was. There, swimming hazily in the air above him was the face of the person he loved most in the whole world. His mouth framed the word 'Kate' but no sound came. His eyes glowed with recognition and then softened in contentment and peace.

Kate knelt beside the bed and kissed her husband's stubble covered cheek. "You are home, darling," she whispered. "You are going to get well" She gazed into the pain-filled eyes, trying to pour the balm of her own love and indomitable spirit into his being. "I need you so much, Jason, you cannot die and leave me. You must live, you must live." She cradled his one remaining hand between her own. That hand, once so tanned and strong, had in a few short days become mere bones from which flesh and strength had drained away.

He was trying to speak and Kate put her ear close to his mouth to hear. It was so faint that the thudding of her heart seemed louder.

"I'm........home........Kate," the words come slowly and painfully, but quite distinctly. "I........will........never........leave."

The surgeon looking down at his erstwhile patient could hardly believe his eyes. He would have sworn that either the moving would have killed the man or he would have drifted into a coma until he died. Yet here he was, conscious and seemingly lucid again. It was as if he had been dead and by some miracle was brought back to life. There was nothing he could do that this formidable woman could not do better. He tiptoed away.

John Denison gave him a drink which he finished in two quick swallows and then accepted a refill. "How is my son-in-law?" Denison asked, his voice trembling with his own distress and wretchedness.

"I really don't know, sir," the surgeon replied. "When it first happened I thought he might have a very slim chance; but sailing here, while he was in the coma, I expected him to slip away at any moment. Now I just don't know. Moving him should have killed him but I have just seen him return to consciousness and speak a few words to his wife. Mrs Cotterel is probably correct, if he is going to recover anywhere it will be here in his own home surrounded by the love and attention of his family. This place must have a strange alchemy all of its own."

"Thank God for that chance at least," murmured Denison fervently, though knowing he was now left to carry the burden of his son's guilt.

They talked on in quiet tones until Kate, having assured herself that Jason was sleeping peacefully, slipped in to thank them and say goodbye. Captain Chapman and the others went on ahead leaving John Thurston for a final word with Kate.

"You know what I think of Jason," he said. "If there is anything further I can do to help, you only have to ask, my dear. And, though I hate to even think it, should the worst happen send a message to Levuka and I'll come straight over."

Kate smiled and put a hand on his arm. "You have no need to worry about Jason," she said confidently. "I have him now and, though it may take time, he will get better. Now that I have Jason safely home beneath my wing, you need not expect to see him in Levuka for a very long time, if indeed ever. But I know it will speed his recovery if he has occasional visits from his friends."

"I hope to God you are right." Thurston said. He looked deadly tired and terribly thin, as if constant worry was sapping the life from his body.

"What about yourself, John?" Kate asked. "You look worn to the bone. This business is driving you into an early grave. I suppose you never see your own home or your poor wife and family.

"I'm not worried about that," said Thurston sincerely. "If you can bring Jason back to life it will be more than enough for me. When he recovers, tell him that I have accepted his resignation from office."

"What a pity you too cannot resign," said Kate. She hated to see the deep lines of worry on John Thurston's face. No one seemed to appreciate what he did and what it cost him to keep the constitution and the monarchy alive.

"You look after Jason and that baby. Don't worry about me. I think we may all be retiring soon, whether we like it or not. To be honest, Kate, the government is on its last legs. Oh, we shall stagger along for a time but it will only be our death throes. Unless there's a miracle, I shall recommend to the King that we make another offer of cession to the British Crown. In fact, if he agrees, Captain Chapman will most likely take the offer back with him."

"After all your worry and work?" asked Kate.

Thurston laughed a little bitterly. "Perhaps it's all for the best. They will never be able to say we didn't try. Jason and I have talked this over dozens of times. Our main concern has been the Fijians. If we can arrange a conditional handover under which the Fijians and their lands are protected, then the British government with its power and financial strength may succeed where we have failed so miserably. Anyway that's my problem not yours, my dear." He kissed her affectionately on the cheek. "My prayers will be with you both."

He walked down the steps and across the lawn, striding quickly to catch up with the others. Kate watched him for a moment. She could not help wondering if the Fijian people realised how fortunate they were to have someone of John Thurston's stature and integrity watching over their interests.

For days which stretched into weeks Jason's condition hardly changed. He drifted along only nominally part of the living world. Kate hardly left his side watching for any movement which might aggravate his wound, tending bandages and dressings, trying to spoon chicken broth into him.

In the interests of the unborn child, Lala and Helen Simpson begged her to consider her own health and delegate the nursing to them, but Kate refused to let anyone else tend her husband. She had it firmly fixed in her mind that he was drawing on her strength in his fight to live and she never doubted that she had strength enough for both him and the baby.

Gradually the dry, fevered look faded from Jason's face and he took on a better colour. The periods of consciousness become more frequent, longer and more lucid. Neither husband nor wife talked much — a smile and the touch of a hand were all they needed to communicate. The wound in the chest finally closed and the stump of his right arm no longer burnt to the touch. Jason would never again be the powerful man she had married, but Kate went down on her knees and thanked the Lord for having returned him to her at all.

Kate came to full term in her pregnancy and passed it — one week, two weeks. She told Helen Simpson, who had come to help with the confinement, that she must have miscalculated. Lala and the other Fijians maintained that the baby was waiting for its father to come back from the dead before it pushed head first into the world.

Whichever theory was correct, on the very day that Jason Cotterel was first able to sit upright and eat solids Kate Cotterel was brought to bed with her third child and second son.

It was John Denison who brought the news to Jason and asked what name the baby would carry. Jason answered without the slightest hesitation, "He is to be named Tobias in memory of his uncle."

Denison put his head in his hands and wept unashamedly. Jason's forgiveness of his son seemed to relieve him of his oppressive burden of guilt.

36

Farewell to a dream

While Jason Cotterel lay recuperating on Vatulevu, John Thurston was still beset with the problems of government. Apart from the King and Fijians like Elija Codrokadroka, his seemed a lone fight against every European in the islands.

The Germans, until then fairly tractable compared to British and American settlers, came out against the government, openly defying them on the payment of taxes. It took the commander of a visiting German gunboat to bring them to heel. But once the Imperial flag dropped below the horizon they were as intractable as before.

As Thurston had foretold, with the approval of the King, a tentative message was sent to London offering for a third time to cede the islands to Britain. But if Thurston thought this would end his troubles and win support he was much mistaken. The diehards continued to abuse him through the columns of the *Fiji Times*, accusing him of, 'Whining for tutelage, surrendering independence and betraying the trust placed in the whites by the Fijian chiefs and people'.

Meetings at which men shouted for the resignation of the Chief Secretary and his ministers would have made ironic listening for Jason. The very things they had fought for were now advanced as those John Thurston had failed to support.

There would never have been the need to approach Britain had Thurston not been at his wits end to safeguard the trust placed in him by the Fijian chiefs and people. Were it not for the King's backing and his own deep sense of personal responsibility Thurston would have gladly followed Jason's example and exchanged the whole sordid mess of politics for the peace and solitude of his plantation.

The Legislature was a farce: only half of those elected ever attended and the rump met with the sole aim of destroying both constitution and the Chief Secretary. They blamed Thurston for the national debt; the slump in the economy; and every murder, rape and incident of drunkenness in the Group.

Far from maintaining the Fijians' trust, they refused to pass the Appropriations Bill authorising government expenditure, and demanded a new constitution in which Fijians were to be refused representation.

If interracial conflict had not been so alarmingly imminent the whole thing would have been laughable, but as Thurston on a visit to Vatulevu told Jason, "I admit I feel like crying at times. We all offered to resign of course."

"I can just imagine the Vunivalu's reaction to that," said Jason. He was really quite fit and, while he found the loss of an arm irksome, he was again taking up work on the plantation. From what Thurston told him, he was thankful to be well removed from the national scene.

"I do seem to recall the King passing a few very pungent comments on white men generally and the members of his Legislature in particular. I tell you Jason, the Fijians have all reached the end of their patience. The King, Ma'afu and Tui Cakau are no fools, they know that the Europeans mean to subordinate them socially, economically and politically.

"We may be up to our ears in debt but, as the Fijians point out, all of the debts have been incurred on the advice of the white men and in the white men's interest. Yet those are the very same men who refuse to pay taxes and try to place the entire responsibility on the shoulders of the Fijians."

"Even though we whites are outnumbered 200:1, let a minister propose in the Legislature any measure which might be construed as being in the Fijian interest and the whole white population howls in derision. Parliamentary institutions are ludicrous in a place like Fiji."

"What did the King say?" Jason asked.

"He heard us out," Thurston smiled to himself as he thought back to the interview. "Then he told us what an unnecessary obstruction he considered the whole parliamentary set-up to be and, by way of contrast, how polite and helpful he found his ministers. In short, he retained us and abolished the Legislature."

"He has virtually torn the constitution to pieces. From being a constitutional monarch he has become an absolute ruler. He had no alternative. Unless the British agree to annexation, what other solution is there?"

"But I thought Gladstone was still opposed to annexation."

"Our latest information is that he has at least agreed to send a commission of inquiry. Sir Hercules Robinson, who has taken over from your friend Belmore in Sydney, wrote to give me official notification. According to letters I have direct from London, there is strong pressure for annexation and Gladstone's position in the House of Commons is so shaky that he gives in on everything these days."

"Anyway, there will be two on the commission: one's a naval chap, Commodore Goodenough; the other's a fellow called Layard, the new Consul."

"Is this commission in answer to your own offer of cession?" asked Jason.

"Oddly enough it isn't, I was only sounding out the ground so to speak. But we were given to understand that there was nothing doing. This commission is entirely a British affair. If they don't want to, they need have nothing to do with either the King or me."

"My God," said Jason scandalised, "if that isn't typical British high-handedness for you. They refuse to consider an offer of voluntary cession but then send a team of their own to decide whether or not they should take over a foreign state. They're surely not going to walk in here without so much as a by-your-leave?"

"Something like that."

"I wouldn't stand for it!" Jason exploded. "Whether Britain likes it or not, Fiji is still an independent state and recognised as such by the United States of America and Germany. I was beginning to think that colonial status under a benevolent governor, someone such as yourself, John, who knows the Fijians, might be a good idea, but if this is the way they operate I want no part of it."

John Thurston was surprisingly calm in the face of Jason's outburst. "I'm going to do exactly nothing," he said. "I'm certainly not going to stop them coming or enquiring about anything they like, but what they must eventually understand is that Britain won't get Fiji unless the Fijian chiefs consent of their own free will."

"The King and chiefs will look to you for advice?"

"Not entirely, but sooner or later the commissioners will have to deal with me and I won't agree to anything that I think is not in the best interests of the Fijians. Not just their interests this year or next, but for as many years as it takes to bring the Fijians to the point where they can govern themselves in the same way as other British subjects in Canada, Victoria, New South Wales, and New Zealand do."

"What the British government must realise is that the Fijians are not a race whom they have conquered, nor is Fiji a vast empty land crying out for settlement. The islands are already settled and the Fijians are an intelligent people requiring time to adjust to the new world that has erupted in their midst. If Britain is not prepared to see Fiji as a gift and a trust, then I'll have no part of cession and I'll make damned certain that the chiefs and other ministers will follow my lead."

For days after Thurston returned to Levuka, Jason thought over what he had said. It was all over bar the shouting. No matter how much they cloaked cession with humanitarian verbiage they were still delivering the Fijians into British bondage. It was years since he had trod American soil, but he was still American enough to remember that his own people had only broken free from that bondage as a result of a long and bloody war.

The dream had been good while it lasted, but the dreamers had different dreams. Cakobau had dreamt of a throne and a Fijian nation powerful enough to withstand foreign intervention. The missionaries dreamt of a theocracy, where priest ruled over magistrate. The European settlers dreamt of a helot state, where they were the lords of creation and the Fijians worked to maintain the white man's comfort. John Thurston's dream was one which only their sons or their grandsons would see.

Jason himself had wanted independence and isolation from the rest of the world, to preserve the charm and simplicity of the islands and their people as it was when he first stepped ashore on Vatulevu all those years before. His dream had been just as impossible as the others.

37

Homecoming

VATULEVU CELEBRATED! Tabua sprouted from every hand; yaqona flowed in an inexhaustible stream; and the kitchens and storerooms of Qaraniqio bulged with tribute — yams, dalo, bunches of bananas and plantains, fish, turtles, baskets of every type of shellfish imaginable and two dozen pigs, until Kate complained that more food was rotting than they could ever eat.

Rolls of magimagi higher than a man, bale after bale of decorated masi, two sailing canoes — there was nothing Vatulevu would not have laid at Ratu Aporosa's feet had he shown the slightest desire for it.

The return of the young chief from Sydney drove all thought of national problems from the minds of the kai-Vatulevu including those of his father and step-mother. The long awaited son had returned.

How could any man be other than proud when he looked on such a son, at 17 already six feet tall and still growing. A copper coloured young giant with the face of an innocent and the body of a Greek athlete, he was intelligent though no genius having more of a practical than an academic bent. There was also something about the way he carried his head, his quiet yet authoritative voice, and a solemnity beyond his years which commanded respect.

Was it is any wonder Jason Cotterel was content to sit back and count his blessings? Let others torment themselves with politics.

Tui Navatulevu would have had his heir in attendance 24 hours of every day had the boy's parents allowed it. As it was, Kate was soon complaining that either she never saw him or when she did, he had 50 Fijians flooding through the house after him.

According to Fijian custom, Ratu Aporosa qualified as a grown man. As a result the village girls were prepared to sing and dance the night through in the hope that they might entice him to take one of them to his bed. It was a measure of his character that after the monastic discipline of a boarding school, he was in no hurry to rush into anything and this included marriage.

He also had the rare gift of being able to refuse what was offered without offending the donor. His father said little; he knew that the old chief in

Lomanikaya was deliberately testing the youth and he was thankful to see his son come through with flying colours.

Tui Navatulevu was no symbolic presence living a life of idleness and comfort. While he might now be very old and physically incapable, in his heyday he had led his people in both work and war. In his younger days, when the blood coursed swiftly through his veins, Tui Navatulevu's food gardens were unrivalled.

Now it was Aporosa's turn to pick up the digging stick and the spade. A few short weeks before he had been cosseted away from the realities of life in a school for the sons of white gentlemen. Now he was expected to become a manual labourer and prove that by virtue of his blood he could out-work and out-fight any other man on Vatulevu.

Jason decided he should talk it over with his son, so that there should be no misunderstandings or hard feelings in the future.

"In spite of your position as chief, yours will be a hard life, boy," he told him bluntly. "Your brothers and sisters will live their lives in comfort. Undoubtedly they will have to work; some may marry and leave the island for all I know, but by comparison theirs will be an easier life than yours."

"The pioneering work is all but done and what Qaraniqio needs now is good management. As my eldest son you might have expected to live here and inherit all of this when I die. But if you take up your title as Tui Navatulevu the people will expect you to live with them. As chief they will want you in Lomanikaya and when they walk to work in the mornings they will want to see you at their head."

Jason watched his half-Fijian, half-American son, whose head was down as if concentrating on some message written at the bottom of his coffee cup. It was impossible to see how he was taking it, but no one liked to hear they were disinherited.

"I don't want you to think Qaraniqio is in any way less your own home," said Jason made anxious by the boy's continued silence. "You come and go the same as ever. All the time your mother and I are living, anything you want from this house is yours. Our children love you and I'm sure that it will stay that way throughout their lifetimes."

"When I die, John as the eldest boy, will be left the plantation intact; there will be provision made for the others, but the remainder of my liquid assets go to you. If God grants me just a few more years you could be a wealthy man."

"But in spite of wealth if you are the Tui you would be deserting your people if you did not fulfil all aspects of your duties to them. John and the others will only be responsible for themselves but you will be responsible for every man, woman and child on Vatulevu. Do you understand what I am trying to get at, Aporosa?"

"Yes sir," the boy answered calmly though he still did not look up.

Jason suddenly felt the gross injustice of asking a mere boy to take responsibility for hundreds of other people's lives. As a hypothetical proposition it was bad enough, but when the boy was your own son it could be tragic.

"You know, you don't have to do this if you don't want to," he said, a lump in his throat. "I could go to Tui Navatulevu and ask him to choose someone else. You could stay here with us or go to Europe or America to one of the universities. Become a doctor or a lawyer if you would rather, it's not too late. No one would think any the less of you, especially not me or your mother."

The boy looked up, but instead of a worried, frightened, or even tearful expression he was smiling at his father. "Would they not, sir?" he quizzed Jason, his direct look making the older man grin a little shamefacedly.

"Well I guess maybe there are a few who would," he admitted. "But dammit, if you do want to toss it in they're nothing to us. We don't care what they think."

"But what about me? If I thought the worse of myself how do I go about the business of living?"

At that moment, Jason, though not a demonstrative man, wanted to kiss his son he felt so proud. At Aporosa's age Jason had been so frightened of his own father that he had felt unable to take an independent line on anything.

"You are worrying about nothing, father. I've given the whole matter more thought than you imagine. I don't suppose it ever really sank in until you and mother visited me in Sydney, but since then I've had plenty of time to work things out for myself."

"Ulamila, John, Katie and baby Toby will have Qaraniqio which you have made into the finest plantation in the Pacific, bar none. But it is barely a tenth of the land I shall control. I'm going to turn Vatulevu into one enormous Qaraniqio and I shall expect you and my brothers to help me do it. The chief already has a gang of men building a bure for me in Lomanikaya and as soon as it is ready I shall move in. I will not surrender every comfort, I shall furnish it from what mother can spare. I'll soon be comfortable, you wait and see. After Spartan school dormitories it will be absolute luxury."

"While you are about it, take the pick of the horses," said Jason expansively.

"A horse!" laughed the boy gleefully. "I'm going to take you down for far more than that! As soon as I am settled I'm going to look through all of your stock. I want my own herds. I have learned quite a bit living with the sons of New South Wales graziers and I've got ideas I want to try out. I shall need horses, cattle, in fact anything you've got. Don't worry about leaving me those liquid assets you mentioned. By the time I've finished milking the estate I shall have had far more than my share."

Jason went over to his son and put his arm around the boy's shoulders, "So you shall my boy, so you shall." He wanted to shout out to the whole world that he had a son he would not change for any other.

"You've given me a day I shall never forget. Were your mother alive today she would be just as happy to know that her own blood will continue to rule in Vatulevu. What she never dreamt was that she gave birth to such a chief as these islands have never before seen. I'll help you boy, you have only to ask and everything I have is yours."

*****

Unnoticed amid all the excitement, Aporosa had not returned to Vatulevu alone. With him was another who had decided to spend the rest of his days there. There were no great presentations but for all that he was highly regarded by all on the island. After 40 years at sea, Peter Bex had decided to swallow the anchor. To Kate and Jason Cotterel his decision to retire to Vatulevu brought a special happiness.

"I always told you I would retire in Fiji," he told Jason. "Anyone can have Sydney or Auckland for my money. If you can get the chief to sell me a plot of land I'd be very obliged. I was thinking about 50 acres somewhere near the beach, so that I can look out to sea every day and thank God I am safe on land."

There was no trouble with Tui Navatulevu, but as a measure of the changing times it was Aporosa who put the old captain's case, not Jason. Apart from the fact that the chief could refuse the boy nothing, Bex was offering £2 per acre, an unheard of price for land. The negotiations were completed in record time and Bex had his 50 acres adjoining Jason's northern boundary.

Soon he moved into a neat cottage built from local timbers by Qaraniqio–trained craftsmen. Despite Bex's protests, Jason refused to accept payment from the man who had acted as Aporosa's guardian for years — the cottage was hardly payment enough for all they owed him.

A cutter full of household furniture arrived from Levuka, together with a plump and rather beautiful Gilbertese housekeeper. An indignant Kate wanted Jason to tell Peter to send her away, but he only laughed uproariously and told her to keep her nose out of Bex's affairs.

Twenty years before, Jason could remember Bex saying that when he retired he meant to have a young thing to warm his old bones; now he had done just that, good luck to him. Jason was quite certain he would be good to the girl and, having once had a Fijian wife himself he could hardly object to his old friend following a similar course.

"You could at least make him marry the girl."

"I'm sure he'd go through the ceremony if he thought if would please you, my dear," laughed Jason, amused by the thought of Bex at the altar. "Not that it would mean anything of course. To my knowledge Peter already has one wife in Sydney and I've heard rumours of another in Auckland; and for all I know there could be umpteen others he hasn't bothered to divorce. What do you expect from a man who has been 40 years at sea?"

Kate escaped, her ears burning and her sense of moral values outraged. She would dutifully follow the instructions of her lord and master, but after that she never saw Peter Bex without wondering just how many wives the old man really had. Bex and her father were approximately the same age, but there was no comparison when it came to virility; Bex was still jumping around like an old goat.

38

Brokering a deal

THE ANTI-CAKOBAU FACTION welcomed the commissioners appointed by the British government with open arms. Deputations of merchants waited upon them with tales of the iniquitous treatment they were receiving at the hands of the King's ministers. Even the criminal fringe, who had nothing to gain except perhaps an amnesty, pandered after Commander Goodenough and his associate Consul Layard.

Jason was kept informed of what was happening by both the Fijians and the ministers and he could only feel tremendous sympathy for John Thurston. The national debt had passed the £90,000 mark; no one was paying taxes; and even the Fijians were in arrears.

Ma'afu, as Lieutenant Governor of Lau, had never paid a cent into the Treasury though it was common knowledge he collected taxes in Lau with all his usual ruthless efficiency. There were also well-founded rumours that the Tovata Confederacy, his alliance against the King, was about to be rejuvenated and hived off as an independent kingdom.

They were supposed to be a purely investigatory commission. Nevertheless Goodenough and Layard could not refrain from meddling in Fiji affairs. Thurston deplored the labour trade, but the only foreseeable source of revenue for the Government lay in the sale of prisoners captured by Fitzgerald and Harding in their successful campaign against the hill tribes.

When they were put up for sale, however, the commissioners threatened the direst repercussions against any British subject who dealt with the government. Instead of the usual scramble to buy, the sale was a fiasco. As a result Thurston had over 1000 prisoners on his hands and not a penny in the Treasury with which to feed them.

It seemed to Jason, observing from the sidelines, that the commissioners were going out of their way to befriend the King's enemies, while insulting his ministers. It was only natural that they received equally cool treatment from Thurston and his colleagues. Even the King, who had been ready to hand his country over to the British, was now reported to have said, 'I shall keep Fiji'.

On Vatulevu, they knew of the commissioners' fact finding tours and it was inevitable they would turn up there sooner or later. Jason's reputation overseas was such that any report on Fiji would have been incomplete if his opinion had not been sought. Jason felt hostile towards Goodenough, but he was not prepared to sully Qaraniqio's reputation by refusing them hospitality. The commission's cutter no sooner dropped anchor than an invitation went out asking both commissioners to dine ashore that evening.

Goodenough had the arrogance and pomposity which seemed inescapable in a senior British naval officer. He considered Fiji a useless piece of real estate which could count itself damned lucky if Britain decided to take it over and he was not particularly interested in other people's opinions.

The other commissioner, Layard, was a pale little man lost in the shadow of his companion. It was noticeable that after any meeting no one could remember just what he had to say and most had difficulty remembering his name.

Goodenough may well have been expecting to find a tin hut or tumbledown shack, and so he could hardly conceal his surprise when he stepped on to the verandah at Qaraniqio. As always, he was correctly dressed but his hosts of late had been lucky if their shirts could muster a full complement of buttons. Now he thanked his lucky stars that he had not relaxed his own standards; the four men present were in formal evening clothes and his hostess wore a gown which would not have been out of place in London.

The house was cool and spacious. Candle light glowed on highly polished furniture and fittings that put his own home in England to shame and spoke volumes for the well-lined pockets of the owners.

The man who came forward to greet him was tall and distinguished, grey at the temples; with one arm of his coat pinned up. Goodenough had already heard of that affair and a little of the man himself. Now that they were meeting in the flesh there was no denying that Jason Cotterel was a far cry from the rest of the planting fraternity.

"Welcome to Qaraniqio, Commodore, Mr Layard. May I present my wife." As Goodenough bowed over Kate's hand he could not help thinking enviously that some men seemed to have all the luck. "The Reverend John Denison my father-in-law, Captain Bex recently retired from the sea, and my eldest son, Ratu Aporosa."

As they shook hands, Goodenough could not hold back a start when his host acknowledged as his eldest son the tall young man who obviously had Fijian blood. He could not avoid an involuntary glance in the direction of his hostess.

Kate moved over to her stepson and stood beside him. "Do I look too young to have such a son, Commodore?" she laughed. "I'm sorry to say that he is my step-son. His mother, who was the Princess of Vatulevu and my husband's first wife, died when he was very young."

"Your servant, sir," said Goodenough, thankful for her effort to cover his social gaffe. I take it you are therefore related to the present chief."

"He is my grandfather, sir."

"The lad is too modest, Goodenough," intervened Bex. "He is the heir apparent. You are talking to the next Tui Navatulevu."

When he returned to the cutter that night, Commodore Goodenough could hardly credit he had spent the evening in Fiji at all. The meal and the wines had been superb, the gleaming silver and well-trained servants better than anything he could have shown a guest. Even down to the light bantering conversation, it had all been unreal.

He had expected a turgid session on island politics, but whenever he raised the subject he had been politely but firmly turned aside. Arrangements had been made for him to speak to the chief the following morning, but when he had asked for Cotterel's own views as a planter he had been put firmly in his place.

"Neither my views nor the views of any white men have bearing on this business. We are here on sufferance. If you are investigating the possibility of British annexation, these islands belong to the Fijians and you must discuss the matter with the Fijian leaders, the King and his chiefs."

It was food for thought, and though Goodenough was not a man who appreciated having lessons read him, nor was he fool enough to deny the underlying truth in what Cotterel said. Perhaps it might be wise to drop the Europeans for a while and start talking directly to the Fijians.

The next morning, when the commissioners were ushered into the presence of the chief, the commodore was irritated by the sight of Cotterel's son sitting on the mats next to Tui Navatulevu. This time he was dressed in the full ceremonial masi befitting a chief about to receive important visitors. After the initial welcome, when the old man spoke it was the boy who translated on his behalf.

"Tui Navatulevu welcomes the representatives of the great Queen Victoria," said the boy. "He wishes to point out that he also has a ruler, King Cakobau."

Goodenough chose to ignore the hint and pressed straight on with his main theme. "Tell the chief that his King, on previous occasions, offered the islands of Fiji to Queen Victoria as a gift. I wish to know what his reaction would be if such an offer was repeated?"

For a moment Ratu Aporosa spoke in an aside to his grandfather, who answered at some length in passionate Fijian.

"The chief says that he has no knowledge of such an offer having been renewed," translated Ratu Aporosa, "and until he is officially informed of such an offer, it is not for him to give an opinion on such subjects. He presumes that King Cakobau will ask both him and the other chiefs for their advice and whatever decision is made will be in the best interests of the Fijian people as a whole."

"Tui Navatulevu has told me to say that he is quite prepared to answer questions about Vatulevu but on subjects affecting Fiji as a whole he says that you should deal directly with King Cakobau and his ministers."

A polite, but very definite rebuff. They obviously thought that the commissioners were soliciting opinions at the back door when they should have been making an open application at the front. Goodenough went red in the face and Ratu Aporosa, with a coolness which belied his 17 years, tried to calm him down.

"You must respect the chief's position in this, Commodore. If another power was considering the annexation of Britain and asked your opinion, and you agreed it might be a good thing, you would be guilty of high treason against your own Queen. Your government may have refused to recognise ours but that omission makes it no less real to us. As the chief has said, it would be better if you continued your discussions with the proper people."

"I do not need young whippersnappers like you to tell me what I should do," barked Goodenough angrily as he stood preparatory to leaving.

There was an angry murmuring from the assembled Fijians, who were not used to seeing their hospitality or their chiefs insulted. Neither Aporosa nor his grandfather were in the least upset and the chief lifted a hand to silence the others. The old man was quite happy to leave the discussions in the younger man's hands, in fact he was delighted by the way the boy had handled the white men. The only loss of dignity was on the part of the commissioners.

Goodenough stalked out in high dudgeon, Layard following meekly behind. All the way back to the cutter he was seething and as soon as they were aboard he called for the captain.

"You can make straight for Bau. I am sick of dealing with under-strappers; it is time we saw the King again and this time we shall include this fellow Thurston."

Layard's jaw dropped in astonishment. His expression of surprise caused a second explosion.

"Just because I refused to give Cotterel's whelp the pleasure of knowing it, doesn't mean to say I don't see sense in what he said. Close your mouth and stop gasping like a stranded fish, man!"

*****

Within days of the commissioners departure from Vatulevu two messengers arrived from the King. One was for Tui Navatulevu summoning him to a meeting of the Great Council of Chiefs to be held on Bau; the second went to Qaraniqio with a similar summons for Jason. With it was a personal letter from John Thurston:

> Dear Jason,
>
> Whatever you said to Goodenough was enough to bring him running to Bau. He now wants to talk to the other Ministers and me about cession. We are at a complete standstill and without British assistance our administration cannot last out the quarter. Even so, provided we play our cards with skill, I am sure we can get conditions which will satisfy Fijian interests.

I need your help. The King has convened a meeting of Chiefs and Ministers here and I need support to counteract the Ma'afu faction. Some of the Ministers are now so determined on Fiji becoming a Colony, they forget all else in the achievement of their objective. If you are not up to it I shall understand of course but having been a prime mover in the game it would be a pity if you were not in on the finale.

Regards,

John

"I'll have to go, Kate," said Jason apologetically. "I am well enough now and I feel an utter fraud sitting here when John needs my help."

She kissed him lovingly on the cheek. "I understand, darling. I will get your clothes ready while you make arrangements for the ketch."

At that moment Aporosa dashed on to the verandah, hot and dusty from a wild gallop from the village. "Father! Mother!" he shouted excitedly. "I am going to the Great Council of Chiefs to be held in Bau."

"Not you too," wailed Kate, "I doubt if I have clean laundry enough for both of you."

Seeing that his news had somehow preceded him, the boy looked crestfallen. His father laughed and clapped him on the shoulder.

"I hope you don't mind, son, but I have just received a similar summons myself. I am still technically a Minister of State and both the King and the Chief Secretary have asked me to go. But tell us more, why are you going?"

"Tui Navatulevu considers himself to be too old to go gadding about in ships. He says the trip would kill him. He's sending me as his official sosomi, his delegate, to speak on his behalf. The matanivanua and five of the other elders are to go with me."

Kate could see that half his pleasure lay in the sharing of such splendid news with his father. The pride in Jason's eyes was such that she could only hope the sons of her own womb would kindle similar warmth when their day came.

"Why, that is a tremendous honour," she said enthusiastically.

"We shall go together," said Jason planning for them both. "I was just about to give orders for the *Albatross* to be got ready for sea."

To Jason's surprise the boy's face fell as if he hesitated to say what was in his mind. "If you don't want to come with me, that's alright," said his father, not fully concealing his disappointment.

"It's not that I personally don't want to go with you, sir, you must understand that," Aporosa begged. "It is just that I know how the people feel about this cession business. The Vatulevu delegation will have to be entirely Fijian. If we arrived together other people would say that we spoke under your direction. We would be thought tools of the white men."

Kate saw from the tenseness about Jason's mouth that he fought to control the shock he felt. She moved to his side and put an arm about his waist.

"Of course you understand, darling, don't you?" she smiled up at him. Kate's back was to the boy and her eyes begged Jason not to vent his wrath on his son. "After all, as Minister for European Affairs, you represent the King's government whereas Aporosa will be giving the independent views of the kai-Vatulevu. His views may even oppose yours."

The hardness faded from Jason's eyes. His good arm came around Kate and squeezed her shoulders reassuringly. "Of course I understand. It wouldn't look at all proper. I presume that means you and your party will be travelling in the *Lovadua II*; if you like we shall race to see who gets there first."

"You're on!" shouted his son with excitement and relief.

"Well, off you go and get your bags ready," said Kate. "I shall be in with your clean things directly."

Aporosa ran off yelling for Lala. Jason disengaged his arm from Kate's waist and sank heavily into a chair. She knelt beside him on the floor. "Don't take it so much to heart, he's only a boy and wouldn't deliberately insult you for anything."

Jason shook his head ruefully. There were tears of mortification in his eyes and he looked drawn and weary.

"You know, Kate, this is the first time anyone on Vatulevu has ever told me I was not wanted. It was not just Aporosa; he was right when he said he knew how the people felt about cession. If he had only had the courage he might have put it in plainer language. They don't want to be represented by a European when it comes to discussing the future of their own country. The chips are well and truly down and they now distrust even me."

"When I first came here I was just another young man. I could live with them, fight and play with the other young men, even choose a bride from the ranks of their young women. But all that has gone. As the years pass and more white men come to islands the Fijians are drawing further and further away. If King Cakobau's flag is replaced by the British flag, the rulers may rule in the best interests of the Fijians but it will not alter the fact that those rulers are white and their subjects are black."

"If white men had dealt honestly with the owners of this country, we could have lived in harmony under Fijian rule, just as I did in those early days. Instead we are to have British rule; race will come to despise race and no man will trust another so long as their skins are of different colours. The old Gods are dead, the old ways are dead and when this kingdom dies, trust and friendship will die with it."

39

Climax

Lovadua II won the race easily, for Jason had no urge to speed towards a meeting which he knew would ring down the final curtain on the Fiji he loved. He sat apart on the cabin roof alone with his memories and left everything to his crew.

The anchorage at Bau was crowded with shipping of all shapes and sizes. Jason was able to pick out Ma'afu's ostentatious schooner; bigger than anything the King could afford. Over to one side, the white ensign on Goodenough's cutter distinguished it from the mass of similar cutters, ketches and yawls that had carried the chiefs to Bau.

There was also a smattering of craft from Levuka. Jason had no difficulty guessing the reason for their presence — their owners would be hawking trade goods to the huge gathering, scavenging for news, or bribing and lobbying influential Fijians to vote in favour of cession.

It was utter bedlam ashore; every house was packed with visitors. Lesser chiefs tried to make up for their lack of importance by the size of their entourage. Their hosts, the Bauans, were frantically preparing food, receiving new delegations as they arrived, and accepting presentations on behalf of their Vunivalu. The huge lali never ceased their booming announcement that some important chief had partaken of yaqona. No sooner had one delegation been settled than the dirge-like drone of conch shells warned that more sails were approaching.

Jason, who was in no mood to be bustled by the mob, sent one of his crew ashore to notify the Chief Secretary of his arrival. The messenger was back within half an hour to tell Jason that he was wanted immediately; preliminary cabinet meetings were already in session. When he reached the meeting house the guards ushered him straight in.

As Jason entered, Thurston stood up from the council table and came forward to greet him. "Jason, old fellow, it is good to see you," he said in a loud voice for the others to hear. But in an undertone he whispered, "You have come just at the right moment, we are having a particularly rough time with our friends from Lau."

Jason approached the King and bowed formally.

On previous occasions they had all sat together on the mat; now the King sat at the head of a long polished table and, to Jason's jaundiced eye, lost some of his presence in western surroundings. Cakobau gave him a friendly if rather weary smile, enquired as to his health, and motioned him to a seat next to Elija Codrokadroka.

At the other end of the table, hatchet-faced and extremely put out by Jason's arrival, was Prince Ma'afu. He had once sworn to have Jason Cotterel's head and they were now to sit at the same council table. Jason knew only too well that that promise had been neither forgotten nor forgiven.

There was a polite hiss of greetings as Jason sat down. The proceedings, which were conducted in Fijian, were brought back to business by the King. But before he could start again on the subject under discussion he was interrupted by the angry Tongan. "Is this Council to understand, Turaga, that Cotterel has been reappointed as one of your Ministers? I had hoped we were well rid of him."

Jason looked down at the papers before him, waiting for the King to speak. He had not expected to enjoy the meeting but he had hardly thought to be personally attacked in the opening few moments. His hand clutched his knee beneath the table as he listened to Cakobau.

"Mr Cotterel, apart from being one of my Ministers, has always been a trusted personal advisor." The King pulled at his beard and looked hard at the Lieutenant-Governor of Lau, supposedly his loyal servant, but in fact as implacable an enemy as ever. "He has always been welcome at my councils, nor had I heard that he had resigned."

"If I may speak for myself Your Majesty," said Jason calmly, "I would inform the noble Prince from Lau that I have been in forced retirement due to wounds received while conducting the King's business."

"So we heard," the Tongan sneered. "You were lucky it was a white man who shot you. Had it been a Tongan behind that trigger you would be dead, otherwise that same man would have had to answer to me."

This brought a coarse belly laugh from his crony, Tui Cakau. The Fijian had the bleary eyes of an alcoholic and from the way he swayed on his seat was already three parts under the weather.

"I seem to remember an occasion when I gave your men a salutary lesson in the use of muskets," snapped Jason, recklessly reopening old wounds. "I don't remember faces, in fact I don't think I saw many, they were forever running or hiding."

Ma'afu was on his feet, eyes blazing, "I have not forgotten you, white pig. You will soon discover to your sorrow that I never forget."

The King was banging the table with a huge brown fist and roaring to attract attention. "Gentlemen! I will not tolerate fighting at the Council table. If you want to remember something, remember where you are now! Sit down at once!"

"I for one will not sit at your council table so long as that valagi pig, that treacherous cur of an American, sits with us." Ma'afu was literally foaming at the mouth.

Tui Cakau heaved his unsteady bulk upright. "Nor will I sit with the white pig." He leant over and spat with great deliberation on the council table. They turned to leave and Swanston, his face expressing disgust at the last display, reluctantly got to his feet to follow.

Jason was dismayed. He had been deliberately provoked and had given back as he had received, but he had no wish to create a breach in the Council. Without Ma'afu and Tui Cakau, the discussions were valueless.

"Your Majesty must pardon me," he said stiffly, "If you so desire, I shall leave the meeting. I came prepared to do all I could to help. I have no wish to add to your difficulties by providing a cause for dissension."

"Sit where you are," the King ordered tersely. "If the Lieutenant-Governor of Lau, Tui Cakau and Mr Swanston wish to desert the Council then we shall be forced to decide the future of Fiji without them."

"You choose this white man over me!" stormed Ma'afu.

"I make no choice whatsoever," said the King in his deep harsh voice. "You are all needed, but no one is indispensable. If you wish to go I will make no move to stop you, nor will I run after you begging for your return. If you go, don't whine to others when decisions are made without your point of view being taken into account."

They glared at each other, their mutual hatred on naked display. The white men were forgotten. No one else in the room dared speak or hardly breathe for fear that the sound might attract their wrath.

It was the Tongan who first gave ground, his eyes flicking aside and down in part submission. It was a measure of Cakobau's personal control and sense of political necessity that he did not push the humiliation to a conclusion from whence there could be no return.

"This meeting is adjourned until tomorrow morning," he said, his voice still hoarse with suppressed rage. "By then let us hope we shall all have come to our senses." He and his personal secretary swept from the room and there was an audible sigh of relief from the other ministers.

Ma'afu paused for long enough to give Jason a lethal glance and then, with his own supporters, left by the main door.

*****

The room was empty apart from Elija, Jason and John Thurston. "I certainly didn't want to create that sort of stir," said Jason to his two friends.

"It wasn't your fault," said Thurston. "Elija will bear me out when I say that this has been coming all day; you were just the match which set off the powder. If anyone started it, it was the King himself. He knows the Tovata are using our present weakness to their own advantage. They are only looking for a reasonable excuse and they will secede and set up independently. The King took Ma'afu to task earlier over the Lau revenues, the money we have never seen, and they have been slashing at each other ever since. Your arrival was just the final blow to Tongan pride."

"But is Ma'afu serious about an independent kingdom?" Jason asked.

"He's serious enough," said Thurston ruefully. "It is what he has always been after really. If it hadn't been for Swanston's constant begging and cajoling he would have taken off long before this."

It was incredible that any man could be blind enough even to contemplate such a course. Secession would mean war to the death; war bloodier by far than anything the islands had known in the old days.

If and when the axe fell, Jason knew that Vatulevu would have the highest priority for attack by the Tovata armies. They had defeated the Tovata once but Jason doubted whether they could repeat that success. The element of surprise was gone and the invaders would be ready to meet their tactics. Moreover, seven years of peace and missionary influence had drained the fighting sap from the people, how badly Jason did not like to guess and felt even less inclined to put the matter to the test.

There was Kate, the children, the plantation and the life he had built from nothing by his own hard labour. Once it had been smashed and he had started again, but he was now seven years older, one-armed and weak. He had been building for a dynasty of Cotterels but now it seemed that the founding generation might not live out its full span. Aporosa, who was to have been the leader in peace and prosperity, would face a baptism in blood. He might have used the years to more purpose if he had kept the boy at home and taught him the art of war, rather than sent him to learn the skills of peace in New South Wales.

"If only I had kept a rein on my tongue," he said to the others. "No matter what went before, I have given him ample excuse to secede."

"Don't blame yourself, Jason. In your place I would have said even more," said Thurston reassuringly, but from the frown on his face it was evident he was deeply worried.

Elija put a hand on Jason's shoulder. Since those days on Vatulevu there had been a special relationship between them and the Fijian could almost guess what Jason was thinking.

"Ma'afu is still unsure of himself. War and the hundreds of resulting deaths do not worry him in the slightest; what does is the uncertainty of victory. He has left his attempt too late and I think he knows this. Swanston is on our side and even now I'll guarantee he is trying to make him see reason."

"Our only hope lies in this offer of cession to Britain, Jason," said Thurston. "We can no longer hold the Kingdom together, we desperately need an outside power which is stronger than any internal faction. Without Britain, Ma'afu and the diehards will come into their own and we shall be back where we were 10 years ago."

"What has Ma'afu said about cession?" Jason asked.

"He is violently against it."

"And the King?"

"Lukewarm. The commissioners themselves are to blame for that. He has turned them down twice, once soon after they arrived and again at the beginning of this week. He wants to maintain his position and independence, but he is not blind to the dangers inherent in the present state of affairs Nor have I any alternatives to offer. I have told Goodenough and Layard not to take the King's latest rebuff as final. So long as he is still prepared to discuss the subject there is hope."

There was no doubt where John Thurston stood despite the fact that he was British himself, and Jason did not doubt that his motives sprang from what he thought was best for Fiji.

"What do you think, Elija?" asked Jason. Elija was one of the Fijians about to be poured into the British mould and he had the intelligence and education necessary for a proper understanding of what it would mean.

"The King is confused, Jason," said the Fijian. "The Europeans have driven him into bankruptcy and now want to swallow him up. Ma'afu threatens a really serious rebellion. Whichever way he turns, his kingdom lies in ruins at his feet. There is so much conflicting advice he is in a quandary as to the best course."

"As one who has not been tarred with the brush of our recent failures, you are certain to be called in and asked for your opinion. Whatever you decide to tell him could well decide the fate of us all."

"What do you think that advice should be?" Jason demanded. "Forget for a moment that you are a Methodist preacher. Should the Fijians fight to maintain their independence or should they place themselves under the yoke of a foreign power?"

Elija paced the room thoughtfully. "We must be careful not to over-glorify our attempts at government. With the greatest respect for both you and Thurston, you could hardly call the present government an independent Fijian state. At best it is a stopgap measure necessitated by Britain's refusals to accept the islands when they were first offered."

"I want to see a Fijian nation. At present we are a multitude of tribes, two or three loose confederations with no nobler purpose than the satisfaction of their leaders' personal ambitions. It will take years, generations, to weld the separate yavusa into one nation with a common identity and purpose."

"And at the same time you will destroy everything good in Fijian life." The rot on Vatulevu most likely started the moment I stepped ashore myself, thought Jason bitterly.

"You are wrong, Jason," said Elija emphatically. "I don't want a Fijian nation which will be a feeble imitation of Britain. Our nation will have its own special character and identity. What is good and useful in our tradition will live but the rest must die. Even in the old days traditions were not immutable. They changed with the needs of the people; and when they no longer served a useful purpose they withered and died, which is the way it should be."

"We need a period of enlightened rule to give us time to develop our nationality. Let them teach us the good and useful things from their culture; let them provide the money we need to develop our resources. Then, when we are ready, we shall take the reins of government back into our own hands."

"Once surrendered, it may take a hundred years or more before you win your freedom back," said Jason angrily.

Elija laughed, "That is American impatience talking; you want everything to happen in your own lifetime. I learnt about America at school. It took 150 years before you were independent, but you needed those years, and you needed the British money which was pumped into America to build yourselves into a nation strong enough to demand independence. New Zealand, Victoria and New South Wales will be the same."

"We have so much more to learn it may take us even longer, but so long as the British are prepared to guarantee the future of the Fijians; to safeguard our lands and our interests above all others; the Fijians will one day rule themselves again. Provided we can incorporate the idea of trusteeship in a binding cession document, I am all for it."

Further discussion between Elija and Jason was stopped by the arrival of a messenger from the King commanding the latter's attendance that evening at nine o'clock.

"What will you say, Jason?" Elija asked.

"I honestly don't know. I want time to think and I want to talk to my son before I decide."

"Is Ratu Aporosa here?"

"He is the head of the Vatulevu delegation," answered Jason proudly. His brow suddenly furrowed with worry as he thought of Ma'afu. "Elija, I want you to promise me something."

"You know that I'll do anything within my power."

"If anything should happen to me, I want you to promise to guard that boy from Ma'afu and see that he comes into his inheritance," Jason's voice was calm and businesslike but it was obvious that he thought his life was seriously threatened. "I have made provision for Kate and the other children, it is only the boy who worries me."

"Of course I'll look after him, Jason," said Elija anxiously, "but surely you don't think Ma'afu would try anything here on Bau?"

"He's in the right mood to try something. You are most likely correct, it won't be here but at sea on my way home." Elija looked frightened and Jason laughed and slapped him on the shoulder. "I am only asking in case Ma'afu's luck changes. He has tried before don't forget, and got more than he bargained for. I may be missing one hand, but I am still more than a match for a bunch of miserable Tongans. Stop worrying, and see if you can get a bure cleared for my use. I want to rest. And then I want to see my boy."

*****

As Jason and Aporosa dined together that night they talked more of home and the boy's plans for the island than of Fiji and the cession offer. In the lamplight, Aporosa's eyes glowed with enthusiasm as he outlined his plans, asking his father's advice on one point, for help on another. Jason listened with affectionate interest. Some of these schemes would come unstuck but it was better the boy had a few failures in his early years to give him experience.

Jason had given his son health, a good home, education and above all pride in himself and now the boy was bursting to test himself against the world. What sort of world would it be? A world of war, massacre and rapine, or a world of peace and plenty? According to Elija Codrokadroka, it could hinge on his advice to the King. Would that be enough or would Ma'afu still use Jason as his *casus belli*? Maybe Jason himself was a threat to the peace and safety of his own wife and family.

Dinner finished, the other kai-Vatulevu were called in and yaqona was mixed. Bowl after bowl passed as they discussed the pros and cons of cession. This was no ceremonial occasion and there was no shyness about expressing opinions. For the most part the Fijians were of Elija's way of thinking. Freedom was a concept hardly understood let alone worried about; they wanted protection from the white men and a cessation of war and both seemed possible under British rule.

Before leaving for his meeting with the king, Jason shook hands with each one. Aporosa accompanied him to the door, "Whatever happens, father, you know what we think and what we shall say when our time comes to speak. You must say what you think; if it is opposed to our views, so be it."

"Don't worry, I shall do my best by you all." Jason leaned over and kissed his son on the forehead.

"Do you want some of us to come with you as an escort, father?" said Aporosa suddenly. "After what the Tongan said, it might be wiser if you had a few of us with you."

"Nonsense," laughed Jason, "I'm as safe on Bau as I would be at home. Take no notice of the Tongans, they would have you believe that I am far more important than I really am. Tongans are more talk than action."

"So long as you are positive there is no danger," said his son doubtfully. "We will wait here to find out how your meeting went. If you are not back within the hour I shall come out and find you." As he watched his father disappear into the darkness Aporosa could not dispel a feeling of foreboding, but in the face of his father's refusal he could hardly force an escort on him.

*****

As Jason walked the short distance to the King's main house there was no movement which might have been construed as a threat. Quite the contrary in fact; he was well-known and well liked and those who recognised his tall figure greeted him courteously. The guards ushered him straight in.

Jason found the King comfortably seated on a pile of mats, attended only by his matanivanua and cupbearer. It occurred to Jason that they were the same two who had listened that night so many years before in Levuka, when the King had first commanded him to take the Denisons to Vatulevu and told him of the threatened Tongan invasion of the island.

There was none of the stiffness of their meeting earlier in the day; none of the hauteur and majesty of the monarch. Cakobau was at home to receive an old friend. He had discarded the outer trappings of the King and wore just a sulu and a loose silk shirt. His dark eyes, which Jason had seen as hard as agate in moments of anger, now welcomed him warmly.

"It is good of you to join me, Jason. Sit up here close to me so that we may talk without shouting. These days it does not do to raise the voice even when talking to friends, you never know who might be listening outside."

"Turaga na Vunivalu, Tui Viti," Jason solemnly accorded him his traditional title. "I am honoured and grateful for your invitation to come here tonight."

Anticipating the King's order, the cupbearer presented Jason with a bowl of yaqona. Jason quaffed it and tossed the empty bowl spinning back to the server. Cakobau waited till his guest had drunk, pulling at his beard, a sure indication that he was about to make a pronouncement.

"For your own safety you must leave Bau tonight. That outburst in Council is but part of it. I have since been forced to listen to Prince Ma'afu'otu'i'toga in private audience; he demands your dismissal, even your head, as the price of his co-operation."

Jason whistled softly. Ma'afu had to be very sure of himself to come out in the open like this. "I sincerely regret that I have been the cause of so much embarrassment to your Majesty."

"You are not to blame but it does not make matters any easier for me. He has never forgiven you for his humiliating defeat at your hands. While you live you are a constant reminder to everyone that the Tongans are not invincible. For your own safety you must walk softly in their presence."

"I am Your Majesty's servant," said Jason with all the calmness he could muster in the face of news that his enemies were closing in on him. "I am here to obey your commands, but if I am to be a continual cause of conflict, just say the word and I shall resign and return to Vatulevu."

"Apart from the political implications, your own safety demands that I must ask you to do just that," said the King apologetically. "Things have come to a wretched pass when I must discard the only men I trust and place myself in the hands of proven traitors. But you of all people realise that I cannot afford a split in our ranks. This is not Britain or America where I am told they expect such things in politics; in Fiji the only alternative to unity is war. I must show the commissioners that I speak for the whole of Fiji."

"Say no more, Turaga, I hereby tender my resignation. I shall leave Bau tonight." These were hard words for Jason to utter. It seemed that he was no longer wanted with the Vatulevu men and now, in spite of all he had done, his presence only added to the King's troubles. After years of working for the Fijians and being forced to suffer abuse at the hands of his fellow whites he was now of no use to anyone.

Cakobau was clearly worried and torn between conflicting emotions. He frowned down at the mat-covered floor. "Before you leave, Jasoni, I want you to know that I respect you more than I do any other European. You have been a true friend both to me and to my people. Once this thing is settled we can be friends again."

This was not true, thought Jason, their relationship could never be the same again. This moment would always stand between them. So far as the Fijians were concerned, from now on he was just another white man.

"Before you leave, I want you to give me the benefit of one last piece of your wisdom," said Cakobau. "Everyone tells me what I should do to safeguard the future of my race. Each tells a different story, each has his own basket to fill. I want you, who have never asked me for anything, to give me your advice. Should I fight for this independence we have or should I agree to give my islands and my people into the safekeeping of Queen Victoria? Shall I tell the commissioners from Peritania to go home empty-handed? Shall we have another attempt at establishing our own government?"

Jason shook his head slowly from side to side as though the weight of his thoughts and his feeling of awful depression were too much for him. It was only with great difficulty that he managed to express his thoughts in words.

"No, Turaga, we tried and we failed," he said hoarsely. "You would be best advised to give Fiji to Queen Victoria. I once thought we could build a Fijian state under your guidance and control, but the forces against us are too powerful to be held back any longer."

"For the good of your people you must seek the aid of Britain. Ma'afu and his puppet chiefs plan civil war. Even if you defeat them you would destroy Fiji in the process. Time and again the Europeans have tried to overthrow your Government. Their ambition is to rule Fiji themselves, to seize your lands and enslave your people. Their fire can only be put out by their own kind."

"If the British promise to rule the islands honestly, you and your people will have the protection you need. There was a time when I thought we had a chance to make something fine, but how could we achieve anything of lasting value when our only source of revenue comes from the sale of slaves?"

The more Jason said, the more weary and defeated became the King's expression. Cakobau had obviously been hoping that even at this, the eleventh hour, Jason might have been able to suggest something which would save his throne. Had Jason said 'fight them, to hell with Ma'afu', it would have so matched the King's own sentiments he might have found himself reinstated on the spot, not just as Minister for European Affairs, but as Chief Secretary. Jason, understanding this, could only bless his lack of political ambition.

"Bargain with the commissioners, Turaga. Don't let them think you have no option but to surrender. Negotiate terms which will safeguard our people — not for today or tomorrow, but until the time comes when they may rule themselves once more."

It had all sounded shallow and hopeless when Elija had expounded the same theme but the more Jason thought about it the more he thought Elija could be right. When he looked again at Cakobau he could see tears in the old man's eyes. The chief had fought all of his life to win his throne and now it was drifting out to sea with the wind like flotsam. Slowly he seemed to gather himself his shoulders straightening as his courage and Fijian pride reasserted control.

"I shall give my islands. But on one thing you are mistaken, I shall not sue for terms. Conditions are not for chiefs," his voice was harsh and proud. He would not beg like a commoner. He was the Vunivalu, to be feared and remembered by his people with pride.

"If I give another chief a canoe and he knows that I expect something in return from him, I do not say, 'I give you this canoe on condition that you only sail it on certain days and certain men of your tribe may not be allowed aboard it!' I give him the canoe outright and trust to his good faith to make me the return he knows I expect."

Jason remained silent and after a pause Cakobau continued. "You have helped to settle my mind and I have no anxiety for the future. You are right. If we try to stay as we are, Fiji will be a piece of driftwood on the beach to be picked up by the first passer-by. The whites who have come to Fiji are an evil lot, scavengers who, like the cormorants, will open their maws and swallow us all if I do not agree to cession."

"We need time all of us, Fijian, Tongan and European; time to live together in peace; time to bind us into one nation. When the day comes when we are so firmly interlaced that nothing can break us apart, that will be the day we shall rule ourselves again."

There was nobility, a depth of understanding, and self-sacrifice which would have graced the greatest of European statesmen. His people would have gladly followed him to war had he decided on independence, but his genuine love of his country and people was enough for him to submerge his personal ambition in order that they might live in peace and security. If only the fools who drank themselves silly every night in MacDonald's could have seen and heard him, thought Jason. If only they had sense enough to appreciate the greatness of this man.

It was time to go. "If the Vunivalu will excuse me, I should like to retire. If I must leave tonight I have arrangements to make and my son to see."

"I heard he was here," Cakobau answered still half lost in his own private thoughts. "He would be Adi Ulamila's son. I saw her once, a very beautiful girl."

Jason decided that the time might be appropriate for him to put in a good word for the boy; with all the uncertainty in the air it might be his only chance. "Ratu Aporosa is his name, Turaga. He has only just returned from Sydney where he was educated. Although he carries my blood in his veins, he fully identifies himself with your own people. It would be a great kindness if you were to watch over him after I leave; with me out of the way, the Prince might strike at him."

"Don't worry about your son, Jasoni, he shall be as my own; no one shall harm a hair on his head. I shall listen to him speak in Council as if you were speaking. But enough of the boy, what of yourself? With so many of Ma'afu's people here, you are not safe even on Bau. Did you bring guards with you? Are you armed?"

"Sega, i'saka," Jason replied, "I didn't consider it necessary. On my way here no one attempted to molest me, I do not need guards."

The King got ponderously to his feet, went over to a wooden chest which stood in a dark corner of the room, and brought back a handsome double-barrelled pistol. It was a beautiful piece, richly engraved and inlaid with gold and silver. At some time or other it must have been a gift to the king from a foreign diplomatic mission. He passed it to Jason.

"Take this, my friend. Be careful, it is charged and primed."

"But I cannot accept this, Turaga." Jason protested.

"You must take it, you need it for your immediate protection. But I would also like you to accept it as a token of our friendship over the years; also as a mark of the respect I have for you and as a remembrance of the night you helped me make a decision which will affect Fiji for the next hundred years. You have refused my gifts before but on this occasion I insist that you accept."

Jason held the magnificent example of the gunsmith's craft in his hand and bowed his head in submission.

"I thank Your Majesty for this gift. It will remain in my family as an heirloom. So long as there are Cotterels on Vatulevu it will remind us that we once served the King of Fiji and are ready to serve him and his descendants when the Fijians come into their own again."

*****

They were waiting, hidden behind another house where the guards in the doorway would not see them. When Jason was well clear of the King's house they rushed him. He could see them running, silhouetted against the light from the house where his son and his friends waited.

There was no point in trying to escape; they were too many and too close. He fired both barrels of the King's pistol, blasting the nearest into eternal damnation. The noise would bring his son running, but Jason knew it was too late. It had been too late from the moment he stepped aboard the *Albatross* to come to Bau. A spear stabbed deep into his stomach and a pineapple club smashed against the side of his head.

The murderers tried to escape into the darkness only to be caught by the crowd which surged out of the houses to find out what was happening. The kai-Vatulevu, hysterical with grief, slaughtered two on the spot and would have cut the remainder to ribbons had they not been held back by Bauan guards.

Jason was carried into the house where, just an hour before, he had laughed and joked with them all. Aporosa cradled his father's shattered head in his arms and wept inconsolably. Both John Thurston and the King were there within a matter of minutes, their faces numb with grief and horror.

He lived for ten minutes. At the very end his lips moved slowly and all heard his last words. "Kate … my Kate." His head lolled on his son's lap and Kate Cotterel was a widow.

King Cakobau got slowly up from his knees, he could hardly credit that Jason Cotterel was dead. Only moments before they had been talking of his plans. John Thurston began to leave.

It was Cakobau who spoke. "Your work has been done for you Mr Chief Secretary. I shall give my country to Queen Victoria as Jasoni advised. I have seen a thousand men die beneath the club, but none loved Fiji like this man. Let Jason Cotterel's blood be the seal of the agreement."

Epilogue

King Cakobau and his chiefs formally ceded the islands of Fiji to Queen Victoria on the afternoon of 10 October 1874. The day was dull and overcast with occasional driving rain and high winds, the sky filled with lowering black clouds. The ceremony was to have taken place in the morning but was delayed so that the ladies hats might not be ruined and the gentlemen's uniforms rain-spotted.

Pulling at their anchors in the harbour were Her Majesty's warships *Pearl* and *Dido*, which had carried Sir Hercules Robinson and the official party from Sydney — King Cakobau and the chiefs waited ashore at Nasova, the government compound just to the south of Levuka.

When the British party came ashore, the entire population of Levuka lined their route. From the numbers of canoes and cutters in harbour, there were representatives from every island in the Fiji Group. A guard of 200 marines and sailors was drawn up in front of the government buildings and HMS *Pearl* had provided a brass band. It was very colourful, very martial and above all, very British.

Katherine Cotterel with her family watched from a special position set aside for her by John Thurston. Some had tried to dissuade her from coming, but she had insisted that her husband would have expected it of her. If anyone was the architect of this moment it was Jason; he had given his life for it. He must have known the Tongans would attack him, but he had deliberately sacrificed himself. As the King had said, his blood was the seal. If he was the creator it behoved his widow to be present at the unveiling.

Sir Hercules Robinson, Governor of New South Wales, inspected the guard. Then, with slow and solemn steps, he marched over to the waiting chiefs and read out the clauses of the Deed of Cession in a booming voice which could be heard by all present.

To Kate the words were unimportant; what mattered was that John Thurston had told her the British government had guaranteed the Fijians ownership of their lands and had promised to create a state based on Christian principles and dedicated to the protection of Fijian interests.

Thurston looked over at her as if worried that she might break down. Kate smiled back reassuringly. Her time for tears was past. Her beloved husband was gone and inwardly she would weep forever, but in public her head was held high. She was Mrs Jason Cotterel of Qaraniqio, Vatulevu. Jason was dead, but his memory continued strong and proud. The plantation, his sons and daughters — the Cotterels — were established in Fiji as a dynasty. This Deed of Cession was a special part of his monument.

They were signing the document now. First, King Cakobau, a dignified and still regal figure despite being in the act of abdication. Kate's heart hardened as she watched Ma'afu's thin sharp face poised above the paper — he still maintained that he was innocent of any part in her husband's death. According to John Thurston, Jason's death had caused such a revulsion of feeling that the Tongan cause was completely ruined by the evil deed.

Chief after chief signed the Deed of Cession in order of precedence. Most made a cross opposite their names, but near the end a younger man stepped forward. Kate was too far away to see the paper, but she knew he was writing, 'Ratu Aporosa, Tui Navatulevu.' He signed with a flourish then, instead of moving on to stand with the other chiefs, he left the main pavilion and walked across to stand by Kate. He looked like a younger, tanned version of Jason; half laughing, half serious. Now, in spite of her resolution she could no longer stem the tears streaming silently down her cheeks.

They stood arm in arm watching King Cakobau's flag come slowly down, then the Union flag being run up to the top of the flagpole. Amid a storm of cheers and booming guns, Kate Cotterel and her stepson stood in silent memory of the husband and father they had lost.

John Thurston was making a final speech. In his hands he held King Cakobau's war club. It was topped with a crown of silver and spiralling down its entire length were silver ferns and doves.

"Your Excellency," said Thurston. There was the slightest tremor in his voice as if the emotion of the moment was almost too much for him." King Cakobau has asked me to speak on his behalf."

"The King wishes to give Her Majesty, Queen Victoria, his favourite war club, the former and until lately the only known law in Fiji. In abandoning club law and adopting the new forms and principles of civilised societies, he has laid aside his old weapon and covered it with it with the emblems of peace. Many of his people died under the old law, but hundreds of thousands survive to enjoy the newer and better state of things."

"With this emblem of the past he sends his felicitations to Her Majesty, saying that he fully confides in her and her children who, upon succeeding her shall become Kings of Fiji, to exercise a watchful control over the welfare of his children and people who, having survived the barbaric law and age, are now submitting themselves under Her Majesty's rule to civilisation."